MASTER AND GOD

MASTER AND GOD

Lindsey Davis

WINDSOR
PARAGON

First published 2011
by Hodder & Stoughton
This Large Print edition published 2013
by AudioGO Ltd
by arrangement with
Hodder & Stoughton

Hardcover   ISBN: 978 1 4713 2510 6
Softcover   ISBN: 978 1 4713 2511 3

Printed and bound in Great Britain by
MPG Books Group Limited

Dedicated to the city of Rome

PART 1
Rome: AD 80–81

Let the Games commence!

1

It was a quiet afternoon on the Via Flaminia. When a wisp of smoke wafted across from the river direction, sheered downwards and dematerialised against a pantile on the roof of the station house, nobody noticed. Rome, the Golden City, went about its business. The vigiles of the First Cohort continued their tasks.

The yard lay still; afternoons were dead time. The tribune was off at his own house. Nobody was doing much. The vigiles had been brought into existence to combat fires, but also covered local law and order. Most action occurred at night. Between lunchtime and dinner their duties were minimal, which was how the day shift liked it.

Titus, their new Emperor, was away in Campania. For the second time now, he was visiting the disaster area after Mount Vesuvius erupted the autumn before. Many people had feared the worst when Titus succeeded his father; despite his charm, Vespasian's son was thought to be ruthless. Yet apparently he had overhauled his personality: renounced vice, promised to execute no more opponents, and even sent away his unpopular lover, Queen Berenice of Judaea, after she scampered to Rome hoping to become his empress. Now every time the wardrobe slaves dressed Titus in his sumptuous robes, he also stepped into a fetching reputation as a benign ruler. After the volcanic catastrophe his people, desperate for reassurance, were forgiving. Titus encouraged them by spending his own money on relief efforts.

3

At forty, he should have a long reign ahead of him but Vesuvius would obviously be its major event—so unexpected, so destructive, so *very* close to Rome. Campania was taking up much of his time. Still, if anything of moment happened back in Rome, his brother Domitian could be roped in as a substitute.

That was unlikely. The Empire and the city rolled along in the safe hands of officials. Though Titus rarely showed open animosity, most people assumed that he intended to prevent Domitian exercising power.

* * *

A couple more threads of smoke drifted above the Field of Mars. Rome's usual hot blue sky was permanently grey that year so these cirrus-light wisps were indistinguishable. Again, no one paid any attention.

The depressing skies had deposited a fine film of dirt over everything. Throughout the Mediterranean the temperature cooled, after Vesuvius flung up millions of tons of ash, its plume blocking out sunlight as far away as North Africa and Syria. In Italy itself, the sea—Mare Nostrum, *our* sea—had been sucked dry then flung back upon the coast. Fish died. Birds died. When spring came, the once-fertile Bay of Naples area lay many feet deep under lava, ash and solidified mud. Instead of three crops a year in Campania, there were no crops at all. Prices shot up. Areas which traditionally fed Rome lay half dead. There was starvation; the populace weakened; an epidemic set in. Thousands were sick and many would die.

So it was already a bad year. Promises of lavish festivities once Titus inaugurated his father's huge new amphitheatre barely kept up the Romans' spirits. Only very expensive public games, with long holidays to enjoy the grunts and gore, would relieve their gloom.

*   *   *

On the station house roof, a dim pigeon spread a wing, vainly hoping to bask in sunshine, while its brighter mate simply sat hunched in the post-Vesuvian murk.

Two levels below, one of the vigiles sniffed the air as if a warning had reached his subconscious, but he continued unconcernedly sharpening fire-axes. All the other smells of Rome competed for his notice, from raw fish and bloody meat to frying food, crushed garlic and herbs; foul stinks from tanneries; wood-burning furnaces; incense and perfumes; whole aromatic warehouses full of fine peppers and cinnamon; middens; drains; pine trees; vagrants, mule dung and dead dogs.

The station house contributed its own odours of scorched ropes and dank esparto-grass mats. On busts of Titus and the old Emperor Vespasian in the shrine at the end of the parade ground, dry wreaths carried pot pourri scents of laurel and cypress. The station house was occupied at various times by a thousand men of lowly origin who engaged in hard physical work; they stank of smoke, sweat and feet, while most of them made powerful use of belches and farts too, using those in conversation like expressive parts of speech.

Few were talking now. Fire buckets were stacked

5

around unfilled. The enormous gates stood all but closed, with only a crack left for access. Some men were catching a nap indoors, though a few lolled outside in the air. They looked up when one of their crime team returned. It was Scorpus, close-cropped and shrewd-eyed, limping since an old accident at a house fire, as so many of them did. He was trailing a young woman.

She must be bound for the investigation officer: Gaius Vinius Clodianus, son of an ex-cohort tribune who managed promotion to the Praetorian Guard; brother of two ex-soldiers; ex the Twentieth legion himself; twenty-three years old, five feet ten, a hundred and seventy pounds; generally competent, pretty well-liked. The men assumed he would hear the story, promise to look into it, deplore the cohort's heavy workload, wink flirtatiously—then send the girl packing.

Sizing up the visitor, they reflected crudely on her youth, her figure and the fact that the lucky Vinius would interview her unchaperoned. She was decent-looking, though here being female was enough.

They all knew Vinius was married. Although he never discussed his private life, the marriage was rumoured to be in trouble (Vinius himself was ignoring their difficulties—which, for his wife, encapsulated the problem). His men assumed that he upheld cohort traditions by chasing other women, though not unmarried girls. They would lay bets on that, just as they were certain that Vinius would always choose the Chicken Frontinian off a menu board or that every time he was shaved he had his barber slap on a plain camomile wash. They served with him, so they knew him. Or so they believed.

*   *   *

As Flavia Lucilla entered, her heart sank. Several men whistled. To them it was appreciative; to her it felt aggressive. She was young enough to blush.

She had found herself in a large open space inside two-storey official premises. Colonnades ran down each long side; another similar courtyard opened ahead, then a third. Just inside the mighty main gates, she had passed between two large water basins. Pieces of equipment were piled in the yards in a way that looked haphazard although perhaps it made items quick to collect in an emergency. It was all alien to her.

She scuttled after Scorpus into the enquiries office, half way down the left colonnade, in one of many small rooms that lay behind the pillars. As they entered, Scorpus pointed an index finger at her in silence, then moved that finger through forty-five degrees to indicate where she was to take a seat. The gesture was not particularly offensive. 'Gaius Vinius will take your story.' The presumed Vinius barely glanced up.

Lucilla dropped onto the centre of a low wooden bench, otherwise unoccupied. She sat on her hands, arms straight and shoulders tight. Clearly, she was a nuisance and she had to wait. That suited her. By now, she wished she had not come.

The enquiry officer was not what she expected; for a start he was young, not some grizzled centurion. Seated at a rustic table placed crossways to the door, he had a good-looking profile and Lucilla felt he knew it. He was working on

7

documents; other men would have had the cohort clerk do the writing, while they dictated. Waxed wooden tablets with a stylus lay in front of Vinius, but he was completing a formal list in ink on a scroll. She watched him sign it then replace the wet pen rather daintily in its inkwell; with this small fancy gesture he seemed to be half-mocking himself for enjoying such work. It suggested Vinius was eccentric; most investigators complained about time-consuming bureaucracy.

'Here, Scorpus. Three to kick upstairs.'

His voice was lower and stronger than Lucilla expected. She guessed 'kicking upstairs' was not a literal command but shorthand for despatching wrongdoers to the Vigiles Prefect. Routine crimes would be dealt with by a thrashing or a local fine. Recalcitrant offenders would be passed to the Prefect of the City, who could send them for a full trial.

Scorpus skimmed the short scroll and, as he went out with it, commented, 'Morena won't be happy!'

Vinius shrugged. Then he waited, idly flipping through the waxed tablets. Lucilla noticed his wedding ring. His hands were clean and neatly manicured. He was blessed with thick, dark hair which he had had extremely well cut, so the young girl was startled by the erotic attraction of expert layering into the nape of his strong male neck.

He continued to ignore her. Increasingly nervous, she tried not to attract his attention. She gazed around but apart from the table and bench there was nothing in the room except a large map on the wall. It showed the Seventh and Eighth Regions, which the First Cohort covered, a segment of the city which ran from the city boundary above the Pincian Hill, down past the Gardens of Sallust and the Quirinal, right into the Forum. It was where she had been brought up so she recognised the main features, even though the street names had faded badly. Occasional newer marks in different inks had been added, as if to pinpoint local incidents.

She should not have come. She should either have left it alone, or made her mother come with her. That had proved impossible; she should have accepted that her mother did not want the vigiles involved.

After various shouts and banging of doors outside, a man burst into the room, grumbling loudly. Some sort of prisoner-escort could be heard in the portico, while Scorpus reappeared and leaned on the doorframe, watching with a smirk.

'Morena!' Vinius greeted the new arrival calmly. The protester was scrawny and seedy-looking, with disastrous combed-over straggles of hair. Lucilla saw he was the kind of man who wasted all day at a street bar counter, making obscene jokes to offend passers-by. From the officer's expression, Vinius would second her: *and then he expects the waitress to fuck him for nothing.* Perhaps adding, if he was particularly depressed, *and the sad little cow probably does it . . .*

'Is it about Isis Street again? You can't do this to me!'

'No option,' Vinius disagreed. 'Morena, I have warned you twice about keeping fire buckets. My duty is to check up on you like a bastard, then your duty is to carry out my orders. But you have persistently done nothing.'

'The tenants keep pinching the water for their

9

balcony flowerpots!'

'Refill the cistern. Evict your tenants for breach of their lease—I presume even speculators like you give the poor sods a lease? We can't do our job without water. Jupiter, man, one dropped lamp in your lousy building and you could burn the city down!'

'Give me another chance.'

'You said that the other times.'

'I just ordered the improvements—'

'My tribune wants arrests.'

'How much?'

In the doorway, Scorpus grinned. Vinius sighed stagily. 'I hope you are not trying to bribe me, Morena?'

'Stuff you then, Vinius, you ugly two-faced skank!'

'Cut it.' Vinius rose to his feet. Ugly was no word for him, though Lucilla would never have admired him openly; he was too sure of himself already. He was tall and well-muscled, entirely self-composed. He barely raised his voice: 'Morena, you are the landlord of a five-storey, ramshackle, multiple-occupancy dump in Isis Street which fails its fire inspection every time we visit. You are a whining, flea-bitten, fine-dodging, mortgage-shovelling, widow-cheating, orphan-starving, small-minded slave-shagger—is that right?'

Morena wilted. 'Fair enough.'

'So bugger off to the Prefect and stop wasting my time.'

Morena was dragged out backwards, with harsh shouts from the vigiles. Gaius Vinius sank back to his seated position, barely winded. Still not turning his head, he looked sideways at Lucilla. 'Right, young lady; what brings you to this fine haven of public order?'

*   *   *

Vinius had already assessed her unobtrusively. He was surprised she arrived alone; young girls usually tripped about in pairs. She would be safe, at least on his watch, but he suspected she had some mischievous purpose in coming. At the first sign of playing up or cheek, she was for it.

She was average height, skinny and flat-chested, though not badly nourished. She, or her parents, had grown up in a household where if they ate scraps the scraps were remains of good meals: leftovers from a well-to-do but wasteful family, typical of the slave-serviced classes. Vinius correctly classified her as a daughter of freed slaves.

Nobody's little princess, she wore a narrow tunic in a cheap natural colour; she had grown out of the garment, so it showed her ankles. Nice ankles, but she wasn't a child now and ought to keep them covered up. Her chestnut hair was twisted and speared with one long pin that surprisingly looked like ivory—a gift? If not a gift, probably filched from a much richer woman's ornament box.

When Gaius Vinius interviewed the public he was businesslike, not one of those enquirers who would banter with women then botch their reports. However, had it been relevant, his assessment was that his visitor would be good-looking when she grew up. Which he prophesied would happen in about a month's time.

He shuffled the wax tablets in front of him, selected one, and smoothed it over with the flat of

11

his stylus, 'Name?'

'Flavia Lucilla.' Her voice came out as a scared little squeak, causing Vinius to check the spelling. 'Flavia' confirmed that her family had obtained citizenship under the current emperors, so in the last generation.

'Age?'

'Seventeen.' *Take away two years,* calculated Vinius.

'Father?' Lucilla stayed silent; Vinius moved on. Many people he interviewed had no idea who their fathers were. 'Mother?'

'Flavia Lachne, imperial freedwoman.'

Vinius felt sceptical of 'imperial'. There were plenty of ex-slaves from the palace, but after three years of dealing with the public he took nothing on trust; he suspected this was merely the child of a fishmonger's filleter, enhancing her status. 'And you live?'

'Opposite the Porticus Vipsania, by the conch fountain.' Vinius could not place it. He had tried to become familiar with all the narrow alleys of the Seventh Region since he was posted in, but he was still learning. The wall map was no help; you could pick out temples and theatres, but finding tenements where the poor lived had never been a vigiles priority. 'An apartment on the fourth floor.' The middle classes lived at ground level; the destitute toiled up six flights of stairs; the fourth floor was close to poverty, yet not absolutely there.

'So what's your problem, darling?'

Lucilla bridled. 'Officer, I am *not* your darling!'

'You'll never be anybody's, with that temper.' Vinius saw the girl take a furious breath so, dropping his stylus onto the table, he made a swift appeasing gesture, open-palmed. Then he linked his hands behind his head and produced a rueful half smile. This generally had a good effect with women. Lucilla glared as if she had paid to see a celebrity gladiator but got stuck with a creaking understudy. 'So, have you come to report a crime or to make a complaint?'

Sensibly, she stifled her indignation. 'We have been burgled.'

'"We"?'

'Me and my mother.'

'Any slaves?' The slaves would be his first suspects.

'Oh our extensive staff!' Lucilla snapped, firing up again. 'A battalion of pastry cooks, three wardrobe women—and we just wouldn't be *anybody* without an unpublished poet who works as our door-porter.'

Vinius looked sour, to stop himself smiling. 'What size apartment?'

'Two rooms; we live in one and my mother works with her clients in the other.'

'Works as . . .'

'A beautician.' Belatedly Lucilla realised how it sounded: as if Lachne was a prostitute.

Vinius wondered if the daughter was being trained in the same trade. He decided that would be a pity. Gods, he must be going soft.

'Mother is a hairdresser, for the Emperor's family,' Lucilla protested.

Vinius did not believe that story. But if Lachne sold herself to men, she must be registered here; he could check the vigiles records, so there was no point in the girl lying. If the woman worked on her back and had *not* registered, it was foolish to attract

13

his attention—which might explain why the girl was sent here by herself, with the mother keeping out of the way.

'Where is your mother now?'

'At home, hysterical.'

'So what happened?'

'Mother came home and found all her jewellery missing.'

'Any of it valuable?'

'All of it!' Lucilla saw the investigator's suspicion. 'Sure it's gone? Mama couldn't have stuffed her beads behind a cushion and forgot?'

'We searched the whole apartment.' Lucilla had done that, and she had been methodical. She had her own doubts about her mother.

Vinius applied a friendly face. 'I shall make a list eventually, so be thinking.' He noted that apart from her ivory hairpin, the waif-like Lucilla wore not so much as a pebble necklace. Nobody would place her as a child of a woman with possessions worth stealing. Jupiter, even among the homeless under the Tiber bridges, mothers usually decked daughters in a string of pebbles. His own toddler wore an amulet. 'So, Mama comes home . . . Any signs of a break-in?'

'No.'

'Damage to your door?'

'None.'

'Would other people have known you would be out?' Lucilla shrugged, implying their movements were random. 'You're on the fourth floor—could anybody climb over from a neighbouring balcony?'

'No, we don't have a balcony, and we keep the shutters closed.'

'So the only way in is through the door? You do

lock it when you're out?'

'Yes, we are not stupid!' Anxiously, the girl lashed out at him again, 'You are not taking any notes!'

All Vinius had scratched on his tablet so far was her name. He never wasted effort. The chances of solving this burglary were slim. Rome was awash with house-breakers, bath house clothes' pilferers, purse-thieves, rogues who pulled packages off the backs of moving carts, dishonest slaves, and walk-in chancers who strolled into houses to empty dining rooms of their silverware. He rarely caught any of them.

'What kind of lock?'

Under his prompting, Lucilla described the pointless inexpensive kind that bad landlords like Morena always installed; at least hers had a key, not merely a latch-lifter. Gaius Vinius, who believed crime prevention was his most useful work, recommended a barrel-lock, suggesting where the women could buy one from a reputable locksmith.

'"Reputable" means . . .?' asked Lucilla cynically.

Vinius had his human side; he was rather enjoying the conversation now. 'The one I always recommend. Then at least I know where to head if someone who has followed my advice is subsequently burgled . . .' More serious, he asked the usual question: 'Does anyone other than your mother or yourself have a key?' This was patronising. On the other hand, there was a good reason why the vigiles always asked it. Lucilla shook her head; victims always denied giving out duplicates. Vinius kept going: 'I know it is very unpleasant to think you might have trusted the wrong person . . . Do you have a boyfriend?'

15

'No.' Lucilla looked embarrassed. He should have known from her absence of ornament; the first crook who came after this girlie would get her in return for a faux-gold snake bangle with glass eyes.

'What about your mother?' Lucilla's silence told its own story. 'I see. Does she have a crowd of followers, or just one at a time?'

'One at a time!'

'So what do you think of the fellows your mother entertains?'

'Not much.' Lucilla was finding the interview more difficult than she had expected. Vinius knew how to break down her defences. 'The present one is a businessman. He doesn't need to steal.'

'Name?'

'Orgilius.'

'How well off?'

'Enough.'

Vinius watched her thoughtfully. He allowed Lucilla time to work out why.

He could see he had upset the girl; he was sorry for that.

* * *

This was the first time in her relationship with her mother that Lucilla took any initiative. Lachne had seemed reluctant to involve the authorities, even though the contents of her jewel box, gifts from important women she had served and men she had attracted, were genuinely expensive. Indignant, and frightened that a thief had been inside their home, Lucilla had flounced off here to report the theft, leaving her mother slumped on a chair. Lachne often played the helpless woman; it had not seemed out of character.

In addressing this crisis, Lucilla had shown new independence. She was already beginning to feel doubts, when the officer's lightly posed question made her see how her mother had duped her.

'One thing I always have to consider,' explained Vinius, 'is whether a reported "burglary" might be an inside job.'

He was right. Lucilla inderstood now. Lachne was preying on her latest man. *Orgilius is such a sweetie; when he sees how unhappy I am, he is bound to replace things* . . . Lachne did not need to report the theft, because it never happened. But she must have decided that letting her unwitting daughter run and appeal to the vigiles would make the story more credible.

Her mother had bamboozled her, lied to her, *used* her. Sitting there under the quizzing of Vinius, Lucilla realised she had been cruelly betrayed by the only person close to her.

Even Vinius, who had never met her before, recognised the hard look as Lucilla decided not to put up with it. She was only fifteen. She had few options. Nevertheless, she would break with her mother over this.

*   *   *

Outside in the yard, there were noises, which Vinius had noticed. His glance went to the door; he was listening, trying to evaluate the activity.

'I'll send someone along. One of your neighbours may have noticed something . . .'

Flavia Lucilla recognised the brush-off. Vinius had not even written down where she lived. No one would be sent. It was a waste of time. Even if one of his troops did investigate, Lachne would simper and giggle, and finger the man's muscles, and let herself be squeezed, until some half-baked understanding was reached, then Lachne and Lucilla would have to spend weeks letting the new hopeful down gently and stopping Orgilius running into him . . .

'So who do you think did your break-in?' Vinius asked: yet another question that the vigiles always put.

'How would we know? It's your job to find out—that's if you can be bothered, *pretty boy*!'

'Ah, sadly, sweetheart, my pretty days are over.'

Vinius swung around in his seat to face Lucilla full on.

* * *

He did it on purpose, intending to shock.

While he was a soldier, he had been seriously wounded. He was smashed in the face by a rebellious tribesman's spear and lost an eye. There was other damage, which an army surgeon who thought his patient was dying had sutured only crudely. The right side of his face, previously hidden as he sat sideways, was disfigured by terrible scars. Shaken up and sight-compromised, Vinius had been posted back to Rome and assigned to the vigiles; he was ugly enough for those tough ex-slaves to accept him.

Lucilla was horrified, but managed to conceal it. 'That must spoil your love life. How did it happen?'

Vinius did not reply. He was on his feet and standing at the door, to see the action in the yard. In any case, he wanted to avoid thinking about his so-called love life.

Someone had already dragged open both main gates. Although the men appeared calm, Vinius sensed the prickle of excitement and apprehension that always accompanied fires. They were hauling a siphon engine from its indoor stall, which told him the alarm was serious.

He glanced up at the sky, which looked simply grey as usual this summer, but smoke in the air was now obvious. Investigators often joined the firemen at a blaze, to show solidarity or to check for arson. Vinius called out to ask Scorpus what was happening, at the same time pulling open a pouch on his belt and pushing in the tablet with the unwritten burglary report.

Lucilla jumped to her feet, scowling. Stalking out, she had to brush past Vinius in the doorway. He let her go, but she felt a light touch of his hand on her shoulder: reassurance and an apology.

It was a casual gesture, but would stay far too long in the memory of a lonely fifteen-year-old girl.

*   *   *

Scorpus lifted an eyebrow, watching Lucilla scurry away.

'A scam.' Vinius shrugged it off. 'Mother fleecing her boyfriend. The girl can't be in on the fiddle—a bit too naïve.' *Who's being naïve now?*

'Seemed sweet!'

'Oh, was she?'

They both grinned.

Then someone appeared in the gateway, calling: 'From the Seventh—assistance sought. It's a big one.'

So Gaius Vinius sent a runner to inform the cohort tribune, and the First rolled out to help with the next great disaster in the reign of the Emperor Titus. Soon they had no time to think about women, not even the women they were married to. For three days and nights without a break, they struggled to control a fire that tore out half the heart of monumental Rome, during which on many occasions they were also fighting for their lives.

2

Old lags in the vigiles loved to describe the Great Fire back in Nero's reign. Vinius had heard them do it. Callow recruits would listen open-mouthed as veterans spun lurid yarns. Up until the fire under Titus, Nero's famous conflagration had been the benchmark by which the vigiles measured all others. In the intervening years, their version had become ever more frightening, and it was technical; they never dwelt on whether the megalomaniac Nero was right to blame the Christians, or whether he started the fire himself in order to obtain prime land in the Forum for his Golden House. Nor did the firefighters bother with stories of him singing 'The Sack of Ilium' in stage costume as he watched the city burn. They even bypassed the alternative version: that Nero, a more caring and energetic ruler than history now recorded, had been away at Antium but rushed back to organise relief efforts, opening his palace to the homeless and arranging urgent food supplies.

For the vigiles, it was a catalogue of effects

and damage. How that fire stormed across Rome for seven days, until three regions were wiped out; seven more were severely damaged; only four survived untouched. How different blazes started on low ground then climbed the hills, but afterwards raced down again. How separate fires joined up. How the blaze out-stripped every counter-measure, how it roared through the narrow winding lanes and close-packed blocks of the old republican neighbourhoods.

Next, the vigiles would list new protective measures imposed under Nero and his successors: height restrictions on apartments, wider streets, enforced use of brick, fire porches to assist emergency access, and water always to be available in buildings. (It was never enough water; that went without saying.) The firefighters would grumble about the public, who moaned that the new broader streets let in too much bright sun, unlike the old shaded alleyways.

If questioned whether all this would work, most vigiles avoided giving answers. Would next time be different? Who knew? There were still too many fires. Rome was a city of portable braziers, unattended lamps and smoking incense. Unsuitable apartments were crammed with home-made griddles and hearths. Religious rites and industrial processes required naked flames. All baths and bakeries had furnaces, with large wood-stores adjacent. Apothecaries, glass-blowers and jewellers contributed to accidents. Every street had multiple eating bars; all used fire. Theatres were always burning down, often not even due to special effects, and brothels were a constant hazard, with their louche lighting, casually draped curtains, and misfit clientele. Anyway, who could counter day-to-day fecklessness? Thoughtless householders, bleary wine-sops, dreamy altar boys, experimental children striking sparks, ostlers setting bonfires in stable yards, and even the occasional witch casting desiccated testicles onto sinister green flames.

Every night the vigiles patrolled. Hardly a night passed without most cohorts sniffing out smoke somewhere. They all knew that sooner or later they faced another big event. Sixteen years after Nero's fire, the First soon realised the next big one was here.

For Vinius and the day shift, the quiet afternoon had ended. They were tackling more than a widow's cat knocking over a lamp in some seedy apartment; wide areas were burning. They were ready, though it fast became apparent they were stretched far too thinly for a major city fire, their nightmare.

Overall control escalated from cohort tribune level to their commander, the Prefect of Vigiles; then the City Prefect took charge. Messengers were despatched, to alert the Emperor and his brother. The first messages were bland, although officials mentioned the risk of wide-scale damage if containment should be difficult.

For three days and nights, containment was impossible.

* * *

Initially, the fire mainly raged through the Circus Flaminius Region, which lay below the citadel. In the low-lying north-western bend of the Tiber, the Campus Martius was devastated.

The Seventh Cohort managed to save the

northern part of the Campus. The Mausoleum of Augustus would continue to dominate the skyline with its great sombre drum and dark terraces planted with cypress trees. The enormous complex of Nero's Baths survived because they were supplied by the Aqua Virgo. Its low-lying destination had enabled that aqueduct to be built underground so water could be taken from an ornamental channel, rather than having to transport it from right over at the river. Saved too, therefore, was the Horologium, an enormous marble pavement with inlaid bronze lines that formed the largest sundial in the world.

Closer to the centre, all the important monuments were lost. Immediately across the Via Lata from the vigiles' station house lay the Saepta Julia, a two-storey, galleried court. This popular haunt of informers, flaneurs and bijouterie boutiques burned down along with the Diribitorium, a huge hall originally used for counting votes which had famous hundred-foot larch roof-beams. Larch was supposedly fire-resistant, but not in a blaze of this intensity. Then they lost the temples of Isis and Serapis where Vespasian and Titus had stayed, the night before their victory triumph for breaking the revolt in Judaea.

Towards the sluggish yellow-grey roll of the Tiber had been the Pantheon, Marcus Agrippa's huge and innovative rotunda to glorify the Julian family; it had an enormous dome above a bronze cornice and amongst the pillars on the portico had stood a statue of Venus; the goddess wore earrings that were a huge pearl halved, twin to the one Cleopatra famously dissolved in vinegar to win a bet with Mark Antony. Firemen stood helpless as they lost the Pantheon, with the adjacent Temple of Neptune and Baths of Agrippa, plus many lesser buildings that had grown up amongst them— houses, shops, clubs, workshops and manufacturing yards where ordinary people lived and carried out their trades.

Southwards towards the Capitol a much older area suffered. Pompey's Theatre lost its recently restored stage, along with the even older Theatre of Balbus and the Theatre of Marcellus, named for Augustus' golden nephew who had died too young to spoil his promise. The Porticus of Pompey perished, one of Rome's most popular recreation areas, with shady walks, antique Greek statues in its porch, and even a fine public lavatory whose seats faced out through a colonnade to a view of the glorious gardens. Gone too the famous statue of its builder, Pompey the Great, at the foot of which Julius Caesar was murdered.

The Circus Flaminius, which gave its name to the region, was at the heart of the fire. Never a venue for chariot racing, it was popular for public meetings, markets and funerals, and when victorious armies returned, their triumphal processions began among the eleven victory temples. Nearby, the Porticus of Octavia was lost, with its famous schools, curia and library. Among its sculpture collection was a huge group by Lysippus, which showed Alexander the Great among twenty-five cavalry leaders at the Battle of Granicus; amazingly, this Lysippus survived. But it was a lone miracle among catastrophic destruction.

*   *   *

Gaius Vinius worked tirelessly throughout all three days. He never identified one certain seat of the fire. Perhaps there were several sources. Professionally, he could tell just from the colour of the smoke that they were fighting a very hot, very intense conflagration. In such heat, even marble would burn.

The afternoon's initial stillness changed to a first night of gusting winds, caused by hot air currents drawn up from the fire. These winds were impossible to predict, with convection columns acting like bellows on structures the vigiles had previously managed to douse, causing spontaneous recombustion. Firebrands were hurled long distances as air currents picked up lighted debris, carrying sparks to new buildings. The winds were erratic, constantly changing direction and force, swirling dust and embers in circular vortices.

People all over Rome woke next morning to find smoke blanketing the city, darkening every street even far from the fire. It was now impossible to tell which regions were actually ablaze. Rumours caused confusion. As the citizens wheezed, panic took hold. Streets were clogged with agitated people trying to escape, dragging their possessions. Terrified mules and horses broke out of stables. Tethered dogs howled desperately. Rats came up from the sewers. The hire-price of wagons and carts shot up, while buckets, tools and materials to shore up collapsing structures became impossible to buy. Looting occurred.

Early in the three-day calamity Vinius worked near the Saepta, helping efforts to prevent the fire from crossing the Via Lata, the city end of the great Via Flaminia. The vigiles were struggling to protect their own station house, and prevent the fire having a free run all across the north of Rome. It was a mixed area with gardens, local markets and ancient temples to obscure gods, as well as some large private homes belonging to senators. Notable among them were the one-time home of Vespasian before he had been Emperor and his late brother's house on Pomegranate Street—to which the First were supposed discreetly to give special attention while never disturbing the current occupants. Vinius commandeered carts and whatever containers looked suitable to supplement the vigiles' buckets and their two creaking siphon engines. Those were constantly refilled, and the men worked the arms until their sinews cracked, but their feeble water streams were no more effective than a lame dog pissing on a funeral pyre. Whenever they could, when they could no longer continue, the First Cohort's shifts staggered back to their station house and collapsed into cubicles, snatching a few hours' rest. Food was provided by grateful neighbours. With the fire so near, they could only doze, anxious that they would waken to find flames sweeping their own building. Disturbed by shouts and crashes nearby and by colleagues' hacking coughs, the unwashed men roused themselves from wild dreams to go out again. As they battled on, many were hurt and some men died. All would be permanently affected. None would ever forget.

Eventually Vinius was in a contingent ordered down to the Forum. When he arrived beyond the flaming porticoes and theatres on the Campus, he found the Capitol itself now threatened. He felt a surge of misery. This had been the heart of Rome through many generations. On the main summit stood the Temple of Jupiter. The Temple of Juno on the second peak called the Arx was almost as significant to the Roman psyche. Between the Capitol and the Arx lay the Saddle, a dip where Romulus, Rome's mythical founder, had offered refuge to the outlaws and misfits who first peopled his new city eight hundred years before.

The foot of the hill was nowadays a great stone-buttressed base called the Tabularium, where records were kept. If flames came down on the Forum side, centuries of city archives would be under threat; the most precious were being carted to a more remote site for safety, though saving them all would be impossible. Down the Forum ran Rome's most important religious, legal and financial buildings, crowded on all sides by columns, arches, statues of heroes, sacred altars and commemorative rostra. At the far end, Vespasian's Flavian Amphitheatre rose, almost complete now. Other cohorts had assembled there to save the precious new arena and to protect buildings such as the House of the Vestal Virgins. Vinius had to concentrate on his own task. He had been ordered up to the citadel.

The Capitol was the smallest of Rome's Seven Hills, but it was steep and rocky, a natural fortress on a high promontory. There were said to be a hundred steps to the top, up which Gaius Vinius toiled, humping on his back heavy esparto mats that the vigiles used to smother flames. He did not count the steps, nor had he breath to curse. Frantic priests and officials buffeted him as they rushed downhill, some lugging statues or treasure chests.

Others even bore in their arms hysterical augury chickens and the geese that had been sacred for hundreds of years since they saved Rome from marauding Gauls. Above the crag, agitated wild birds were circling in dense smoke. Wails rose from onlookers clustered in the Forum below. As Vinius staggered skywards, he felt he was climbing to the roof of a world he was losing for ever, staggering into a flame-lit hell where all he knew and loved was about to die.

On the summit, the main temple was on fire.

The renowned temple of Jupiter Best and Greatest was the centre of the state religion. Here, magistrates began their term of office with solemn sacrifices, and the Senate held its first meeting of each year. It was the culmination of victory parades, where heroic generals vowed their arms to Jupiter. This mighty temple with its gilded roof was the largest of its type ever built, created on a massive square podium in ancient Etruscan style, with eighteen giant columns standing in three rows on its daunting portico. Destroyed by fire in the last days of civil wars only ten years before, its loss then had been traumatic. During the violent change of emperors, Vespasian's brother, Sabinus, had made a last stand there, barricading the citadel while opponents pointlessly held out; at the last hour, Vespasian's brother was hacked to death and his cadaver dumped on the very Gemonian Stairs that Gaius Vinius had just climbed with his deadweight burden of equipment. Vespasian's younger son Domitian had had a hair-raising escape.

That burning of the temple had symbolised terrible times that everyone now prayed were ended for good. The Temple of Jupiter had been restored by Vespasian, who hauled off the first basket of rubble himself when the site was cleared. Enormous care had been taken to find or replace the hundreds of ancient bronze tablets that had adorned the building. When it rose again at last, it seemed a sign that Rome would once more be great, its people fortunate under a worthy and energetic emperor. Now Vinius saw that the recently reinaugurated temple was burning so fiercely it could never be saved.

Choking and completely spent, the vigiles had given up and were starting to retreat. Blackened faces told of their soul-destroying efforts. Vinius was signalled to stay back. Flames had reached the roof. The temple was too high, too isolated; there was no way for them to send up water to its cloud-scraping pediments, even if water had been available.

Then someone shouted that priests were still inside. The cry of 'persons reported', dreaded by all firefighters, roused Vinius. Marginally fresher than the men who had been here before him, he ran up the great steps and through the massive portico columns. He heard protesting voices, but instinct propelled him on.

Inside, the heat was so intense, air seemed to burn in his throat and lungs so that every breath scared him. The spectacle was lurid. The ceiling was hidden by thick smoke, but three enormous crowned cult statues of Jupiter, Juno and Minerva were lit by flickering red light. Vinius was no more religious than the next man in the armed forces; he honoured the rituals because you had to, prayed to be saved from danger, but had already learned that divinities had no compassion for humans.

No calm-browed god had stepped in to protect
him when the British homunculus launched the
spear that nearly killed him. Even so, as the light
from sheets of flame flickered across the towering
statues, it was hard not to feel he stood in the
presence of the gods.

It was crazy to stay. Slabs of dissolving marble
the size of serving trays were dropping from on
high. Oil or incense must have spilled, so vaporous
licks of blue flame were creating a molten floor
carpet. Amidst the continuous roar of fire,
Vinius heard louder cracks as massive columns
and masonry began to break apart. The whole
enormous building was groaning in what he knew
must be its death throes.

He glimpsed one body, prostrate before the
statue of Minerva, in the skullcap with a pointed
prong that marked a senior priest. Somehow he
crossed the interior and found he had carried with
him an esparto mat; he flung it over the priest
then summoned the strength to haul man and mat
backwards out of the sanctum. As he fled, the cult
statues seemed to loom and sway as if they were
about to fall. Smoke blinded him. Heat flayed him.
His skin seemed to melt. Even the intolerable noise
was distressing.

Outside, the terrified Vinius hauled the priest
free of the mat, got a shoulder under him and
stumbled down the steps. Colleagues ran to relieve
him of the burden, then they hustled Vinius from
the temple forecourt, beating at his clothing which
was now on fire. Behind him the roof must have
failed almost immediately, with a tremendous
crash, then sheets of flame poured skywards
through it.

The man he saved was stretchered away at a run. Vinius forgot about him immediately. Once his burning clothes were extinguished, he squatted on his haunches in the rags of his tunic, with a raw face, charred hair and eyebrows, burned arms and shins, and despair in his heart.

They stayed up there, huddled in an open space where omens were taken, in case the Temple of Juno was threatened, but an alteration in the wind saved it. So although sometimes they had to beat out spot-fires, mostly they took a grim kind of rest, standing or sitting in silence as they watched the larger temple being consumed, counting the crashes as its huge columns keeled over. Each collapse seemed to mark their helplessness; each fall emphasised their failure.

*   *   *

For Vinius that was the worst time. It ended in one last terrible night of exhaustion and despair. But it did end. A quieter dawn came, where cries and crashes continued, but the heat and smoke were noticeably more subdued, the fire at last starved and dying.

Sporadic flames still danced amidst the havoc on Capitol and Campus as the stunned vigiles surveyed what they had lost and what they had saved. They were all at their physical limits. Some who seemed unharmed would yet succumb to the effects of smoke and evil particles inhaled in confined places; others would be tormented for years by nightmares. Now they regrouped raggedly, while officers unfeelingly gave new orders. Those who had been on the Capitol then came very slowly down to the

31

Forum, where crowds stood waiting. People broke out into applause. Gratitude seemed too terrible to bear. Men in the ranks wept. Unbearable emotion swept over them. Though he thought himself tough, Gaius Vinius too felt hot tears rush down his burned cheeks.

* * *

Cruelly, they were not yet dismissed. Those of the vigiles who could still keep upright had to parade at the foot of the Capitol. It was explained to them, with a caustic undernote, that a good show must be put on: a party of horrified magistrates and other senators were coming to view the extent of the damage.

Foremost among the dignitaries, acting as imperial representative, would be Titus' younger brother and heir, Domitian Caesar.

3

Domitian arrived by litter. That was his style. Throughout his life—his adult life in the imperial family, when funds were no problem—he preferred to travel carried by bearers. He lounged aloft like an exotic potentate, which gave an impression of importance, while he could draw all the privacy curtains, indulging his love of solitude.

Inspecting the fire damage on behalf of Titus produced mixed feelings. It recalled his father's accession ten years ago, when Domitian had had a taste of direct power as he represented Vespasian for a few delicious weeks; he made the most of it. A decade later he was used to playing substitute. If second place riled him, he had learned to conceal his feelings. He knew how to appear modest too; he was as good an actor as his brother. He had inherited all the family talents.

Patrician families in Rome, a select group of famous names who had multiple consuls and generals among their ancestors, believed what mattered was a pedigree that ran back to some moss-covered hutment next door to Romulus. Even without, the once-obscure, up-country Flavians had moved themselves in merely three generations into proximity with gods. They achieved it on ability. They were astute and intelligent; they knew how to position themselves politically; they were diplomats. Domitian, when he chose, had all those qualities.

Above all, the Flavians were clannish. They supported each other financially and socially, gave each other jobs, married their cousins. Domitian had been born and partly brought up in his uncle's house. Uncle Sabinus had seemingly felt no grudge when his younger brother was bidding for the throne, only proud that it was 'one of us'. Two of us, as it turned out. Vespasian (with Titus alongside) became emperor. Vespasian (with Titus) was awarded a Triumph for subduing the Jewish Rebellion. Vespasian (and Titus) then ruled the Empire like unofficial partners. Titus now possessed it.

As the spare heir, Domitian was sidelined. Everyone knew that his father and brother had argued about his capabilities and whether he was reliable. *He* knew it, which certainly rankled.

33

They awarded him a few minor priesthoods, then relegated him to organising poetry competitions. Fortunately he liked poetry. Indeed, the young Caesar wrote and performed verse himself which, naturally, was well-received. It was said that the multi-skilled Titus wrote poetry *almost as well as Domitian*, though praise for Domitian came from critics who were nervous of him—an aspect which did not escape his notice.

Vespasian died. Titus took over. If Titus, who was currently unmarried, never had male children and if his daughter Julia had no sons, Domitian would succeed to the Empire. Mind you, if Titus lived as long as their father, he could be waiting thirty years.

Understandably, people presumed Domitian was plotting against his brother. Romans were power-hungry. Anyone in his position would try to remove his rival. You had to be practical, and recent precedents existed. Most of the ambitious Julio-Claudian dynasty, with or without assistance from their noble wives and mothers, had had a hand in murdering some relative who stood in their way. The Empress Livia kept in constant touch with a poisoner. Sending soldiers to despatch rivals with swords happened on a routine basis.

In contrast, officially the Flavian creed was to admire 'traditional Roman values'. That dull ideal meant spending their summers in the country and deploring scandal. Instead of eliminating each other, they glued together in a patriarchal huddle. It was said that once, when Domitian had angered Vespasian, Titus generously urged their father to be lenient, because blood was thicker than water. Now Titus gave a very sincere impression that he loved his ten-years-younger brother, admired him, confided in him, valued him, relied on him, would bequeath him everything in full confidence of excellent stewardship—and that he never felt any tendency to wring Domitian's sturdy neck until the untrustworthy little bugger croaked.

Domitian kept his own counsel. This is always viewed as moody and suspicious.

Being intelligent, he could presumably see that bringing about the death of an emperor would carry a pervasive after-taint. Assassination sets a bad precedent; historians cluttered up the court, expertly pointing that out, albeit in undertones. If he really did have designs on his brother, he was hampered by the fact that from the start of Vespasian's reign Titus had appointed himself Prefect of the Praetorian Guard, nine thousand battle-hardened men whose job was to protect their emperor day and night, which they now did with the devotion of uncomplicated soldiers he had personally commanded for ten years. Men to whom Titus had also given a massive donation of cash on his accession, the usual way to guarantee the Guards' loyalty; their loyalty code was simple.

Topping Titus while nine thousand armoured toughs were looking after him would be difficult. So stabbing Titus at the baths or the Games was out. Even putting arsenic into the cherry preserve at breakfast time, though feasible for a family member, would be the act of an idiot.

Nevertheless, on the twenty-mile journey down from Alba, secluded in his palanquin, it must be natural for a frustrated Caesar, an emperor-in-waiting who might never succeed, to let his thoughts dwell privately on possibilities for becoming an emperor-in-fact. For three or four hours he had not much else to do. He was not a great reader. A bumping litter was no place for entertainments to take his mind off his feelings. Belly-dancers or flautists were out. You could fuck a concubine or eunuch if you really wanted a challenge, but there were easier ways to give yourself a hernia. The Emperor Claudius was supposed to have invented a special chessboard for his carriage, but Domitian's game was dice, solo. His personality was obsessive enough to throw dice repeatedly for a whole journey to Rome, but in a bumping litter dice got lost too often. He never coped well with that kind of frustration.

It had not struck him that he would not cope with the burned Capitol either.

*　　*　　*

On arrival, the usual flummery set in. Stretching irritably, he waited for things to start, while as always it took longer than he could bear. He watched people around him in silence, which always worried them. They were scared of him. He recognised it, with a mixture of resentment and bitter glee. All the time a part of him wanted instead to be loved, as his father had been, as his brother still was. Knowing that it would never happen just made him colder and more autocratic.

He gazed up from the Forum to where the Temple of Jupiter should be. Once again it was gone. Its absence took him back to the worst night of his life, that night of terror when he was eighteen.

He had had an unextravagant childhood. They

were always short of money. Nonetheless, by the time Domitian was born, Vespasian had become a man of importance, one of the victors of the Roman invasion of Britain and a consul; during those years he was a remote figure to his younger son, often serving abroad. Domitian had been home-schooled whereas Titus, previously, was educated at court with the Emperor Claudius' son, Britannicus. But Domitian had expected the kind of career his brother had: the army at officer rank, formal entry to the Senate, diplomatic posts abroad, maybe training as a barrister. None of that happened, because his father became emperor.

During Domitian's teens Vespasian left Rome again, accompanying Nero on a cultural tour of Greece. It unexpectedly led to a further three years away, subduing a revolt in Judaea. Vespasian won the command because Nero had jealously executed a more prominent and popular general, Corbulo, who was probably plotting (though possibly not). Titus went east with Vespasian, first on his father's staff, but before long leading troops as a general in his own right. Domitian had been left behind in Rome, deposited with his uncle, Flavius Sabinus.

Nero's antics finally offended Roman taste too much; he was pressured into suicide. A tussle for power ensued. Three new emperors came and went, each lasting only months, each dying violently. Finally, to the astonishment of the snobs in Rome, Vespasian emerged the winner. Having four legions in his command had helped. Another virtue was that his two grown sons guaranteed an enduring succession. He did not venture home to Rome until the situation stabilised; in the last months there was bloody turmoil as his predecessor

Vitellius clung on in power.

Flavius Sabinus, one of the most respected men in Rome, was Prefect of the City; he held that post for many years, even under the rival Vitellius. With the Empire and city suffering terribly, Sabinus struggled to clinch his brother's bid for the throne, desperately brokering peace. Domitian found himself in a thrilling position, though much overshadowed by his uncle and with house arrest imposed by Vitellius.

As Vespasian's troops marched through Italy towards Rome, Vitellius agreed to abdicate. Prematurely, Sabinus allowed exulting Flavian supporters to congregate outside his house. They were attacked by a furious mob of opponents. By that time, Vitellius was unwell and had no power to control this situation even if he had wanted to. Sabinus took refuge on the Capitol with a motley group of followers; he sent for his own sons and Domitian, who managed to evade his guards and reach the citadel.

Frantic, the Flavians barricaded themselves in. They used statues to block routes up the hill and threw roof tiles down on the Vitellian troops who surrounded them. It became a debacle. Unknown arsonists set fire to the Capitol buildings. Suddenly, everything had gone wrong for the Flavians; in a frantic race against time their army struggled to reach Rome to achieve a rescue. The Vitellians stormed the Capitol before the troops arrived. Sabinus was captured and killed; his mutilated body thrown on the Gemonian Stairs like a traitor's. Through the flames and smoke, chaos and mangled corpses, Domitian managed to evade the Vitellians who were hunting him down. As

Vespasian's son, he would have been at best a hostage, but he knew they wanted him dead.

A brave caretaker of the Temple of Jupiter concealed him in his hut through one terrifying night. Next morning, assisted by a loyal freedman, Domitian escaped down to the Campus where he mingled with bare-chested priests of Isis, dressed as one of their exotic number as they went in procession to the sound of sistrums. He made it across the river to the house of a schoolfriend, whose mother hid him. Only when the Flavian army arrived in Rome, two days later, was it safe to emerge and scramble to them. He gave a speech to the soldiers, who then acclaimed Domitian with the title of Caesar and carried him in triumph to his father's house.

Heady moments followed. He appeared in the Senate, speaking for his father, and acquitted himself well. He handed out honours. He was courted by greybeards and sycophants alike. Women flung themselves at him; he lured one senator's young wife—one of Corbulo's daughters—to Pompey's villa in the Alban Hills where he persuaded her to leave her husband for him.

But the events on the Capitol had affected him for life. His equilibrium was shaken. The sights and sounds of fire and mob violence, and his uncle's ghastly fate, embedded themselves in his mind. From then on, Domitian trusted nobody and no situation. He had witnessed how good fortune could be snatched away. If the most senior and worthy men could end their lives torn limb from limb, what hope was there for anyone? At eighteen, having never held a military post, he was affected by this violence. His need for disguise and elusion that bleak night had taught him deep reserve, a personal wariness which he never again put off. Ten years later, the smell of the burnt temple on the Capitol was threatening to unman him.

He had to go up there. It was expected.

He stared as deferential vigiles produced protective boots and thick, hooded cloaks for the milling dignitaries. Someone must have hastily raided the cohorts' stores for brand new boots. It would be unacceptable to push the illustrious corns of a consul into a pair that had been worn already by some horny-soled freedman stomping out sticky embers at a grain warehouse. *Nice thought, though!* As the Emperor's brother, Domitian was provided with gear by slaves from the palace. He joked with an impassive dresser that a special battalion had charge of imperial disaster uniforms: National Emergency coveralls with delicious purple accents, boots with little gold wings on them for flying above catastrophes ... Once kitted out himself, he coolly observed how the officers who were helping the others glanced at each other as they tried to advise the doddery old fools who now intended to go clambering over smoking ruins where there was still danger of collapse.

The Prefect of Vigiles gave a short, sensible safety lecture. Half the dignitaries were talking among themselves or wandering off. None of the great seemed to see the point of thick-soled boots, even though up on the Capitol the ground might be still red hot.

Domitian caught the Prefect's eye and let a flicker of sympathy show. He had been taught to respect efficient men. After all, his down-to-earth father had viewed his role as emperor as merely doing an honest job. Vespasian also set an example of scoffing, in coarse language, at high-ranking droolers who had reached the limit of their competence but were still cluttering up the Senate.

Far too many introductions were made. A discreet official stood behind him, mentioning names so Domitian could greet people as if he remembered them. He made it plain he hated shaking hands, but merely inclined his head as long queues of officials paraded. However, he embraced the two consuls, because he knew Titus would have done so: mighty men sharing public grief for their damaged city. Titus would have freely wept on their togaed shoulders, but Domitian's eyes stayed dry.

He reviewed the weary vigiles with respect for what the firemen had gone through. Their achievement in saving the main Forum and his father's new amphitheatre deserved genuine thanks. A small number were presented to him while their Prefect read hastily scribbled accounts of individual bravery. Domitian made awards. Although in theory every honour needed the personal sanction of the absent Titus, his brother was permitted to make on-the-spot announcements of diplomas and cash gifts. Domitian brought it off with grace. He knew how to behave.

One man's heroics caught his interest. The Prefect explained that this young fellow, one-eyed and hideously battle-scarred, had plucked a priest from certain death in front of the cult statues in the Temple of Jupiter. Domitian, who credited Jupiter with saving his own life on that terrible night on the Capitol, paid close attention. He seemed fascinated by the man's scars too.

41

Later, the Prefect of Vigiles remembered this. By then the inspection party had snaked up the Gemonian Stairs to the heights, where they gasped at the ruined Temple and gasped again as they surveyed the destruction that stretched across the Field of Mars below. Lists of lost monuments were read out by a sombre works official. Then vigiles tribunes made themselves available to take questions. The senators all liked to think they were bright and well-informed. Some of their queries about how the fire had behaved and how the firemen tackled it were apt; some were stupid. After they had expressed horror over the tragedy, they began talking about rebuilding.

Classicus was on hand. He was secretary of finance to Titus; he normally stuck with the Emperor day and night, so Domitian wondered if Titus had sent him to spy on what happened today. If Domitian ever became emperor, this freedman would be the first retainer to go.

Classicus stated quickly that the Emperor would have to be consulted about costs. He had had no chance yet to ascertain how far Titus wanted to empty the Treasury and whether, given how generously he was already paying out after Vesuvius, he would contribute money of his own. Domitian, who was itching to involve himself but who had no remit, stayed silent but looked pinched. As the VIPs pontificated, the troops were under orders to stick close and make sure none of the noble ones dithered into an unstable building or had half a column crack down on his head. Domitian had been frowning and withdrawn for a while. Suddenly he announced that he wanted to explore alone.

The City Prefect nudged the Prefect of Vigiles. This was an awkward breach of protocol. As a member of the imperial family, Domitian was entitled to bodyguards especially when he was representing his brother, but he had not asked and no Praetorian Guards had been arranged. It was still highly dangerous up here and no one who valued his job wanted to take responsibility for the young Caesar if he went off on his own. So the quick-thinking vigiles commander suggested that one of his own men should accompany the prince at a distance, to ensure his safety. He gave the nod to the man who had saved the priest. That was how, while Domitian went as close as possible to the Temple of Jupiter, Gaius Vinius trailed three yards behind.

They could feel heat still radiating from the ruins, so intense that the building seemed liable to burst into flames again. Enormous broken columns blocked their path. What remained of the gigantic building groaned afresh. Vinius knew that when you started to hear new creaks and shifts, it was time to leave. He wondered if he was allowed to speak up and alert his charge.

Domitian must have sensed danger; of his own accord he moved back and strode around the summit to the far side of the hill. Now they were isolated together, out of sight of the rest.

Domitian stood for a long time, gazing across the devastation below. Vinius placed himself nearby, also staring out over the Tiber, in that apparent trance good soldiers adopt to avoid irritating their officers. Domitian considered ordering him away but chose not to. He decided the man was not as dumb as he appeared, simply discreet. Vinius

43

looked a little slumped, clearly having no energy left for the ramrod position his superiors would have wanted.

In turn, Gaius Vinius weighed up his companion. Domitian Caesar was not yet thirty, Vinius in his early twenties, so they had one thing in common: among the party who had come up to survey the scene—officers, magistrates and officials all in their fifth or sixth decade—they two were the youngest. Domitian was taller than Titus which probably pleased him, though shorter than Vinius. He was good-looking and well-made, though not muscular because he rarely took exercise. Around the eyes there was a noticeable resemblance to his father Vespasian, though unlike his brother he had a silly mouth, Vinius reckoned. Wrong teeth? Receding jaw? A section of his upper lip twisted slightly. The cause was not obvious. The mouth gave him a pleasant expression from one side, though from the other he looked weak.

Domitian turned his head. Vinius was staring directly at him. Since it was impossible to disguise this, he cleared his throat and said, 'I see you looking down the Via Flaminia, sir. That was the natural limit of the fire, because the intense heat on the Campus Martius caused an in-draught. Air rushing over the Campus created a natural firebreak.'

For speaking uninvited, Domitian could have dismissed him. Vinius stared woodenly across the distant Campus. His princely companion elected to be gracious. Vespasian, superb general that he was, had been good with common soldiers; there could be nothing but credit in talking to this one about his speciality, fire.

'The Temple of Isis is gone, I see, soldier.'

Vinius picked up on the statement's significance at once. He knew how Domitian had disguised himself as a devotee of Isis during his escape from the Vitellians. Dropping his voice, he acknowledged the young Caesar's inevitable stress. 'This must be very hard for you, sir.'

He understood why Domitian had wanted to escape from observation by his companions. He had hidden it, but all through this official visit he had been fighting down panic. He had tested himself by inspecting the Temple of Jupiter and forcing himself to look down where the Temple of Isis had been, but if he didn't get away soon it would be too much for him. Now he urgently wanted the Capitol visit to be over, but had to make himself steady before he could return to the others and conclude it.

Vinius, who regularly endured his own nightmares, knew what was going on here. Domitian's heart would be pounding erratically. Sweat gleamed on his high forehead. Mentally, he was back in that violent climax to the Year of the Four Emperors, shaken by terrible memories.

'One who knows, soldier?'

'I would not presume, Caesar.'

They shared a brief moment of fellow-feeling nonetheless. The paramilitary stood quietly; the prince's hands were gripped in fists. Domitian admitted, 'I nearly died that night. One assumes the memories will fade. That's a mistake.' Vinius glanced over again, so Domitian indicated his striking scars. 'You must have experience of the after-effects of trauma.'

Vinius nodded. 'Unfortunately, sir! A major

45

shock, especially when you're young, seems to stay with you for life.' Since the sky failed to fall in, he continued: 'And when the nightmares come, every man is on his own. Just when you think you are safe from the horrors, you get tired, or drunk, or simply the Fates think you are enjoying yourself too much and need to be reined in . . . But sometimes it's bloody obvious why it all comes rushing back. So pardon me, Caesar, I know exactly what's churning you up today and I don't mean that disrespectfully. I myself wouldn't want ever again to find whooping barbarians throwing spears towards me.'

'Yet you are a brave man.'

'If you say so.' A soldier's answer. Slightly sullen. False modesty, no doubt. *I only did my duty, sir.* Or true modesty perhaps. The man was visibly too tired to care. He talked, almost to keep himself awake: 'I just know that any more action in the field would give me the shakes, I couldn't help it. After I was wounded, I was glad to be sent back to Rome to avoid that situation. For you, sir, at the age you were that awful night, and with what happened to your uncle, coming back on the Capitol, with the Temple burned down once again, must be unbearable.'

If this conversation with Vinius had any palliative effect, Domitian would never admit it. Their exchange abruptly ended. Imperial distance resumed very fast. Without a word more, Domitian set off back towards the others.

Watch your step, Caesar.

Don't give me orders, soldier.

*　　　*　　　*

46

The exchange had results, unfortunately.

After Vinius resumed his place with the troops, Domitian stood with the Prefect of Vigiles and asked the man's history. By then the Prefect had quickly checked the investigator's background, so he was able to explain the scars, another story of heroics. He also knew that Vinius Clodianus was the youngest of three sons of a dedicated officer, all three young men serving in the military. The father had been tribune of the vigiles' Fourth Cohort, before transferring to the Praetorian Guard. He died a mere six weeks later. (The Prefect censored out how the father had spent all six weeks celebrating the achievement of his lifetime dream, drinking gross amounts of wine until, according to the medic, his brain just went off pop.)

A tragic story. Something should be done for the son, said Domitian.

People would learn that Domitian only spoke when he had darkly worked a subject through. He had a plan in mind that would meddle where Titus held authority. The idea provided a reward for Vinius and his bravery, whilst also reflecting his father's service over many years and the disappointment that must have been felt in this whole loyal military family when the father died so suddenly. Titus, who claimed he counted a day lost if he had failed to do good to somebody, would find it impossible to quibble.

*　　　*　　　*

Ignorant of his fate, Gaius Vinius went home that day and slept like the dead until his wife decided he had slumbered in his filth long enough. Cruelly

47

woken, he retreated to a cell at the station house, until eventually someone had to root him out to see their tribune.

Shambling blearily, grumbling, and still dripping from a hasty bathe, Vinius was informed of an unexpected honour: he had been posted out of the vigiles and into the Praetorian Guard.

'Shit on a stick!'

'This is for carrying out that charred priest, I imagine. Look as if you're delighted.' The tribune spoke dryly. He knew Vinius liked to keep his head down. 'They are all foul-mouthed, arrogant bastards. You should fit in. You'll be among the youngest,' he added a little spitefully. Some vigiles had to yearn for this for years; most never made it. 'They will love you like a new little kitten.'

'Stuff that for a lark,' growled Vinius at this sinister promise. *He* was now stuffed. His life, as he saw it, was ruined. He knew the constraints. The only benefit was that the unwanted advancement put an end to his marriage problems. He could live in the camp and never go home. He *had* to live in the camp, in fact.

'From what I've heard of your father, he would be delighted.'

'Yes, sir. He would be very proud.'

It must be the after-effects of the fire; as Vinius faced his future, even with his dead father's imagined blessing, he felt sick.

4

The Flavian Amphitheatre was paid for by Vespasian's booty from the Judaean wars. It took ten years to build, required a whole new quarry to provide its travertine marble fittings and facings, remained incomplete when its venerable founder passed away and was formally opened by his son Titus. The enormous and iconic gift to the people of Rome would one day be known as the Colosseum because of an adjacent hundred-foot bronze statue of Nero, which stood in the vestibule of the Golden House. All memory of Nero was being obliterated in Rome so Vespasian had added a sunray crown to reconfigure the gigantic figure as a tribute to Sol Invictus, the undying sun. He was not a man to waste anything expensive. So in his ever-genial way, he set a precedent that statues to an emperor who was *damned to the memory*—written out of history for abominable crimes—should be recycled. Vespasian had probably not envisaged that one day the head of the Emperor Nerva would replace that of his own son Domitian.

Since the amphitheatre was slathered in many other statues, sculptors were happy; their agents and middlemen, who took the larger share of their fees, wore even bigger smiles. When Titus dedicated the arena after the fire, suppliers of exotic animals and gladiators enjoyed a smackeroo bonanza. The opening games lasted around a hundred days, with nine thousand wild beasts slain in the process—together with some humans. The knock-on effects as obscene profits were splurged would bring joy for years to bankers, builders, silver- and goldsmiths, gourmet chefs, marble importers, traders in silks and spices, providers of carriages with expensive coachwork, undercover betting agents, suppliers of performing dwarves, and everyone in the multiple branches of the sex trade.

Less obvious was that a hundred days of public partying were a boon to hairdressers. Every woman who disported in the spanking new seats, and many men too, wanted to look smart. Although some relationships would break apart under the strain of so much enjoyment, numerous other pairings were begun, developed or cemented, during the arena games. This required endless work with curling irons, colours and conditioners, wigs, toupees and topknots.

Though still a young girl, Flavia Lucilla worked hard while she had that chance. She earned good money. She even won more, because one day when she was sprucing up imperial locks that had drooped in the hot sun, her quick fingers managed to grasp and hold one of the gift balls that Titus flung into the crowd; some were for clothing or food, but hers gave a cash prize. At the same time, she established a presence, gained her confidence, and acquired clients who would stay faithful to her throughout her working life. Titus' inaugural Games left her just about safe financially, although immediately beforehand—during the few months after she went to the vigiles—her life had been perilous and maturity dropped on her abruptly.

The first shock was the unexpected loss of her mother. Lucilla had furiously planned a break with Lachne straight after her interview with Gaius

Vinius, but a quarrel was pre-empted by the fire raging so close to where they lived. She found Lachne hysterically running up and down stairs from their apartment and loading their possessions onto a cart sent by her lover, Orgilius. Smoke filled their street, yet members of the vigiles were telling everyone to wait, though to be ready to evacuate if the fire crossed the Via Flaminia. It never did. People disobeyed the orders anyway.

Lucilla deferred her quarrel. She helped Lachne load the cart, then struggle through the crowded streets to another apartment that Orgilius put at their disposal. This would have been generous, Lucilla thought, if he had not so obviously been protecting his own sex-life. The place was better— one storey lower—though it was not where Orgilius lived himself. Lucilla was sure he must be married. Oblivious to this glaring conclusion, her mother declared how useful it was that he owned so many properties. Lachne settled into the improved accommodation like a smart limpet who had drifted to a more promising rock. Even if their old apartment survived, she was not going back.

Flavia Lachne had the fine features that were common among slaves and ex-slaves of the aristocracy, who could afford to buy their staff not simply for potential use but for appearance. The Flavians were a frugal family who usually picked their slaves because they were affordable, yet Lachne had been ornamental too. In later life she inclined to stoutness, but she always had a striking, regular face with large dark eyes and a figure she made the most of. She looked like a woman who was up for anything; Lucilla presumed she was.

As far as anyone knew her origins, Lachne came

from the Aegean coast of Asia, somewhere south of Troy and east of Lesbos. This happened to be a region with olive oil production and the related creation of cosmetics, but although a knowledge of beauty treatments was later useful, Lachne had in fact wangled a career ornamenting the adult Flavian women simply because she wanted to avoid getting stuck as a nursery carer. So another slave called Phyllis was subsequently able to boast she had looked after the infant Domitian and Titus' daughter Julia, while instead Lachne plaited and coiffed her mistresses. It appeared, even to her own offspring, that she did not like children. This was felt keenly by her daughter Lucilla.

Like most mothers, Lachne believed she had brought up her children well. Nobody could complain there was a lack of love (thought Lachne) yet there was little demonstration of it (thought Lucilla). The pair had lived together for fifteen years, shared meals and chores, sometimes went shopping, very occasionally had outings to see acquaintances, rarely quarrelled, but often failed to communicate. Lachne would have said she knew her daughter inside out; the reserved Lucilla would have scoffed. But Lucilla did know Lachne. There was much about her mother that she tended to despise, though she generally refrained from argument or attempting to change her.

Lucilla had barely reached her teens when a subtle shift in their relationship came, and it was over the famous Flavian hairstyle. Then, Lachne seriously needed her.

*   *   *

52

The Flavian women were not tall. This was never recorded by poets or historians who, unless there was scandal to report, only cared to mention women's names and their marriages. Up until now no Flavian ladies had inspired scurrilous writing, where physical attributes might have been mocked. Even the existence of Antonia Caenis, Vespasian's ex-slave concubine, had caused more surprise than censure. Julia's reputation would be fouled, though not yet. Domitian's wife was said to brag about her conquests, though perhaps this was a vindictive slur, retaliation because she was proud and ignored critics contemptuously. Most Flavian women stayed silent and practically invisible. That included Flavia Domitilla whom Lachne and Lucilla knew best. Her mother had been Vespasian's daughter.

The Flavian ladies' moderate height can be deduced from the extremely tall hairstyle that Lachne devised for them. She was a good hairdresser. She understood impact. Despite moving with the slow sway of a pregnant dairy cow, as the darting Lucilla saw it, Lachne always did her job. She knew how to suggest brightly that a rather dumpy, ordinary-featured, unassuming, no-longer-young woman, perhaps wearied by pregnancies and children dying, or simply depressed by long years of humouring a husband, might cheer herself up with a new look. This carried a promise of renewed marital excitement, not to mention a subtle gloss that the put-upon client was a woman of worth; she still possessed needs, desires, allure and sexual fire of her own.

Having a good eye and more creativity than her sleepy manner implied, Lachne became so much loved by the Flavian ladies that she won her freedom on the strength of it, though on condition that as a member of the extended Flavian *'familia'* she would always remain available to do her ladies' hair. Intent on escaping drudgery, Lachne moved out—one advantage of becoming a freedwoman was that she had now some choice in this—but she always lived very close to the most important Flavian women. She could be summoned in an emergency, though was not on instant call. Lachne had time to herself and if she shooed Lucilla out of doors she could freely entertain men.

So Lucilla had grown up near the Quirinal Hill in the Seventh Region. By the age of fifteen, part of the tension with her mother came from Lachne's determination to keep control of her. Lachne herself no longer had nimble hands. Lucilla's small, extremely dexterous fingers were essential for constructing the court ladies' hairstyle.

Nothing like this startling edifice had been worn before. In previous times, Roman women harped piously on 'traditional simplicity'. The more ostentatiously virtuous relatives of the Emperor Augustus, starting with his chilly sister Octavia, had scraped modest ringlets on the nape of their necks. Some parted the front and took their hair down each side to their bejewelled ears, an effect that could be achieved naturally, though it was in hairdressers' interests to suggest waves either side of the parting, which required curling rods. Other women had a rolled topknot just above the forehead. It looked severe but added 'lift'. This noun is frequently dropped into hairdressers' conversation. 'Lift' needs assistance, whatever the hair type.

Lachne's new style had stupendous lift. It

consisted of a comical crescent of false or real hair, covered all over with a crush of pincurls. It lofted above the wearer's face from ear to ear, like a curly tiara. Of course the look required support, either a wire framework, which was lighter, or padding, which was more comfortable but heavier—though women found it altered how they held their heads and gave them a sense of dignity. Their own hair, which was redundant to the effect, would be plaited and coiled on the back of their heads. False curls allowed the whole front structure to be removed, which saved having to sleep upright.

The rows of frontal curls were a challenge for sculptors. Apart from the technical difficulty, it is not easy to ply a chisel while trying not to grin.

Wearing this hairstyle women could not judge how odd they looked. In boudoirs of the day, even the most beautifully ornamented bronze or silver hand-mirrors had polished metal surfaces that showed only blurred images.

The curly coronet was as hot as a bearskin to wear. From the side, it seemed liable to topple off. From behind, joins showed. Yearning to be fashionistas, Flavian ladies were nevertheless convinced by their attendants that they looked quite lovely. Other people that they might have consulted were no help. What husband, when asked, 'How is my hair today, Septimus?' was ever going to answer, 'Bunnikins, you look ridiculous'? Septimus was probably miles away, dreaming of screwing that kitchen girl with the enormous breasts, or wistfully lusting after his favourite altar-boy, the one who wore his tunics unbelievably short to display those pert buttocks ready for rodding . . . Even down-to-earth husbands would be just as vague, as they groaned over the price of oxen or wondered how to catch out a business manager who was blatantly fiddling. Perhaps a rare wholesome specimen might instead be philosophising on human goodness—though on the whole Roman men were more fascinated by badness.

From a young age, Flavia Lucilla had helped create the crazy concoctions with which women of the Flavian family turned themselves into trendsetters. Even under Vespasian, an emperor whose political appeal was 'old country values', it was permissible for respectable women to spend hours having their hair tended. Some women enjoyed being viciously cruel to the slaves who had to work on them; they could pinch and punch and beat unhappy foreign girls while they were themselves beautified. All knew that complicated hair made them expensive ornaments to their noble menfolk, which the men liked, and which showed that the upper classes were special because they had leisure and money for time-consuming processes. Their men were taught to go along with it. For one thing they reassured themselves that while wives were being combed endlessly indoors, they were not out committing adultery with charioteers. (Men believed that was what all wives dreamed of; wives gossiped that some of their number indeed managed it.)

Lucilla always smiled wryly at the concept of her mother as a guardian of morals. But she did admire a woman who could persuade her clients to deck themselves out so crankily, and to pay handsomely for it. Only much later, much too late, did Lucilla concede that, creatively, her mother must have possessed an impish sense of humour.

56

By that time, Lachne was gone. During their flight from home in the terrible fire, she was already breathless. She must have been affected by smoke, yet was also sickening. Lucilla had supposed she was terrified that her jewellery collection, hastily retrieved, would be lost in the crush or discovered by Orgilius, who would realise she had tried to dupe him. Mother and daughter quarrelled, badly. Already feeling ill in truth, Lachne forgot her need for Lucilla's dexterity. She goaded the girl, who had nowhere else to go, no means to support herself—unless she wanted to become a waitress in a street bar, which was the same as being a prostitute. Lucilla in response made vicious comments on her mother's men. 'That would include my father—if I knew who he was. But even *you* don't know, Mother, do you?'

If Lachne did, she took the secret to her grave. As the quarrel flared more violently, Lucilla fled. She went back to their old apartment, but Lachne had paid rent only sporadically, so very soon the landlord kicked her out and put in new tenants. Helpless, the unhappy girl slunk back to see Lachne, only to learn that her mother had caught the plague that was running through Rome in a populace weakened by famine after the eruption of Vesuvius.

The epidemic was virulent. Lachne had died.

There was a funeral. People Lucilla barely knew

turned up, one of them Lara, whom Lucilla had always believed was a young aunt. Fellow slaves of Lachne's had clubbed together to put up a memorial.

To Flavia Lachne, freedwoman of Domitilla, hairdresser. She lived forty-three years. This was made by Flavius Endymon, clothes mender; Flavius Nepos, cook; Flavius Afranius, litter-bearer; Flavia Lara, hairdresser.

Lucilla wondered whether Endymon, Nepos or Afranius could be her father, though she felt no affinity with any of them.

Members of the Flavian family sent gifts, there was never any suggestion these imperial patrons might attend in person; the gifts were selected on their behalf by the same freedmen and women who supplied the undertakers and provided the inscription stone. Since those who had generously paid for the stone wanted their names listed on it to advertise their piety, there was no room to mention Lucilla.

*   *   *

She was terrified about her future. People at the funeral had fallen upon Lachne's clothes and other possessions, taking them away as 'keepsakes'. The young woman Lara, who had a useless husband and several small children, was particularly eager to gather up mementos. All Lucilla kept was the famous jewellery collection. It was her only fallback. Otherwise, her choices were to work or to marry someone with a job or little business; marriage

58

would probably entail hard work in any case. Lucilla ought to be entitled to a basic corn dole, but it was never enough to live on and had to be claimed by her male head of household; Lucilla had no head of household.

Orgilius said she could stay at the apartment for a while. How long, or on what terms, he did not specify. Lucilla soon found out. One evening he visited, plied her with drink, pleaded with her to be nice to him, and seduced her.

It was no surprise. Nor was it brutal rape. Lucilla knew the rapid coupling was no different from abuse meted out daily to slaves in most homes. Orgilius felt he had inherited the girl, a fair return for financial investment in her mother. True, Lucilla was young, but much younger children had to service the rich. He blamed Lucilla, murmuring, 'You encouraged me, you naughty minx!' as he slunk off.

Lucilla saw that Orgilius had some shame and would stay away for a while—a short while. Inevitably, he would return. He took her compliance for granted. Who could blame him? Though he had made her tipsy, she had not tried to fight him off.

Lucilla tried not to feel wanton, though she was a normal girl, already intrigued about sex. Even with a horrible partner, and with such cursory manoeuvres, her body had to some extent responded. So she viewed what had happened with detachment. That did not mean she wanted more of this.

Orgilius was rich, but he was overweight and pudding-faced. He made her flesh creep. She suspected he could turn nasty and Lachne had complained of his interest in experimental sexual acts. He was sixty. He had warts. He thought a young girl should take orders and be grateful. Next time he grabbed Lucilla, their congress would go on very much longer and she would be expected to participate vigorously.

She seemed stuck with Orgilius, as a provider. If she fell pregnant, however, he would evict her. She had no knowledge of prevention, nor of where to go for an abortion, which was illegal anyway. To be publicly linked to the businessman carried a penalty. Unless she kept this secret and lied, she would be spoiled for marriage, with its poisonous reliance on a bride's supposed virginity.

She opted to flee.

Her one hope lay in Lara. Lara had left her address, as if inviting contact. When Lucilla turned up, tearfully begging for help, Lara immediately took her in. Lucilla's vague hope that she could simply stay with this family in their admittedly crowded apartment and help look after the children ended as soon as Junius, Lara's husband, wandered in. Junius worked in some unspecified branch of the leather trade. He was small and shifty; it was difficult to see why Lara, a beautiful young woman with a pleasant personality, had married him. Maybe he had seemed her only option for security, though he oozed various kinds of unreliability and smelt of tannin. His speculative glance at Lucilla spoke volumes. She saw at once that Lara would want her to find other accommodation quickly, lest things go badly wrong. She herself now had no wish to dally.

By then she had had a new shock. Lara was not an aunt. Apparently Lachne was her mother too.

She and Lucilla, Lara explained, were sisters.

That was not the entire truth; the truth was another family secret which Lucilla would be a long time discovering.

*   *   *

The story Lara told was that Flavia Lachne had been only thirteen when she was first made pregnant. As with Lucilla later, she had never said whether her elder daughter Lara was fathered by a fellow slave, someone outside the house, or one of the family. Any of these was possible in most households. It was a slave's lot to be sexually exploited, though the lucky ones passed puberty first. Lucilla sometimes thought her sister had a Flavian air, though slaves often took on the mannerisms of the family they lived with. Her origins were best unexplored. Lara herself showed no curiosity and trying to associate herself closely with one of the imperial family would do her no good. Slaves and ex-slaves were used to not knowing their paternity.

As a slave's child, Lara had had minimal contact with her birth mother. Eventually Lachne bore a second daughter, Lucilla, with about fifteen years between the two. Neither ever knew of Lachne having other children, though she could have done. Both daughters became free when Flavia Lachne was manumitted; she bought their freedom herself.

Lara married young, then she and Lucilla, who was still an infant, rarely met. Looking back, Lucilla remembered her mother had from time to time left the apartment, mentioning that she was off to visit Lara, though she was always reticent about it.

Lucilla liked Lara. Lara had a good opinion of everyone and always expected every event to turn out well; perhaps this challenging viewpoint explained why she married Junius.

Lara explained to Lucilla that, as the children of a freedwoman, they did have connections. They could claim the Flavians as patrons and extended family. The orphaned Lucilla could ask for their help. She would have a duty to them, but they had responsibilities to her and should ensure she did not starve.

Accompanying their mother, Lara had regularly groomed the Flavians. With Lachne gone, she went independently. She now took Lucilla to meet Flavia Domitilla, Vespasian's granddaughter, who had freed Lachne. The sisters would work together, even after Lucilla found her own place to stay. Lara quickly trained Lucilla in all aspects of hairdressing, not just building towers of curls. Quietly and pleasantly, like her mother and sister, Lucilla made the Flavian ladies feel she turned them out like goddesses.

When Lara was caught up in domestic affairs, Lucilla visited the Flavian women on her own. They paid a small, rather unreliable retainer, but soon Lara's other private clients were introducing her to their friends. She and Lara had also become known for attending at weddings: they adorned the brides, who traditionally had their hair arranged in a special style like that of the Vestal Virgins. This generally led to extra work on the brides' female relatives. Tips on wedding days were good. Then when the amphitheatre opened, Lucilla set herself to work long hours to build up her savings.

The cash gift she collected at the Games allowed her to move out from Lara's to a tiny one-room lodging. Her long-term dream was to rent a much better apartment where she could both live and work. It had to be pleasant, with space for customers and running water so she could wash clients' hair. This would be expensive. Lucilla's nest-egg slowly grew but for a long time the kind of place she wanted remained beyond her reach.

*   *   *

Times changed. After ruling for only two years, the Emperor Titus collapsed with a fever, just as his father had done. When Titus died, everyone immediately understood that Rome was entering a period which would have a very different flavour. Domitian Caesar snatched the throne, almost too impatient to wait for the Senate's approval.

From the start there was consternation. While it was true that the beloved Titus had turned out well, nobody ever expected Domitian to flower like his brother. He was damned before he began—and he diligently lived up to people's fears. The Senate was tense. Artists hoped for benefits, though imperial patronage was always uncertain. The armed forces had mixed expectations because to date Domitian had had no military career. Traders grumbled, even though most businessmen remained confident. Lucilla and her sister, whose clients included members of the imperial family, watched events with heightened curiosity and from close at hand.

Lucilla occasionally attended Domitia Longina, the Emperor's wife, a woman she did not take to much, though it was not her place to refuse the work. She mainly continued to look after Flavia Domitilla, who was a mother of seven and much in need of pampering. Through her, Lucilla met Domitilla's cousin Julia, Titus' daughter, after being sent along to revive Julia's spirits after her father died. Romans were supposed to have unkempt hair when mourning, but behind discreet veils most aristocratic women preferred to stay neat. One never knew (Lachne had always said) when a lover might manage to creep up the back stairs with a practical suggestion for consoling one's grief.

Of course Flavia Julia, admired daughter of the beloved Titus and respected young wife of her cousin Flavius Sabinus, did not have lovers.

Well, not at that time.

And perhaps never.

*　　　*　　　*

Being single, Lucilla was more readily mobile than her sister. Whenever the court moved out to one of Domitian's villas in the summer, it was Lucilla who went. His favourites were at the Alban lake, or his father's birthplace in the Sabine Hills, but there were also imperial villas at Circeii on the Neapolis coast, at Tusculum, Antium, Gaeta, Anxur and Baiae, not to mention extensive property that the Emperor's wife Domitia Longina had inherited from her father Corbulo. Lucilla loved to go, though she worked for other clients too, and resisted being a permanent member of the imperial entourage; she always kept a base in Rome.

Alba was special to her. She could see just why, on his father's accession, the young Domitian

64

Caesar had grabbed Pompey's villa, which was part of the imperial portfolio; why he had chosen this fabulous setting for his seduction of Domitia Longina, who was at the time married to another man; and why after he became Emperor he made this his most frequent retreat, his summer court. Associated with that court, Lucilla herself acquired new confidence. Her duties often left her with free time. Before she was twenty, she had grown into her looks and shone with personality. As Gaius Vinius had once prophesied, she was becoming attractive. She began to make friends.

Plenty of people at Alba knew Flavia Lucilla. She made contacts, many of them very close to Domitian: she met and befriended his eunuchs and his dwarf, musicians, sculptors, architects and poets. She never associated with the upper classes, the senators who were part of his advisory circle—although their wives knew who to visit when they wanted a decent stylist for something a little ambitious. Lucilla was familiar with the imperial secretaries since many of them, like her, were freedmen either of the Flavians or their imperial predecessors; wives of several prominent bureaucrats were also among her customers. She knew by sight a few of the Praetorian Guards, though she tended to avoid soldiers. Likewise, she had little to do with the athletes who came for Domitian's new Games, and she fastidiously shunned contact with his gladiators.

She had certain special dealings with the Emperor's bedchamber barber. This fraught freedman was handling an obsessive ruler who was notoriously upset by his receding hairline. It had become well known that Flavia Lucilla had flying fingers and was utterly discreet; she was the best maker of undetectable wigs.

Given the sensitive nature of these consultations with the barber, she never talked about the subject.

5

Gaius Vinius Clodianus did *not* want to be his father. The late Marcus Rubella had passionately yearned to be a Praetorian, but his youngest son had no similar desire. His unnamed patron had badly misjudged the situation—or was cruelly indifferent to his feelings. His brothers, of course, called it 'bloody brilliant'. They would be living through him. That was his first problem.

Next, the Praetorians hated it as much as he did. That was much worse. To have Vinius foisted on them at twenty-three, after only two years in the army and three years in the vigiles, was extremely unpopular; the Guards wanted hoary veterans with long personal histories on the lines of some glorious fantasy: *Gaius Vinius Clodianus, son of Marcus, first rank of the Praetorian Cohorts of the divine Augustus, chief centurion of the Twentieth Valeria Victrix legion, awarded two headless spears and gold crowns, military tribune of a cohort of vigiles, military tribune of an urban cohort, military tribune of a praetorian cohort, prefect of engineers, duumvir for the administration of justice, priest of the Augustan cult . . .*

'So what have you done, son?'

The officer who asked this was like all of them: older and heavier than Vinius, built like a

66

mortuary slab, tough and terse, none too clever. He resembled Vinius' father closely, though the late Marcus had at least been bright.

The admissions procedure had established that the newcomer met the requirement of being born in Italy, and that he had undergone basic training, though not to the Guards' immaculate standards. Being able to run, ride, read, swim, make bricks, hurl javelins, build roads, cook soup, stab and stamp, put up a fort from a pre-formed kit, hold your beer, screw a peasant girl behind her parents' backs then march for hours in full tackle were nowhere near enough. The Praetorian ideal was a special course on swaggering, bragging, breastplate buffing and trampling on the public's toes.

'Done?' Gaius Vinius took a snap decision: 'Not enough, I'm afraid. I pulled a priest out of a burning temple; maybe a watching god was grateful. Otherwise, all I can offer is that I won the civic crown.'

The Guard snapped to attention. 'That we like!'

Vinius tapped his face to illustrate his tale. Being ugly would help. Most of these big brutes were seamed with old wounds like crumpled laundry.

With genuine modesty, he never normally discussed it. People knew; he just left it at that. He would rather have kept his full eyesight and not had a cheekful of scars that got cut open again every time a barber shaved him. But if there was one moment in his life when he needed to assert the honour he had won, this was it. The civic crown was a wreath of oak leaves, awarded for saving the life of a comrade in great danger. It was awarded very rarely indeed.

Vinius explained how he had been in the

Twentieth legion in Britain, a province which he was careful not to criticise in case his interrogator had served there in some fondly remembered youth; the Praetorian was not old enough to have jollied around the south beating up hill forts under the young Vespasian, but he could well have fought Queen Boudicca under Nero. Vinius had been in Britain later, when Julius Agricola was governor, pressing into new territory to the west and north. Annoyed by Roman expansion, a tribe called the Ordovices had ambushed parties of troops. On arrival in his province, where he had served before, Agricola wasted no time on familiarisation but launched a surprise attack to write the Ordovices out of history.

'He did it too—annihilation. They won't resist us again: they won't be there. When the missiles started coming, I shoved a tribune out of the way. It was how I lost the eye. I failed to jump fast enough. I took the spear in the face.'

'Bit of luck, for you?' suggested the Guard. That was how these Praetorian idiots saw it. Even getting yourself half killed was clever, so long as you emerged with a bauble to show off on your tombstone when the time came. Some of the bastards had a torque, bracelets and nine breastplate disks. They went on parade so highly decorated they glistened with gold like girls.

'You just do what you have to,' murmured Vinius.

'Now you're talking our language.'

That was it, then. He just had to bluff, like his father boozing among old comrades at some grisly cohort dinner. They were turning him into his father, however hard he fought against it.

Vinius and his father had in fact enjoyed a fair relationship. This was mainly because young Gaius was too peaceful to start confrontations. His father and two half-brothers had conditioned him to do what they said. For instance, they had all told him to go into the army, which fortunately he had not minded. As far as they knew—so far—he never minded anything. He grew up letting them push him around, which in some odd way made him feel comfortable. He was saving rebellion for when something really mattered. With his father dead at fifty-two, whatever he was waiting to kick against would never happen.

His father had been a solid, steady, military man. In Rome he had run his vigiles cohort with the right mix of rigidity, contempt for bureaucracy and loathing for the public; he terrorised petty criminals, slammed major gangsters, and out-schemed fraudsters of all kinds, while his firefighting successes were legendary. He kept the Aventine Hill, a lawless district full of poets and freed slaves, running as smoothly as anybody could.

Flouting the rules, as was traditional in all branches of the military, he had married and produced two sons, Marcus Vinius Felix and Marcus Vinius Fortunatus. Their mother died when they were in their teens. The father coped for a time, then brought in a young woman to help with the house and his unruly lads. After a flurry of initial suspicion, all three came to adore her. It worked so well the father married her to secure her.

Clodia was sweet, slight and babyishly pretty, yet

they all did what she said. She gave her menfolk routines they had badly craved. She could cook. She made them leave dirty boots at the front door and tidy up their mess. She loved them all, gaining in return a devotion that came close to the religious. When she presented them with a baby, the family seemed perfect. The older boys treated their little brother Gaius as if he were an intriguing pet. Clodia persuaded them to be gentle, or at least not to pull his legs off.

Gaius was three years old when Clodia died. Even while their father was still living, Felix and Fortunatus took it upon themselves to look after him. Like many bullies, they were violently protective of the young in their own family. He was never bullied by anybody else, for certain. Only they could and did push him around, a system they continued into his adulthood. That he might not need their interference never occurred to them.

Their father was too dispirited by Clodia's death to remarry again. While still small, Gaius was passed into the daily care of his grandmother, Clodia's mother, a tough, even-handed woman at whose house the boy often slept. He also had a slew of aunts. Most were Clodia's sisters, but there were a couple on his father's side too, which made two competing groups. The aunts, who were at various times single, married, widowed or divorced, came and went but always spoiled Gaius. Rome was a paternalist society, but aunts who have an appealing, motherless little boy to dote on sweep aside such nonsense.

So Gaius Vinius grew up in the company of strong men, but with the influence of powerful women. His two elder brothers had always seemed

70

like adults to him; he could only ever remember them shaving and drinking and talking about girls. Being so much younger, his position was almost that of an only child. A quiet, self-sufficient boy, he kept any sadness to himself, but he longed for the mother he could not remember, especially since Clodia was so frequently mentioned in conversation by his father, and by Felix and Fortunatus.

His grandmother and aunts were proud of him. Always good-looking, he was easygoing and rarely in trouble. He also had more intelligence and courage than people realised. His talents came as a shock, because his brothers had instilled in him that he was a milksop who needed tireless looking after. His father, too, had always made it plain he thought that Felix and Fortunatus would excel in the army while Gaius might struggle. Even so, they expected him to join up. He enlisted at eighteen, as each of them had done.

Oddly enough, Vinius was a relaxed soldier who did well. In Britain, he was loved like a son by a benign centurion who brought him on, then noticed favourably by their commander and, as the glaze on the almond cake, he saved the life of that senior tribune. The tribune was a young man from a senatorial family whose death would have been defined as a major social tragedy. High-class relatives might even have cried negligence though in fact when spears started flying the tribune, who was debonair but dim, had been looking the wrong way even though he had been warned not to. He was an idiot. Given time to think, Vinius would not have saved his life at all. Still, in a split-second decision his decency won out; he paid a high price physically.

The legionary legate recommended Vinius for one of Rome's most coveted awards, amidst collective relief among the province's high command. The governor, Agricola, personally signed off the citation before it went to Rome. The old emperor, Vespasian, approved it.

By way of thanks, the young tribune sent Vinius an amphora of extremely fine wine which, since he was still on his sickbed, his comrades drank for him.

His civic crown had been despatched to him in Britain, arriving after he was sent home. Three years later, he had still not seen the thing. Maybe it would never catch up with him.

*   *   *

Just before Vinius returned to Rome, his father achieved his lifelong ambition of a transfer to the Praetorian Guards. He died only six weeks later, without ever being on duty beside the Emperor. Of those other great military men, Felix and Fortunatus, there was little better to record. Whilst on service in Germany, Felix had had an accident involving a cartload of liquor barrels (he was larking about), acquiring a limp and a medical discharge. In Syria, Fortunatus had made it to centurion but was subsequently dismissed, clearly under a cloud. He made light of it, but Gaius suspected there had been some fiddling of legionary stores. Fortunatus worked for a builder when he came back to Rome; pieces of wood and hand tools were always coming home with him. Felix, who had no sense of irony, now earned his keep driving delivery carts.

Vinius was left to sustain the family tradition of military service, so after his convalescence he accepted a posting to the vigiles. Felix and Fortunatus pushed him into it, knowing their father would have approved. It allowed him to feel he was not written off. He quickly found his niche as an investigator. He enjoyed the work, and was good at it.

No one in the armed services could marry; many ignored the rule. Vinius had married before he joined up, which briefly solved the problem of sexual release, that ever-pressing matter for a seventeen-year-old. Felix and Fortunatus had been suggesting women they thought suitable, all rejected by Vinius, who gave them a hint of his independent spirit when he chose Arruntia for himself. They were childhood sweethearts, genuinely in love. The marriage was passionate, even romantic; he and Arruntia could hardly keep their hands off one another. Gaius also enjoyed extricating himself from his male and female relatives' supervision.

Then the dream ended. Arruntia was horrified to learn he intended to join the legions; she could not believe he would leave home indefinitely, leave her, and do it voluntarily. Somebody warned her that legionary service was twenty years, plus more in the reserves—then another so-called friend pointed out that soldiers were not allowed to marry so she was in effect divorced. She felt utterly rejected. Coming from such a military family, the blasé Vinius had taken his future for granted. He had not intended to deceive Arruntia; he was a lad, and just never thought about it.

He did not know, when he departed for Britain, that he was leaving his wife pregnant.

When Vinius then came home out of the blue,

expecting to pick up their previous life, he fell over the cradle as he entered their rented room, and was severely knocked back. His wife's angry mood over his career choice was also outside his experience; worse, she no longer had much interest in sexual relations. Had pregnancy and labour been frightening? Was she overwhelmed by domestic responsibility? Although she devoted herself to the child she now had, perhaps she did not want another baby. Perhaps, Vinius darkly suspected, she no longer wanted him. As far as he could tell (and he brooded on this continually) there had been no other man.

He knew for sure his damaged appearance horrified Arruntia. She shrieked and burst into tears when she first saw him; even their tiny daughter took the apparition more quietly.

He had no idea how to deal with an infant. Arruntia biffed him away when he tried. On rare occasions when he found himself alone with the baby, he picked her up gingerly but felt as guilty as if he had taken a secret lover. Once, the tiny child fell asleep clinging onto his tunic and Vinius found himself weeping, he did not know why.

Older now, and shaken by his army experience, he dimly recognised that Arruntia must have felt desperate when he left, though this understanding did not improve his subsequent behaviour. No teenaged girl would enjoy being shackled to a man she might not see again for twenty years; when she unexpectedly got him back, he was hideous, plagued with night terrors and moody with it. He made no real move to discuss this situation; he matured in his working life with the vigiles, but barely adjusted at home. He felt alienated and disappointed. Marriage, he discovered, was one thing he would *never* be good at.

So, joining the Praetorians who were barracked in an enormous camp outside the city relieved him of some stress by letting him escape arguments. For a man this was ideal. For Arruntia it was just another downhill lurch in their deteriorating life together.

But even Vinius himself was depressed; his transfer seemed a sixteen-year prison sentence (sixteen years was the Praetorian term of service, though he was appalled to hear that many Guards were so keen they stayed longer). His short stint in the army had instilled in him a loathing for this special corps; it rankled with regular legionaries that the Guards not only received pay-and-a-half but wallowed in a life of ease at home. Now Vinius suspected that there was no guarantee of the supposed easy life; the Praetorians were the emperor's bodyguard, his personal regiment. If your august leader developed military ambitions, you went on campaign. Vinius, who had thought his fighting days were over, faced the unwelcome possibility of more overseas travel and more active service. Should Titus fancy roughing up barbarians, there would be no getting out of it.

Duty in Rome was a mix of luxury and tedium, he soon found. One cohort at a time, carrying weapons but in civilian dress, accompanied their emperor wherever he went. Since Vespasian, Praetorian cohorts had each been bumped up to close on a thousand men. At every change of the guard, they marched down from the Viminal Gate through the Fifth and Third Regions, crossed the Forum and stomped up the Palatine Hill; reverberations shook flagons from shelves in wine bars and made wet sheets slither off washing lines. Standing guard at a palace or a villa, a cohort of Guards filled up a lot of corridor.

Eight other cohorts would be left to hang around the camp. There, a tiresome amount of unnecessary drill occurred, plus occasional homosexuality and much undercover gambling. Sick leave was high. Vinius informed his wife that staying in the camp was rigidly enforced, though Arruntia could hardly miss the fact that off-duty Praetorians ran rife through the city like rats in a granary.

Vinius had a hard time fitting in at first. Nobody wanted him. He was too young. His service record was too short. He arrived with mysterious patronage, which gave no protection because if he had been favoured by Domitian Caesar that counted against him with Titus' men. He did his best to survive. With what he had learned from his father, he managed to dodge various raucous clubs that had unpleasant initiation rituals. Many Praetorians wore beards; he grew one, found it disgusting and had it shaved off, which at least gave him impressive scabs temporarily. He followed his father in using only two of his three names, dropping 'Clodianus' and saying two had been good enough for Mark Antony, always the soldiers' hero. Otherwise he lay low. Keeping to himself in such a fraternal environment marked him as antisocial, which to Praetorians meant plain disloyal. Loners cannot hope to be popular.

*　　　*　　　*

Joining in the reign of Titus, his first major exercise

was the opening of the Flavian Amphitheatre. This helped his colleagues forget their antagonism. The Guards now had too much to do to waste energy on bullying him. Vinius was too busy perfecting new skills to worry about them.

The Praetorians were supposed to look friendly to the public, but their role was to scrutinise faces. While everyone else was staring at the Emperor, they would pack around their charge looking outwards, searching for signs of trouble. Soon it came as second nature. Vinius knew to the inch where Titus was sitting or standing, but he never glanced that way. Instead, his one good eye was constantly moving, raking the crowds. With forty or fifty thousand seats in the elegant new amphitheatre, this was a damned large crowd.

'Still, we're all having fun, aren't we?' was the sarcastic comment each centurion barked. For them, the inauguration was a nightmare. They wanted their man back in his easily patrolled throne room.

There were a hundred days of celebration, with Titus attending all the shows and constantly needing the ultimate security. Often his brother and other relatives came with him, so extra bodyguards were detailed. The imperial box, with its private access corridor, gave protection, but once on show the gregarious Titus liked to throw himself into the occasion. He was never the sort of Games president who just dropped the white scarf to signal the start, then sat like an automaton. Titus was always bobbing up to throw balls labelled with lottery prizes into the crowd, or enjoying arguments with them about contestants' merits, especially Thracian gladiators who were his favourites. Whenever he leapt to his feet, decor?ative ranks of Praetorians in celebration uniforms cheered nearby; their breastplates flashed in the sunlight and their tall helmet plumes bristled. But a small, almost invisible cadre of duty Guards in civilian dress were closest to Titus, watching for any suspicious movements that could threaten him, grim faced and with hands on their sword pommels.

The Prefect was twitchy. All the cohort tribunes were jerky in reaction, so the centurions found it hard to relax and they took it out on the men. This made it easier for newcomers to bond, as everyone suffered. At least, on duty or off, they regularly got the best seats.

The order of play was similar on most days: animal entertainments in the morning; at midday criminals were executed in various inventive ways, at which point the Emperor and fastidious audience members slipped away for lunch; on their return in the afternoon there were races or gladiatorial displays. Sometimes the arena was flooded for mock sea battles. These were conducted briskly, before the waves leaked out; subsequent performers had a soggy time of it until the arena floor dried.

Anyone had to marvel at the building's beauty and efficiency. But its greatest achievement was imperial propaganda. Nero had offended people by commandeering the Forum to build his Golden House, turning the whole centre of the city into one man's private home and grounds. In giving back the stolen site for public use Vespasian had imposed benign rulership in place of maniacal despotism. When Vespasian returned the Forum to the people, he restored Rome to itself. The massive crowds who assembled in the marble-clad arena, including groups from faraway parts of the world with their colourful robes and outlandish turbans and hairstyles, were staring at the ultimate in statement architecture. Here, sport was pursued not as mystic religion in the way of the Greeks, but as part of the pragmatic politics of Rome.

The programme made available that August was one nobody present would ever forget. Wild animals had been gathered from all over the Empire for the hunting scenes and beast contests. Elephants, lions, leopards, panthers and tigers; boars and bears from the north; desert ostriches, camels and crocodiles; even cranes and rabbits—

Rabbits?

Oh killer bunnies pack a mean thump, Gaius Vinius.

Don't even try to tell me how!

It was exciting when the nervous trainers managed to persuade unusual combinations to fight, and even more exciting when uncooperative animals ran amuck, throwing things in the air and threatening to clamber over the safety barrier right beside the marble seats on the front rows where the senators sat. Fortunately—or not, if you loathed the aristocracy—the barrier was a cunning arrangement of vertical rollers that defeated both animals and gladiators who tried to escape. The maverick rhinoceros was a firm favourite. The bull maddened by torches briefly had his fan club. The trained elephant that approached the royal box then knelt submissively before Titus showed the Emperor as a man with so much charisma he could control wild creatures, while the lion that let a hare play harmlessly between his paws was generally thought adorable. Less appealing was another lion, who unsportingly mauled his trainer.

Gaius Vinius had never been cold-blooded; he was generally pleased that Titus left for lunch so he could miss the execution interlude. That had fairly routine pitting of thieves and army deserters against ferocious wild beasts—or sulky beasts that had to be goaded to attack the cringing convicts. There were also lurid re-enactments of scenes from mythology and theatre: Pasiphae being raped by a bull, supposedly for real; crucifixion of a bandit in a notorious play, adapted to a gory new version where Prometheus had his liver torn out by a Caledonian boar; the Orpheus myth cruelly perverted so that although the pinioned criminal who was acting the lyre player did seem to tame various creatures with his exquisite melodies, a wild bear who was presumably tone-deaf then tore him to pieces.

After this basic stuff, professional gladiatorial combat seemed to represent pure skill. There were single bouts and group fights. To meet the Roman fascination with the exotic there were female contestants and dwarves. At one point, Titus presided over a record-breaking combat: two evenly matched fighters called Verus and Priscus slogged it out for hours, neither able to break his opponent, neither willing to concede defeat. A draw was not unknown but a draw with honour was unheard of. When Titus eventually persuaded the crowd to allow him to declare equal rewards for these fabulous contestants, giving both gladiators their freedom, the occasion crowned the Games.

This inauguration would be the highlight of his reign. Nevertheless, a sense of anticlimax visibly

80

began to affect the Emperor. Perhaps it was exhaustion, perhaps he was grieving his father's demise, perhaps he was already in poor health. On the final day, Titus dedicated the building formally, along with the nearby public baths that he had built in his own name. Something went wrong at the sacrifice, and the bull escaped, which was a bad omen. It was said that Titus wept.

Vinius was not on duty but he heard about it. Many of the Guards were unsettled.

*   *   *

There were no more celebrations. The following September, Titus set off from Rome along the Via Salaria towards the Sabine Hills, his father's place of origin and a long-time family resort in summer. They owned a beautiful villa above Falacrina where Vespasian had been born. On the way, at Aqua Cutiliae, where only two years previously Vespasian had developed a fatal fever after bathing in the ice-cold springs, Titus also fell sick. Immediately his condition must have looked serious. He was taken on to Falacrina, clearly aware that he was dying. His brother must either have been travelling with him or was called to the scene. Lack of clarity about Domitian's whereabouts and role would add to subsequent suspicions over what happened.

Back in Rome, the first Gaius Vinius knew was a clamour in the Praetorian Camp. When he emerged from his barracks block to investigate, he was told all leave had been cancelled and a full parade summoned. News had flown round. Men reappeared from all quarters of the city. The camp was soon packed. Tension was so palpable the air tingled.

It seemed Domitian Caesar had arrived in a state of high excitement. He galloped in and demanded the Guards' protection and acclamation. Vinius saw him a short time later, his eyes so bright that he looked drugged, his face flushed, heavy sweat stains on his tunic. Any of Vinius' resourceful aunts would have made the agitated prince open wide for a big spoonful of calming syrup, followed by a lie-down. Vinius himself thought the man needed a stiff drink among older, more equable friends, then a siesta with a couple of well-articulated dancing girls to put life in perspective. But real life had ended for ever for the impatient Caesar.

Domitian insisted his brother was dead. The Praetorian Prefect responded with caution, still nominally Titus' man; he probably thought his own days would be numbered from the moment Titus was officially declared dead. Troops began talking amongst themselves of a large accession bonus—for most of them, their second in two years. Somebody said to Vinius in a speculative voice, 'This should be good news for you!' but the prospect of Domitian coming to power failed to fill him with joy.

A small mounted squadron was quietly despatched to Falacrina but met a sobbing messenger who confirmed the news. All kinds of rumours rapidly circulated. Most fanciful was the Jewish belief that when he destroyed the Temple at Jerusalem, Titus had slept with a prostitute and a gnat entered his ear, growing inside his head for years until he could no longer bear the noise of it. Perhaps the headaches he suffered were really malarial, though doctors seemed to doubt that. Popular belief was that Domitian's plots had

82

finally succeeded; one way or another, he had murdered Titus. More believable was that he had ordered Titus to be finished off by putting him into an ice-bath; but could this be a proper medical recourse for a patient with such a high fever? The certain truth was that Domitian abandoned Titus to die alone while he raced to Rome, indecently eager to replace his brother.

*   *   *

An announcement was sent from Domitian to the Senate. To his pique, the senators spent all the rest of that day applauding the virtues of Titus and grieving their loss of such a beloved leader. Theoretically they could hail anyone to follow him, which was the reason Domitian so hurriedly pleaded for Praetorian support. Only the next day did the senators appoint Domitian formally as successor. They would pay for their delay.

The Praetorian Prefect lined up the ranks. To a man, the nine thousand Guards dutifully swore the oath of allegiance to their new master, their mighty shout audible across large parts of the city and intentionally threatening. So, apart from the first year, Gaius Vinius would spend his service as a Praetorian Guard with Domitian as his emperor.

He swore the oath. He took the money. He supposed that he would do his duty.

6

Alba. The Alba Longa of the ancients, pride of Latium, chief city of the Latin League, whose kings claimed an unbroken line from Ascanius, son of Trojan Aeneas, to Romulus, founder of Rome. The lake, a deep volcanic crater with sheer sides is accounted the most beautiful in Italy. On a high sunlit ridge stands a five and a half square mile compound of elegant white buildings, centred on the Emperor's enormous villa, built over the citadel of the old, lost town. This has been and will always be a holiday retreat for the best people. Its devotees say it has the best views in the world.

In high summer, it has the best houseflies. Or so the Alban flies believe.

*   *   *

High on a fold of drapery indoors, motionless against its deep Tyrrhenian purple hue, Musca broods, thinking up her next move. Her six feet have suckered onto the sumptuous cloth, so she hangs head-down with ease. Close by is an ornate plaster cove, creamy and delicate, its soft surface always welcoming. Less appeal belongs to the smooth polish of marble columns, though their patterning offers greater camouflage.

She fixes her attention on the human below. He sits, almost as motionless as she. He is a man who has obtained what he yearned for and now has to think what to do with it. By definition the people he most wanted to impress have died before him.

He could be asleep, but it is the fly's business to be certain and she knows he is not.

*   *   *

He has failed to settle easily into his coveted role. He is the foremost man in the civilised world. Twenty nine legions in the front line provinces, plus nine elite cohorts of Praetorian Guards, three of the Urban Cohorts and seven of the vigiles, have all sworn, every man in them, allegiance to their new emperor. Son of a divine father, sibling to a newly deified brother, husband to an august wife, father of an august son. In Italy, and in every province throughout Europe, Asia and Africa, each man, woman and child now knows his name. They speak it with as much familiarity as if he were a relative; most honour him; some already revere him as a god. They erect statues of his wife; they love his infant son. Soon they will see his profile every time they hold coins. His statues will dominate marketplaces and basilicas at the ends of the Empire. Camel drovers and peat choppers, date harvesters and cinnabar miners, oyster fishers and ivory merchants will all be aware of him, the ruler who nominally cares for their welfare; has them counted; sends them benign instructions, grinds them into poverty with impossible demands for taxes.

To Musca he is merely a motionless figure. He is dressed in loathsomely clean robes, robes that are changed several times daily to meet the demands of protocol. At least the oils that scent those garments hold some fascination; even from her perch high above, Musca detects enticing undernotes of fish organs and long-fermented rotten flower-petals.

Her olfactory equipment is perfect. Musca can smell death from ten miles away, then be there in an hour laying eggs in the corpse. Most attractive to her here are the teetering gold comports of ripe fruit, where pears and apples hold a sensuous hint of decay. She notices the bold stickiness left on a porphyry table, where a goblet has been carried away by a painted slaveboy, leaving dark fluff to accumulate where the cleaners' sponges have continually missed a three-week-old circle of dripped wine.

Musca sees possibilities for a landing place on the man's partly bald head. To a housefly, as to anybody else, this cavernous room is the height of luxury. Too much is inhospitable for Musca, though. True, high up in these festoons of drapery lie ancient seams of dust, while the comings and goings of numerous people far below have tramped in dropped hair, dander and street detritus—sometimes even a sublime slick of dog or donkey faeces or a drunk's vomit. But too many surfaces are hard and bare. Pre-dawn, the court has been prepared with busy activity, polishing its expensive sheen to befit its occupant. Some places have even been properly washed.

Not all. Slaves have no incentive to reach high or sponge crannies.

The solitary man promises entertainment. Taking off with a light spring, Musca begins a slow test run, at first swooping gently from one side of the room to the other. She alights upon a branch of an ornate, five-foot-high candelabrum, gazing around. Though he seems to sleep, she remains watchful. With large eyes that have many lenses and all-round vision, she can see everything within the room. That includes the broken bodies of several of her relatives, prone on the surface of a marble table in front of the human. The stabbed corpses lie around an expensive writing pen with a sharp nib. She sees this, but learns little from it. Dead relations hold no interest. Suspicion is Musca's watchword, yet flies are not sentimental.

On a side buffet stand interesting treats. There are flagons, conical sieves, little bowls of appetisers, spice grinders and goblets. Musca soars gently in that direction, criss-crossing with anticipation above the wine equipment before landing on the cold, curved rim of a silver water ewer. Head down again, she tiptoes, then sips. Buzzing happily to another container she tastes wine. After each visit she leaves behind traces of all the disgusting places she has been that day. She slicks saliva onto her front legs, considering whether to lay eggs on the food remains.

Illness has carried off the human's father and brother. Illness will take his young son soon. He lost his own mother before he could remember her, his sister not long after. He lives in the utmost luxury, yet disease threatens continually. No one will ever explain to him that Musca and the millions like her are the biggest enemy he has. Nobody knows.

Two major bereavements in less than two years have affected him more deeply than he will ever acknowledge. He has honoured his father and brother: announced them as gods, planned monuments in their name. This does not compensate his loss. Vespasian and Titus were men of great physical and mental energy, characters who filled a house with their presence. However much he fretted against those warm-hearted heavyweights, with them both gone, his isolation weighs oppressively. His female relatives eye him up too coolly; even his wife is too conscious of her own status as Corbulo's daughter. Distrust and disinterest sour the atmosphere around family dinner couches; there will be no comfort there. His surviving male relatives, his cousins, all have to be seen as rivals. Enough said. If they push him, he will deal with them.

He sits, as he has done now for many hours, sluggish and barely moving, in chronic depression. He stares emptily. He neither thinks, nor works, nor even enjoys the solitude he has demanded. He has realised a dismal truth. He is the Emperor. He is trapped in his role forever, not freed from impositions but doomed to spend his every hour according to the expectations of others. He must live as emperor until he dies, yet the joy he had expected eludes him. A worm of despondency gnaws; this despair will never leave him.

He will be a good emperor. Work diligently. Take a meticulous interest in all aspects of administering the Empire. Honour the gods. Rebuild, replenish coffers, tackle moral degeneration, crush revolt, initiate festivals, encourage artistic and athletic achievement, leave Rome flourishing and ready for a Golden Age. His name will reverberate through history. His fame will be perpetual.

Knowing these things is not enough.

*   *   *

Voices are audible beyond the massive double doors. Dimly they reach Musca, who does not react.

88

But the human listens intently, knowing they will be talking of him. There is no other subject in his villa at Alba, only the Emperor.

The men outside, like all at the court, are waiting to see how he will behave; most are already anxious. The precedents are bad. Generally, emperors of stature came to the post when they were mature and experienced. Titus, at a mere forty, was unusual. He defied doubters, in only two years establishing himself as much-admired. Who could say whether, given time, he would have degenerated? Yet that no longer matters. His good reputation will last.

Everyone is remembering the two very young emperors: Gaius, who was known as Caligula, and Nero. Both were bywords for extravagance, cruelty and madness. Domitian is thirty. People call him the new Nero, pretending it reflects his cultural interests, yet hinting at the worse traits that brought the Senate to declare Nero an enemy of the state. Nero, too, was believed to have poisoned his brother. Will Domitian follow Gaius and Nero into tyranny, or will he develop more benignly?

Is his character already formed, his destiny predetermined? Will he have any choice?

He owns everything he could ever want. He can do anything.

He is human. Megalomania beckons alluringly.

*   *   *

One voice outside the room is too quiet to distinguish but the speaker's companion is Vibius Crispus: bland, confident, self-interested, supposedly witty. Crispus trims his barque to any current. First he flourished as an informer for Nero; his own brother was accused of extortion as a provincial governor but Crispus managed to reduce the sentence. Without breaking stroke, when most Neronian informers went down, Crispus reconfigured himself to become a close associate of Vespasian and Titus. Now he manages to hold on at court as Domitian creates his own circle of advisers: Caesar's friends, some of whom actually like their Caesar. Men who either enjoy risk, or cannot think up an excuse to avoid his notice.

These souls attempt their duties, their role as advisors, yet the new Emperor thwarts them and causes perturbation. He takes long solitary walks; fails to confide; gloomily spends hours all alone in closed rooms, doing nothing. No one thinks that he may be suffering mentally after the loss of his father and brother. Even he fails to recognise it as bereavement.

The 'villa' at Alba is an enormous complex, peopled by an entourage that runs into hundreds. He ought to lead them; show himself; thrill them with his presence and personality. People judge as peculiar his sitting alone for many hours, killing flies with his pen. In stuffy, traditional, upper-class Rome, it amounts to a breach of etiquette, one they will not forgive.

'Is anybody with him?'

The reply is sarcastic: 'No, not even a fly!'

Wrong, Crispus.

Musca is here, about to have fun. She begins her plan to annoy the man at the table. She zooms at high speed from one side of him to the other, as if winding invisible wool-skeins through the room, buzzing loudly as she goes. She dive-bombs him.

90

She taunts him, rushing past his ear, so close he feels air shimmer with her wings. He gives no sign of noticing. He stares ahead, slowly twirling his pen between his fingers, apparently unaware of the housefly trying to torment him.

She ***!!***

*　　　*　　　*

Musca will not be appearing in this story again.

PART 2

Rome: AD 82–84

You think he is going mad?

7

Tiberius Decius Gracilis was posted to Rome for Domitian's new Praetorian unit. The incoming emperor felt the need to show his importance by raising the number protecting him from nine to ten cohorts. It brought almost a thousand extra Guards onto the complement, including ten centurions. Gracilis had been a centurion for a number of years, rising to *primipilus*, 'first-spear', or chief centurion in a legion. It was a venerated post, dedicated to ensuring continuity and discipline. These officers did much more than nurture continuity, so the character of any legion owed much to the individual strengths and prejudices of its primipilus. Wielding such power could make a man seriously corrupt, though by the time anyone reached first-spear in a Roman legion, he had learned how to get away with almost anything. Oddly, some of these heroes were surprisingly straight.

It went without saying that where centurions were traditionally reckoned to be bastards, chief centurions were the bloodiest bastards of all, a role they much enjoyed.

It was a one-year post. Afterwards, the holder was entitled to take his retirement, leaving with an enhanced discharge grant and an impressive detail for the mason to chip onto his memorial stone. Yet most wanted to stay as long as possible in their army life, which offered so much simple joy and prestige. They applied to be chief centurions of further legions, taking along increasingly colourful reputations and the elaborate investment portfolios they had put together from their rewards as the army's super-bastards.

Gracilis arrived at the Praetorian Camp with his decorations in a casket he had designed himself; first-spears adored fancy equipment. Special luggage enhanced their status, if greater status were needed. His box had neat, removable cloth-lined trays for his nine gold *phalerae*, the heavy round breastplate badges that soldiers who cared about such things jealously collected, and cedarwood inserts to hold his other awards: all his little spears and torcs and honorary bracelets, together with diplomas listing citations. When Gracilis stowed the box in his newly allocated officer's suite, he gave it a casual kick into position as if the baubles meant little to him. However, he then instructed his servant that nobody else was to touch that casket or he would personally remove their balls with his dagger, barbecue those stinking items with rosemary, and eat them.

The servant, who had looked after Gracilis for years, smiled politely.

The centurion chewed a thumbnail. His expression was that of an overseer as he checked that a crucified thief had been nailed up straight. 'Or I may decide on marjoram—if that's not too girlie.'

*   *   *

Nobody—that is, nobody who wanted to keep his spleen intact—would call Decius Gracilis girlie.

He was sturdy, short-legged, short-armed, shrewd and competent. At forty-five, he weighed two hundred and ten pounds naked and barefoot, with a body he was still proud to own. By descent he was Spanish, though born in Northern Italy. His heavily tanned face had wide-set eyes, which gave him a startled, boyish look, and eyebrows which, despite his thinning grey hair, were still brown. In the last year of Vespasian's reign he had been promoted out of the XX Valeria Victrix in Britain (one of the utterly glorious legions that defeated Queen Boudicca) to be first-spear of the IX Hispana (glorious for the same heroic reason), which had happened to be his grandfather's legion, as it once served in their home province. Under the Emperor Titus, Gracilis moved on, far across Europe to Moesia, where he served in the I Italica at Novae, staring across the Danube in case the barbarians did something stupid, then further upriver to the V Macedonica at Oescus; he had been expected to shift even deeper into the interior to the VII Claudii at Viminacium, but he had heard a rumour about a new Guards cohort so applied himself to the challenge of obtaining a transfer. He got his wish; now he was here. He had never been to Rome before yet stalked the streets like a man who thought Rome should be glad to have him.

The new cohort's formation allowed him to skip the vigiles and Urbans to enter directly at the top. Like others, he had volunteered to take a demotion to ordinary centurion to secure this Praetorian post. Though he would have denied being arrogant, Gracilis believed he would soon move up a notch again to his rightful rank as primipilus. All the Guards centurions thought that of themselves, though he might actually achieve it.

Once assigned to a cohort, a vital task was to appoint his assistant, his *beneficarius*. There was always pressure to look at those who had been selected for promotion to centurion but who were awaiting a vacancy. Gracilis had no particular beef against such hopefuls since he had been one himself once, but he was an individual who took his time. He looked around. Picking his beneficarius was highly personal; by definition the two men had to get along. It was also one of the favours centurions could bestow, part of their much-loved power.

When he noticed a soldier he already knew, the decision made itself. Gracilis remembered Gaius Vinius. Back in the Twentieth, he had liked this legionary's talent and attitude. The centurion believed he never had favourites, but he had known the young man's father, Marcus Rubella, in the army years before so naturally he took an interest in his colleague's son. He had nurtured the recruit, seeing him grow in a couple of years from a casual lad to a highly professional soldier. When, after his wounding, Vinius lay all night unconscious in the sanatorium, Gracilis had watched over him obsessively, alternately raging at the Ordovices and yelling abuse at the surgeon. He knew that if Vinius died, he would have to write and explain to his old friend. Since both men thought saving idiot tribunes' lives was an insult to the gods, this would not have been easy.

When Vinius came round, it was Gracilis who told him, as considerately as possible, that he had lost his right eye and his good looks.

*　　　*　　　*

They were reunited in Rome on the Praetorian Campus, an enormous parade ground that sprawled between the barracks and the city walls. Gracilis was there knocking his cohort into shape with what he believed was a light hand and the men regarded as unnatural punishment. They were all tough, yet Gracilis had them whimpering. There had been rebellious mutters, comparing his treatment to that of Nero's intractable general, Corbulo, who took troops who needed hardening up to an icy boot camp in remote Armenia, where several died of exposure and harsh treatment . . .

Vinius and a few comrades had been watching. They were standing on the edge of the parade ground, letting the straining bunch of new boys know by means of 'helpful' comments that their performance did not impress. Vinius had now achieved his own acceptance, so he could enjoy handing out this welcome to newcomers. His scars had faded, but his battered face, once so handsome, was instantly recognisable; he in turn quickly remembered his one-time centurion. When Gracilis concluded the exercise, he called Vinius over.

Formality was needed in public but once off duty they retired to the privacy of one of many bars near the camp. These were serious places where a capacity for hard drinking was the entry ticket, yet landlords knew they had to keep order or they would be closed down. The whole point of bringing the Praetorians all together in one place, back under the Emperor Tiberius, had been to impose more discipline than when they were originally billeted throughout the city and caused havoc. Guards were now discouraged from mingling with civilians. They had their own social venues. If members of the public accidentally wandered in they were served and no one bothered them, but the atmosphere soon persuaded them to drink up and leave.

Gracilis and Vinius settled down. Gracilis bought the first round, claiming seniority. They caught up on news. For the centurion this merely consisted of listing his appointments. Vinius had more to say, explaining his sudden move to the Guards and his regret at leaving the vigiles. 'I really miss being an enquirer. I'm just a face in the ranks now.'

'Investigators work without much supervision?' This mattered. A centurion's assistant would have to know his thoughts before he had them, and act on his own initiative.

'Complete independence. I loved it,' answered Vinius ruefully.

'Were you any good?'

'Shaping up.'

'What was involved?'

'Monitoring undesirables—prostitutes, religious fanatics, philosophers, astrologers. I investigated pilfering at the baths. Crimes in the Forum, domestic disturbances, knife fights in bars, mad dogs, street ambushes at night . . . On a good day,' he reminisced, 'I'd have some charming young lady trip in to report a home burglary.'

'I can't remember—are you single?' Gracilis noticed Vinius wore a gold ring, but that could mark the equestrian rank he had acquired from his father.

A distinct shadow crossed the soldier's scarred face. Vinius was polishing off a bowl of olives, not greedily but throwing them into his mouth with a relentless action that disguised emotion. 'My wife died—the city epidemic. Our child too.'

Gracilis could not fully interpret the expression

100

Vinius wore. Arruntia and their young daughter had died very recently. Vinius was still suffering a lot of family blame. One of his aunts, speaking for them all, had attacked him bluntly for not making a home visit when his dependants were sick. His last contact with Arruntia had been a typical blazing row. The next time he showed his face was at the funeral.

Losing his family had plunged him into guilt and despair. However, other women were disturbingly eager to console him. Foremost was a smart and sassy young matron called Pollia, supposedly his wife's best friend. She had left her husband so was free to cosy up to the widower; she explained that immediate remarriage was the best way for Vinius to regain his equilibrium. He fell for it. His aunts were disgusted, though Pollia, a subtle operator, made him feel this was expected by everyone.

I give it two months! said her mother.

They lived with Pollia's mother. Too late, Gaius saw this as a mistake. Guilt over his dead wife was expressing itself as lust (which had to be modified because of poor sound proofing in the mother's apartment). Sex attracted him, but sex with Pollia never seemed a complete foundation for thirty years of mild debate over whether he liked carrots or how many relatives to invite for Saturnalia—family life as his aunts had drilled him to expect it. He and Pollia were not soulmates. He was glad he could flee to the camp.

Pollia had a child, not previously mentioned. Fortunately, Vinius took to the little boy.

He had made up his mind to be a better father this time.

Don't bet on it! sniffed his aunts.

101

He outlined the situation to Gracilis; he even admitted he had been hustled: 'I discovered the Praetorian salary and big bonuses make us a great catch.'

Decius Gracilis had never married. There was no idealised young girl left behind in his birthplace whom he mourned in his cups; no smelly little bundle he had visited in a native hut in Britain or Moesia, promising to regularise the arrangement once he became a veteran; no scandalous affair with a commander's wife. It was possible his interest in Vinius had a suppressed homosexual element, though if so the centurion himself failed to recognise it and Vinius, whose attributes were clear, had never felt threatened. 'Does this marriage mean you keep trying to wangle home leave?'

Vinius grinned. 'No, sir; I manage to avoid domestication.' *Excellent.* The centurion mentally dismissed the wife, not giving her another thought for all the rest of their service together. How Vinius would elude Pollia had yet to emerge.

*   *   *

The olive dish was empty and Vinius pushed it away across the table; they went through a brief mime querying whether to order another but deciding to stay as they were. Gracilis plucked at a still unfinished saucer of shellfish. Vinius signalled to a waiter for another round of drinks, his turn. They were emptying beakers at a steady pace, nothing

102

excessive but no holding back. It indicated their complete off-duty relaxation and let Vinius forget his personal life.

He looked as if he felt better for talking. Gracilis supposed Vinius had just needed a few drinks.

'So . . .' Here came the inevitable question from Gracilis. A new Praetorian wanted to evaluate their Emperor. 'He's been in for a year. What's he like?'

Vinius glanced around before he answered. They were seated on benches in a small internal courtyard, beneath a pergola vine. Sparrows minded their own business as they hopped after crumbs. Other customers were taken up with their own conversation and none were sitting too close. But Gracilis noticed the look and approved.

Vinius took his time answering: 'Well—he's not Titus.'

Gracilis cocked his head, unfazed. 'A complete bastard? Well, we like a challenge.'

'I think he'll give us that.'

'You've been up close?'

'Comes with the job, sir.'

'So is he your magic sponsor?' This complication had to be factored in before Gracilis definitely invited Vinius to work with him.

'I bloody well hope not. I know when I may have caught his eye, but nothing definite was ever said. I like to keep my head below the parapet.'

Good lad! 'So does he talk to his Guards?'

'No.'

'Does he talk to *you*?'

'No.' Vinius preferred to forget their odd moment on the Capitol after the fire.

'Thank you, Mars! . . . I might have been worried about you, young man.'

103

'I would be anxious myself! But he doesn't talk to anybody. If there is a problem, it's that he keeps his own company—too much, some say. He locks himself away. He goes for long walks, alone. Nobody knows what to make of him—and if you ask me, he does it all on purpose; he likes creating anxiety.'

'Does protecting him get awkward?'

'No.' Vinius considered the question further, but stuck with his initial assessment. 'No, he accepts protection.'

'Is he concerned about his safety?'

'Very much.'

'Well that helps!' Gracilis took a deep swallow of his wine. He was thinking. In the opinion of the other ranks, chief centurions did not bother with thought. He, like most centurions, saw himself as different, more astute, more intense, thoroughly commendable.

He reckoned Vinius had spotted being assessed. Vinius had changed since Britain. He had become fatalistic. There was a hard edge to him. That could do no harm. The world was hard.

A waiter brought new wine. Gracilis watched Vinius pour, steadying the flagon's neck on the rim of the beaker instead of holding it above as most people thought good-mannered. Noticing his stare, Vinius explained that after losing his eye he could no longer focus length. Generally he managed. His one-eyed field of vision was almost as wide as it would be with two; only objects on his far right required him to turn his head. But, he freely told Gracilis, he was apt to tip liquor all over the table, even when sober, and he loathed going down steps.

'Does it affect your weapon-handling?'

'No, sir.' The Guards would have rejected him otherwise; rightly so. 'Well, to be honest, I'm lousy with a javelin and I couldn't set a catapult, but at least I know my weakness. Hand-to-hand is fine. I function.'

With that cleared up, Gracilis continued to gnaw at the subject of Domitian. 'So what's the new boy done so far? What's his style?'

'Besides forming an extra Guards cohort? He caused a flurry by deciding he requires twenty-four lictors.' Lictors were the attendants who walked ahead of a great man to let everyone know he was coming. They carried a bundle of rods, to symbolise an official's right to impose punishments, sometimes with axes to indicate his power to execute. They cleared a passage through the crowds, though were not allowed to disturb Roman matrons—something those doughty women always reckoned a fair return for their obligation to be noble, virtuous, fertile and decorous.

The norm was twelve lictors for a consul; six for a lesser magistrate; one for a Vestal Virgin. It had been twelve for an emperor—in keeping with the original myth that an emperor was simply a leading citizen, albeit for life. Demanding twenty-four raised eyebrows.

'Let him. Who would want to guard a no-account?' shrugged Gracilis, unmoved. '*He* knows his place in the cosmos now, by all accounts: I hear he really throws himself into using his power of life and death!'

Vinius paused, warily. 'Yes, he had a cull. Men who had been too closely associated with Vespasian or Titus were rapidly removed.'

'Exile?'

'No; a short march to Hades.'

'Well that stops plotting.'

'And it sends warnings. The Flavians are not soft. Vespasian used to boast that he put no man to death after becoming emperor, but that was a technicality; in reality he used Titus for the dirty work.'

Gracilis said, 'I gather Titus was never the cuddly lambkin people now choose to believe?'

'Not in those days. Almost his last act before his father died was to invite Caecina to dinner, then signal a Guard and have him killed when he got up to leave.'

'Caecina?'

'The tale was that Caecina and a colleague called Marcellus were plotting to kill Vespasian—though he was seventy, so why bother? More likely they posed a future threat to Titus. Marcellus was to go on trial, but he gave up and cut his throat.' Gracilis winced at the method. 'An autographed speech that Caecina "planned to make to the Guards" was "discovered", to justify the execution, if you believe it.'

'Do you, Vinius?'

'No. Who carefully signs draft notes—especially if they're treason? Besides, Titus was, by his own account, a clever forger . . . Make your own deductions. At least Caecina went out on a full stomach,' said Vinius in a dry tone. 'Titus gave great banquets, by all accounts.'

Gracilis belched demurely.

*　　　*　　　*

The centurion continued his questions. Vinius liked

106

his attitude: professional interest as a Guard, not leering after scandal or construing political science. With a soldier he trusted, Gracilis was diligently building a picture of the man they had to protect. He wanted to understand the Emperor, and the situation surrounding him.

Vinius offered: 'Talking of executions, head of his hit-list was Flavius Sabinus.'

'Cousin?'

'Top cousin. He out-ranked Domitian at a family dinner table.'

'Tricky situation?'

Vinius snorted. 'For Sabinus.'

As the elder son of Vespasian's elder brother, this Sabinus had been the most senior member of the Flavian clan. Initially, his position looked secure. He was appointed consul in Domitian's first year, continuing the Flavian tradition of surrounding themselves with relatives. But Sabinus had already offended Domitian by having his household retainers dressed in white, which was imperial livery; Domitian had darkly implied the world was not big enough for both of them.

'So when his consulship ended, Sabinus was executed.'

'The heir presumptive? Just like that?'

Vinius croaked, 'It didn't exactly help him look harmless when a herald at the Games accidentally announced Sabinus as not *consul* but *emperor*.'

'In Domitian's presence?' Gracilis winced.

'Let's be realistic. The herald probably got a reward for giving him a reason to lop the cousin.'

Gracilis pursed his lips. 'Do doctors hand out diarrhoea pills in the palace?'

'Are the rest shit scared? Too right.' Vinius

smiled, then continued in a neutral voice, 'I haven't heard anyone else say this, but I think it was significant that the Emperor had just lost his young son. Maybe his cousin openly presumed too much after the boy's death. The other problem was— and you may think, still is—Sabinus was married to Titus' daughter, Julia.'

'She a threat?'

'No signs so far, but she could theoretically become a figurehead for devotees of Titus.'

'Even if she's loyal?' Gracilis grimly added Julia to his list of Praetorian concerns.

'Julia must be ten years younger than the Emperor,' said Vinius. 'But I believe they were brought up together. Vespasian had offered her in marriage to Domitian for dynastic reasons, but Julia was a child and he was in love with Domitia Longina. Julia's later marriage to Sabinus was equally political.' Vinius sounded cynical, though it was not obvious whether he disapproved of how noblewomen were shunted into bed with their cousins or if he had come to despise marriage in general.

'They had children?'

'Luckily for the children, no. *"Oh precious nephew, sweet innocent niece, come and sit on Uncle's knee—let Rome's great leader wrap his friendly hands around your little rival throats . . ."*'

Gracilis sent Vinius a reproving look, but pressed on. 'What's he like with the Senate?'

'Ignores them as much as possible.'

'Vespasian and Titus at least paid lip service.'

'Domitian doesn't bother.'

'Advisers? Any powers behind the throne that we need to watch?'

Vinius took a deep swallow of his wine as a punctuation mark. His tone was dry. 'There is an ad hoc council of *amici*, Caesar's Friends.'

Gracilis picked up on his scepticism. 'How does that work?'

'About twenty advisers. He summons them periodically to watch him announce decisions. Every man is bloody scared stiff. They tremble and burble admiringly. So much for the venerated Roman system,' said Vinius. 'Surely the whole point is for a man's private circle to tell him what nobody else dares say?'

Gracilis pulled a face. 'So who is his confidante? The Empress?' A powerful empress could be a nightmare for imperial bodyguards.

Domitia's role seemed merely ceremonial, her influence of no concern. Vinius dismissed the suggestion.

They next discussed how Domitian treated the imperial bureaucracy, those influential freedmen running the palace with whom the Guards had to liaise. 'He kept the most loyal of his father's private associates, but the palace staff—whom you could say really wield administrative power—were comprehensively weeded.' Vinius gave examples: 'He started with Classicus, who had been close to Titus. Classicus was in charge of Titus' personal finances plus, as chamberlain, he spent a lot of time in the Emperor's presence, and controlled access. He was swiftly chopped. Also pensioned off was Tiberius Julius, who ran the public funds—there were rumours of embezzlement, possibly trumped up to get rid of him—along with anyone else who seemed too significant in the previous administration, or whose face simply didn't fit.'

'Ditching staff-in-post is a good rule,' said Gracilis approvingly. 'Shake them up. Put in your own. Make them grateful.' *That's why I'm looking at you, Gaius Vinius . . .*

'To his credit, he takes care with appointments. Demotion or promotion, he vets every one. If scribes don't meet his standards, the duds don't linger. And we are talking about a huge complement, Gracilis. There are scores of staff in the secretariats.' They both grimaced. 'He's into everything as well. The bureaucrats hate his interference—though it's a dilemma because this could be a good time for them if they want to be associated with a big programme of work. Titus left a full Treasury and if Domitian has inherited their father's way with making money, funds won't be a problem. But he demands details; he won't let the secretaries move on anything until he gives personal approval.'

'So what's your overall assessment?'

Vinius had thoroughly warmed up and had answers ready: 'He wants to be the new Augustus. People are calling him the new Nero, but they can't see further than his youth and his love for the arts.'

'We have to attend a lot of recitals?'

'Afraid so! But he also loves gladiators.'

'And long term? Is he ambitious?'

'As Hades.'

'I like it!' Ambitious emperors were good news for troops. 'So he's thirty,' murmured Gracilis. 'Are we going a long way with him?'

'Well, bodily, he does not impress—' Vinius, a fit man in a physical profession, was frank. 'Mentally, I'd say he packs power. No question about his intelligence—or his determination. He has the will, he should make his mark. He's rebuilding the city, revamping the currency, re-establishing old-fashioned morals . . .'

'Jupiter! What does that mean?'

'As Pontifex Maximus he cleaned up the Vestal Virgins—'

'*Cleaned them up?* The most revered women in Rome? What did they do? Let the sacred flame go out once too often?'

'All very sad,' murmured Vinius, with a trace of disrespect. 'Brought to trial for taking lovers. Varronilla, and the Oculata sisters . . .'

'Half the establishment! Found guilty?'

'Their affairs were blatant. But to demonstrate his mercy, our leader stopped short of the traditional burial alive. They were allowed to choose how they died.'

'A delicate touch!'

'Feather light. Other than that, reforming morals means restating the Augustan marriage laws. Everyone should have at least three children, preferably by fathers who can be identified; widows have to remarry smartish; and the spoilsport has outlawed adultery.' Cautious again, Vinius dropped his voice: 'No doubt with the usual proviso that everyone else has to give up their private fun, but not the Emperor.'

'So what's *his* private fun?' Past Caesars who indulged themselves had had disgusting habits. Gracilis acquired the anxious look of a man with no sexual history himself, fearing the worst.

'Founding new cultural festivals,' replied the soldier gravely. 'Our leader is a married man, who is famously infatuated with his wife—a general's daughter, who may even be faithful to him—well, if Domitia Longina has any sense she'll bloody well make sure she is.'

Only when the centurion thought this subject safely disposed of did Gaius Vinius revive it mischievously, saying that nonetheless Domitian's anterooms were packed with throngs of pretty boy eunuchs, scantily-clad imperial playthings who called themselves cup-bearers.

Decius Gracilis understood this was a tease. He swallowed his prudery. 'Convenient. If the catamites are half naked, we don't have to search them for concealed weapons.'

'No, we can see straightaway whether the buggers are carrying . . . Sorry, sir; "buggers" was ill-chosen, in context.'

They both cleared their throats.

By this point, Decius Gracilis felt the conversation showed the right meeting of minds. Without more ado, he made the offer of becoming his beneficarius.

Encouraged by drink, Gaius Vinius was still amused by a mental picture of the upright centurion forced to overcome his natural distaste and frisk oriental eunuchs . . . He accepted straightaway.

8

The Insula of the Muses on Plum Street stood in the Sixth Region, the Alta Semita or High Lanes. This insignificant byway ran down the western slope of the Quirinal Hill and descended to the Vicus Longus. To the north were the extensive Gardens of Sallust and across the dip was the Viminal ridge. In this district, which had been favoured by the Flavians in their shabby days, were other substantial houses owned by senators nobody had ever heard of, families clinging on by their supposedly noble fingertips to uncertain status and rusty prestige. As the Senate mouldered under Domitian, they started losing their grip.

Bounded by narrow roads on all sides, the small block contained one of those houses. It was owned by the Crettici, who still lived there, though their fortunes were declining. The lack of heirs meant failure to bring in money through adept marriages, the elderly patriarch was now frail, and on good advice they were seeking to exploit their property. Ground floor rooms that faced onto streets were already leased out as shops or offices. Faded tenants in despised professions occupied single rooms on the top two storeys: honest accountants, engineers with no grasp of physics, half-blind bead threaders, a retired armed robber with quiet habits . . . Adaptations had recently begun on the first floor, carving up family accommodation in order to make bijou apartments, where a good class of person might be lured, guaranteed not to affront the owners, since the Crettici were hanging on in their original suites around the interior courtyard.

They still wanted to believe the house was their own, though in truth many other people had possession. A takeaway food and wine bar on one corner started slowly but as it became popular with passing workers, there were noisy periods. A religious statuette boutique attracted obsessed old widows who shouted strange abuse at harmless passers-by. The stationer served odd bods, in the

113

form of would-be writers. They were believed responsible for a rash of subversive and not very funny graffiti. A stray dog solved that by biting a culprit.

Facing onto Plum Street were now a fringe-and-tassel shop (struggling) and a booth where a slightly peculiar man sold multi-bladed pocket-knives to soldiers and shy adolescent boys buying birthday presents for their fathers (a galloping trade). Between them, newly built steep stone steps disappeared under a tall arch, leading up to a discreet apartment. This was 'strikingly renovated, with fine art frescos and high-end fittings'; Melissus, business manager for the Crettici, was attempting to sell a long-term lease to 'discerning clients' (anyone daft enough to believe his patter). A discreetly veiled imperial freedwoman seemed a good prospect, until she explained, 'People who can afford exquisite frescos are looking for more space than this, while people who only want four rooms won't pay your price.'

'What about the decor?'

'It's beautiful.'

'You dislike it?'

'I cannot afford it.'

'You need to make up your mind quickly,' oozed Melissus, deaf to obscenities like 'cannot afford'. 'Somebody else is interested.'

You're bluffing.

Right.

You invented him?

He can't afford it either.

*   *   *

114

A few weeks went by. There was no other interest. This was mainly because the pocket-knife vendor, who had fallen out with Melissus, was telling enquirers the place had been taken off the market. Melissus had not paid him attention, being concerned only to live the classic life of an owner's agent: eating pies in his little office, conversing with associates in the Roman Forum, or sleeping with one of his mistresses. Neither was young any more; he was getting his action before they both packed him in.

Things became pressing. The Crettici were desperate to recoup their expenditure on the misconceived revamp. Their contractors wanted payment. Melissus had promised he would install tenants by the first of July, the traditional start of annual rents in expensive properties. Tenants had to pay upfront. It was attractive for owners, though a burden for tenants.

Melissus concocted a compromise. He told both potential clients that he was willing to split the apartment. It was laid out with two rooms each side of a central corridor. They could occupy half each. A lightweight partition could be put up as a divider. Melissus presumed these cheapskates would not object to shared facilities. Instead, he talked up how rare it was to have water, a clanking pipe linked to the supply the Crettici paid for from the nearest aqueduct: this was official, so no danger of being fined for illegal access. Melissus went into ecstasies over the tap in a cubby-hole that served as a kitchenette where a clever run-off then sluiced out a tiny lavatory, giving personal privacy as well as immediate convenience . . .

This apartment was indeed elegant, by Roman

standards. The Crettici had had no idea how to cut corners for their own commercial benefit.

*   *   *

The freedwoman learned that her co-lessee would be a serving soldier. She pouted.

'Not to worry,' Melissus assured her. 'The Emperor is taking the troops abroad, Germany, Gaul, some horrible place—by the way, I never told you that; it's a state secret.'

'Yes, I know.' Demurely she implied she had better contacts than his.

'Oh! The man's brother is one of the builders, Fortunatus; you may have seen him working here—"Those steps will last a hundred years . . . That's a lovely bit of travertine!" He put his brother onto this, as an investment opportunity. The fellow just got married. He wants to salt away some capital, a secret from the wife. He's looking for a business partner, if you're interested.'

'How does that work? To earn off the place he must intend to install tenants of his own?' Clearly, like so many in Rome, the soldier intended to sublet at a profit. Some buildings had so many tiers of renters, no one could work out who owned the head lease.

'He is leaving the country so that's months away . . .' The agent was bluffing; the soldier would want to have his sub-tenants in place before he left. Then he would be away, so if they turned out unsatisfactory, the freedwoman would find herself stuck with the problem. 'Now I do need to move quickly, so let's get this lease signed.' Melissus winked. 'You will be first in; you can make the

116

place your own.'

'I suppose you told this soldier, "She's a woman alone; you can push her around" . . . Does the bullyboy have references?'

'He is a Praetorian Guard, so have no qualms. A centurion's assistant. Handsome fellow. Perfect manners. Absolutely responsible.'

'A woman has to be careful.'

'He will not make advances. I told you, he's newly married. Besides, this is business for him; he won't muck about. Maybe you know of him? His name is Vinius.'

'Never heard of him,' she answered, not believing in coincidence.

What Melissus had told Gaius Vinius was that he, the helpful Melissus, had with great difficulty persuaded an influential freedwoman to relinquish part of her space, given that she would be infrequently in Rome due to her duties attending on the imperial ladies.

'Know anything about this bint?' growled Vinius, when he made contact just before the troops left Rome. 'Is she a good businesswoman? I want solvency.'

'Naturally I ran checks.' Melissus had merely asked his wife. 'She only accepts select clients. Noblewomen flock to her, wanting to be beautified like princesses. She will not default.'

'I don't want upsets on my premises. Is there a man in tow?'

Must be. They all have one. 'No follower is obvious. And I have guaranteed that *you* won't cause offence, by the way. This woman seems very respectable, hard-working, honest—just don't jeopardise everything by trying to grope her.'

117

'Not interested,' scoffed Gaius Vinius. 'I'm in enough trouble. I'm on my third damned wife!'

Pollia had kicked him out after only six weeks. She said she found Vinius unbearable; she claimed he was mean with money, always absent, humourless, unkind to her mother and fell asleep while making love. (He denied the last point.) Insultingly, she went back to the husband she had previously left, a violent swine by all accounts. She took her son. Vinius regretted losing contact with the child.

To help him forget, Felix and Fortunatus swiftly fixed him up with Verania. A priest was booked to take auguries at the wedding before Vinius knew anything about it, and his brothers did later sheepishly confess that the new bride could have been better vetted. Within a week Vinius discovered Verania had schmoozed his banker and was stealing from him. Convinced he had funds salted away (as he did), she was to be a tenacious wife.

'So what's her name, this investor I'm roped up with?'

'Flavia Lucilla.'

After years in the vigiles, listening to unlikely stories of coincidence, Vinius remained expressionless.

Their coming together here was not entirely chance. The Cretticus house stood in a position that suited both of them. Lucilla wanted to be near to the Flavians' private homes; Vinius was looking at property en route to the Praetorian Camp. She could easily access her ladies; he could check on his investment when passing. The time was right; they both had savings. Since Domitian started a

118

massive building programme, all Rome was full of dust and marble carts. Builders were flourishing and Vinius' brother Fortunatus had just set up on his own account, renovating apartments. As an entrepreneur, to further his own sticky operation, he was quick to nudge unlikely investors into partnership. He assumed Vinius would eventually buy out the freedwoman and make double profits by subletting her rooms too.

She hoped to earn enough to purchase his lease and rid herself of him.

*   *   *

On the Kalends of July, first day of the month, Lucilla moved in. The promised dividing partition had yet to appear and since it would destroy the proportions of the frescoed corridor, she did not remind the agent. She had first choice of rooms, assigning herself the two that overlooked the interior courtyard, while leaving the absent Praetorian, or his tenants, to suffer the noises from the street. Although shutters cut down some of the clamour, whoever lived there would have to endure night-time delivery carts, tedious street-cries, and the buzz from a small market. She would be shielded, and more importantly for her work, one of her rooms had access to a balcony, with doors that could be opened to flood the place with light.

The apartment had once been a suite of family bedrooms with interior access. Blocked off from the main house, it was now reached through double doors off a private little landing at the top of its own new stairs from the street. Inside, the proportions were still grand. It had wooden floors and ceilings throughout. The central corridor was painted in muted shades of green and turquoise, relieved with flashes of chalk white. The four main rooms were decorated in dark red, with coloured tendrils and flowers, executed finely as dados and cornices. At the far end, informal curtains hid the domestic facilities, a scullery and lavatory; these were basic, though their very existence was a rarity.

Lucilla's previous building had been a purpose-built lodging house with forty tenants crammed in on many floors. Her single room there was dilapidated and draughty, containing only a low bed, a lopsided cupboard and a few secondhand pots; she did little more than sleep in it. Now she had this new apartment, she could invite private clients and have leisure herself. Some women wanted her to visit their homes, but others welcomed a chance to go out; these civilised surroundings, with a discreet entrance and elegant decor, were ideal. She seated them in the room with the balcony to have their hair styled; she could wash their locks and make them drinks, while she heated hot curling irons. Once her clients all left, she could relax in the styling room, with its comfortable wicker armchairs. Lucilla slept in the second room and kept her own things there.

Carefully, for she was terrified of poverty and hardly dared spend money, she had begun to buy furniture. She spent more readily on the tools of her work: combs, scissors, mirrors, cosmetics, footstools and side-tables.

As Melissus promised the Praetorian, she was solvent. She had cashed in most of her mother's jewellery; she still had some money from the arena lottery; then, as well as the earnings she and her sister Lara made, Lucilla had a discreet source of income from her own commission making hairpieces for her anonymous male client at the palace. She had set a high price for that.

Life in the new apartment had, for her, as much luxury as she could ever need. She welcomed periods of solitude. She loved the privacy and peace. She badly hoped the Praetorian would continue to ignore the place. For almost a year she was thoroughly spoiled, having sole possession while the Emperor and his soldiers were away.

Domitian had gone to Gaul, on the excuse of overseeing a census; then he suddenly swerved across Germany where he built roads to take troops over the River Rhine. His trip to the north had been planned in advance, with a military purpose from the start. There was detailed pre-consultation at Alba with the Emperor's council. Enormous forces had been gathered for the expedition, with detachments from all four legions in Britain, for instance, even though the governor there, Agricola, was conducting troop-hungry military expansion. A new legion was created, the I Flavia Minervia, named for Domitian's patron deity. He was desperate to achieve military glory to set him alongside his father and brother: Vespasian the conqueror of Britain, Titus the victor of Judaea.

He entered the territory of a tribe called the Chatti on the unconquered east bank of the Rhine; he established a presence and subdued the Chatti, who had a warlike reputation. Although on Domitian's return the joke ran that the Chatti were 'more triumphed over than conquered', he did surprise them and pen them into their fortresses. Rome now straddled the southern Rhine, with

121

a new frontier thirty miles beyond the river and control over main roads used by various tribes to pass north and south. Domitian had annexed a strategic bight of Germany and put himself in a good position to tackle the dangerous gap between the Rhine and the Danube, which served as a funnel for aggressive tribes who were seeking to move west.

Hostile commentators would portray this campaign as whimsy on Domitian's part, but it was a continuing move to strengthen the frontier in Europe, a process begun by his respected father.

The following summer Domitian arrived back in Rome, styling himself a conqueror. The Senate was prompted to award him a formal Triumph.

Domitian assumed the honorary name of 'Germanicus' as if he had won a tremendous victory. His critics made much of it. The previous Germanicus had been a much-respected soldier and commander, elder brother to the Emperor Claudius, who went into a hostile district to recover the bodies from three legions slaughtered in a disaster, thereby restoring the national psyche. Chipping into the lands of the Chatti was modest by comparison, and spoilsports whispered that neither Domitian's father nor brother had claimed equivalent titles for their genuine military exploits . . . Deeply sensitive, Domitian took note of who was whispering.

The imperial ladies, who had enjoyed a relaxed holiday for many months, threw themselves into a flurry of treatments and primping. Lucilla and Lara had a hot time meeting their requirements. The Triumph only lasted a day, but it was a long one, from a dawn start, through an interminable procession at a snail's pace, to a public banquet. The ladies had to be on show for most of it, prepared to be stared at even though most of the crowd's attention would be fixed on the endless marching groups of proud officials, seedy priests, tetchy sacrificial animals, exhausted musicians, bored soldiers, the painted floats that constantly creaked to a standstill, wobbly bearers carrying slightly suspect booty, and glum prisoners. At last came the gleaming chariot which carried the Emperor, dressed in white in the role of Jupiter, while a slave supposedly muttered, 'Remember, you are only mortal.'

'Germanicus is deaf to that!' scoffed Lara.

Lucilla was rarely at home while they were preparing their charges for greeting the victorious general, but once the Triumph was over she knew that the Praetorian's half of the apartment might be claimed. Despite this, she was so used to being alone there that she was badly startled one evening. As she prepared her supper, she heard noises; someone was in the house.

'Sorry,' said the man in the corridor, seeing her alarm. 'I am—'

'I know who you are.'

'Your co-tenant. Name of Vinius, Gaius Vinius.'

'Gaius Vinius what?'

'I only use two names.' *What a poser!*

'You could have knocked.' Lucilla glared at him.

'I'm not a passing sponge salesman.' No help from him. He softened. 'Yes, I need a way to let you know it's me.'

'Whistle a tune?'

'I'm not the bread boy either.' He looked disdainful. 'I'll call out, "It's me—Vinius".'

123

'Yes, that should work,' snorted Lucilla sarcastically, as she turned away. He had not changed; she still found his attitude overbearing.

His damaged face was unforgettable. His current wife had said, in a rare moment of discernment, that some people would see Gaius Vinius as half disfigured, some as half handsome. Now meeting him for the second time, Lucilla was still making up her mind.

She had forgotten he was taller than average and subtly powerful despite a medium build. He wore a plain grey tunic, with a worn belt and boots; reassuringly he was unarmed. Lucilla noticed again how his dark hair looked finely trimmed, his hands beautifully kept. She liked his grooming. He seemed fastidious, though not offensively vain. She noted his wedding ring again and, now, a signet ring.

If he remembered her, he gave no sign.

*   *   *

Vinius looked around his investment. It was a year since he had been here, at a time when the renovations were still incomplete, with dust sheets and scaffolding everywhere. Now it was cleaned up and occupied, it looked, felt and even smelt different. He was pleased with what he had taken on. Fortunatus had given him a good tip.

After he eyed up the corridor, he came to the doorway of the tiny kitchen. There was no room for two, so he leaned against the gathered curtain. He saw a stone bowl beneath the tap, a counter barely a plank's width, high shelves, a low-level rubbish bucket. Nosily, he watched Lucilla cutting sheep's

124

cheese into a bowl of lettuce. Refusing to feel intimidated, she mentioned the suggested partition.

'Yes, that should ruin the aspect successfully!' He gazed back at the corridor. 'I suppose you are anxious in case I put in sub-tenants?' Vinius clearly thought himself a wit: 'I've offered it to a large family with no sense of hygiene and four screaming brats.'

'That's a relief.' Calmly Lucilla tossed olives into her bowl. She had huge qualms about the other rooms' future. 'I was dreading you would dump some ghastly mistress on me. You'd both have noisy intercourse; she'd be a spiteful piece who would leave dirty bowls in the sink until she forced me to wash up after her . . .'

'I like the sound of that!' He grinned. He seemed more hollow-cheeked and unhappy than Lucilla remembered, perhaps less sure that grin of his would impress. He need not have worried. 'Honestly, I have not decided what to do. I apologise for taking my time. I promise to discuss any plans with you.'

'Thanks,' said Lucilla coldly.

More relieved than she would admit to him, she scattered pine nuts on her food; she did not offer Vinius anything. They were equals as co-tenants. If he felt peckish, he could bring in a hot pie.

He made a fuss checking the miniature griddle, said it was dangerous and he would speak to the letting agent about putting in protection at the back of the fire basket. When she first arranged her own bowls and cutlery, Lucilla had left one empty shelf for his use; she watched him wondering whether to challenge this. He crossed to his own two rooms, working out which she had allocated; he checked dimensions with a folding measure his brother had lent him, then appeared to be about to poke his nose into her rooms too.

Lucilla blocked his path. Vinius stopped, reassessed his rights, grudgingly revised his view of hers. They had a short face-off.

*   *   *

Vinius cleared his throat. He looked her in the eye, finally acknowledging that day at the station house. 'Flavia Lucilla. I see you grew up nicely.'

'Oh, have we met before, soldier?' Since his face was unforgettable, this amounted to an insult.

Oddly, he just smiled. 'I let you down, I know . . . You did stay on my conscience but I was transferred out straight after the fire. I hope someone else came to look into your loss.'

'There was no loss.'

'Ah.'

They stood, three feet apart, in the corridor, either side of where the partition would be, if the agent ever had one constructed.

'Your mother had a lover back then. What happened to him?'

'I have no idea.' Lucilla moved back towards the kitchen, not wanting to think about Orgilius, not wanting Gaius Vinius to sense that the man had seduced her. He would probably say he could tell that someone had. Still, that was how a man saw things.

Vinius was smitten by the alteration in Flavia Lucilla. She had changed much more than him. No longer a neglected child, she was neat, vibrant and kitted out daintily, in the tradition of her trade.

126

Strappy sandals. Fancy hems on her dress. Plaits tied into a topknot with ribbons. In quiet moments, she and Lara did each other's hair, nails, pedicure, brows. Lucilla frequently changed her appearance, enough to show she had an eye for fashion while never looking like a rival to the women she tended.

'How is your mother?'

'She died.'

'Sorry to hear it.'

'At least I found my sister. We work together now.'

'What's her name?'

'Lara—why?' Lucilla asked truculently; Vinius was questioning her as if he were still an investigator.

'Calm down! If I'm knocking about here, I may run into her.' It was meant to make Lucilla feel unreasonable, though Vinius noted she merely scowled. He knew he could sound high-handed. 'So your sister does not live with you?'

'She is married with a family.'

His inquisitiveness was annoying. It forced Lucilla to retaliate: 'You're not dossing here with your wife then?'

Vinius looked surprised at the idea. 'We live near the Market of Livia, by the Servian Wall . . .' He pushed away the thought of Verania. They had a couple of rooms in a tenement, adequate (in his opinion) but cruder than this place.

'Oh yes, I heard you keep secrets. You don't intend your wife to know you have this place.'

He flinched. 'My damned brother talks too much.'

'He does!' scoffed Lucilla, to make him wonder.

'What other nonsense has Fortunatus regaled

the whole neighbourhood with?'

Lucilla raised her neatly shaped eyebrows. 'Not too much. What's exciting you? Everyone around here thinks you are a man of mystery.'

'That's good!' answered Vinius through gritted teeth. 'That's exactly how I like it!' Then he slipped in vindictively, 'So: who is Junius? Your boyfriend?'

Lucilla blinked. 'My brother-in-law.'

'I saw his name on our lease. I want to know what he's like,' Vinius growled. 'Don't tell me it's not my business; it is. I don't care for unknowns.'

'He is my guardian—supposedly. I just put him down to keep Melissus happy.' A Roman woman could not engage in business on her own account. If she lacked a father and husband, then for anything legal or financial she was obliged to have a male 'guardian' to act and sign for her. 'Forget him, Vinius. He doesn't know anything about it.'

'So how did he sign the lease?'

'My sister wrote his name in.'

'Right!'

'Soldier, your only worry is whether I pay up. I feel the same about you; the second-year rent is due now, incidentally.'

Vinius pre-empted her; he had paid Melissus that day. He had his Triumphal bonus to keep out of his wife's grasp. To protect the cash from Verania, he was spending more of it on material goods and warned Lucilla he intended to have furniture delivered.

Putting on a show of competence, Vinius inspected the front door lock. 'We need this changed. I don't want the agent, or even my brother, or anyone else who may have obtained keys wandering in. One for you; one for me. No

128

duplicates. Agreed?'

Lucilla nodded, looking amused. *Nothing for wifey?*

Don't be cheeky!

Vinius had a thought. 'Doesn't the agent have responsibilities—cleaning? maintenance?'

'I already gave instructions,' Lucilla informed him. 'The slaves have to knock and wait to be admitted. They must keep the entrance tidy so the apartment looks lived in, but they can only work indoors when one of us is here to supervise.'

'That man Melissus wanted me to pay for a porter and a cook.'

'I said no. He wasn't happy.'

'Good girl. Those bastards try anything to push the price up . . . That seems to cover everything.' Vinius sounded almost disappointed.

Before he left, Gaius Vinius held out one hand and they formally shook on their partnership. Both kept it brisk.

Oddly, when Lucilla ate her supper that evening, the apartment seemed unduly still. Their choppy conversation had affected her; she noticed her heart pattering.

Gaius Vinius was a man; he expected to dominate. He would learn better.

*　　　*　　　*

On leaving Plum Street, Vinius met his brother in a bar, as he did from time to time. Naturally Flavia Lucilla became a subject of conversation. Fortunatus needed to be reassured that his young brother would be able to tolerate her; there was nothing so awkward as a financial arrangement that failed to work out . . . 'I only saw her all veiled up, but they say she's tasty.'

'Passable,' shrugged Gaius.

With male complacence, he reflected that his assessment that first time he met her had been right; Flavia Lucilla had grown up quite attractively. The scrawny girl had filled out and fluffed up, fulfilling his prophecy to such an extent Gaius Vinius preened himself on his astuteness.

Fortunatus led a blameless life. His wife ensured that he ate dinner at home, every night without exception. She was also prone to turning up at whatever site he was working on, to bring his lunch, or for some other domestic reason, at unexpected times of day. His men joked that Galatia came to pick him up and take him home safely when they knocked off work, though that was untrue; she frequently left Fortunatus to find his own way home since, after all, he was not a schoolboy.

He was eager that his young brother should enjoy more excitement.

'Are you screwing her?'

'Not yet.' Out of pity, Gaius went along with his brother's need to be titillated. As Fortunatus drooled with jealousy, Gaius quipped, 'She will have to wait until I'm in a good mood.'

O Jupiter. Gaius, you lucky beggar!

Fortunatus concluded their gossip in his favourite way. He was master of the well-placed fart.

*   *   *

Vinius went home to his own house where in due course he made love to his wife. There was no point

130

a man being married unless he availed himself of his rights if ever, and indeed whenever, he had the opportunity.

Supposing that intercourse would make him approachable, Verania afterwards asked if it was true that the Emperor had raised the pay of the armed forces. Vinius pretended it was just a rumour. Luckily his salary, after deductions, was paid into the soldiers' savings bank; that was kept in armoured chests under the shrine at the Praetorian Camp, well beyond the grasp of wives who were, after all, not supposed to exist.

Domitian had in truth given the troops an astonishing raise; he had increased pay across the board by a third. Who knew what the damage to the Treasury was—but who cared? It made the soldiers happy and secured the army's loyalty.

They approved of more than that. Although the literary commentators who had stayed in Rome picking their noses all satirised the new Germanicus for indulging in a fake Triumph, the soldiers assessed his expedition differently. They could see how invading the Chatti formed part of the careful strategy to beef up frontiers against the very real threat of invasion. And Domitian now had another success. News came that Agricola, the governor of Britain, had won a major battle against the northern British tribes in some wild place called Mons Graupius; he brought more of the island under Roman control than had ever happened before (or would ever happen again).

All this made for a good mood in the army. The legions might never love Domitian as they had Vespasian and Titus, with their grasp of logistics, brilliance at siege warfare and willingness to be in the thick of it, fighting hand to hand. But Domitian had won the troops over.

He would need that. Because it soon became clear he was gripped by an obsession that he had enemies everywhere.

9

Paris. Paris the actor and dancer . . . Domitian decided that Paris had become Domitia Longina's lover. The Emperor frequently brooded alone on this subject, but once he began goading his suspect wife, everyone was mesmerised.

When are you going to confess?
Oh please! Not that again.
He is your lover; admit it.
I would not demean myself.
You must take me for an idiot.
No, dear; you're just sick . . .

*   *   *

Lucilla and Lara witnessed some of the upsets.

As Lara said, it must be hard trying to throw yourself into a rampaging private quarrel, when so many other people surrounded you. The Empress always had her attendants; the Emperor trailed his bodyguard. Scores of other functionaries roamed adjacent staterooms and corridors, with hundreds elsewhere in the palace. Their presence was physically oppressive and accompanied by a permanent level of noise. Slaves had no incentive to do their work quietly. People waiting for an audience would gossip, cough and make complaints. Freedmen from the imperial secretariats called out to one another loudly as they traversed intersections or bent their heads over scrolls in corners of peristyle gardens, speaking up over the mumbling of gardeners and the splash of fountains.

They were in Rome. The Emperor needed to be on the spot; he was reviewing his huge city rebuild. Civic works took precedence, as his architects reconstructed the fire damage; there would be many new buildings too: a remodelled overflow forum, new temples for the deified Vespasian and Titus and for Domitian's favourite gods, extra entertainment facilities. Until he fulfilled plans to monumentalise imperial accommodation on the Palatine, his family stayed in the Domus Aurea, Nero's Golden House; the Flavians had always indicated they would only be lodgers in that notorious extravaganza but so far other building projects took priority and after more than ten years they were still here. The exquisitely decorated corridors and intricately linked rooms gave ample opportunity for sweeping about in a rage.

Flavia Domitilla, who was herself pregnant again and lumbering uncomfortably, had lent Lara and Lucilla to her cousin the Empress, to ease well-reported marital problems. Nothing had been mentioned openly—nothing ever was—but they understood it was their task to support Domitia Longina as she tried to prevent her marriage unravelling. She was a woman who looked too determined to be beaten by a quarrel. She had a strong hooked nose any general would be proud of, full cheeks and an incipient double chin; yet she was pampered enough to believe in her own looks, and of course still young.

Within the suite where they were styling Domitia, cushion-plumpers and tray-bearers came and went as if their minor errands were all important. The surroundings were sumptuous, wearying to the eye, a clutter of overstuffed upholstery, drapes and often startling statues. A rash of ornate daybeds and side-tables filled the cavernous room, among towering stone candelabra whose last night's smoke still lingered.

The day began as routine. When Domitian burst in, everyone froze. Always prone to blushing, he had coloured up. His wife tensed, though she hid it. The two sisters saw a marital fight coming. Some attendants scattered. Lara and Lucilla followed protocol, abruptly standing still with lowered eyes. Domitian was prowling between them and the double doors he had flung open; they could not make a discreet withdrawal.

Domitia had had ten years of practice with her husband. The trick was to let him be the centre of attention.

I know you had an affair.
You are winding yourself up needlessly.
Stop lying to me . . .

*   *   *

There had certainly been a shift in this famous marriage. Domitian had returned from Europe suffering agonies of jealousy. It seemed to blow up from nowhere, though Lucilla suspected Domitia Longina had unwittingly contributed. She had misplayed her position when left behind in Rome. In the anticlimax after his campaign and triumph, the new Germanicus was now all too ready to ponder uncomfortably on what might have happened in his absence. Domitian never liked feeling left out, even though he preferred solitude. Now he had a new game: brooding over these fears that his wife had been unfaithful.

If the 'visit to Gaul' had been merely ceremonial, Domitia Longina might have gone abroad with him. Although he took courtiers, she did not escort her husband. She was Corbulo's daughter. She could have stomached a few weeks of pecking at unusual titbits among men with moustaches and trousers. But Roman commanders did not take high-born wives into battle, which had always been the expedition's real purpose. So she was left in Rome.

Problems had begun when their son died. They had lost their young boy and were not coping well. Domitia was both grieving and resenting any pressure for her to immediately produce another heir. Breeding called for conjugal relations. There were doubts whether that was happening.

The couple guarded their privacy. People were not even sure how many children they had produced; if they ever had a daughter too, as some believed, her little life must have been even shorter than the boy's. His existence was recorded; he was pictured on coins; now he was shown among the stars, dead and deified.

Neither of his parents could open up and talk about it. In a festering atmosphere of secrecy, Domitian's response to loss was as strangulated as always. They gave each other no consolation. Domitia froze; Domitian consorted with his eunuchs. Domitia tolerated that, since at least he had not taken a senatorial mistress who would usurp her position. There had been strife, though not a rift, but when he left for the north it must have been a relief to both of them. For Domitia, his absence brought unprecedented freedom.

If you worked it out, as Lucilla thoughtfully did, Corbulo's daughter had never before been allowed any independence. Second child of a strong father, she was married very young, to Aelius Lamia; she was still an inexperienced bride when Domitian invited her to Alba and persuaded her to divorce her husband. Domitian was eighteen, Domitia even younger. Adolescents. Immature and thrilled. Lucilla imagined them marvelling that after both being children of disgraced fathers under Nero, they now had a glorious reprieve. Domitian was a star in a brand new ruling dynasty and, during the first heady days of their love affair, he was even his father's representative in Rome.

They faced a wobble when Vespasian pressed Domitian to marry his brother's daughter, but Domitian held out for his soulmate. The link to Corbulo's family had attractions so they were allowed their wish. Domitia moved from one marriage directly into another, but Vespasian insisted they lived with him; it was to enable Domitian's initiation into government, but it meant that for ten years they never had a home of their own.

Now she was Domitia Augusta, first lady of the Empire; her image was on the currency; she had the same privileges as the Vestal Virgins. So what did she do when, for almost a year, she was left to her own devices with no head of household? Domitia Longina spent long hours flopping on couches, bored. She chatted to friends. She visited her sister. She spent money. She spent more money—though not too much because the Flavians were infamously frugal. In private she dwelt on her loss as a mother, which was not only tragic but diminished her influence as Domitian's Empress. Then, she ordered up her curtained litter and went to the theatre.

Of course she admired Paris. Paris was brilliant.

*   *   *

The Roman establishment had a mixed reaction to pantomime. It was a form of dramatic performance that came from the east, particularly Syria, although Paris—this particular Paris, for he used a traditional stage name—was Egyptian. Exotic, risqué cultures raised hackles in grumpy Roman conservatives. Rome's founding fathers, lean men ploughing cold furrows in between fighting fierce enemies, would find this theatrical genre distasteful, while the danger that posturing matinee idols would seduce noblewomen caused horror. Mimes came into frequent contact with such ladies, who threw themselves at performers.

Pantomime presentations, retelling Greek myths, had spectacular stage effects and lavish costumes, so productions were expensive. It was a callisthenic art. It featured rhythmic dance. Sometimes there was an orchestra or merely a sinuous flute, but always percussion. One man, mysteriously masked and with a well-honed body, would perform all the parts in a story while a soloist or chorus sang the lyrics. It was said that a good pantomime talked with his hands. Husbands knew what they thought that meant. They knew where the bastard's hands were likely to be put when offstage.

Pantomime artistes made extravagant claims on their tombstones that they had led chaste lives. This was to refute satirists, who told the public that pantomimes corrupted morals, the morals of women in particular, although everyone thought the dancing bastards were not picky. They, or at least the theatrical masks they wore, had long hair, which always offends traditionalists. The greatest performer of his day, Mnester, had been put to death for an affair with that byword for voracious sexuality, the Empress Messalina. The Senate had banned mime performances in private homes, and forbade the aristocratic young from joining in dancers' processions. Rivalry between their fans occasionally led to riots. Sometimes pantomime artistes were exiled—not often enough, said the prudish.

Nevertheless, these cult performers flourished. With huge incomes and celebrity acclaim, plus close contact with the upper classes, they easily became arrogant. Their influence at court was wildly over-estimated; Paris was reputed to control army postings and other rewards, though that hardly squared with the Emperor's own determination to supervise all appointments himself.

Always caught between his liking for the arts and his self-imposed role as moral arbiter, Domitian enjoyed the pantomime and had seriously admired Paris. That was until he convinced himself that Paris had slept with his wife.

*　　　*　　　*

138

Lara and Lucilla had been to watch Paris perform, though at long distance because their tickets consigned them to the upper rows of the theatre, where women and slaves were segregated. They could see enough to understand his powerful stage presence. Exhilarated themselves by the stirring dance rhythms and by his acting, they had realised that in gazing too long at Paris Domitia Longina was courting trouble. Rumours started. Whether there was anything in those rumours then hardly mattered.

Naturally she was chaperoned. She arrived by closed litter, though the imperial litter was instantly recognisable. To those wanting scandal its curtains, though normal, suggested concealment. Then if she sat, veiled, in the imperial box, there were plenty who would criticise her for appearing in public at all during her husband's absence. Besides, an imperial lady's veil tended to be pinned on behind her coronet of curls, leaving her face visible.

Perhaps Domitia did make contact with Paris, though Lucilla thought a face-to-face meeting would put her off sex. She could imagine it. Tiptoeing to the dressing room door with the frisson of danger . . . Then finding that the actor-dancer was older, less cultured and more paunchy than he appeared on stage. Inevitable disappointment. Backstage was hardly glamorous: the aura of liquor, the actual shabbiness of seemingly fabulous costumes, the dancer's skin coarsened and greasy from the stage makeup, the poverty of conversation from a person who relied on scripts, his difficult Egyptian Greek, his caricature Greek Latin . . . Still, nobody went to a heart-throb to talk.

Was the man one of those easterners who were 'not safe in palanquins'? Did he have the oriental habit (Lucilla and Lara had both endured it) of backing any woman into a corner, or even launching himself upon her, never caring about witnesses and not hearing protests?

Or perhaps it was all as Domitian dreaded. Perhaps the Empress really had tripped off to some dangerous rendezvous, where she betrayed her husband.

I must tell you my admiration for your delightful and moving performance.

Augusta, the delight is mine! Please let me move you some more by tumbling you lasciviously among these convenient stage-props.

Oh I can't—Oh I want to—I can . . .

*   *   *

The Emperor believed what he wanted to believe.

Tell me what you did, every detail.

There is nothing to tell.

Domitian remained wildly distrustful. His misery gnawed; he bitterly analysed every facet of his wife's behaviour. It got him nowhere; there was no evidence. Even if there had been proof of her innocence, he would have disbelieved it. Her declarations of good faith went unheard. Failing to prove the unprovable made him more aggressive. Lara thought Domitia Longina was afraid he would become violent.

So the couple tussled endlessly. They were equally matched, both strong personalities. Neither had had many friends; they had always relied on each other. Nothing would dissuade Domitian.

140

Nothing would cow Domitia. Their quarrels surged and died, then flared again. One or the other would brood on the latest slights, then rampage through anterooms seeking a new fight.

I've been watching you.

You saw nothing then.

I'll be the judge . . .

On that fatal day when Domitian stormed in, the sisters were eventually shooed out by a chamberlain. Uncertain what would happen next, they sat side by side on stone benches outside the room. The corridor was crammed. Attendants of all sorts waited for the current tempest to die down.

That was the day he ordered her to leave.

Sharp intake of breath from everybody. The court was riveted.

*   *   *

It was a shock, but Corbulo's daughter would not plead. For one thing, he threatened to execute her, so it made sense to get away fast. Once Domitian told her to go, she just packed a few things (by an empress's standards; her luggage required a mule train). Then she left him.

Domitian was caught on the hop. That must have consoled her—though with him so volatile, she remained at risk.

*   *   *

Life at court deteriorated. Rome was shocked that the Empress, whom most people reckoned innocent, had been wrongfully divorced. Old stories did resurface that Domitia Longina had had an

141

affair with Titus, although the view prevailed that if she had done, she would have boasted of it. New mutterings started about the Emperor's relationship with Julia.

Julia was living with Domitian. This had been the situation ever since her husband was killed; it was not really odd in Roman terms. With her grandfather and father dead, when Domitian executed her husband Sabinus he made himself her nearest male relation. He was, incontrovertibly, the widowed Flavia Julia's head of household. Had she been older, married for longer, or a mother, particularly the mother of three children which conferred special rights, then Julia might have lived apart, mistress of her own house.

But she was not yet twenty, and childless.

*   *   *

The Guards had plenty to say about the Julia problem. Gracilis told his beneficarius, 'It's perfectly bloody obvious. He has to keep Julia at the court. She is the only child of Titus, eternally beloved. She is an orphan and a widow. She is good looking, wealthy, no one has a word to say against her, and she's either too shrewd to make waves or a genuinely pleasant girl. By the moral legislation our leader loves, Julia should be remarried pronto and made to carry children. Of course the minute she does that, she becomes a threat to him. He's stuck. He has to ensure that no other bugger ever marries Julia—and while he keeps her close, everyone is bound to say it's because Uncle Domitian is fucking her.'

Gaius Vinius quietly overlooked the fact that

142

much of this excellent theory had been his. 'So what can he do?'

'Bring the wife back. No bloody option.'

'What about the mess he's invented with Paris?'

'Send the pirouetting poppy into exile.'

Vinius knew his centurion was thinking, thank you, Jove, it was some bloody ballet-dancer their leader had fixed upon. It could have been one of his Praetorians, who sometimes had to escort imperial women. That nightmare of a princess taking a shine to one of her fit and fearless bodyguards; the discipline dilemma and ensuing stink, if a nervous soldier could not think up a polite way to say no . . .

So thank you, thank you all the gods in the pantheon. Whatever else the stupid skirt had done, there was no suggestion she did that.

*   *   *

It was on their watch that Domitian dealt with Paris.

The Emperor was being carried through the streets. Gaius Vinius wondered afterwards if he was actually cruising, on the look-out for the miserable dancer. Certainly, Domitian had had too much time for thinking. In the litter, he had got himself properly churned up again.

Gracilis and some of the cohort were on escort detail, Vinius among them. Domitian abruptly ordered the bearers to stop. He leapt out, highly agitated, his face already flushed. Guards tightened their formation around him, uncertain what he was up to. It was an ordinary street, with clogged gullies along the cobbles and full washing-lines overhead: vegetable stalls, urchins, businessmen, slaves carrying the daily bread. Too many witnesses—even the stray bloody dogs were gawping.

'Give me a sword!'

Vinius had the misfortune to be nearest. Like all of them he was dressed in a discreet civilian tunic, but was carrying his short military sword in its handsome decorated scabbard. Some colleagues, since they were not bearing shields, had their weapons slung from belts on the left, but Vinius continued to wear his gladius under his right arm as he had learned in the army.

Using the regular move, a smooth right-handed pull and flip, he drew out his sword. Mid-action, Domitian snatched it. Vinius had to whip his hand away to avoid severed tendons.

He himself had identified Paris. Paris had spotted Domitian; watched him grab the weapon. Paris guessed his fate.

So did Gaius Vinius.

Unlike Titus, who had been drilled at court by Nero's bullish Praetorian Prefect, Burrus, Domitian probably never did much basic training. Becoming the son of an emperor at eighteen had exempted him from the course of honour, the normal series of military and admin posts that conditioned young men of the upper classes. He was at one time called Prince of Youth, which was meaningless. His honours had been all concerned with priesthoods and poetry. He had a reputation for squeamishness and had even discussed abolishing animal sacrifice in religious ceremonial. Though officially a general, the triumphant Germanicus had spilt no blood personally while they were campaigning.

Paris—effete, bejewelled, gorgeously clad, his features cosmetically emphasised—backed against a house wall. It was a sensible move, had this been a mugger after his purse.

Domitian rushed him. To a soldier, it was a disaster. The way the sword point was wavering, Vinius could tell that Domitian would make a mess of the kill. He would probably be hurt himself. Close by, Gracilis spat an obscenity. But Vinius was still nearest.

Nothing for it.

Vinius stepped up behind the Emperor. He felt like a trainer with a raw recruit. He dropped his own fist over the Emperor's hand on the sword pommel and guided Domitian's aim. He grasped Domitian's left shoulder, leant against his back for a firm stance, then shoved the sword for him with the right strength. Paris would have felt as if he had been punched hard in the ribs, but he would not have felt it long. He died there as Vinius wrenched out the blade, with a twist to make sure. Vinius let go of the Emperor; he could feel Domitian shaking. He took a step back.

Gracilis bumped past him. Retrieving the sword from their master, the centurion wiped off most of the blood on the dead actor's pretty tunic. Knowing him, Vinius believed he was disgusted by this fiasco. 'Help the Emperor into his litter, make it quick. Someone, fetch the Urbans to control the mob and clear this corpse away . . .' Respectfully he spoke to Domitian, like a mother rescuing a child: 'Well done, sir, but that's enough excitement. Let's get you home, shall we?'

As the Emperor clambered back into his litter, a crowd collected, too stupid to know what was good for them. Shutters were opening overhead, women calling out to their neighbours. Decius Gracilis spoke urgently in a lower voice: 'Vinius! Go to the camp. Go straight there. Don't speak to anyone. Clean up, clean your weapon, leave it with my batman. Is there somewhere you can hide up? Get there and stay there, until we can assess the fallout. Scramble!'

Not your best move, soldier.

I get it.

A Roman whose wife committed adultery in his home had the right to kill her lover on the spot. But Domitian had slain Paris in cold blood. He had not caught him in the act, nor discovered him in his house. Any good defence lawyer would accuse Domitian of forethought, deliberately seeking Paris out, well exceeding his traditional rights.

Being realistic, if the Emperor owned this openly, he would get away with it. Even so, technically, killing Paris was unlawful. If Domitian was accused and wanted to distance himself, Gaius Vinius might be charged with the murder. It would be unfair, but Roman law could be harsh.

Vinius made himself scarce.

*   *   *

In markets and food shops in adjacent neighbourhoods, flies noticed a new scent in the air, calling to them. Musca's descendants responded. Paris was still warm on the cobbles as they rose in slow circles and unhurriedly approached to lay eggs in the carrion.

10

Safety.

The apartment. Four quiet rooms. Dim light. Life went on here on a decent domestic basis, orderly, ordinary, private. Someone was trying out a floor rug in the corridor. Not a success. It was tripping up clients and the cleaning slave loathed it; the experiment would be discontinued.

All the internal doors were closed. Street noises were muffled: shouts; harness bells; chickens in cages; children's squeals. Indoors, silence.

An island of serenity in a troubled world. Few people knew his link to this place. Nobody knew he was here.

Having the apartment was starting to matter.

*　　*　　*

Flavia Lucilla opened a door suddenly and bounced from her workroom, her mouth full of hairpins. Annoyed, she found the soldier standing just indoors, key still in his hand. 'Vinius!' Hairpins scattered.

Once again his unexpected arrival had startled her. He, too, wished she had not been here. Without a word he strode to his room, closing the double doors. He stood there, leaning back against the wood, desperate, shaken by today's experience.

Lucilla knocked briskly, trying to push open the doors. A furious Vinius faced her, snarling: 'We need some rules around here! Doors open: permit to treat. Doors shut: bloody well keep out!'

She returned to her client. The woman sensed a desire to be rid of her. She hung on, asking questions about maintenance of her new hairstyle, wondering about lotions, describing dull antics of grandchildren.

Once freed, Lucilla prowled about, making it obvious she was now alone, but no sound came from the soldier.

*   *   *

Hours later, she was finishing in the kitchen when she heard Vinius emerge quietly and use the facilities. He came in. Though a little more benign after her supper, Lucilla cold-shouldered him. He barely seemed to notice. A married man, he was used to the silent treatment.

He stared at his shelf as if he had never seen the things that now stood there. She had presumed he chose them: two sets of ceramic redware bowls in three sizes, small, medium, generous; knives and spoons wrapped in a dinner napkin; a small frying pan with a folding handle; another flat pan with two handles; a set of four beakers; two pottery lamps (with designs of ducks, nothing pornographic); and a flagon of lamp oil. All were new. All had arrived the same day as the furniture she had seen in one of his rooms: a bed-frame with a neat pile of folded blanket, sheet and pillow; a stool beside the bed; a chest. The chest was locked; she had tested it shamelessly, then scurried from the room as if she feared Vinius had an invisible gryphon watching his belongings.

Conscious he needed rehydration, Vinius selected a beaker. In a world of his own, and with

148

his one-eyed focussing trouble, when he turned on the bronze tap he partly missed the water flow. Splashes went everywhere; he stood transfixed.

Lucilla dropped one hand on his wrist to steady the beaker. She turned off the tap. Vinius greedily swallowed down the half cup.

Lucilla had recognised there was some real crisis. She touched his arm again, using the back of her hand so it was as neutral as the touch of a medical orderly. 'You're freezing cold! Are you ill?'

He stared dully. 'Shock . . . I had a shock.'

Amazed, she saw his teeth chatter briefly. She took control; she steered the man to her workroom, where she sat him in one of the armchairs. She fetched the blanket from his room, shook it open and draped it over him, saying she would make him a hot drink. Vinius allowing her to take charge was sufficiently uncharacteristic to cause concern.

It took time to heat anything on the small cooking fire. While he was alone, Vinius roused himself a little, looking around. He stood up, clutching the blanket, and went to the open door which led onto a veranda; it ran around four sides of an internal courtyard but had been sectioned off with trellis outside their apartment, providing a small place to sit out, dappled with sunlight on this long summer evening. He heard voices below, must be old man Cretticus, talking to a slave.

Back indoors, Vinius deduced much about Flavia Lucilla's life. Her situation had changed from when he first met her, scratching an existence, with the blowsy mother he had suspected was almost a prostitute, Lucilla then a girl who seemed only one step from the same fate. Clearly she had talent. Apart from what he had heard about her from

149

Melissus, he could tell from this workroom. Two exuberantly curly female headpieces sat on a shelf, one of them half-finished. She had assembled kit, all organised with systematic neatness on shelves or in trays in a way that appealed to a soldier. The Empire permitted social advancement, but that was commonest among men who could rise from slave to free citizen through business, then with enough application and patronage reach the equestrian rank and even senator. Flavia Lucilla was a rare woman to seize on the possibilities. Vinius was not surprised, but impressed by her swift progress.

He was back in the chair looking meek when Lucilla returned, bringing heated wine with honey and a hint of spice. Vinius cradled the cup in both hands. He gulped, then shuddered, but it hit the spot. 'You're wonderful!'

With a sniff at his cliché, she took the second wicker chair, pushing a cushion into the small of her back. She was wearing the same blue dress as last time, but with casual slippers. Her hair was different, looped in a heavy plait behind her head; Vinius thought it too severe but guessed the style was temporary. She positioned her feet on a footstool, pair to one Vinius had kicked aside, then laced her fingers together, leaning her chin on them. 'I think you ought to tell me what happened.'

'Can't do that.'

'I am a hairdresser, Vinius. We see everything and say nothing.'

Vinius remained stubbornly silent to begin with. He gazed around Lucilla's room, as he had done while she was brewing his hot drink. To delay answering her question, he indicated a large divided basket in which were laid hanks of human hair in different colours.

'Imported,' Lucilla explained, matter-of-factly. She kept talking to settle him: 'The blonde comes from Germania, the blue-black from India. Don't worry; I pick it all over and give it a wash before I bring a bundle into the house. Expensive stuff, but I get access to the importers and special rates because of who I work for ... Sometimes I wonder about the story behind it. For a woman in abject poverty, selling your hair beats selling your body— and, unlike a virginity, you can grow it back and sell it more than once.'

Vinius at last smiled faintly. He did not remark that, as he knew from the vigiles, in the sex trade repeat virginities were two a *quadrans*.

Next, he cocked his head at a stone bust of a male head, stylised yet familiar, alongside which lay a hairpiece on which Lucilla had been working after her client left. It was not one of her fanciful fondant crests for her ladies, but a flat band of cloth onto which she was slowly knotting a dense row of identical formal curls. *'Is that—?'*

'If it is, you'll see him wearing it, won't you, Praetorian?'

She rose, and planted the hairpiece on the model's smooth crown; she made a mock obeisance, then snorted. She put away the bust in a cupboard, where she must normally hide it out of sight.

They were connected closely through their work, with its demands of confidentiality. Anyway, the death of Paris was public. Vinius made his decision. 'I killed a man today—at least, helped somebody do it.'

Lucilla took his empty beaker, lest it slip from his fingers and shatter. She resumed her chair, sitting

151

very still. Oddly, she felt no fear at all at the fact he said he had killed someone. 'Who's dead?'

'Paris,' said Gaius Vinius in a drab voice. 'Paris, the actor-dancer. Paris who may have been the Empress's lover.'

'Or not!' commented Lucilla. 'Paris who was merely suspected by her husband, the maniac.'

We live in dark times.

We have seen nothing yet.

*   *   *

Gaius told her what had happened and his part in it. Lucilla merely asked, 'What was your thinking, when you involved yourself?'

'Paris was going to die anyway. No need to prolong his agony. He was terrified, but he meant to resist, and whatever you think of theatrical types, he was extremely fit and athletic—which Domitian is not. I didn't want to let the public see Paris being mangled. There would have been screaming. And scrabbling around on the ground. It would have lasted a long time. Blood everywhere. Maybe the Emperor himself wounded.'

'I see,' said Lucilla.

Words were coming freely now. 'We bundled Domitian off the scene as fast as possible. My centurion told me to lie low—a good man, old school. We work very closely . . . He is scared I may have to take the blame.'

Lucilla considered. 'No. No, it won't happen. The Emperor will want to see himself as a hero.'

'He killed an unarmed man!'

'A soldier's viewpoint, Vinius. Anyway, you will be deleted from his version.'

152

'He may want me deleted permanently.'

'Then your centurion is right. Disappearing will help Domitian misremember how things happened. Soon you won't count.'

'I just did my job.'

'Oh how conventional.' Lucilla's jibe was gentle and Gaius smiled at it.

He finished his drink, feeling it reheat his body-core as intended. He was at ease with the girl now, any predatory interest in her neutralised. All it took, apparently, was just one kindly brew to reposition Flavia Lucilla among his grandmother, aunts and the mother he could not remember. Or he viewed her, perhaps, as a man might think of an elderly prostitute who was content to listen, or some friendly landlady, detached from his real life but with a warm heart.

She saw him just as before: a typical man, a menace, a potential lecher, an idiot.

*   *   *

Vinius remained at the apartment for the next three days, but Lucilla rearranged her appointments so she saw her customers in their own homes—as a favour to him, as she saw it—and she spent a lot of time elsewhere with Lara. She and Vinius barely saw each other.

After the Praetorian returned to the camp, the apartment seemed somehow less empty to her. She had accepted that they shared the place. He would be coming back and, on the whole, Lucilla no longer minded.

153

11

Themison of Miletus had his lunch on a tray. Bad for digestion, any doctor knew, but he had convinced himself the demands of his private patients left no alternative. It had worthy ingredients: lettuce, radishes, celery, hard-boiled eggs, olives, capers, sliced onion, curls of hard cheese, squares of soft sheep's cheese, pine nuts, anchovies . . . In truth, there was rather a lot of it.

Still, he only drank cold water. Well, he did today. His home appointments were over-running and just when he planned to finish for the morning, two new patients had wormed themselves onto his list. He had no idea how they managed to persuade his usher to slot them in. Themison harboured growing suspicions that the usher had started to disobey instructions deliberately. He also suspected the man accepted bribes.

He wanted to be brooding about his festering feud with his rival, Pharoun of Naxos, who was trying to do down Themison with all the obnoxiousness and deceit of an islander. He could dwell on Pharoun's wiles while he was eating, even though he should not be torturing himself during the digestion process. He had been looking forward to an hour of seething about Pharoun as much as he looked forward to the bliss of regular bowel movements.

Irritably he agreed that the two men could come in.

*   *   *

154

They were soldiers. Although they were not in uniform, interpretation of body language was a professional skill. Also, they were carrying swords and when he asked, they immediately owned up to being Praetorians.

Themison observed they were both anxious. While they were in his waiting room they must have seen a young woman totter out, needing the support of two attendants. ('Speculum examination,' one man had guessed in a hollow voice to his companion. Growing up among many aunts, he knew about gynaecological torment.) Next, a waiting child had screamed so much he had to be taken home without seeing the doctor; the painfully thin lad's grey complexion indicated that there was no hope anyway. Finally, a man they recognised as a top gladiator hopped through, muttering curses and with bloody bandages on his bunions.

When they were called in, they nearly went home instead.

In the consultation room, they stared around, then glanced at one another. They took another penetrating look at Themison: a middle-aged, bearded Greek in a long but sleeveless tunic. He had humourless, searching eyes. His sense of importance implied that his curriculum vitae went back as far as the Parthenon's. However, his attitude was just the same as the legionary doctors who, even before a new patient had crept shamefaced through the door, started dispensing advice that the best treatment for a bad back was to keep marching, not spend three days malingering in bed.

They already knew Themison was a gladiators' doctor; he held a senior position at the Ludus Magnus and what they witnessed here—the wealthy class of his patients, the discreet slaves padding to and fro, the bloody great size of his lunch—confirmed he must have a good reputation. He probably rarely killed people, or not so their relatives noticed.

Themison produced one of the waxed tablets he kept for patient records; when he asked their names, surprisingly the men supplied them. He wrote them down neatly, with the date, then looked up nervously.

'Write what you like,' smiled the younger one, Gaius Vinius. *That doesn't mean I'm going to let you keep the tablet.*

Themison assessed them. One was a wide-bodied, short, aggressive man with Iberian looks; his subordinate was a taller, younger fellow who at first pretended to be a patient. This Vinius presented with an interesting set of facial scars. Themison told him what the soldier knew already: it was too late to improve his appearance, though if Themison had been present when he was first wounded, much could have been done to save him not only from disfigurement but a lifetime of discomfort. He was too kindly to say he might have saved the eye; of course as a gladiators' doctor, he believed he could have done.

'You need to look after your skin. Do not regard this as effeminate. I suppose you spend much time out of doors? Follow my advice and you will feel an improvement. Keep your scars moisturised. I will give you a pot of my lubricant and a prescription any apothecary will make up when you need more.

156

Rub it in daily. A woman's touch is helpful, if you have a girlfriend.'

The soldier accepted the ointment pot but barely listened. Vinius knew Verania would have no interest in massaging pungent wax into his face, even if he trusted her with the task.

Themison decided there must be some more sinister reason for their visit. He felt panicky, as if he might be about to vomit.

Decius Gracilis put down the money for the consultation. It was a large amount; his hand lingered on the leather purse. Neither man moved. Yes, their enquiry about Vinius had been a ploy. Themison's heart sank further. Involuntarily he analysed the symptom. It could not be a physical movement, a literal migration of the beating organ, although clearly not a fantasy either; he wondered what really caused the lurching sensation and how he might use this to prevent terror in gladiators.

'Is there something else I can help you with?'

'We hope so.'

Themison abandoned all hope of enjoying his lunch in the near future. He carried the tray to a side-table, where he covered it with his napkin to keep off flies. A fly did settle on the napkin shortly afterwards, but Themison had tucked in the cloth so the weight of the tray held it down and prevented access.

*　　　*　　　*

'So,' began the centurion, conversationally. 'You are a doctor. How good are you? What do *you* think Titus died of?'

Zeus!

157

Appalled, Themison laid down his stylus. 'Classic marsh fever. Don't quote me.'

'What do you base that on?'

'Time of year, overheating, and the headaches. It would be unprofessional to give a more detailed opinion when I never examined him.'

'Any views on the rumour he was poisoned with a hare fish?' *By his brother Domitian.*

Please, please don't ask me that . . .

'Reminds us of the old story that Caligula used such methods.' Decius Gracilis flexed his fingers. Either he had arthritis, or he was making veiled threats. 'Maybe someone snooping round the palace found a big old jar labelled *Danger, Hare Fish Poison*, with an imperial seal and a picture of a skeleton? And they tried it out?'

Themison began showing symptoms of hysteria: pallor, acute sweats, agitation. He looked as if he was about to faint. The soldiers were not worried. They knew enough battlefield first-aid to revive him.

It was still the centurion testing him. The other man was roaming about the consulting room, peering at equipment. Themison had the usual display of surgical saws. In addition to models of feet, ears and internal organs, presumably parts he had successfully treated, there was a sculpture of the medical god Aesculapius with his snaky staff among many small statuettes of gladiators. Vinius opened up pillboxes, dropped roundels on his palm, put them back again. Themison suspected this bullying was intended to terrify and control him. Then they would make him say treasonous things. After that he was utterly done for.

'Any comment on the ice-box story?'

'The patient needed cooling.'

'You wouldn't just dump Titus in a bed of ice and leave him, though?'

'Obviously *I* would not. Look—what is this?'

'Just curious.' *Just testing . . .*

Oh mother, I need a potty!

* * *

The Praetorians had chosen Themison because he was easy to access. He was an imperial servant as they were; he worked at the Ludus Magnus, the big gladiators' barracks that Domitian had built close to the new amphitheatre. Those fighters were not criminals being sent for slaughter, but highly trained professionals, expensive slabs of beef who were looked after by the best doctors in the world. A spin-off for the doctors was lucrative private practice. Some wrote best-selling medical manuals. Themison himself was secretly scribbling a set of lurid memoirs. He would have to be dead before publishing was safe.

Gracilis and Vinius had not wanted to approach any of the gruesomely expensive society physicians who blew magistrates' noses and carried out their wives' abortions. Nor, in view of Titus' fate, did they trust the palace freedmen who tended Domitian's health. They needed discretion and, as the gladiators' medico, Themison counted as official.

'What exactly can I help you with, Praetorians?'

Gaius Vinius stopped prowling. He returned to his seat, taking out a waxed note tablet and stylus of his own as if used to sitting in on interrogations— probably ones that proved fatal for the victims, thought Themison. The centurion sat leaning forward intently with his elbows on his knees. Themison clutched his left wrist with his right hand, as if taking his own pulse; the result was not good.

* * *

It was a few weeks since Vinius had gone back to the camp after the Paris murder. It was clear that, as Flavia Lucilla prophesied, he had been wiped from the record. Domitian wanted to believe killing his rival made him a figure of authority. The avenging husband. The moral judge. The new Augustus—utterly hypocritical.

The Emperor recalled Domitia Longina from exile almost immediately, 'summoning her back to his divine bed'. Nobody was clear whether her removal had counted as divorce—which, legally, Domitian should have insisted upon if he believed she had committed adultery. He claimed he was forced by a public outcry to forgive her. Most people thought their reconciliation was really because he missed her.

Others muttered that it was a ploy to cover up his incestuous affair with his niece Julia. Julia stayed at court, making an awkward family threesome.

If there were recriminations, they were kept behind closed doors. It would be rumoured that the Empress took lovers, though no one specifically named these brave men. Domitian kept his body-beautiful eunuchs, though Vinius had never seen him in a bunk-up. Nor had he ever witnessed him canoodling with Julia. In fact, Vinius wondered if the Emperor now avoided sex, which might explain a lot. The imperial couple would remain married throughout Domitian's reign, even though

Domitia never produced more children.

She knew how to handle Domitian. Possibly she had missed him too.

*   *   *

The ructions should have all died down. But the Emperor learned that people had been leaving flowers and perfumes in the street at the spot where Paris died. Domitian angrily ordered their removal. People who persisted in bringing tributes were dragged off and never seen again. Domitian himself haunted the area obsessively, until he noticed one of the actor's apprentices, paying his respects to his mentor. For modelling himself too closely on Paris and even having an unfortunate facial resemblance, Domitian had the young dancer executed.

At this point, the centurion Decius Gracilis became so concerned about his charge's state of mind, he decided to take medical advice.

*   *   *

'We haven't come for ourselves,' Gaius Vinius explained to Themison. 'We are worried about a friend.'

Caesar's friends. Not the amici in his council, those friends he didn't want. These were trusty amici Caesar never knew he had.

Some people might question their actions, but Decius Gracilis was the kind of stubborn, diligent centurion who took protecting the Emperor to the highest level. For him, the task included protecting the Emperor from himself. Never insubordinate, he had discussed his idea with the Praetorian Prefect.

Cornelius Fuscus was an old ally of the Flavians, the man who had brought the province of Illyria over to Vespasian's cause and helped secure his bid for Emperor. Appointed Prefect by Domitian on his succession, Fuscus was too canny to join in this. He allowed Gracilis to make medical enquiries, but on the usual cynical terms of 'get found out and you can catch the shit on your own shield'.

Themison wiped his sweating face on his sleeve. He had heard 'for a friend' before, often. Normally it meant patients were too embarrassed about a symptom that was going to require tunic-lifting: sexual dysfunction; something they caught from a prostitute; or worst of all, haemorrhoids. If all these men wanted was to discuss an anal fissure, he would have a lucky escape. 'Tell me about your friend.'

'A bit of an odd personality.' The centurion spoke. His assistant took notes. Themison certainly did not. Taking notes about personalities was a sure way to end up looking an arena lion in the teeth.

'In what way?'

'Solitary. Unduly watchful.'

'Unpredictable?'

'No, I think we can predict him: if any idea has no possible basis in fact, he'll love it.'

'Excessively sensitive? Cannot cope with criticism? Imagines the world revolves around what other people think of him? Needlessly worries about his appearance?'

'Sounds like you've met him!'

The doctor remained expressionless; he was trained not to be susceptible to what patients thought he wanted them to say. The Praetorians, like all patients, found this off-putting. From the vigiles, Vinius recognised the deadpan method; he

162

thought Themison was overdoing it.

'Has he always been this way? Or did it come on, for instance, in early adulthood?'

'Could be.' Vinius took this question, remembering that scene on the Capitol.

'Was it triggered by an extended period of stress, or some catastrophic event? Witnessing a violent death, for instance?'

'That fits.'

'How old was he?'

'Eighteen.'

For once Themison nodded. 'That would be typical . . . And what about his childhood? Did he suffer deprivation?'

'There is said to have been relative poverty—no family silver on the sideboard, if you count that as hard luck.'

'I meant in another way. Could your friend when young have felt he was somehow insignificant? Unloved? Considered worthless?'

It was still Vinius supplying answers: 'His mother died, his father spent a lot of time away. I don't know what happened domestically; he may have been passed around family members, but they were a clannish family and I doubt he was really neglected. He may have been jealous of an older brother who was always a favourite. Well, he must have been. Very jealous. He probably grew up thinking whatever *he* did, it would never be good enough.'

He thought briefly of Felix and Fortunatus. There were ways to live with strong older brothers, without losing your sense of self.

'And what brought you here now?' asked Themison. 'Is his intellectual capacity suffering?

163

Does he function normally?'

Gracilis took the lead again. 'He is bright, energetic, takes an interest in everything. He functions, functions well. Generally.'

'But?'

'Very extreme behaviour on occasions. Unreasonable. Dangerous.'

'You mean you think he is going mad?'

*   *   *

There was a long pause. All three men breathed a little faster than previously.

Themison, frightened, attempted to react as if they had merely said their friend had a septic rash. 'I shall need more details.'

'He believes his wife has been unfaithful.'

This time Themison shocked the Praetorians by exploding with laughter: 'You call that extreme? Every husband in Rome believes the same. A large proportion are correct.' Gracilis and Vinius exchanged glances, each wondering what the doctor's wife had to put up with. Apparently unaware of his self-revelation, Themison continued, 'I am not joking. Always remember that when patients seem to harbour delusions, there may be a grain of truth there. It confirms their fears and makes it harder either to diagnose their illness, or to convince them there is anything wrong . . . Has your friend been violent?'

They nodded.

'Has he harmed anyone? Do you need an opinion for legal purposes? Has a victim pressed charges?'

Gracilis laughed harshly. 'Won't happen.'

'But you have approached me because you feel deep concern.' Themison now sat up more. 'I can give guidance on patient management, though most of my work concerns wounds to the body, as you know.'

'You do study the mind, doctor?'

'Oh yes. I tend gladiators. Preparation for physical combat includes good mental health.'

'I am glad you think that—' The centurion looked as though he would like to discuss this thesis professionally.

But Themison had reached the point where he was ready to contribute, a moment in any consultation where he expected to hold the floor while patients, or their concerned 'friends', listened admiringly. 'This is my opinion, based on what you say. You may have been describing a condition we call "paranoia". From *para* meaning "beyond" and *noos*, "the mind". Do you know Greek?'

'Enough to be xenophobic!' scoffed Gracilis rudely. 'So if "paranoia" means "beyond the mind", what does "beyond the mind" mean in good Latin?'

'Outside the boundaries of reason,' Themison explained crisply. His actions and speech became much more comfortable. 'We all carry the seeds of paranoia within us. However, most people can tell when their fancies have no reality, and often holding crazy ideas is temporary. With paranoia, extreme suspicions last. It can be as mild as "that slave gave me a funny look just now" or as severe as "the plotters have cunningly drilled a hole in the ceiling to spy on me". Let me outline some symptoms you may recognise: anxiety, feelings of being threatened, difficulty forming social relationships, jealousies regarding the sexual fidelity of a spouse, preferring his own company, secretiveness, eccentric and aggressive behaviour, a heightened sense of self-importance . . .'

'Exactly.'

'Does he suffer hallucinations?'

'Not that we know.'

'Is he hearing voices?'

'Seems not. Is that good?' queried Vinius.

'Better than nothing.'

'Can you do anything?' asked Gracilis.

'Even if I could, such patients are not amenable to being treated. Their suspicion that people are plotting against them leads them to resist any suggestion they are ill; they see this as part of the sinister plan, the plan they must try to outwit. Even if they do seek help, they tend to disrupt any prescribed regime, toss away medicine, obstinately take against their doctors—'

'It's a waste of time trying?'

'There is no cure.'

'He will never get better?'

'The condition is chronic. He may perhaps get worse.'

'That could be unfortunate! So what do you advise?'

'It is important to resist his crazy ideas. Stand firm. Do not undermine the poor fellow, but tell him firmly you assume he has his reasons for thinking that way, but you cannot agree with him. This condition is very hard on friends and family, because of the unremitting need to deal with someone who denies he is afflicted and resents help. Such patients are wearing to live with and, as you probably appreciate, to be constantly under suspicion while innocent may exasperate his

166

associates until they do turn against him. Those who love him will feel rejected.'

'Those who love him may *be* rejected.'

'Exactly.'

'This is bleak.'

'Not entirely. Such patients can have great creative talent—and can be capable of immense kindness to others—but even those who admire him may not dare to reassure him, in case the slightest phrase is misinterpreted.'

Themison paused. The Praetorians were too despondent to react.

'Well, at least from your friend's point of view, although he suffers terribly—and believe me, his delusions do make him truly miserable—even so, his affliction is not fatal . . . Though we must all die,' said the doctor lugubriously.

'That's what you think!' snapped Decius Gracilis dryly. 'He's almost a god. Half the buggers sitting up among the constellations nowadays are his dead relatives.'

This plain speaking went too far for Themison. With the patient's identity brought into the open so dangerously, he broke down under the pressure.

He jumped from his chair and fell on his knees. 'Is this a test? Has some patient complained? Is a rival playing tricks on me? *Pharoun of Naxos?* What can I have done to displease the Emperor? Are you going to send troops to arrest me?' He sounded quite delusional.

They would achieve nothing more from the interview. The Praetorians went to the panicking doctor, lifted him considerately from his cracking knees like a sack of hay, and replaced him in his consulting chair. Vinius fetched his lunch tray and laid it in the doctor's lap, then wiped Themison's brow with his linen napkin and waved a fly away. After these gentle courtesies, the two soldiers left.

*   *   *

Outside in the street, Gracilis and Vinius breathed deeply as if they had been stifled in the consulting room; heads back, they gazed for a moment at the mild autumnal sky.

'Well, we tried our best. There's nothing we can do for him. "We all carry the seeds of it within us"—how good to know!'

'And what hope is there for anyone, when even the doctor is paranoid?'

PART 3

Rome, Alba and Dacia: AD 85–89

All roads lead to . . .

12

Life went on.

For nearly two years the Emperor was absorbed in running Rome. To demonstrate stability, he reorganised the Mint and upgraded the currency's metal content to the high quality it had contained in the reign of Augustus. This standard was hard to maintain. But Domitian boosted the Treasury by confiscating property; it was said he relied on trumped-up charges laid by informers. At the start of his reign he had expressed abhorrence for informers; now he was less fastidious. On the other hand, his management of the courts was scrupulous; he purged juries of undesirables and, when he was involved personally, gave high-quality judgements.

The most visible result of his rule was the city revamp. Almost all the buildings destroyed in the fire were reconstructed within a few years. The Campus Martius was completely redeveloped, with even the gnomon on the Horologium straightened up to tell the time correctly; the Pantheon and Saepta were restored, with an enhanced Temple of Isis to celebrate Domitian's dramatic escape in the Year of the Four Emperors. How much his youthful experience affected him was displayed in his new treatment of the caretaker's hut where he had been hidden overnight; the original shrine he constructed during his father's reign, with its altar picturing his exploits, was replaced by a large Temple of Jupiter the Guardian.

The main temple to Jupiter Optimus Maximus

on the Capitol was lavishly restored. Using its original footprint, the massive Etruscan base, Domitian created a dramatic new building with a hexastyle Corinthian portico in white Pentelic marble, which had never been used in Rome before. The doors were plated with gold and the bronze roof-tiles gilded. The new chief cult statue of gold and ivory rivalled the masterpiece of Phidias, the statue of Zeus at Olympia.

Carpers might accuse Domitian of ignoring his father and brother, yet he willingly completed the Temple of the Deified Vespasian in the Forum, plus a Flavian Tribunal on the Capitol where discharged soldiers were listed under the aegis of all three Flavian emperors; he commissioned the Arch of Titus, a superb and enduring monument that celebrated his brother's Judaean victory. Close by, Domitian created new underground systems in the Flavian Amphitheatre, where gladiators and animals were assembled before fights, and crowned the building with a fourth storey, decorated with bronze shields just below its cornice and supporting famous canvas coverings that were operated by sailors from the Misenum Fleet, to shade the audience. He installed the curious Sweating Fountain and built four training schools for gladiators, one directly linked to the amphitheatre. In Vespasian's forum, he completed the Temple of Peace, adding his own Forum Transitorium, which ingeniously utilised a narrow space to provide a linking walkway, at the heart of which was a Temple of Minerva, Domitian's favourite deity.

His works included every kind of amenity and monument: warehouses, gates, arches, baths. He renovated the public libraries, and spared no efforts

172

to stock them, sending scribes to Alexandria to copy all existing literature. To persuade the gods to ward off future conflagrations, in every region of Rome he paid for the substantial altars that had been promised since Nero's Great Fire, yet never before provided.

There were many more projects in planning, not least a dramatic new palace on the Palatine Hill. Although credit for much of this massive building programme would be claimed by his successors, Nerva and Trajan, it was Domitian who instigated many buildings that would become the famous face of imperial Rome.

This great statement Flavian city did have an unsettling effect on people who felt unsafe with the unfamiliar. Altering the time-honoured centre of an ancient urban scene is not immediately popular. But generations would soon grow up who had only known the new. For them, Rome was now more magnificent and impressive than it had been before, both a source of pride for its own citizens and a magnet to awe-struck visitors.

*   *   *

In Plum Street, by contrast, the Insula of the Muses looked much the same. Agents for the Crettici kept the building secure and watertight, though they tended to leave shutters and doors with a sun-bleached, shabby look. The porticos were swept most days by a group of slaves who worked slowly and liked leaning on their besoms, but who did deter vagrants. Many tenants supplied balcony troughs or flowerpots on steps; some even put out lamps in the evening, though these were regularly stolen by burglars or mischief-making revellers.

The ailing tassel business finally went under, which made Lucilla assess her own plans. She would have liked to rent the vacant shop, starting a local beauty parlour, but so far her ambitions were grander than her cashbox allowed. After a sad discussion with Melissus, she saw the new lease given to a couple of pumice-and-sponge sellers. Like the soft-furniture people before them, they had silly taste and little business sense, so Lucilla was biding her time.

Gaius Vinius somehow acquired a disassembled couch from the tassel shop. Typically, the desultory designer had always intended to use this to show off his stock, yet he never created the display. Lucilla one day heard a strange croaking sound and found Vinius in his second room, assembling the couch, whilst apparently singing. He claimed to be musical. Unmoved, Lucilla watched for a while, as he sorted a big bag of bronze fitments and systematically laid out parts in rows on the floor. 'I snapped this up from Droopy-Tunic. He reckoned it could be bolted together by a semi-nude fan-dancer in half an afternoon . . . Total tit, no wonder he's bust. Here, hold up the frame for me. Keep it level.'

Lucilla could follow instructions. She could also spot when Vinius had missed out a necessary joint, though he ignored her warning, which delayed the finished product by an hour or so. Brought up and working among women, she had learned enough about men and their foibles to bite her tongue.

Vinius decided to run down and buy a multi-bladed tool to help as he fixed webbing; he got talking to the knife-seller, leaving Lucilla standing with the couch. When he reappeared,

Lucilla had gone back to what she herself had been doing. She noticed that Vinius made no complaint. He resumed work alone. She waited long enough to make her point, then took him a pistachio biscuit and continued helping again.

Their relationship was neither warm nor cold. In eighteen months, they met at Plum Street on maybe a score of occasions. Since Vinius sometimes had had a quarrel with his wife, on those occasions he was uncommunicative. He shut himself in his bedroom, lay on his mattress and waited to calm down. Lucilla deduced what had probably upset him; he never said anything.

Other times, he brought knick-knacks or collected clothes. A stringed instrument appeared, which Lucilla heard him tuning and strumming. Once, with unusual diffidence, he asked Lucilla about the pot of ointment the doctor Themison had given him. She sniffed it, identified herbal ingredients and urged him to use it. Vinius told her, grinning cheekily, that Themison had said a woman's touch was best, but she made him rub it in himself.

He and Lucilla would nod to one another if she had a client, or otherwise exchange the time of day blandly. They had, however, adopted their catchphrase:

'It's me—'

'—Vinius!'

If Flavia Lucilla had shown any encouragement, an entanglement might have ensued. But the last thing she wanted was to complicate her life with a married man. She liked the look of the Praetorian, she could not help it; she welcomed his steady tread and did not object to him singing when he was happy (though she never joined in). But she was self-protective. Even if she had wanted to flirt, there were other men on the periphery of her life. Some were handsomer and even seemed more pleasant, although any belief in their good nature was probably rash. Many had two eyes not one, but most clearly lacked brains.

Gaius Vinius was bright, she thought. From their first meeting she had seen him as almost dangerously clever, though she had heard enough about him to know he was hopeless with women. Who wanted that?

* * *

Generally, Lucilla understood that any affair, or even marriage, would mean she lost control of her career. Men took up your time. They resented you having other interests. They made demands, even if you could avoid bearing their children. So although her women clients regularly asked when she was going to get a love-life, Lucilla murmured obliquely that she was still looking.

The avoidance of pregnancy was a subject on which she and Lara were seen as professional consultants, an offshoot of their trade. They gave discreet advice—not that Lara ever seemed to follow it. Along with handing out pots of face cream and other cosmetics, they would dispense discreet recommendations: how honey, gum or olive oil might make men's seeds sluggish; the usefulness of ground acacia, cedar or white lead in creams or vaginal tampons; and even the possibilities of goatskin sheaths, though these were generally seen as mythical and nobody knew how to obtain them.

In disasters, they would whisper an address for the Sixth Region's abortionist, although she operated discreetly because while it was permissible to prevent conception, killing a foetus was illegal. It denied a father his rights.

Getting pregnant could be problematical, even for women who wanted it. Others were relentlessly fertile—their main client, Flavia Domitilla, was one of those, either carrying or breastfeeding most of the time they knew her. Equally fertile was Lara herself. As the two suffered in the summer heat or risked pain and death at every birth, Lucilla saw enough to be wary of motherhood.

Lara, her closest friend and confidante, had married young but somehow avoided pregnancy for several years. Perhaps then Junius found out what she was doing and forbade such measures. He took little interest in their children but their existence proved his manhood; Lucilla thought privately, it also kept control of Lara. Her sister's eldest son was fourteen, about seven years younger than Lucilla. Lara had borne several more children who died at birth or very young; in all there were six survivors—three boys around their teens, two little girls, a sickly baby—and that year Lara was pregnant again.

While Flavia Domitilla could take her ease at such times, looked after in every way by batteries of slaves, Lara had no such luxury. If she had not had a mother-in-law who took in her children by day, Lara would have been stuck. She worked right up until she felt her birth pangs, from necessity. She and Junius paid their rent and had food on the table; their children possessed an outfit and sandals each; Junius could drink in bars often enough.

Mostly, they managed to avoid moneylenders. But Lara's income was as important to their budget as her husband's. She needed Domitilla, she needed all the sisters' private clients and weddings. Any loss would have a serious financial effect. This never perturbed her, as far as Lucilla could see. Lara was an easygoing character who kept afloat by never worrying. She remained true to her personality, but her life was hard.

By contrast, Lucilla was wary and anxiety-prone. She could not risk being drained in the way Lara was. Scrimping and saving, or being dragged down by a man who could never quite be trusted, were not what Lucilla yearned for. She saw her sister's life and feared ending up that way.

*   *   *

Lucilla had no real friends other than Lara. Lara taught her, shared their work, laughed with her, and gave her a home to visit for a share in family life. Lucilla generally spent birthdays and the great winter holiday of Saturnalia at Lara's house. Lara had a deep affection for her, loving Lucilla equally with her own children. It was a devastating blow when, a couple of days after giving birth for the final time, Lara died. By the time Lucilla reached the house, the newborn baby had gone too.

Juno, what was the point of any of it?

*   *   *

Lucilla felt completely cast adrift again. Worse, she found tremendous pressure building for her to look after Lara's children. For her sister's sake

178

she wanted to do right but the consequences, if she agreed, would be grim. Yet Lara's children were her only blood relations.

Junius openly hoped she would move in. Just as when her mother died and Orgilius expected to inherit his lover's daughter, Lucilla sensed that the tanner aimed to have her replace Lara in his home and bed. That would never happen, but his calculating, sordid gaze depressed her. Arrangements for her sister's burial were mainly left to her.

It was at this point, immediately after the funeral, that the Praetorian found her sobbing.

*   *   *

'It's me—Vinius!'

Gaius had assumed Lucilla would be there, and was surprised to hear no answer to his cheery call. It was evening, when she rarely had clients. He had brought a goat-legged bronze side-table for the room where he had his couch. Dumping the furniture, he stood in the still corridor, listening.

He had never been at the apartment when Lucilla was absent, and he found it much less appealing.

A surprisingly dark thought came: that she might be entertaining a lover. Nothing to do with him, and it would be unpardonable to barge in. The lover would certainly get the wrong idea. Cringing, he imagined Lucilla's reaction . . .

It was a courtesy between them that they never went into each other's bedrooms. (That was what Vinius believed; Lucilla had no compunction about his when he was not there.) Her workroom was free

179

ground; he tapped the door, strode in and came upon her sobbing broken-heartedly. Gaius Vinius jack-knifed through horror and fear of involvement, followed by a quick review of his own recent actions in case this was his fault. Then he flung open his arms, offering to comfort her.

Lucilla shook her head, impatiently lifting her lightweight chair to turn away from him.

Vinius folded his arms, looking resigned as he waited for her to finish crying. He ignored any instinct to pick her up like a bedraggled leveret. In the vigiles he had dealt with distraught women; he knew she would tire herself out, then speak coherently. He had learned this through dealing with the widow who had given away her savings to a fraudster who 'seemed such a nice man, with such beautiful manners', and that barmaid at the Fighting Cock who murdered her two-timing lover with a fish-kettle, beating his head as flat as a bread-paddle before begging the vigiles to bring the louse back to life . . .

Lucilla was an efficient nose-blower. With dried tears, she seemed quite winsome. Still, Vinius was a stalwart; he ignored any urge to set his co-tenant on his knee and kiss her better. Or indeed, kiss her until he felt better himself, now that he had started to think that his knee was a good place to put her.

Jupiter. With Verania still hung around his neck like a leadweight amulet, he had to treat Lucilla like a sister. He had always wanted a sister. As a good-looking young soldier, when he met other people's sisters, he had gained the impression they were always very sweet.

'Finished?' A nod. 'So what was all that about? A man caused the problem, I suppose?'

'Only a man would say that!' Lucilla jumped up from her chair, looking as if she wanted to stick a hairpin in his good eye. She swiftly informed him about Lara, whose funeral had been that afternoon.

Vinius was crushed. 'Oh gods, I am sorry.'

Lucilla could not afford to quarrel because she had decided to ask a favour that she feared would not go down well. Seeing no alternative but to take Lara's children and bring them up herself, she had a confused proposal: she would rent Gaius Vinius' two rooms. 'You wanted an investment—'

'Stop it! This is a bloody ridiculous idea.' Vinius clamped his hands on her shoulders and shook her. He seemed genuinely angry. 'They have a father, don't they?'

'He's useless; he's revolting—'

'Oh I get it—he groped you over the pyre today? Still, use your brain. How can you earn your living with a bunch of infants under your feet, especially if you try to take on double rent for this place?' Everything Vinius said was obvious, but as Lucilla crumpled under his stern onslaught, he softened. 'Ah Lucilla! Don't throw away your precious life. Now you're breaking my heart—please: let's see your old spark again.'

At that moment Lucilla would, for once, have fallen on the Praetorian's neck. Unfortunately, his arms remained rigid as he still gripped her shoulders, so she was unable to collapse into that inevitable disaster.

'What am I to do then?' Tears were about to gush again. Vinius let go of her quickly.

'Buck up, girl. There has to be a solution. I'll sort you out.'

'I can sort myself,' Lucilla whimpered

ungraciously.

Vinius scoffed. 'Doesn't look like it to me! I'll help. I don't want snotty brats ruining my elegant investment, not to mention you blarting and reneging on your rent.' Knowing when things were swinging his way, he changed his tone. 'The best way to plot is over a food bowl. I'm ravenous and I don't suppose you bothered to eat today? Does that bar down on Plum Street run to a Chicken Frontinian? Get your stole; I'll treat you.'

'I can pay my way.'

'I'm offering street food, not a banquet.'

Lucilla unbent a little. 'Thank you.'

'My pleasure.'

'The Scallopshell does chicken dumplings or pork morsels,' Lucilla told him. 'You have to wink first.' The old emperor Vespasian had banned everything except pulses in food shops. Tiresome gruels discouraged people from lingering at the counter so long they started muttering against the political regime. In his previous existence, Vinius had policed the edict in a desultory fashion; when barkeepers were found selling meats instead of lentil pottage, the vigiles could lean on them, extracting information by threats to suspend their licences.

He could live with dumplings if Frontinian was unavailable. Eating out in public was safe. It held fewer temptations than being alone together in the apartment—provided his wife never heard about it. He had no evil intentions. He was too committed to thinking up a way to solve Lucilla's problem.

*　　　*　　　*

182

Vinius found a solution quite easily.

He consulted Lucilla, then next morning took her to visit his brother. Felix and his wife, Paulina, had had a young son and daughter who both died of a childhood ailment the previous year, a common tragedy. Paulina had been a good mother and was desperate for more children. She had even suggested searching rubbish-dumps for abandoned babies. She felt apprehensive about risking pregnancy at her age, but longed for children so badly she was contemplating it—'Though my husband drives, which means he works at night. Not much chance of anything happening!'

During that remark, Lucilla saw Gaius Vinius was amused at the suggestion a couple might only make love in bed and at night; she looked away quickly.

'The only other thing,' said Felix, 'is to buy a healthy slave girl. I can father a couple of nippers on her, no sweat.'

Paulina was a woman of few words, but said what she thought about that. Although Felix was a big man with bigoted opinions it was clear that in their house Paulina held sway. He pulled a face at his brother, but backed down, appearing oddly proud of his strong wife.

Vinius lost no time in taking his brother aside to broach his idea. Paulina was ahead of him. As soon as Lara's orphans were mentioned, she showed Lucilla the room where her own children had once slept, an untouched shrine still containing their two tiny beds and pathetic row of clay animal figurines; she produced a copy of their memorial stone with its sad picture of the children, their pet duck and puppy.

183

Lucilla described the two little girls, whom Lara had named Marcia and Julia after the months of their birth; they were about five and six. If they could be taken care of, Junius' mother would bring up the three older boys, who needed less attention; as lads, Junius took more interest in them anyway. Everyone thought the baby, Titus, who was about fifteen months old, was too sickly to live.

Without delay, Paulina asked for a meeting; Vinius shepherded her and Lucilla to Lara's house. Since their mother died, the younger children had become very subdued. The boys had the same shifty manner as their father; they would be fine with him. The two girls were pretty, like their mother; Paulina instantly took to them.

Junius fairly readily agreed to give up his daughters. His only tricky reaction involved him taxing Vinius: 'Your connection with my wife's sister is *what*, exactly?'

'I am Flavia Lucilla's guardian,' replied the Praetorian, unfazed. His sister-in-law glanced at him quickly.

'How did that happen?'

'I appointed him,' Lucilla interrupted. 'I met Gaius Vinius through official channels when he was very helpful to Mother and me. I would not dream of taking any important decision without his advice first.'

Even Gaius looked startled by this declaration, though he rallied enough to wink at Lucilla, a curious gesture from a one-eyed man.

'Vinius Felix insists on proper arrangements,' Paulina butted in, anxious to pin down Junius, of whom she clearly shared Lucilla's low opinion. 'If everyone settles down nicely, we will adopt

184

formally.' Her eyes narrowed at the whimpering Titus, whom Lucilla was tending. 'What about that little mite?'

'Don't worry about him,' shrugged Junius. 'He won't last the week.'

'Give him to me as well then. I'll comfort him on his way out.'

He might not die. Lucilla reckoned that if the toddler could be saved, this stern woman would achieve it.

They went in a quiet crocodile to Felix and Paulina's house. The two little girls, in their matching pigtails that Lara herself had plaited a fortnight before, walked one each side of their new mother, with Paulina grasping each by the hand. Paulina seemed abrupt at first meeting, but the children had immediately accepted her gruff kindness. Lucilla carried the frail Titus in a basket. Vinius shouldered a small pack with the children's meagre belongings, together with professional equipment of Lara's that Junius had passed on to Lucilla.

Paulina gave them a meal, during which Lucilla had an odd feeling that her introduction to Felix and his wife might have wider repercussions. Paulina had encouraged her to see the girls whenever she wanted. She would be invited to their home again.

When she and Vinius were leaving, Felix came and thanked her for making his wife so happy with this ready-made family. Lucilla began to feel tearful again.

*　　　*　　　*

Vinius walked her back to Plum Street. 'You did the right thing. Paulina is strict and Felix will spoil them silly; it's perfect. Then of course, I make a wonderful uncle.'

Lucilla felt their relationship shift disconcertingly.

Vinius had to go to the Camp, or so he said. Lucilla wondered if he was really intending to visit his wife at the marital apartment. Whatever his destination, he seemed in no hurry to be there. Before he left that evening, he carried two chairs to the balcony. Felix had given him a flask of wine which Vinius poured into beakers. Feeling calmer about the future, but suddenly exhausted, Lucilla slumped in her chair beside his.

They sat for some time enjoying their drinks in silence. It was good wine. As a carter, Felix sometimes drove for a wine importer.

'You will be all right,' Vinius encouraged. 'If you need any kind of help come to the Camp and ask me.' Silence. 'You *can* ask.'

'Yes.' Lucilla held up a hand, palm towards him. 'You are a good friend, Gaius; I understand that.'

This was the first time she ever called him Gaius. It was a slip. Too personal. Even though he had become her nieces' uncle, she would not repeat it.

It was then that Vinius turned his chair so he sat directly facing Lucilla. He could have reached out and taken her hand, though he did not do so. 'I want to ask you some questions.'

Lucilla placed her beaker on the ground, immediately on the defensive. 'What questions?'

'Tell me about Lara.'

'You met Lara once. She was here one day when you came, about six months ago.'

Vinius did remember. The women were very alike to look at. He had heard Lara in the workroom, sounding cheery; then she came out to be introduced. A pretty woman, though with dispirited eyes. They had barely met, yet to his mind the sister had stared at him as if she did not trust him near her Lucilla.

'She loved her children?'

'Yes. She kept them immaculate. She would have been horrified to see them today, all grubby and tearful.' Children were like that all over the Empire though many others, even in gruelling poverty, were given the best of everything possible. Lara had been devoted. Please gods, Paulina and Felix would be too.

'And she loved you too,' commented Vinius. *She thought I was after you. She reckoned I was trouble* . . . 'How old was Lara, would you say?'

'She was thirty-six this year.'

She looked forty, Vinius thought; forty at least. 'Thirty-six; and a mother how many times?'

'Oh about ten,' groaned Lucilla unhappily. 'Some died. She still looked so young, to me, because of her happy nature, but she was worn out. And don't say, "Never let that happen to you, Lucilla", because she told me herself often enough.'

'I bet she did!' Vinius was still pursuing some mysterious line of thought. 'When you were born, Lara would have been how old?'

'Fifteen. She was fifteen years older than me.'

'When did she marry Junius? He's a horror, by the way.'

'When I was a baby, I think. Very young—too young. She married and she moved away. So I never really knew Lara during my childhood.'

187

'While you were being brought up by her mother, Lachne.'

'*My* mother! How do you remember her name?'

'You told me, at the station house. The day the big fire started. Most vigiles remember that day all too well . . . When did Flavia Lachne become a freedwoman?'

'Soon after I was born. She must have been thirty; those are the rules. Flavia Domitilla granted her freedom—or perhaps Mother had to pay for her manumission; she never said. One thing she was very proud of, Lara told me, was that she managed to save enough of a nest-egg to buy freedom for Lara and me.'

'But at the time when you must have been conceived, both Lachne and Lara were still slaves?'

'I suppose so.' Lucilla was too intrigued to object to these questions, though she felt uneasy.

'Let me guess—Lara was sunny in temperament, pretty, a very appealing young girl?'

'Yes. You met her. You just saw her daughters. Our mother was good-looking too. Lara must always have been beautiful. Vinius, what is your point?'

'Think, Lucilla.'

Consciously or subconsciously, Lucilla resisted what he wanted her to see.

Vinius left the suggestion, temporarily. He picked up her beaker and shared out between them what remained in the wine flask. He tilted his cup, saluting her, and waited. Vigiles interrogations had made him a patient man. 'Sweetheart, it happens.'

'What happens?'

'Slavegirls are seduced when very young.'

'You are beginning to offend me.'

'Don't be silly.' His motives were good, in his opinion, so Vinius pressed on. 'Lara meant so much to you and she obviously cared very dearly for you—even a stranger could see that. I just wondered if you ever thought of the possibility that Lara, and not Lachne, might have been your real mother?'

*   *   *

Lucilla had never imagined this.

Once before, at the vigiles station house, Gaius Vinius had said something that disturbed her family ties. Now he was doing it again. He knew life. He knew people. He picked up clues from nowhere and analysed them forensically; he shook out the truth like moths from an old cloak. As soon as he made the suggestion, Lucilla felt it was probable. Many things became clear. Lachne's occasional air of resentment; Lara being kept out of sight during Lucilla's childhood; Lara's tender reception of Lucilla after Lachne died . . .

It must have been agreed that Lachne would bring up Lucilla so Lara could marry and have a life—if marriage to seedy Junius, with its endless pregnancies, could be called life. It was respectable, and less precarious than Lachne's own existence relying on a series of lovers, but had Lachne later regretted what happened to her elder daughter? Lucilla remembered Lachne speaking sourly of Lara's family arrangements.

'Don't be upset,' Vinius soothed her. 'I only wish I had thought of saying something when Lara was alive, so you could have asked her . . . This would not be unique, you know. Mothers do step in to help very young daughters in that predicament.'

'Oh history had repeated itself,' agreed Lucilla in a dull voice. 'Lachne bore Lara at an even younger age. The same, presumably: a slavegirl seduced, whether she wanted it or not.'

Lara's and Lucilla's father could even be the same man, Vinius thought; he was too considerate to say so. 'Forgive me for speaking?'

'I suppose so.'

Vinius let a little lightness into his voice and did, finally, tease her: 'After all, I am your guardian.'

Lucilla gave him the dirty look he wanted, burying her nose in her wine beaker. Vinius smiled slightly.

After a moment, Lucilla let herself smile too.

*   *   *

This was dangerous. Assuming responsibility for a woman in trouble was something Gaius Vinius had never done. His own wives, except his first and youngest, barely needed him for emotional support. What they wanted was his money and the social status of marriage, especially marriage to a Praetorian. He was pretty sure that Verania required him to be faithful yet herself strayed. She had never sought his advice, offered advice to him, nor wanted consolation of any sort. Keeping their distance suited both of them.

A quiet voice in his head warned him to watch out.

Then again, he rather enjoyed the warm feeling he experienced when this vulnerable soul looked to him for help. A vulnerable soul with melting brown eyes and—he let himself notice as she reclined in dappled sunshine—an inviting body.

I don't suppose if I stayed here tonight, you would sleep with me?

Get lost, Vinius!

*　　　*　　　*

When she seemed composed, Vinius left Lucilla to herself. Though she bore no grudge for his raising the subject, he saw she wanted to think about her mother and sister in solitude. Her family connections were so very few, and now they all needed to be reconsidered.

He had intended to visit his wife that evening. But Verania was like a jealous dog or cat; she would smell other people on him and their aura would make her sulk. Their relationship was sketchy, yet any hint that he had other interests inflamed her. Even the touch of melancholia that crept over him when he left Plum Street was liable to drizzle into Verania's mind and affect her as if he had committed some act of blistering disloyalty. When in fact (Vinius convinced himself) all he had done was a kindness to someone.

As he neared the Market of Livia, within reach of their apartment, he changed his mind abruptly. An insistent voice urged him to return to Plum Street. But Vinius turned his steps up along the ancient Servian Walls and returned via the Viminal Gate to the Praetorian Camp.

191

13

In Sarmizegetusa the balance of power shifted.

In *where*?

Sarmizegetusa Regia, the royal citadel of the Dacians, lay four thousand feet up in the Carpathian Mountains, the hub of a string of powerful fortresses from which Dacia would wage war upon the Romans and their emperors for the next thirty years. The very fact that the name of their citadel was a tongue-twisting hexasyllable indicated the Dacians' attitude to the outside world. They were a warrior people. They did not give a toss.

Sarmizegetusa had a military purpose but was also a political and religious centre of greater sophistication than enemies might suppose. Its people, who mined for gold, silver, iron and salt, had long been wealthy and had a very high standard of living. On a daunting approach road, which climbed steeply through leaf-littered woods where exquisitely cold mountain streams rattled over pebbles, no milestones signed the citadel. Sarmizegetusa was too long to carve on a stone. If you had a right to go there, you would know where it was. If not, then keep out.

The heartland of Dacia was a remote area that would one day be called Transylvania, almost entirely surrounded by the crescent of the forbidding Carpathians. This heart-stirring enclave was a mix of striking crags, rolling meadows, delightful forests, fast rivers and scenic plains. There were alluring volcanic lakes, wild bogs and mysterious caves. Wildlife teemed in bounding abundance, with every kind of creature from bears, boars, lynxes and wolves, various deer and chamois. Fish filled the brooks, lakes and rivers. Fabulous butterflies roamed over hay meadows. Wild flowers crowded everywhere. Eagles slowly soared above. Nobody gave a second thought to the odd vampire bat.

A few forbidding routes led in from the exterior over high, well-guarded mountain passes. It was hostile terrain, especially in winter, when all strategists agreed that approaches should be tackled only in dire necessity, or for a very dubious advantage of surprise. A winter invasion would certainly be a surprise—because it would be madness.

In the interior were impregnable hilltop fortresses, plus an old royal city and others no one else had ever heard of, of which the capital was the most magnificent. Any Dacian might well believe that all roads led to Sarmizegetusa. Though not snappy in any language, it had a certain portentous quality, whereas 'all roads lead to Rome' can sound by comparison like a line in a comedy musical.

At Sarmizegetusa, the four-sided fortress crowning the hill was guarded by massive masonry, enormous blocks that were known as Dacian Walls, with monumental gates. As a military building it was equal to any Greek acropolis, on a scale with the Cyclopian Walls of ancient Mycenae, though a Dacian engineer would claim they had better setting-out and better-dressed masonry. Dacian Walls were tremendous structures, with a double skin of stonework that was bonded with timbers and a hard-packed earth and rubble core. Outside the fortress, civilian areas occupied a hundred or so great man-made terraces to east and west. Their buildings were sophisticated, often polygonal or circular, created with great precision. There were domestic compounds, workshops, stores and warehouses. Water was pumped through a sophisticated system, with ceramic pipes feeding the homes of the well-born. The citadel had all the accoutrements of a thriving population who benefited from a rich economy.

The ancient Dacian language was spoken all over central Europe, used commercially and politically by many other tribes. Dacians were masters of ethics, philosophy and science, including physics and astronomy; they toyed with Egyptian divination; they had contact with Greeks. With their spirits lifted by their beautiful country—and boosted by their enormous wealth—the Dacians were famously religious. At Sarmizegetusa they had created a sanctuary where a great sun disc showed their mastery of their own solar calendar while a combined stone- and wood-henge allowed them to honour the winter solstice, winters there being bone-hard. Long, dark nights of yearning for the sun's renewal gave them, like all northern people, morose tendencies.

They lived at the crossroads of central Europe. Their choice, therefore, was either to be downtrodden by everyone who passed through, or fight them. They took the latter course. Dacians had no reputation for diffidence.

*   *   *

From the Roman point of view, Dacia had been

quiescent for a hundred years after a king called Burebista was quashed by the Emperor Augustus. For the Dacians, Burebista was never quashed and would remain a mythical ideal. He was killed off by jealous aristocrats of his own nation, a local difficulty which was a mere kink in history. For them, it had no bearing on Dacia's potential as a world power.

One of King Burebista's measures, it was said, was to uproot Dacian vineyards and persuade his warriors to stop drinking the robust red wines of their homeland. These wines may provide a clue to why Dacian pre-eminence had been slow in coming. And why, after the vines were replanted, Dacian fortunes slumped again for a long time.

Under King Burebista, Dacian territorial influence had extended to its widest, from the Black Sea to the Adriatic, and from the Balkans to Bohemia, always with Transylvania as its political core. Burebista had consolidated the Dacian tribes including the influential Getae, or Goths, who had made their mark in the past and would do so again. However, he made the mistake of siding with Pompey against Julius Caesar. This alienated not just Caesar but his gut-wrenchingly ambitious young successor, Augustus, who invaded Dacia intent on diminishing its status. Before he arrived, however, Burebista was killed. The coalition disintegrated into ineffective warring factions. For a century afterwards, Dacians held a truce with Rome, which meant they took any money Rome offered and in return were thoroughly unreliable allies.

Assassinating their leader was an error, yet one from which it was possible to learn. In the opinion of the Dacian who would become known as Decebalus, quiescence to Rome had endured long enough. This man began establishing himself around the time of the Roman Flavians. There was absolutely no question that he was persuasive and intelligent. Like many heroes he must have been aware of his own potential from an early age, taking up the burden of becoming great, always a lonely destiny but much better than no destiny at all.

He was a commanding figure. Thickset and jowly, he wore traditional Dacian costume which, unlike Mediterranean dress, was designed for warmth: full-length woollen trousers gathered in at the ankle, a long, long-sleeved tunic, a short cloak with fringed or furred edges, caught on one shoulder with a massive brooch. His romping curls were topped with a cap, its long peak turned over to provide an extra insulating air pocket. Unlike the Emperor Domitian, Decebalus had no problem with middle-aged baldness and also boasted a rampant curly beard. Totemic carvings of him, hewn from bedrock on Dacian approach roads, showed a heavily pugnacious face.

The Romans were so indifferent to anyone they called a barbarian, they were unclear whether this man's name was Duras, or Diurpaneus, or whether the original Diurpaneus was the same person as the later Decebalus, or was a king who abdicated his leadership to Decebalus because he was the better warrior. Diurpaneus/Decebalus did not care what the Romans called him; he knew who he was.

He knew a lot about Rome too. He listened; he talked to those passing through; he observed. He knew as much about what the Romans were doing on the Rhine and the Danube as they did, more than most citizens of their empire, whose ill-informed commentators saw him as a shadowy forest-dweller, whose nation existed solely to be overrun by Rome.

He nursed another dream. Other than the fact 'Roman Empire' was easier to enunciate, there was no reason why Europe should be rich pickings for fish-eating, olive-oily, beardless, bare-legged southerners, most of whom could not ride a horse. As he planned to combine the Dacians into one force (no easy task) it seemed feasible that under decent leadership (his, for instance), a 'Sarmizegetusan Empire' should arise instead, of equal significance to anything Roman, though admittedly a tad trickier to say.

*   *   *

For over ten years, Diurpaneus had watched the strategic adjustments on what the Romans thought was their frontier. They held the west, temporarily perhaps, but in central Europe the geography was dominated by two enormous rivers. The Rhine ran north-south through Germany. Its eastern forests were sparsely populated and comparatively peaceful. The Danube, an even longer watercourse, started north of the Alps, not twenty miles from the Rhine in Raetia, which left a narrow corridor through which migrating peoples could emerge on a millennial east-to-west cycle without getting their feet wet. The Danube ran east across Raetia and Noricum, before it plunged almost directly south into the heart of Pannonia, increasing in power, then heading east again across the top of Moesia until its many branches poured their waters through a mesh of channels into the Black Sea. For Rome, that was the end of the world. A place to exile poets. A fate far worse than death.

It was generally accepted that the Romans must accept these rivers as natural limits. Beyond, lay enormous tracts of territory with no other patrollable boundaries, lands which would be impossible to conquer, or if conquered impossible to hold, with no viable reason to do so. The Danube was for much of its length difficult to cross, so except when it froze—which was regular and historically known to be dangerous—this frontier could be controlled.

Along the Rhine and Danube the Romans had established themselves, abutting nose to nose the fractious tribes who lived beyond. Diurpaneus was aware that first Vespasian and now his son Domitian saw the position as dangerous. Whether the barbarian tribes were in search of new territory themselves, whether they were being pushed in the rear by other land-hungry peoples from deeper in Europe, or whether they just came for a fight because that was what they liked, the Romans needed to strengthen their frontier. Vespasian, Domitian and their eventual successors followed a consistent policy of tightening their grip. Domitian's crushing of the Chatti, therefore, was much more significant than it seemed to his critics in Rome, who accused him of over-ambition and wanting a fake triumph. Dacia took it seriously.

First, the Chatti were a major military power. As warriors, they claimed respect. They were powerful and daunting. Males were trained to kill, and were expected to do so before they counted as full members of their tribe. Their strongholds were stone-built and almost impossible to access. Even the Romans said that where other tribes merely fought battles, the Chatti waged war. They elected officers and even obeyed them. On campaign, they carried tools as well as weapons and made proper camps at night, just like the Romans. Every day they planned their strategy and worked out a timetable, a system which to other tribes seemed unnecessarily organised. It worked. Domitian's campaign against them had been hard-fought and bitter; the tussle was still ongoing in the forests of unconquered Germany even two years after his official triumph.

The fact that Domitian had named himself 'Germanicus' after he dealt with the Chatti showed he understood the crucial importance of his victory. By annexing their territory, he had cut off an awkward acute angle in the enormous Roman frontier, reducing by many miles the length that needed guarding. He had penned the belligerent Chatti into their strongholds, safeguarding trade routes—including the Baltic amber route—with his new frontier. There, he was constructing a regular series of wooden watchtowers that guarded a military road. Rumours rippled around that an earthwork or at least a palisade was being planned for the whole length. The new frontier would be Domitian's enduring legacy, enabling Roman oversight of the German tribes for the next two centuries.

Logically, as Diurpaneus recognised, Domitian must be coming for Dacia. Although he had not yet changed the number of legions, which remained as they had been since Nero's day, those in Moesia which lay immediately opposite Dacia were being beefed up by units drawn from his British and German auxiliaries. So far, there were two legions in Pannonia, one in Dalmatia and three in Moesia, which was not much for such an extended frontier, but both Vespasian and Domitian had steadily reinforced the river defences. They had quietly built new forts. They had established extra bases for the Pannonian and Moesian fleets which patrolled the Lower Danube.

As Diurpaneus of the Dacians weighed up the fine tuning opposite, he knew that Domitian's arrival on the Danube must be only a matter of time. He was a comparatively young emperor, son and brother of famous generals, who wanted to make his own name. Diurpaneus could sit and wait for it to happen—or he could strike first.

He struck—and he struck hard.

*　　　*　　　*

There had been a long history of hit-and-run raids across the river, but this was different. Newly bonded under Diurpaneus, the Dacians came snarling across near Novae. It was an ancient Thracian settlement at an important strategic position in Moesia, dominating a road junction on the south bank and controlling one of the easier Danube crossings. Although the soldiers in the line of Roman forts had been staring north for years in anticipation of exactly this, they were taken completely by surprise. Scads of Dacians attacked and overran the province. They laid waste the riverbank. Penetrating far to the south, they destroyed towns and fortifications. There was great loss of life. A wide area collapsed in chaos. Then the

200

Dacians did not simply plunder and retreat; despite the inevitability of Roman reprisals, they dug in and stayed.

The Dacian weapon of choice was a long sword with its end curved like a harvest sickle, which the Romans called a *falx*. Opposing strategists claimed it was cumbersome, and useless against shields, but Dacian warriors knew how to handle it. At close quarters it served efficiently for disembowelling. It was very sharp and could be used in other ways. When Diurpaneus and his rampaging Dacians captured the Roman governor, Oppius Sabinus, he was killed by decapitation.

It took a month for the news to reach Rome.

14

Lara's death inevitably marked a shift in Lucilla's life. For the first three years of Domitian's reign she and her sister—or was she really her mother?—had been extremely close. Their difference in ages always made Lara the leader; Lucilla could now see that it was more than simple seniority. Lara had skills to teach and at first she provided their customer base. In retrospect, Lara always made their choices—who to work for, how to organise appointments, even what colour a client's hair would be or the right moment to refresh a woman's style. Lucilla, using her nimble skill with hairpieces, had had her own expertise so there had never been struggles for supremacy. It had always seemed natural that Lara took the lead.

Now, Lucilla had to make all the choices.

Although forlorn and insecure, she never neglected her business. Work offered itself as a natural solace. She was good at what she did; she could work even when her mind was wandering into thoughts of Lara and Lachne. Covering every task that she and Lara had once shared kept her intensely busy. One or two clients who had been particularly attached to Lara slipped away, but most stayed loyal. It became necessary to consider training an assistant.

She bought a slave. It was troubling for Lucilla, herself a freedwoman's child, but she was at least able to purchase the girl from Flavia Domitilla. Lucilla did not have to venture into a slave market where the overseers treated their wares worse than animals, pulling open mouths to show how many teeth slaves had, letting lewd male customers fondle young girls' breasts, loudly making coarse assertions about their sexual pasts and future possibilities. Instead, Domitilla's girl, whose name was Glyke, could be quietly looked over at the house, then without embarrassment obtained from the steward; Stephanus only demanded a modest bribe for fixing the transaction.

A freedwoman's slave could face a life of particular cruelty. Those who had endured beatings and other abuse in their early life sometimes imposed worse on their own slaves. Lucilla presumed Glyke would appreciate that this never happened to her. But after a year, the ungrateful Glyke ran away with a baker's delivery boy. Lucilla could have reported this to the vigiles and had her runaway slave hunted, but she forbore. Glyke was in love. The baker's boy might have pretended affection but he would dump her eventually. He had that look in his eye. For a girl so young, being abandoned would be enough punishment.

Glyke may never have realised she was only a few years younger than her new mistress. There was a world of difference between them in judgement and poise.

Nevertheless, Lucilla was hiding deep uncertainties. In some ways she was fortunate. She would survive financially. Her client base was sufficient. She might build a much bigger business; that would be hard work, though work she found a pleasure. Yet it would take all her time. Acquiring Glyke showed her the problems of management. Yes, the girl shared her labour, but Lucilla spent too much time training and supervising; with her own reputation at stake she could not trust the young slave to work on her own initiative. She had to house and feed her too. At the apartment Glyke slept in the workroom, but constantly nagged to be allowed into the Praetorian's accommodation. She seemed unable to grasp that his rooms were outside Lucilla's control and that Lucilla had no wish to put herself under any obligation to Vinius.

When Glyke ran away, Lucilla's strongest feeling was relief. She bore the financial loss, which was compensated by being once more alone at home and unpressured. Having the apartment to herself again was wonderful. Vinius had said she could use the room with the couch as her private area; without Glyke, Lucilla did so.

Her ease with her own company did not mean she hankered for a reclusive life. At twenty-one, her unmarried state was becoming a source of unhappiness. She shrank from being trapped with the wrong partner but if she ever dreamed of her future, she imagined someone in her bed and at her table. Like Lachne, and Lara too, presumably, she was drawn to men. Despite her grim knowledge of life, as much as she yearned for physical love she harboured idealistic hopes. She wanted true male companionship; also, she believed she could be a good mother, if she ever had children.

She had few affairs. Nevertheless, she knew about men's behaviour. At work she spent most of her days listening to women on this subject, usually complaining. A woman and her hairdresser might never spend time together socially, yet they were intimately acquainted with the fabric of each other's lives. Husbands and sons, fathers and brothers, were routinely discussed. Their characters and careers were catalogued, their habits and adventures followed over time. Lucilla, who was a good listener, absorbed this and acquired more wisdom than she realised.

It would be wasted if she never found a man.

*   *   *

The place to look was obviously Alba. Lucilla had always loved Alba, and now without Lara dragging on her to stay in Rome near her children, Lucilla could go whenever she wanted. If the court was at Alba she could spend the whole summer there.

It was truly beautiful. On one side was a breathtaking view down a precipitous wooded hillside to the perfection of the lake bowl, its surface often turquoise in reflection of the sky, a scatter of water birds bobbing midway. A nymphaeum, or water-feature, had been cut into the shoreline rock, its entrance dramatically framing the view to Mount Albanus, which was topped by the glittering white Temple of Jupiter Latiarius. In the other direction enormous garden terraces faced towards Rome and the Tyrrhenian Sea, which could be glimpsed in the far distance.

Alba was called Domitian's villa but was like a small city. There were women present though, apart from a few noblewomen, they tended to be employed either in menial tasks or predatory occupations. Of the men, Lucilla knew her first serious choice ought to have been easy: the freed slaves of the imperial family. But they seemed like strangers. After Lachne was freed and left the household, Lucilla had lost the advantages of knowing and being known well by any potential candidates.

It would appear she had plenty of alternatives: the Emperor's advisers and personal attendants; artists, musicians, poets and learned men; architects, engineers; finance experts, secretaries, soldiers; athletes and professional gladiators. Some were married, though many left their wives elsewhere. Of those, some noble sorts were restrained and faithful: not many. Occasionally one of the better men would develop a soft spot for Lucilla and engage in cheery, acceptably flirtatious banter.

Most were to be avoided. They were, openly, just looking for a good time. In her early naïve search for friendship, Lucilla struggled. As a hairdresser she was viewed as a cheaper, cleaner, patriotically home-grown version of the sordid Syrian flute girls or notorious Spanish dancers, just an easy lay for whom men would not even pay. Nobody admired a hairdresser for chastity. That she resisted encounters only raised a greater challenge to those men who believed they were special, where in their view 'special' meant sexually irresistible.

Others were available to Lucilla because they were so gauche that no woman with any sense would touch them. The fact that she appeared unconnected seemed to draw these hopeless characters to her; they were then outraged if she said no to them.

Some adventurers took an interest because they had assessed her success and were after her money. One even told her so; his honesty had a passing allure but she still refused him.

*   *   *

To find a loyal companion from among these potential disasters began to appear impossible. Lucilla could certainly have a string of sexual partners, if she could endure brief conjunctions, one-sided action, men who nervously checked the time of day to find excuses to leave, raw panic on their part if she ever seemed to grow needy. Occasionally she went to bed with someone, but she failed to find permanence or real pleasure.

She needed a man who would neither resent her talent nor try to take her over. He must have either a business or professional career, but not one where he needed a wife's unpaid assistance; Lucilla wanted to continue her own work. It would be best if he was connected with the court, Lucilla's world. He should have the same mobility as she did, for the same reasons.

However, the way Lucilla moved on a whim

between Alba and Rome was in itself off-putting to many men. She looked flighty. Her freedom to wander hinted she might lead a double life: if she was not doing so now, she could do it in future, betraying any poor mongrel who kennelled with her permanently. Each knew about two-timing because they, men, did it all the time. They made duplicate assignations; flitted to new partners; lied and got away with it. Alba had many a careerist who for years kept a wife and children, dumped in some small town, on a farm, in a back-street of the capital, but who, in the separate world of the villa, lived it up with a dancer or singer or an imperial servant—a dresser, an embroiderer, a jewel-casket-minder, a *hairdresser*. Some moved around skeins of these ladies in an ever-changing country dance. Inevitably on retirement they would slink back to the small town or farm.

A problem was the subtly unreal atmosphere. Much as Lucilla loved the vast villa complex, she recognised its falsehoods. Alba lay twenty miles from Rome, which was just near enough to make the journey down the Via Appia in one day with the best transport. It seemed accessible; yet was remote. It seemed cosmopolitan, yet was intimate. Everything suggested simple country life, though a life suffused with luxury. Attendants padded everywhere in their resplendent white uniforms with gold decoration; white roses were brought in enormous quantities from Egypt to adorn and perfume the marble halls. Reality died at the entrance gates.

Domitian aimed to prove that 'Rome' was the Emperor. Power no longer resided in the Senate, which was physically tied to the Curia in the city

Forum; power now centred on him. He had not retreated to Alba in the same way as Tiberius, the emperor he most studied, a grim figure who had exiled himself in Capri in order to lead a life of morose perversion, set apart from Roman society. Instead, Domitian made Alba the heart of things that mattered.

His villa was regarded as a gloomy citadel, full of suspicion and menace. Its beauty and amenities belied that. His architect, Rabirius, who was now creating a staggering new palace in Rome too, had devised at Alba a building with sophisticated use of space and materials. Domitian's personal pleasures were cultural. He surrounded himself with music and poetry, plays and readings in his theatre, athletics and gladiating in his arena. He also loved hunting. Despite spindly legs and a pot belly, he had become a notably good archer, capable of shooting two arrows into the skull of a deer so they looked like horns. Once he made a slave hold up his fingers, and shot arrows through them, causing no wounds. And he spent many hours walking in his magnificent gardens.

In addition to outdoor activities he gave dinners, dinners which were almost a chore to him because he preferred to eat his main meal at lunchtime in private. In the evening he merely watched others, blighting their enjoyment as he stared and munched an apple glumly. His social reticence stood for his austere moral authority. Even so, for those privileged to share his life at Alba, he kept a famously elegant table, though he tended to terminate banquets early then retreat to his private quarters.

Once Domitian was out of sight anything went.

Each evening came a sense of restraint being lifted. Lucilla felt temptation, though usually she shied from the decadence. Yet sometimes her loneliness became too much to bear.

*   *   *

It was late summer, the days already shortening though they were very hot and their evenings sultry. The Emperor was gathering an army for Moesia. Domitian was heading there in person, soon. His advisers, his freedmen, his Praetorians would accompany him. The Guards' Commander, Cornelius Fuscus, had been given overall command.

They were all keyed up. The court's impending shift had imposed an end-of-term atmosphere that unsettled both those who must go and those who would remain in Rome.

Lucilla became unbearably restless. Last time, when the Emperor went to Germany, her sister had still been alive and in order to spend time with Lara she had accepted that the removal of the court simply meant the sisters would for a time exist more quietly in Rome. Now a greater sense of loss hung over her. Not only was her domestic life solitary, but with the big masculine exodus she lost all chance to make connections. In over a year she had made *no* connections that she valued. She had no lover. She could not envisage ever acquiring one. Looking around at the men she encountered, she was as half-hearted about them as they were towards her. Her faith in herself diminished. She was not only frustrated, but intensely lonely.

On one particular evening, any man who deployed a scruple of charm could have had her. A few shared jokes would have done it. A gift of half a bowl of cherries, some tame philosophical theory, caressing the arch of her foot as she sat on a flight of steps, all would have been sufficient. Perhaps luckily for her, this wild mood that laid her open to seduction was too scary for most of them.

On the main terrace the Emperor was attending a concert in his miniature theatre. It was a perfect gem, marble-decorated, intimate and exclusive. Twenty or so tiers of stone seats formed a tight semi-circle, so close that friends on one side could converse across the centre with others opposite, while from his marble throne midway, Domitian could preside and feel himself the centre of a sophisticated gathering.

Tonight's elegant music was too refined for many hangers-on, who had stayed outside, too rowdy, too impatient and shallow to appreciate measured cadences of lyre and flute. People had clustered in small groups on a terrace with an enormous fountain bowl, waiting for Domitian to emerge with his immediate coterie. They were quiet but louche. Flagons were being passed around, strong perfumes filled the air, lewd jokes flickered through every verbal exchange and it was blatantly assumed everyone present had world-weary hopes of copulation.

Lucilla drifted among them, in a set centred on Earinus, Domitian's eunuch. He was an exquisite youth, selected in Pergamum to be sent to Rome for the Emperor, then too beautiful to be sent back after the Emperor took a new moral stance. Domitian had decided to shame his brother Titus, who had once kept eunuchs, by banning male castration as an unnatural outrage; even so, he

210

ignored his own strictures by favouring this smooth, scented boy in his bracelets and necklaces. Earinus tasted the Emperor's wine, then passed him his rare fluorspar cups like Ganymede attending Jupiter, an analogy Domitian adored since it made him godlike.

As ever, prurient talk dwelt on just how much the cup-bearer had lost in his castration, and what sexual acts Earinus could still perform. People harped on his painful snip obscenely. Unabashed, he lapped up attention. According to him, he was much in demand among senators' wives, especially as there was no risk of pregnancy. Despite any diminution of his sexual drive, he slept with anyone. He even offered himself to Lucilla, not entirely joking.

'Do you want a bunk-up—half price to you?'

Lucilla was exasperated by the self-centred toyboy, who she knew had actually cut off his hair and sent locks to his hometown of Pergamum in a gold box; he had begged a poet to write a celebratory lyric about it, as if he were a person of account.

'Wobble yourself, Earinus. I like a lover with balls.'

Just at that moment she saw Gaius Vinius.

Vinius, who had a true love of music, had emerged from the theatre. Off duty and unarmed, he came at a fast clip up a short flight of marble-veneered steps to where Lucilla and her companions were noisily clustered on the flat terrace. He must have left the concert early, apparently overcome by tristesse. Lucilla thought she even saw him wipe away a tear.

She knew he had spotted her. He obviously

heard the conversation. His expression of contempt was searing. They did not speak. Vinius disappeared. Lucilla felt cheap—then annoyed, because what she did and who she knew were her own affair, whatever the Praetorian thought.

What he thought suddenly mattered to her. That made her more angry.

When Domitian emerged and his party flocked after him out of the theatre, Lucilla severed herself from the group she had been with. Her mood was sour, not least because she had been drinking wine after little to eat. Wine had a crazy attraction that night, so she was carrying a flagon as she walked off by herself. She went just fast enough to deter anyone from trying to speak to her.

There was a long promenade, sheltered by a high hillside wall, which led away from the theatre. On her left, a line of narrow flower beds with low walls carrying water channels was graced at intervals with grottos, statues and fountains. More formal planting with topiary lay to her right. Everywhere seemed to be full of entwined couples and people laughing, with distant screams that were impossible to interpret: silliness, feigned protest, or even real cries for help, though nobody took any notice. Part way along this terrace a tunnel under the hillside had steps leading down, then a passage wide enough for four abreast that went to the upper terrace and living quarters. Her original thought had been to head back to her room that way. Furious, wretched and befuddled, Lucilla missed the entrance.

*　　　*　　　*

Someone, a man, started following her.

After a lurch of panic she recognised that level tread. Surreptitiously, she confirmed it was Vinius. Lucilla flounced off. His slow footfall continued.

At the farthermost end of the promenade, where hardly anyone else had wandered, she reached a small garden room enclosed by high walls and foliage, with a petal-shaped pool decorated with ornamental shrubs. Lucilla stopped and waited, with a pitter-patter of anticipation, for Vinius to catch up.

He was not happy with her. 'What in Hades are you doing?'

'Walking.'

'Crap. For what reason are you tripping around in a dream by yourself, carrying a wine flagon?'

'I want to get away from people.'

'By inviting the wrong attention? These gardens are my bored colleagues' domain. They judge women on a sliding scale—that's from slag through slut, via filthy tambourine dancer, and ending up only with eminently fuckable—'

'None of them came near me.'

'Only because I gave them all the evil eye.'

Vinius was right. A number of the men sauntering on the terrace were Praetorians, enjoying their regular evening haunt. It was an empty kind of recreation and they might well be looking for trouble. A woman could tell herself the Guards didn't frighten her; any woman who genuinely thought that was stupid. Yet here Lucilla was, a long way from other people, and alone with one of them. 'I don't need your protection.'

'You need a good hiding. You've gone wild here. For some dumb, ethical reason I feel called to intervene.'

Lucilla took off again, but this time with Vinius alongside. Now that they had spoken he seemed to calm down. They strode along together as if simply admiring the topiary until they reached the great viewing area, a balcony that gave a wonderful panorama with views of Rome and the sea. They fetched up by its balustrade, which bore massive plant pots, its rough stone still warm from heat beating on it all day.

To cover their awkwardness, Lucilla began asking questions. 'I saw you come out of the music.'

'Yes.'

'Do you go to hear concerts by yourself?'

'I like concerts.'

'It seemed to have upset you.'

'I was moved. That doesn't have to be a bad thing.'

'I don't think of you as emotional.'

'Then you don't know me.'

'No.' Lucilla's voice was drab, but firm. 'And maybe you don't know me either. You put yourself in judgement on me tonight, unfairly.'

'Those people are trash.' It was a harsh denunciation, a soldier's. 'It's not only tonight. I've watched you when you didn't know. I've seen you among real lowlifes here. Wallowing with the squeaky-boys. You keep atrocious company.'

'Earinus is harmless.'

'No; he's vile!'

Blinking back tears, Lucilla blundered away from him, alone this time, and plunged down to a flight of steps which led into a huge underground hall like a grandiose passageway that was called the cryptoporticus. At the end where she entered,

Domitian had built a great platform from which he could survey the length of the grandiose gallery. Sometimes he summoned the Senate there and glowered down at them from his vantage point.

There were few people about because most preferred to be outside, but some small groups were in the giant vaulted passage, talking quietly. To avoid unwelcome overtures, Lucilla had to act as if she was going to meet someone. She teetered down the wide, steep stairs, realising she was more tipsy than she liked. She reached the flat, a long gallery that must be over three hundred yards long. This part had small high windows, designed to flood the passage with sunlight that would reflect off the highly polished marble walls and provide almost theatrical illumination for the Emperor on his podium. With few oil lamps, the place was deeply gloomy after dark.

People stared at her. Becoming nervous, she found an exit.

*   *   *

A new broad terrace opened out of doors, with the cryptoporticus forming its back wall. More peaceful parterres, with neatly trimmed hedges and topiary, extended to far vistas. Statues climbed out of tangles of roses in graceful allées. Enormous trees of unimaginable antiquity reached for the sky.

She turned right and marched quickly to the end of the gardens, where a statue made a feature among a semi-circle of stone benches, with curtains of tall, trimmed cypress trees behind. She slumped on one of the benches.

Feet crunching on the path announced that

Vinius was joining her again; she was not entirely surprised. He sat down a couple of yards from her, watching her disapprovingly although the mood between them seemed less hostile now.

'You're a strange girl.' He said it with a half-admiring, half-troubled tone. 'Why don't you find yourself a boyfriend to keep you out of mischief, or get married nicely?'

'Because I've had a look at what's available.'

She heard Vinius laughing. 'Fair enough!'

There was a silence, after which he shuffled along towards her, holding out his hand for her wine flagon. Lucilla gave up custody. He gulped, let out a disparaging noise; it was white, girlie wine, too acid. Nonetheless he drank greedily. When he stopped he offered the flagon back, but she had had sufficient earlier. Vinius sat, with his head flung back, looking up at the early stars.

'So you approve of marriage,' Lucilla challenged. 'Well, I hear you've done it enough times.'

'Marriage has its uses.'

'Did you ever have children?'

'One.'

'Boy or girl?' There was such a long pause, Lucilla rounded on him: 'Juno, you are appalling; you don't even remember!'

'I was thinking about my daughter,' Vinius responded coldly. *Vinia Arruntina. A grand name for such a tiny tot. She would have been, what—eight? nine? now. Her father's little girl; his lost princess; forever his baby . . .*

Lucilla watched Vinius. She was surprised that his mood tonight was so strained. When she changed the subject, intuition nudged her to ask, 'Will you tell me about Dacia?'

216

'What do you want to know? Why?'

'Not many people will discuss such things with a hairdresser. It's all, "So does Julia *really* sleep with him?" As if while I'm pinning up a curl Flavia Julia would exclaim, "Uncle Domitian had incest with me again last night!", then allot him a score as a lover.'

Gaius Vinius let out an uncharacteristic giggle. He gulped more wine to calm down. 'So that's what hairdressers talk about . . . Well, *does* he sleep with Julia?'

'I don't know. You're as well-placed as me to observe.'

'We don't do bedroom duty. Thank the gods.' After another pause, Vinius said not unsympathetically, 'I see him with the imperial ladies. I'd say he does have genuine affection for the women in his family. The niece. The wife too. They say Julia is the one person who can exert a softening influence on him.'

'I believe it's true.'

'Do you reckon she is frightened of the situation?'

'She must be. I feel sorry for her. She can never remarry; it would be the man's death sentence. I just think,' said Lucilla, 'as long as Domitian is alive, Julia will have to act sweet, look trusting, appear entirely happy with her fate—and never, ever share her thoughts with anybody.'

In silence, they considered Julia's loneliness. Vinius offered the wine flask. This time Lucilla had some, then he took it back and drank again, hard.

Vinius was looking at her rather intently.

He changed the mood. He jumped to his feet, exclaiming, 'We got distracted. So—Dacia!' He was holding out his hand to her, so although she did not take it, Lucilla stood too and they walked. With night air cooling her flushed face, she felt much calmer; she now allowed herself to enjoy the beautiful location as they sauntered back down the gardens to where a large fountain had been built into the outer wall of the cryptoporticus.

They stopped to admire. Neptune. Two fellows on dolphins, wrestling snakes. Creepers ran up the high walls.

Vinius provided an epitome of the frontier arrangement, the recent Moesian disaster and the ongoing Dacian situation. 'Free Europe is a vast area and the tribes there are very mobile, constantly roaming, hard to pin down. Gracilis, my centurion, served in Moesia. He says the Dacians live between two different groups of Sarmatians—the Iazyges on the great plains to their west and the Roxolani on their eastern flank—so he reckons they may feel pincered. It is a fluid situation, though. This side of the Sarmatians, the Suebi, who are Marcomanni and Quadi, are clearly eyeing up Pannonia. All these peoples are looking across the frontiers and seeing our Empire, so prosperous and well-organised, so *civilised,* just beckoning to them.'

He explained it well. Lucilla congratulated him and he said it was because his centurion had to instruct the men; as beneficarius, Vinius had to write the brief for the centurion. Lucilla suddenly remembered him at the vigiles station house, dipping pen into ink with a playfully fancy gesture.

Something in his tone had given her another flash of insight: 'You don't want to go!'

'You will never persuade a soldier to say he does not want to fight.'

218

'Do you like being a Praetorian?'

'It's probably treason to say anything different. You'll get me sent to the beasts.'

'You still don't want to go. I know you, Gaius Vinius.'

'Yes,' he said gravely, as if noticing something significant, or seeing a truth for the first time. 'I believe you do, Lucilla.'

When they began walking on again something—everything?—was different. They were hand in hand, their fingers intertwined.

* * *

Close to the fountain, clipped fretwork hedges allowed people to look out again at the panorama, though from intimate niches in the hedge. They stood there and gazed. Neither was seeing much.

Vinius spoke. His voice, that baritone that had always stirred Lucilla, was low: 'Be true to yourself, girl. Look after yourself.'

'I am better than you think.'

'I think you're adorable.'

'Don't talk like that.'

'Don't push me then. Don't make me the guardian of your morals. Don't be unfair on both of us.'

In two heartbeats the conversation had plunged into dangerous areas.

* * *

They walked again, now like close friends. They were two of a kind, like-minded, both outsiders, naturally bonded, mutually rueful. Whether friends

219

or something else, both knew what was happening between them.

The night grew quiet. Though far from other people, they had a clear sense that elsewhere revellers had dispersed. Scents of roses, lilies and cypresses had whispered around them unnoticed. They descended to lower levels. They passed sunken gardens, parklike areas, belvederes, gazebos, galleries of statues, circular promenades, vistas to ornamental specimen trees or fishponds.

They came across a pavilion, empty now, though it had been occupied earlier. A fastidious man, Vinius wondered by whom? There were still sun-bleached cushions on couches, among abandoned flower garlands, cold perfume burners, and half-eaten bowls of tiny wild strawberries from Nemi.

By a pillar, they stopped. Vinius turned Lucilla towards him. They kissed quietly, without prior fuss. It seemed inevitable.

'This is not a good idea.' A cliché, but Vinius was fumbling to express reluctance while not really feeling it. He let her go. They were still close. They could not bear to draw apart.

'A man of honour.'

'Probably insane.'

Lucilla forced herself to support his decision. 'We should go back, before we do something we shall both regret forever.'

'And regret it all night if we don't . . .' Vinius was almost laughing. Both knew: they thought they were strong-willed but the attraction between them had become intense.

'You go.'

'I want to see you safe.'

220

'I shall be. Let me stay here by myself a little longer, then when no one is about I'll walk up quietly.' To encourage him to go, Lucilla moved away, further into the pavilion, where she perched on a couch hugging her knees lightly. It was a flat stone structure, made like a triple dining-couch for picnicking in this dainty gazebo which in daylight would have dramatic views. Head back, she savoured the warm night air.

Gaius Vinius decided to take himself off. 'Goodnight then.'

'Goodnight.'

*   *   *

Next minute he was back, urgently leaning down over Lucilla. 'Stuff honour!' His lips were on hers. He was so aroused that to refuse him would be frightening.

Lucilla did not want to refuse. She kissed him back, much more intently than the first time. Juno—just for once it was her turn. Time to forget rectitude, time to ignore caution, time for what she so much needed, all she sensed this man would give her . . .

'Agreed?'

'Once!'

'Once then,' said Gaius, terse. His hands were moving over her. She was reaching for him . . . Lucilla seemed to hesitate. Still just in command of himself, Gaius cancelled her objections. 'Accept it. You're desperate. I'm going to Dacia and may never come back.'

'No cheap excuses,' said Lucilla.

He laughed quietly. Gaius Vinius showed

221

amusement more often than she had realised; he could be full of warmth, overwhelming the affection-starved Lucilla. 'No excuses at all!'

He was unfixing the roundel fasteners of her sleeves, tugging and trying not to seem like a man who had undressed too many women. Lucilla pulled the tang on his belt to release the buckle, hoping not to reveal how rarely she had undressed men. He took her in his arms, with a suppressed groan. For a short, wild moment she wished she had a better body, bigger breasts, more energy, enough experience—before, for the first time in her life, Lucilla gave herself into the care of a man whose competence, as a matter of pride, included both their needs.

He was not normally one who boasted, but he heard himself declare to her crazily, 'If it's only once, it must be good! Flavia Lucilla, I am going to make love to you all the way to the gates of Hades, then all through the Elysian Fields and all the way back here. You won't know whether to beg me to stop or plead with me for more . . .'

Gaius Vinius knew all about routine love-making in some anaemic relationship for his own swift relief. He wanted better, much better tonight. He was ready to deploy heart, lungs, muscles, imagination, and an unlikely sensitivity in order to achieve it. He wanted to blot bloody Dacia from his consciousness, his reluctance to go there, his centurion's dark premonitions, his own emptiness at what his life had been so far and its pointlessness if he should not survive battle. He wanted to purge the profound sadness that had swept through him at the music recital. To do so, every fibre of him wanted this girl who could be so sweet, and who was so worth saving, and with whom on this strange evening he had felt such extraordinary closeness.

You fuck to forget. Every soldier knows that. On the eve of departure, you fuck blindly to create memories to see you through that long march which may be your last . . . Yet there could be more. Gaius Vinius believed in it, and that night he found it: in not just extreme physical passion, but complete exultant joy.

15

Domitian travelled via Dalmatia, bringing five legions. The Romans' arrival in what they called Moesia was swifter than Diurpaneus had hoped. They came the same autumn; they marched in by October. He would have liked to have deterred them longer. If they had stayed away until winter he could have established firmer footings, but they came, and with them their bald, bewigged Emperor. His presence with them was bound to give his soldiers heart, whatever stories these Romans had heard of the Dacians' fierceness.

The Emperor entrusted command to the chief of his own Guards, Fuscus. Domitian had appointed him, weeding out Titus' previous incumbent, so he had been in post as Praetorian Prefect for almost five years. It was normal to have an aristocrat as general to a field army, but Cornelius Fuscus was from the middle rank which Domitian preferred to trust (although the Prefect came from a rich family and had remained an equestrian by choice). A fiery supporter of Vespasian, Fuscus' reputation was for seeking novelty and risk.

So the Emperor's own corps was to take prime position in clearing out the invaders. The message was clear: defeating Dacia was personal. That kind of edge to a campaign suited Diurpaneus.

The Roman battle-force was powerful. After a first, fast scramble out of the way upon their sudden appearance, the Dacian retreated carefully. He eased his troops back to the brim of the Danube, then slipped away across the river. He seemed to have given back to Domitian what the warriors had seized in Moesia that summer, but although the Roman counter-offensive appeared successful, their opponent's response to it was reactive only; he had fight in him yet. For Diurpaneus, a good tactician, the struggle against Rome was only beginning. Shooing the invaders out of Moesia might temporarily satisfy the Romans, but both sides knew the Dacians would be back.

*   *   *

On the south bank, the Romans restored order as systematically as always. They rebuilt the forts, gave at least cursory protection to the native civilians, scoured the country for unwanted foreigners. They made occasional use of scouts and informers. There had to be a new governor; and once on the spot Domitian began to consider splitting Moesia in two, which would strengthen it administratively. Few people remembered that Domitian had a connection with the area; his Uncle Sabinus had been governor of Moesia for about seven years, an unusually long period. He had been hearing about this part of the world from childhood.

224

Denigrating stories circulated that while on the Danube, Domitian abandoned himself to loose living. His troops scoffed that this presupposed Moesian cities offered licentious possibilities. It was one thing to have live oysters delivered overland for Roman commanders, but supping shellfish was not quite a life of riot. As the soldiers knew (for they had looked into this diligently), Moesia suffered from a perennial shortage of dancing-girls, not to mention a complete famine of fancy boys.

The Dacians meanwhile sought to return to their previous relationship with Rome, suing for peace. Domitian rejected their overtures.

Satisfied that Moesia had been restored to order by these few months of his glorious presence, late in the year Domitian left Fuscus to it and returned home. There the returning victorious commander-in-chief, resplendent with triumphal honours, could call on the services not only of well-drilled belly-dancers, but impossibly handsome cup-bearing catamites, and if he was really desperate—or gracious—his wife.

Some Praetorians had to be in Rome to guard the Emperor, but many stayed on campaign with their commander. This included the century of Decius Gracilis, who had had useful experience in Moesia previously. Now Vinius frequently heard him grumbling, convinced that the apparently dispersed enemy were not being taken seriously, muttering that crisis-management was slack and everything bound to go wrong . . .

They spent the winter consolidating. With the province's whole infrastructure needing to be rebuilt, the soldiers were constantly busy, but sometimes the weather prevented effort and they had rest periods. At such times, Gaius Vinius found his thoughts straying to his own unresolved issues back in Rome.

*   *   *

As dawn broke on the morning of their unexpected tryst at Alba, he had awoken with Lucilla on what he assumed were affectionate terms.

Better?
Much better . . .
Want more?
You can't.
I bet I could . . .

He had left her briefly, to carry out basic ablutions: a long pee, a quick wash in a fountain, a deep breath while thinking *now get out of this, lad* . . . When he looked for the girl again, he discovered that she had slithered off somewhere, presumably for a pee, a wash and thinking what a wonderful lover fortune had gifted her. Then he realised she had disappeared completely. At least that saved embarrassing conversation, was his first thought.

As Gaius plodded back up through the gardens alone, he found he regretted that attitude. He walked very slowly, absorbing the beautiful day and delightful surroundings. To his surprise, he felt there was unfinished business between them, and not merely a longing for more sexual contact. He wanted to see her, to find her. He wanted to talk things over. She had charmed him, astonished him, devastated him.

He was highly annoyed when discreet enquiries revealed that Flavia Lucilla had left Alba

226

altogether.

Gaius was a man; he had no grasp of the turmoil he had imposed on her. He presumed, insofar as he faced up to it, that if he could accept being unfaithful to his wife, it was his quibble, not Lucilla's. Her position was easy, or seemed so to him.

He had no idea whether their relationship would develop. He had not planned to make love to her last night. Now, he was not necessarily expecting more—but nor was he clear there would be *no* more. He simply had not thought about it.

She had left, left him without a word. He felt he had been used and dumped.

Of course it was irrational. Though annoyed with himself for feeling that way, he had enough humanity to imagine why Lucilla might have fled. Not necessary, girl! He would never have allowed any awkwardness afterwards. He would have let her down gently if needed; he felt she could have given him the same consideration.

He did not suppose she was really upset; the night had been too good for that. He would sort this out.

Vinius knew the theory that sex was best when accompanied by love. That did not rule out love developing from sex. Perhaps it was happening to him. He was guarded in his relationships, to the extent that wives had called him cold, but he was self-aware. He knew some affection coloured his attitude to Flavia Lucilla. He viewed his plight now with curiosity, as if he were watching an insect crawl up a window frame.

Just before leaving for Dacia, the Guards were in Rome so Gaius looked for Lucilla at Plum Street.

There was no sign of her. She must be deliberately avoiding him. Duty called. There was nothing he could do.

He did take one action, however: something he should have tackled long before. He went to see his wife Verania and announced that their life together was over.

Verania was so surprised to hear he had finally bestirred himself to divorce her, she took it quietly. He gave her enough money to grease the process. She was amazed at how generous he was, given that throughout their marriage he had been obsessed with suspicions that she was relieving him of cash (which, indeed, she had progressively done, by giving shameless hand-massages to his banker).

Vinius also made his will. Soldiers could write a basic testament in the field prior to battle but the Praetorians had a headquarters staff, under an officer called the *cornicularius*, which included a clerk who kept their wills. This was his first real contact with the office of the cornicularius whose work, Vinius thought, looked interesting.

*   *   *

From Novae, all this seemed a long way away and lacking urgency. Still, thoughts of home kept him occupied in lazy moments, and thoughts of Flavia Lucilla provided a future goal, of sorts.

Spring arrived. Cornelius Fuscus took the initiative: he built a bridge of boats across the Danube then led detachments from all his five legions, with his Praetorian unit, to the Dacian side. Whether or not this manoeuvre had been discussed with Domitian, let alone approved by him, was never clear.

Diurpaneus patiently let the Romans come. In a classic bluff, he gave them free access across the plain on the north bank of the Danube, then into the Dacian heartland via one of the high passes. The legions invaded the mountain-cradled interior, and Vinius noticed that Decius Gracilis had stopped his usual complaining; he was not a man to depress morale when courage was required. His beneficarius could tell from the set of his face, however, that Gracilis believed they were going too far from secure bases, with inadequate supply lines and no backup.

Still, the Romans pressed forwards in their classic line of march. Auxiliary cavalry went first to reconnoitre, with a light backup of bowmen, followed by half the auxiliary infantry, some legionary cavalry, a group of heavier infantry, a colour party and the all-important engineers. At the head of his legions rode the army commander, Fuscus, with his own cavalry and infantry escort, then the artillery—battering rams and catapults—before flank guards for the legionary commanders and officers, who were followed by a marching body of standard bearers and trumpeters. The main army came next, one legion at a time, shoulder to shoulder, six men abreast. Finally, after servants and baggage, the second half of the auxiliaries and the last cavalry formed a rear-guard.

Diurpaneus watched them coming. They never saw him.

They kept a tight line of march, all the way protected by flurries of cavalry, but the scouts reported few enemy sightings. Encounters with Dacians were noticeably scarce, though when they

229

ran into any cowherds these were dealt with briskly. Native peoples within the Empire were tolerated with little worse than contempt, but natives outside were there to learn what the Roman army was made of. There was occasional rape. There was modest pillage. No army passed through enemy territory without imposing itself on the women or putting old men and boys to the sword. Fuscus' troops met no armed resistance and optimists could convince themselves Diurpaneus was unaware of their arrival.

At night they made temporary camps, meticulously guarded by sentries who were under pain of death should they neglect their duties. Gaius Vinius watched Gracilis doing the rounds each evening, checking up on the men in his century, still saying nothing. He seemed to listen a lot. Gracilis was listening to the Dacian countryside, discounting the birdsong and animal cries, straining eyes and ears for suggestions of troop movement; the very soles of his feet were on the alert for reverberations in the ground that could indicate approaching cavalry. The further they went, the more grim his response to the absence of opposition.

They had come over sixty miles. Needing speed and any chance of surprise, they were using a paved Dacian road, unwillingly impressed by its high quality. As far as they knew, Sarmizegetusa lay up ahead. *All roads lead to Sarmizegetusa* . . . Much of Dacia was upland but they could see the rising heights where the citadel was thought to be. Thirty miles off, maybe? Forty at most. Two days.

Tapae. It was not much more than a village, a hamlet even, with a few pigs and chickens. The

230

place appeared deserted, with signs of the locals' hurried departure, although Vinius caught hints of wood smoke on the damp air.

Tapae. Roman armies were used to winning, used to the notion that unlike barbarians they were well-armed, well-drilled, an utterly formidable victory machine. Even when their battles were hard fought, those they won were often glorious. But they had always been beatable and when Rome lost, Rome lost on a big scale. Historic defeats still resonated. Every schoolboy learned the names of the battle of the Allia, the Caudine Forks, Carrhae, Cannae, Trasimene, the Varus disaster when Germanic tribesmen lured three legions into a trap and annihilated them . . . A trap deep in enemy territory.

Tapae. That was where Diurpaneus fell upon the army of Cornelius Fuscus in a well-planned ambush. From that time Diurpaneus would be known to his people as Decebalus, which meant a warrior ten times as great as others.

The Dacians appeared out of nowhere. There was a flash off a helmet, perhaps more glints of sunlight on metal; the first signs seemed unreal, almost passed unnoticed in the distance—then the enemy were upon the Romans. Most warriors were on horseback, shrieking and brandishing fearsome weapons. Fuscus and his men scrambled into well-practised action. The Romans had no battle plan; there was barely time to form up to face the hordes of warriors descending on them. After the long silence from the enemy, some men looked exhilarated at this chance for action but Vinius saw his centurion deplored their confidence. Gracilis had been waiting for this; he anticipated disaster.

231

A few frantic horn calls sounded, their meaning incomprehensible, then further down the line behind, sudden uproar announced that the fight had begun. Never having been in a pitched battle, Vinius was shocked by the chaos. They were fighting for hours, and for hours it was impossible to tell what was happening. He now understood why sometimes when a battle ended, exhausted participants were too confused even to know which side had won. At Tapae, eventually the outcome became bitterly clear. The Dacians with their long swords and sickles were carving up the Roman army, end to end. The Roman invasion force was being wiped out. They were all going to die, here in this godforsaken village, here on this bloody Dacian road.

The butchery horrified Vinius. He found himself trampling over dead and wounded, discarded shields and weapons; sliding on blood and guts and brains; stabbing and slashing, sometimes to good purpose yet sometimes aimlessly, while blinded by a mist of sweat and blood. The relentless noise appalled him. Not only the endlessly clashing weapons, but the terrible squealing of horses, the hideous screaming of men. The conflict just went on and on. He had never known such weariness, nor such spirit-sapping misery.

The Guards stuck solidly by their commander, knowing he would be a target. Diurpaneus habitually closed in on an enemy leader. The Praetorians therefore took the brunt of a deliberate Dacian onrush and suffered enormous casualties from the start. Heavily outnumbered, the remainder fought on even after they had seen Fuscus picked off; he was surrounded by intent

232

warriors, dragged from his horse, and cut to pieces. With Fuscus killed, his men's hopes for survival died too. The Praetorian battle standard had already disappeared, their trophy now a Dacian victory symbol. Screams and shouts intensified as the Dacians gloried in their success and the desperate Guards were systematically massacred.

The centurion Gracilis was last glimpsed by his beneficarius taking out opponents to the last, still showing his exasperation at the sheer bloody stupidity of this ill-planned operation imposed on good soldiers by an impetuous leader. Decius Gracilis, who would obey orders even when they were suicidal, died in that field of gore. Vinius saw him go down, bucking in agony yet wielding his sword valiantly even as life left him. His own heart burst with grief as he himself went on fighting— because that was what they were there for and there was no escape now—until a Dacian came up on his blind side. His helmet barely withstood the mighty blow that finished him, adrenalin carried him forwards momentarily, but he felt his sight blur and his legs give way. Vinius was finished. He knew it as, bitterly struggling against the darkness, he dropped to his knees then fell headlong among the dead and dying, helplessly submerged in carnage.

16

Certain moments would never be the same again. A garden at dusk in late summer would always remind Lucilla of her tryst with Vinius, and now mid-mornings when street-life was going on outside the shutters would sometimes catch her out too, making her weep. That was the time when Paulina had come to tell her what had happened. Instead of her usual cheery appearance, carrying little Titus, with the two girls scampering ahead and squealing for their aunt, Paulina was alone and solemn. She and Lucilla sat down together with hot beakers of flavoured borage tea, and then Paulina broke the news.

Reports of the tragic rout at Tapae had reached Rome. Felix and Fortunatus had gone to the Praetorian Camp, pleading for word of their younger brother. They learned that when Decebalus chased the remnants of Fuscus' troops back through the mountains, so few soldiers scrambled back to the Danube that the cormorants on the riverbank scarcely bothered to lift off at their coming. None of the Praetorian contingent made it back. Their battle standard had been captured, which told its own story.

The Guards at the Camp had been sympathetic, until the brothers' persistence became a menace; then the Guards' own dismay at the loss of colleagues made them rougher. They shouted at Felix and Fortunatus to give up. There was no point repeatedly beseeching answers. Gaps in the Praetorian cohorts were to be filled immediately; any Guard who had stayed in Moesia with Fuscus was presumed missing in action. Fuscus, the Prefect, was definitely dead. A great many good men had died with him. Decius Gracilis and his century had been wiped out. The beneficarius was lost with his centurion. Felix and Fortunatus must stop causing trouble and accept it. Gaius Vinius was dead.

Dead. He was dead.

'We all thought,' said Paulina, with delicacy, 'Gaius had a soft spot for you, Lucilla.' Silence. 'He never said anything?'

'No.'

Paulina was not easily deflected. 'Did you know that he divorced his wife? Just before he went away ... She was very surprised. We all were.'

'I am too,' replied Lucilla honestly.

Not half as surprised as when the Praetorians supplied Felix and Fortunatus with their brother's will. Gaius had made them his heirs and executors, not unexpectedly. He left them everything, with one surprising exception. A bequest 'to Flavia Lucilla, well-deserving of me' gave her all the contents of his rooms at Plum Street. 'Well-deserving' was a phrase used on tombstones for a spouse or lover, though presumably he intended simply to deter legal quibbles. Felix and Fortunatus added Gaius to their father's memorial tablet near the Camp, but Lucilla was not invited to appear on it.

Everyone found it convenient to make out that Lucilla's odd inheritance was just a few sticks of furniture and old keepsakes.

The furniture was better than her own, and Lucilla would take care of it for his sake. The keepsakes turned up when she unlocked the great chest in his bedroom. She made sure she was alone when she explored it.

Inside were his birth certificate and proof of Roman citizenship; army papers; two phalerae, which were his medals for army service in Britain

235

and for saving a priest's life in the vigiles. A flat gilded box that she remembered him bringing contained the gold oak wreath he won in action when he was a young soldier. She visualised him carrying that box into the apartment, clamped under one arm as if nothing special; he never said what it was.

Some items were everyday: a draughtsboard with two sets of glass counters, a toy ceramic chariot Gaius must have had in his childhood, favourite belts and a scabbard, the bronze multiple tool she remembered him buying, with its ingenious fold-up spoon, fork, cutting blade, toothpick, spatula and spike.

There was an amulet on a very short string, such as an infant might wear; his daughter's? Lucilla lifted out personal treasures carefully, guessing what each possession might have meant.

Wrapped in a piece of soft cloth was a small collection of jewellery. She did ask his brothers about that; they were vague, but Paulina consulted an aunt who said the simple rings, silver bangle, gold chains and various earrings had belonged to Clodia, his mother. His father had called him after his mother, Lucilla learned. The formal documents and citations gave his full title. Gaius Vinius Clodianus: that had been his name.

* * *

What Lucilla never told the others was that the chest he left her contained a large amount of money.

The soldier's savings took the form of aurei— each worth twenty-five denarii or a hundred sesterces—those big gold coins that people rarely used but hoarded. Perhaps it was true that when Domitian took the throne he had awarded soldiers a bonus of twenty thousand sesterces, the huge sum first given by the Emperor Claudius. Lucilla never actually counted, but the quantity took her breath away. Knowing this gift was intentional, yet hardly daring to touch it, she thought very carefully about how to use the cash. In the end when their rent fell due she paid Vinius' regular share out of his money. That way, she could keep the apartment as he must have intended. Years were to pass while Lucilla continued to pay rent as if for Gaius.

She used his second room as her evening refuge, altering it to suit her, but kept his bedroom just as he had left it. She even left an old cloak of his on a door peg, but she brought out the toy chariot and placed it on the stool beside the bed. Nobody else went in there. She cleaned, tidied, occasionally lay on his neat bed, thinking. She never felt able to wear most of the jewellery, apart from one set of earrings with pearl drops which she chose and wore in the Praetorian's memory.

In the months after the news came, she discovered unexpected things about him. First, in the apartment itself, she noticed a wall niche in the corridor. It must always have existed. Before he left, Vinius had placed there two small bronze statues, the 'Lares and Penates' who traditionally guarded the fortunes of a Roman home: he had left Lucilla with her own household gods. His gods too, perhaps. Had he taken them when he divorced Verania? The bronze had no patina; the little statues looked new.

Lying on the ledge where flowers and offerings

could be placed, he had left his front door key—
One for you; one for me. No duplicates. Agreed?

People continually talked about him.
Paulina reminisced about his youth. 'He was so
good-looking before that happened with his eye.
Lovely hair, and such long eyelashes—oh he was
gorgeous! Very quiet as a lad, but he seemed
happy. You want to talk to his aunties about him . .
.'

The old man who owned the main house
called Lucilla one day. Cretticus senior, his face
seamed, rather staring eyes; he spent his time in
a long daybed in the peristyle garden, apparently
snoozing, in a nonagenarian's dream-state. He was
all there if you spoke to him though. 'Sound fellow,
your Praetorian.'

'Not mine!'

'Decent manners. Wonderful patience. Knew a
thing or two; he took a lot of interest in the world.
He always had time for an old codger. I shall miss
our talks . . . Let me know if you need anything,
Flavia Lucilla. So long as I am still here.'

Did he ask you to look out for me?

He would have done, if he had thought of it. 'That
man was a hero, girl. Did you know he won the civic
crown for saving a life in battle?'

'I found it. It is a little crumpled, but very
beautiful.'

'Keep it safe for him.'

You speak as if he is coming back.

'He knew I had a weakness for hazelnut slices.
He would often bring me one from the fine bakery
on Ten Taverns Street. So thoughtful.'

Whenever Lucilla passed the bakery now, she
bought pastries for Cretticus and chatted to him.

238

When the pumice-seller gave up, the old man told Melissus to give her a good price on the lease for the spare shop, which he knew she wanted. 'Trust a pretty woman to wind a helpless old-timer around her sneaky little finger!' complained the agent. But he too was growing older and lazier, so he went along with it. Thus Lucilla was able to open a neighbourhood manicure and hair business as she had always wanted. Two lively girls worked for her; they tended customers on the street or indoors, and lived in an upstairs mezzanine. One was her slave Glyke, now returned without the baker's boy though with suspicious bruises and unfeasibly good intentions.

* * *

After Alba, Lucilla had wondered if Vinius might have left her a farewell note at Plum Street, but there was nothing. Only his bequest now silently gave her comfort as she grieved; perhaps in some friendly way he had wanted that for her.

She never regretted running away from him. She believed he was not for her. She felt he had always made that clear. She could never have resolved the conflict she perceived between how much she wanted him and its impossibility. So at Alba, when he left her alone briefly, she bolted from their pavilion, rushed to the residential quarters, gathered her things and fled down the hill to the Via Appia. She hitched a lift on a cart, right then in the clear air of dawn, before most people were stirring. She went not towards Rome, but down south to the Bay of Naples, where she stayed at another imperial villa until she could be certain

239

Vinius had left Rome.

Afterwards, sometimes she dared to remember being in his arms. How, after only clumsy couplings with others, she and this man had straightway come together as a perfect fit. How they moved together, in effortless synchronicity and with such deep pleasure. How when their exercise left them exhausted, she cried a little, so Vinius wiped her eye with his index finger, murmuring kindly, 'No tears!' before they both fell into profound sleep.

How her troubled mind had drowned in peace, her body melting against his . . .

*　　　*　　　*

He was dead. No point speculating. Cherish the past for what it was, an ideal, a signal that human happiness might be a possibility. Raise your standards. Make a decent life, Lucilla. Life is all there is. *If it's only once, it must be good* . . . He had been right. If perfection only happened once, that was better than never. Now nothing for her would ever again entail complete despair. So thank you, Gaius Vinius Clodianus, son of Marcus, thank you for your good deed, a deed that brightened somebody's dark world.

Onwards then. Life had to be gone through. In the year of the news of the Battle of Tapae, sad as she was, Flavia Lucilla picked herself up. Determined to improve herself, she stopped dallying with awkward lovers and ignored the fast set. She attached herself to a more cultured circle, keen to educate her mind. She dressed smartly but with taste. She was chaste, or at least careful, even though nobody knew it. She listened, learned to judge, tolerated many fools, made a few good friends, and eventually she suggested to a man she knew that they should be married.

He was a teacher. What could be better than that?

*   *   *

How she came to this marriage eventually was through mutual friends. By that time, Lucilla knew a lot of people. Many were at Alba, to which she returned whenever the imperial ladies went. There in particular she now explored society with better discrimination. At one point, as a tribute to Vinius, she tried to appreciate music; this was not a success, partly because it made her miserable on his behalf but also because she tended to drift off into her own thoughts.

For a brief period she dallied among the building project teams. Hearing one of the great Rabirius' drawing assistants one day discussing business with a site supervisor, she had been struck by the power of professional men, relaxed in their expertise. It had an almost erotic effect, although subsequently when an architect tried to take up with her, Lucilla found him deceitful and indecisive, which soon cured her.

Eventually she alighted instead on the verge of Domitian's literary circle.

Joining a writers' group is a mistake even for professional writers—especially for them, if they have any self-respect. Lucilla was too inexperienced, so far, to take that attitude.

The girl would learn.

Although life on the frontiers was tricky, back in Rome it was a time of civic certainty. Domitian had returned from his initial success in Moesia to hold a Dacian Triumph (spurious, in the light of the coming defeat at Tapae) and to appoint himself Censor. Unlike his predecessors in that role, he held the post alone and was to be censor for life. This would involve him enforcing much moral legislation, particularly the Augustan divorce laws. He enjoyed regulating conduct. The main point was that the censor reviewed the lists and supervised the political orders; this gave Domitian full control of the Senate.

In case anybody ever missed his significance, he took to appearing at all public occasions, including Senate meetings, in full triumphal uniform. That meant parading with a laurel wreath on his best toupee, a gold and ivory sceptre, and elaborate white robes that signified the honorand was representing Jupiter. The one-day ceremonial regalia for a general had been extended to permanently suggest divinity.

Domitian felt himself to be under Jupiter's personal protection, but his foremost devotion was to the goddess Minerva. Minerva was sometimes equated with the Greek Athene, though she had very ancient roots in Etruscan Italy. Helmeted and depicted carrying a tall spear, she was a goddess of war and warriors, but her patronage extended to significant peacetime activities: wisdom in general, medicine, commerce, crafts, music and poetry. At Domitian's court this was particularly good news for poets, who cluttered up audience rooms, all hoping a well-disposed attendant would place an elegy in the Emperor's bedroom, or a well-timed public recital would have them reading aloud just as he dropped by. Domitian had apparently stopped writing himself, but loved the tyranny of patronage.

Lucilla first engaged with this circle originally through Claudia, a pleasant woman married to the poet Statius; she had a daughter by a previous marriage to a different poet, a young girl who was extremely musical and whom Claudia closely chaperoned. Lucilla met mother and daughter at a recital, then heard a reading by Statius who had a famously good voice. He, like his father before him, had been a prize-winner in the literary category at the Naples Games, which were now defunct after the eruption of Mount Vesuvius. Coming to Alba, he hoped to become known for his magnum opus, an epic in twelve books called the *Thebaid.* He was still polishing this piece of work, though he regularly read excerpts. It told the story of the Seven Against Thebes, a Greek power struggle which involved episodes of extreme violence; that was not to Lucilla's taste, especially in the period after Vinius died. However, the writer was a man much-liked, and with good reason, she thought; she learned simply to wonder quietly at the subjects authors choose.

An overheard discussion of the *Thebaid* one day made her realise her education's deficiencies. Statius was not present, which was as well because he was so sensitive about reception of his work it was painful to watch. The discussion was about whether his poem, which might reflect on Domitian's court, was either slathered with the grossest flattery or instead was deeply subversive and critical of the Emperor's authoritarianism and the violence which underlay society. The concept that words could be so ambiguous was new to Lucilla. She was also straining to define phrases like 'dactylic hexameters', and to grasp whether she ought to regard these as thudding poetic metre or storytelling elegance.

Feeling disadvantaged, Lucilla might have gone off to some other clique, had she not come across the epigrams of Martial. His first book was recently published. These poems were easy: they were short, rude, witty and unpretentious—so readable that Lucilla could now see no reason to bother with any verse that was long-winded, overwrought and obscure. She began to discriminate between what she liked and what was fashionable. Such naïve honesty would, of course, bar her from the intelligentsia.

Lucilla battled with epic. The success of Virgil's *Aeneid*, with its undisguised grovelling to the Emperor Augustus, had encouraged writers of long heroic poems. Professionals like Statius blatantly hoped to win handouts whereas the upper classes, the amateurs, dreamed of retirement from public life, devoting themselves to ten-year labours over cherished epic manuscripts. Hence the *Thebaid* of Statius was now only one in a plethora of grandiose efforts: Valerius Flaccus, in his *Argonautica*, had begun the modern trend when he used Jason's quest for the Golden Fleece as a metaphor for the youthful Vespasian's involvement in the invasion of Britain. It was Statius' friend, the teacher Nemurus, who advised Lucilla against reading this; he told her the central hypothesis—that in capturing Britannia, Vespasian had opened up the seas in the same way as Jason—was so flimsy, the bluff old emperor himself must have guffawed. 'All you get are tedious displays of erudition, exaggerated imagery, monotonous style and wilful dullness.'

This was when Lucilla first decided Nemurus was worth cultivating.

Epicry was like a plague. Rutilius Gallicus, the newly appointed Prefect of the City, was thought to be penning a little something. A career administrator from Northern Italy, he was such a plodder, nobody would even ask him about it. Silius Italicus, a lawyer with a suspect past (he had worked as an informer for Nero), kept his head down these days too, devoting himself to his *Punica,* which in a mammoth seventeen books related the conflict between Scipio and Hannibal. From what had leaked into public circulation (given a good shove off the slipway by the author, said Nemurus), his models were the historian Livy, Virgil naturally, and Lucan's *Pharsalia,* written under Nero, which had retold the rivalry of Caesar and Pompey. Lucilla was disappointed to hear this was not glittering heroics. Caesar came across as unpleasant, Pompey as ineffectual. 'However,' (Nemurus again) 'Pompey goes to his treacherous death with stoic poise.'

Lucilla, usually so diffident, lost her temper. 'That's insulting to our soldiers. I knew a Guard who was killed in Dacia. Nobody will ever even learn what happened to him, but he too was ambushed and I don't imagine he went down with "stoic poise". I see him covered in blood, fighting to exhaustion; I hear him saying "bloody well annoyed to be landed in this shit by idiots" . . . Why can't poetry be real?'

The satirist Juvenal, happening to be present, fetched out a note tablet and scribbled words that he would work up later, excoriating Domitian and his advisory council by portraying them in a mock-debate about how to cook a monstrous turbot, when they ought to be applying themselves to Dacia.

Lucilla never cared for Juvenal, not socially. His targets were indiscriminate; he had even insulted Statius, saying he prostituted his art by pandering to the popular taste, so desperate that he had once sold ballet scripts to Paris. Juvenal could be extremely funny, but like Martial he was always depicting his life as a desperate struggle to obtain money from disinterested patrons, rushing about in the hope someone would invite him to dinner, or attaching himself to the gullible rich in order to screw legacies out of them. Martial was warmer, and at least said he never used real people in his epigrams. Juvenal did, and had a bad habit of brutal exaggeration. Once he knew who she worked for, he was always asking Lucilla about the Emperor's relationship with Julia, trying to get her to say Julia had experienced a whole series of abortions, all supposedly forced on her as a result of sex with her imperial uncle. Telling Juvenal it was untrue never deterred him.

Lucilla had a distaste for men who chose not to work yet bewailed their poverty. So her preference was for the professional poets and other learned men who made up an income giving lessons. That said, even career teachers hung around hoping for imperial appointments, but as the Emperor and Empress continued to have no children, this was futile.

Good poets had opportunities. In the year of the Fuscus disaster at Tapae, Domitian's chief project at home had been reinstituting the Capitoline Games, in honour of Jupiter, for which he built a new Odeum and Stadium, deemed two of the most beautiful buildings in Rome. Held from then on every four years, these games were modelled on the ancient Olympics and attracted international competitors, though Domitian extended the repertoire to include not only athletics but literature and music. Two years later, after Tettius Julianus won the second Battle at Tapae and reversed Roman fortunes in Dacia, the Emperor would hold the Secular Games in Rome, which were by tradition only held once in anyone's lifetime. He then founded the Alban Games, held annually at his summer court in honour of his patron goddess Minerva. He liked to attend the Games in Greek dress, wearing a gold crown.

These years seemed to pass drably for Lucilla as her ache for Gaius Vinius slowly dulled. Finally, in the lull after the Alban Games, when those in her particular circle were upbeat and optimistic for their future because they were winning prizes, she decided to improve herself and first went to Nemurus to ask him to give her lessons. Although he felt instructing a female, a hairdresser, was demeaning for a man of his intellect, lack of a regular salary forced him to look receptive. Lucilla persisted; he agreed. He had been poor and had a one-time pauper's terror of being poor again.

They got off on the wrong foot. Nemurus mistakenly assumed she was illiterate. He began showing her the alphabet on placards. Lucilla explained gravely that, even if most were not

247

trained to the standards of a Greek secretary, slaves in upper-class homes, as her mother had been, were required to be basically literate and numerate. Lachne had sent Lucilla herself to a morning infant school.

'So what are you asking?'

'I want to learn to read a poem and understand it.'

Under encouragement from their mutual acquaintance, Statius, Nemurus caved in. The lessons had been Statius' idea, in fact, because his own father was a teacher.

Lucilla's critical education began and seemed successful. Nemurus could be an unsympathetic taskmaster, but she bore it. Reproof made her concentrate harder. For one thing, she was paying with her own money, and had no intention of wasting it, so strictness worked. She was determined to siphon off everything Nemurus had to give her intellectually. She fell upon reading and only needed to be given guidance.

For a time Nemurus was proud of her, or at least proud of his own achievement. They were on good terms—so good that Statius and his wife Claudia suggested that since both were single, they should get married. Though initially startled, Lucilla indicated that she would entertain the idea. Nemurus withdrew into himself, repeatedly begging advice from his male friends. But eventually he announced, as if the whole thing had been his idea, that this was what he wanted.

A teacher? Dear gods, that stinks!
Who are you with your unsolicited opinions?
The name's Vinius. Gaius Vinius.
Go away; you're a dead man.

248

At least I don't have to see you being shafted by an inkblot—who, I see, wears socks . . .

* * *

Nemurus did wear socks, though Lucilla thought she could put up with it.

Romans did occasionally wear socks. Nemurus adopted the fashion preferred by Egyptian pharaohs; his had separately knitted big toes, to enable toe-post sandals. When venturing into cold climates, anyone could stuff their boots with woollen or fur linings—most soldiers who had gone to Moesia would be doing that, while at the ends of the earth, for instance in Britain, the men would demand underpants. But on the Bay of Naples or in Rome, Lucilla knew in her heart, socks were inelegant and mildly eccentric.

The socks would come to signify everything wrong about Nemurus. But at first, she told herself they were a positive sign of character.

This was the only visible disadvantage Nemurus exhibited. In his twenties, he was educated and well spoken, slightly old-fashioned in social matters maybe, but in a scenario full of dissipated eunuchs and slobbering fat cats, Lucilla found that reassuring. He had manners. He was extremely precise about eating in public; shepherding women through doorways; deferring to men with superior intellects.

A lot of those, presumably!
Oh get lost, Vinius.

* * *

249

Apart from the fact that since she had no father, Lucilla could not be collected from her paternal home by her bridegroom, they had a full wedding. It took place in Rome, which allowed many women at whose marriages she and Lara had assisted to flock excitedly to hers. Suddenly she was the centre of attention as a bride should be, and realising how many good women cared about her.

It was extremely odd, after preparing so many other brides, to have her own hair formally divided with a sword and arranged in seven locks, to have attendants putting her under a saffron veil. She knew, but had forgotten, that at a formal wedding the old-fashioned rubric—and Nemurus, naturally, went for the traditional version—included the vows *ego Gaius, tu Gaia*: 'I am Gaius, you are Gaia . . .'

Lucilla was nearly sick. Twittering women whisked her to one side and gave her water, telling everyone she was overcome by nerves.

* * *

The marriage was a mistake. Still, teachers are generally civilised people and, as mistakes go, it was by no means fatal. They had never been to bed beforehand, or Lucilla might not have gone through with the wedding. She was also surprised to learn that her new husband was a year younger than she was; he always seemed quite a lot older.

Lucilla realised on their wedding night that what she had construed as a promise of passion was only her husband's urgency to achieve his own release. He must have slept with women, but not many, she decided. For Lucilla, their love life was to be disappointing. He would never improve. He was a three-minute jiggler. He slipped into her and out again, like an uncertain minnow, then occasionally turned her over and repeated the procedure, his idea of sophisticated sex.

Nemurus had seen on the walls of taverns and bath houses pictures of women wearing nothing but a bustband, providing bedroom entertainment to well-endowed fellows, sometimes in intriguing threesomes, and with bug-eyed servants watching. *That* looked like a lot of fun, but he loathed himself for hankering after it. He did not believe such behaviour belonged in a harmonious marriage. He wanted a wife he could respect who would not try to alter his already settled habits. If he sought Lucilla in bed after their first few nights, it was merely for comfort, like a child falling asleep sucking a piece of old cloth. He had no interest in her feelings or her needs.

He believed he treated her in an exemplary fashion. There was no point complaining; it would only lead to a quarrel. He was clever and extremely widely read, but it had given him no aptitude for real life.

*   *   *

It worked for a year; they even stayed together longer.

Soon Lucilla learned to hide her intellectual development. As her husband watched her bounding progress, he was no longer proud but jealous, resenting her loss of reliance on him for teaching. Still, his world was full of books. She could devour those, especially when he was not at home with her, which happened increasingly. He

251

spent much of his time with male friends. This soon involved dicing and drinking, though in keeping with his character, he was restrained and wary, which at least saved him losing too much money. Lucilla heard herself say, 'Well, if it keeps him happy . . .' As she said it, she knew everything was all up with her.

Lucilla was following the traditional wives' habit of slipping the leash, though hardly in the traditional way. While Nemurus thought she was following his prescriptive curriculum, which involved intense study of many, many books of the historian Livy, Lucilla had discovered the erotic love poems of Catullus. These she read all the more joyously because she knew Nemurus would be annoyed.

When she finally defied him and openly refused to read any more Livy, Nemurus let her try Ovid's *Metamorphoses*. Lucilla had become a tricky student. 'That Apollo—what a hunk! Now I'd really like to do *his* hair!'

'Be serious.'

'I am, dear.' They called one another 'dear', instead of risking the intimacy of names. 'For instance, I know that when a lecher, man or demigod, chases after a girl intending to rape her, she does not get conveniently turned into a tree. She will be raped.'

'Is that your critical appreciation of Ovid?'

'I think it's my appreciation of all poets.'

And people who teach poetry.

You cannot mean that, dear.

'Anyway,' snarled Lucilla. 'Who wants to be a laurel bush?'

Julia died.

She had been ill for a short time, but the situation had been covered up at court, with the usual whispers, hastily closed doors, hurrying feet, and sudden unexplained visits, sometimes at night, from medical practitioners. Even so, her death came unexpectedly. She was twenty-five, little older than Lucilla. Those who had attended her, especially her women, wept and were stricken. Though Lucilla knew Julia only tangentially, she was bonded in her colleagues' heartbreak.

Domitian was away at the time, either in Germany or Pannonia; there were dark fears how he was going to take this.

Juvenal came nagging, 'Was it an abortion that went wrong?'

Lucilla was furious.

After Julia's funeral she withdrew into herself. When Lucilla and Nemurus were in Rome rather than at Alba, officially they lived with his parents. His mother inevitably thought Lucilla too common; she believed Nemurus had an exceptional talent, an opinion he encouraged. The good thing about coming from slave stock was that you had an endless facility for silent insubordination. Lachne had taught Lucilla how to put up with anything and to appear meek, while being insidiously mutinous. But it was no way to live.

Now, citing the needs of her business, Lucilla returned most days to Plum Street, which had always been her refuge. Her husband never came. He liked the fact she had her own money; it saved her making demands on his. He generally enjoyed her connection with the imperial family, which he saw as potentially a useful connection for him. Otherwise, he took absolutely no interest in her work.

The couple remained married, because it was convenient. But increasingly they were leading separate lives.

Nemurus did not accept his fate meekly. As soon as he sensed Lucilla's growing independence, he had recourse to the Roman husband's most hackneyed weapon: he accused her of intending to commit adultery. Like many a Roman wife, Lucilla played the wounded innocent. While she dramatically bemoaned her husband's injustice, she never confessed the truth: that her entire marriage felt to her, and had always felt, like a betrayal of her feelings for the lost Gaius Vinius.

17

It had rained all day and now there was snow again. 'Crapping caryatids!' groaned Gaius Vinius. 'I have had enough of this.'

Vinius, not dead. Vinius, utterly depressed and irritable.

His head hurt. The ache was at last diminishing slightly, so he thought he would escape brain damage, although when he first regained consciousness he had self-diagnosed, in the absence of any medical aid, that he had suffered concussion and permanent harm was possible. More likely, he would simply go mad trying to endure life as a captive. The boredom and claustrophobia were dire.

What in the world could be worse than to be stuck in an isolated mountain-girt, barbarian land on the wrong side of the frontier, a thousand miles from home, never knowing if or when they might be released, or whether anybody of their own even knew they were there?

They thought nobody did know.

The prisoners taken at Tapae, a mere handful of Roman survivors, had been picked up and transferred in crude carts to a half-deserted citadel whose name they were not told. They were dumped in a dilapidated compound on a small hillside terrace, over twenty men crammed into space once built for one family. Their shelter comprised a couple of clay-floored rotten wattle huts that were too grim even to be pigsties, though their stink was distinctly animal. This was to be their home indefinitely.

If the men had realised how many years it would be, how many years before any chance of rescue, they would have given up. All that kept them going was that the Dacians neither killed them nor made slaves of them. Dark stories were told of Dacians sacrificing defeated enemies to their warrior gods and hanging up armour as trophies in trees; these Romans had lost their weapons and valuables but were spared. It had to mean they were hostages, and for hostages there must always be a glimmering mirage, that thin possibility which they must never see as false: belief in returning to safety one day.

Some died. There would be no return for them.

*   *   *

They were all going to die, of dirt, disease and dismal despair, unless someone made an effort to preserve their health and sanity. Vinius had realised this in the first weeks, around the time he slowly ceased feeling nothing but distraught over losing his centurion and the battle, the time when he knew he would have to start fighting for his own survival, which at least was what Gracilis would have done and what he would want Vinius to do.

The prisoners were an assortment from several legions. Numbers were few, though as time passed, Vinius picked up signals from occasional Dacians who did communicate; he suspected there were others held elsewhere. None in his group were officers. Vinius was the only Praetorian; moreover, he had been a centurion's beneficarius. So, once he hauled himself out of his initial misery, he tried to pull everyone together. Vinius had to assume leadership. He must do what Gracilis would have done, what the mystic voice of Gracilis was even now instructing: rally them, keep up their spirits, drag them through this ordeal however long it lasted, find a way to co-exist with their captors, look for ways to escape but never try anything stupid.

They agreed. None had the energy to resent him; none wanted to take charge themselves. Anyway, he was a Guard—so they may as well let Vinius do it. If there was any trouble, he could take the blame.

'Right. We have to take care of ourselves. Scrupulous hygiene, as far as we can manage—' There were mountain streams and they were allowed to collect water. 'Anything we can do to keep mentally alert. Just don't ask me to tell you bedtime stories. Daily exercise.' They did press-ups and lunges, and after some months acquired an extremely old, unwanted horse, too far gone even for eating, which they all learned to ride. The Dacians let them keep the horse because, as Vinius remarked, there was no way twenty-three of them were going to escape on him. It was like some horrible team-bonding task in the new recruits' manual, something the old general Corbulo might have come up with: *get out of Dacia without being killed in the mountains, using only one arthritic horse, four billycans with holes in them and a set of panpipes* . . . The panpipes were whittled by Vinius; once he had finished, the others made it plain that, officer or not, he should refrain from playing them.

He knew how to make himself even more unpopular: 'I expect you to be clean-living.'

'What, no singing "The Girl I Kissed at Clusium" while we're having a wank?'

'That's up to you. I meant no humming of "The Boy I Kissed at Colonia Agrippinensis" while you're buggering your tent-mate for the ninety-fifth time.'

'Ninety-five times! Do you think we'll be here a whole month?'

Gaius Vinius feared they might be there forever. It was one of the burdens of office that he had to keep this thought to himself.

'Sir, sir—is this the official new policy on wanking then?'

'Senatorial edict, sunshine. Enacted in the consulship of two most noble wotsits with five hundred years of donkey dung on their fancy boots and so inbred they've got three heads, who voted in the Curia that anything is permitted if it's exercise . . . Jupiter, I hope you horrible beggars know what I am rambling about, because mountain air makes me light-headed . . . There is to be no attempted conversation with the flower of Dacian womanhood, incidentally. We are in enough trouble.'

That last instruction was hardly needed. Dacian women wanted nothing to do with them. They had enough virile Dacian warriors at their disposal, or if they wanted variety, thrusting Suebi who only lived on horseback and in wagons, Sarmatians who tied their hair back in curious topknots, or even Scythians—those barbarians that even barbarians thought were scary wild men—who sometimes passed through for cosy tribal fraternisation and plotting against Rome.

Dacian adult men thought guarding foreigners far beneath them. This at first left the Roman prisoners in the care of a bunch of spotty, slouching youths, the lowest tranche of Dacian society. It was a first taste of power for the adolescents, who loved the excitement of beating up helpless victims for no reason.

Eventually Vinius had had enough of that, as well as the rain and snow, so in a spurt of energy he rounded up their tormentors, split them into teams, instructed them to bring him the head of a dead goat, and got them playing football like urchins in a Mediterranean back alley. This worked until the wrong team won, when the losers became sulky. The Roman prisoners consoled them by organising a pissing-up-a-door competition, a game in which the lads needed no education, though one giggling idiot must have let something slip because a few days later a group of infuriated mothers came from their village to screech blood-curdling insults and take their babies safely home.

The boys were replaced with apprentice warriors, who were bored but harmless.

'If I'd known all it would take to get rid of the little bastards,' said Vinius, 'was to make their mothers think you lot were teaching them Greek gymnasium perversions, we'd have lost them bloody weeks ago.' To a soldier who looked puzzled, he added, 'Women think playing with your dingle-dangle makes you go blind.'

After a short pause, naturally someone asked him if that was how he lost his right eye, at which Vinius smiled patiently. As an officer he had a tolerance his old centurion would have despised. Still, Gracilis had always known, Vinius did everything his own way.

The soldiers went back to singing incorrigible ditties about persons they claimed to have kissed, and much else, in various towns of the Empire, with accompanying gestures according to taste. Vinius did not sing; he was too unhappy. But when he wanted a treat in the long cold nights, he lay on his back and allowed himself to remember his experience at Alba Longa with Flavia Lucilla in his arms. He understood his feelings now. She was in his blood and in his soul. Bored and bereft, he rationed the memory, as if fearful that each time he replayed the experience in his head, it would be subtly worn away. He could not bear it to fade.

To preserve that memory he varied the special reminiscence with other incidents. He liked recalling the evening he had taken Lucilla to eat at the bar down in Plum Street, after he found her crying when her sister died. The food place—the Pisces? Aquarius?—the Scallopshell—was local and convenient, not good, though not as grim as many on the streets of Rome. A dead fly floated in the gravy among his chicken dumplings. Despite her wan face over Lara, Lucilla had giggled, 'Do you want to send it back? Why Vinius—are you hoping for a bigger fly in your next bowlful?'

A little joke, but one which now exquisitely cheered his bleak existence. Sometimes he imagined what he would have done or should have done, if he had realised at the time how he felt about her.

Go back and <u>think</u>: you would have told her. You would say you cared.

No. Alba would have been too soon. Take it slowly. Not the right moment.

Be realistic: for some men it is never the right moment. They expect the woman to discover for herself, winkle it out of her fellow, guess, deduce or decide, choose the occasion (too soon for him of course), then helpfully say the words for him.

Praetorians should have more gumption, Gaius.

I'm shy with women.

Don't be an idiot.

*   *   *

He kept all these thoughts to himself, being the kind who needed privacy to stay sane.

As soldiers, most prisoners had reserves to see them through their exile. Some failed to cope, however, cracking up either slowly or very suddenly. Their isolation and interminable uncertainty broke them. There was no way to predict who would mentally collapse, old or young, tough or vulnerable. The others had to nurse their comrades when a breakdown happened. They lost a couple. One ran mad and threw himself off a crag, one simply pined away.

When these tragedies happened, the Dacians appeared indifferent, although Vinius noticed the quality of their food improved temporarily. Mainly they were fed on thin pottage and a little salty sheep's cheese. During festivals, they were treated to spiced meatballs, which for the Romans led to inevitable periods sweating in a Dacian shit-house. They called these Mars' Balls, which Vinius thought sounded like some sweet Saturnalia treat such as those his aunts and sisters-in-law carried around on trays at family parties . . .

One of the soldiers said that, according to Virgil, the god Mars was born among the Goths, or Dacians. Vinius replied straight-faced that he would make it his rule from now on never to be captured unless it was with someone who read literature. *'Aeneid,'* the man came back at him sadly. 'Book Three.' *Jupiter!*

Once when they had all been sick, they were given some badly cured animal skins to help them keep warm. Someone was monitoring them, in a crude fashion. That made it worse in a way. They had not been forgotten. They were being stored in their run-down hutment like pieces of old fruit that no one cared for much, not allowed to rot, though not expected to be brought out except in an emergency.

Every New Year, Gaius lined up his men, delivered a sharp pep talk on being Romans, and made them take the Oath of Loyalty to the Emperor. He was to do that three times.

After Tapae a winter passed, during which they learned that they would shiver above the snowline for a hundred days a year. Another year went by with no change in their situation. This was to be a long haul, possibly forever. The prisoners discussed it endlessly. They had no way of knowing what happened in Rome.

*   *   *

Domitian spent a full year preparing his retaliation for the Tapae disaster, determined not to repeat the planning and reconnaissance failures that caused it. He was a man who constantly brooded. That helped get logistics right.

He mobilised troops from other provinces: Britain, Germany and Dalmatia. Although it caused controversy, he insisted that the legions in Britain had to withdraw from the north where there was too much demand on manpower in return for too little gain. The legions reluctantly pulled out of Caledonia, which Agricola had won such a short time previously, and the II Adiutrix was brought south to cover the Danube emergency. Domitian increased the legions stationed in Moesia from three to six. They carried out detailed reconnaissance. As he had planned, he rejigged the province, dividing it so there were two governors, who could concentrate their energies. Avid attention to revenge was his lifetime speciality. Doggedly, he refused to be hurried.

The prisoners did find out that the next year, their second in captivity, the Emperor at last sent a new army. It was led by Tettius Julianus; unlike the flighty Fuscus, he was an old-style general with a reputation for enforcing discipline. He advanced from Viminacium, crossed the Danube and invaded

262

Dacia. As far as Vinius could glean, it sounded as if Julianus used the same route through the Transylvanian Iron Gates as his predecessor, which could have been equally disastrous. Warned by what happened to Fuscus, however, Julianus must have prepared tactically for an ambush. He was enticing Decebalus to repeat his previous moves.

This time fortunes were reversed. At the same place, again at Tapae, Tettius Julianus fought Decebalus, imposing defeat on him. The Dacian second-in-command, Veizinas, had to pretend to be dead in order to escape under cover of night. The Dacians were crushed—though not annihilated. Their Roman prisoners from the previous battle were kept alive but were abruptly moved to a two-storey tower in Sarmizegetusa. They were knocked about during the journey. The upsurge of vicious treatment helped Vinius deduce that Rome had had a success. But it also warned him: a Roman victory might put the prisoners-of-war in extreme danger.

They were not rescued, even if the Roman high command knew of their existence—which probably they did not. The advance by Julianus had taken time. After the second battle at Tapae, he decided it was unsafe to press on to Sarmizegetusa so late in the year. Struggling to get information, the prisoners could not argue with the strategy, however dearly they wanted to see Roman troops arriving. Lines of communication and supply back to Moesia would be under threat in winter. The approaches to the citadel were difficult. Large units would struggle in the hills, while smaller contingents would be prey to guerrilla attacks.

Their third dreary year of imprisonment began

for Vinius and his companions.

The Dacian maids Vinius had warned the men to ignore were beginning to look as bright and beautiful as meadow orchids.

*   *   *

At this terrible moment, with help so close and yet hope so unreliable, near disaster struck. It happened on the Rhine. Antonius Saturninus, a man nobody had ever heard of and who could have slipped from history a complete unknown, made a surprise play for fame. He was Domitian's appointee as governor of Upper Germany, once the base from which Vitellius, Vespasian's rival, had launched his bid for supreme power. From the huge double legionary fort in Moguntiacum, Saturninus also declared himself emperor; he chose the first of January, the day on which he was supposed to give his troops the oath to Domitian. It was twenty years since Vitellius had seized the title; choosing the anniversary was a pointed attempt to oust the Flavian dynasty.

There was a murky conspiracy, one which would never be completely unravelled. There must certainly have been contact between Saturninus' supporters in Germany and the elite at Rome, because only a madman would try to become emperor unless he believed his elevation would be well received. With a significant number of troops at his disposal and ample funding in the savings banks of two legions, Saturninus had precipitated a serious crisis. But his attempt was rushed, and some said that since he was openly homosexual he had prematurely reacted, or overreacted, to Domitian's new morality laws.

At the same time, and presumably in cahoots with Saturninus, the Free German Chatti assembled on the far bank of the frozen Rhine, apparently preparing to invade over the ice. Other tribes, a branch of Sarmatians called the Iazyges, plus the Suebian Marcomanni and Quadi, who had previously recognised Rome, menaced the province of Pannonia. With these frontier systems enflamed, Roman activity in Dacia was seriously compromised.

Warnings of what Saturninus might be planning had reached Domitian from his own supporters, who did exist, back in December.

Always alert for threats against him, whether real or imaginary, his response to this true emergency was electric. He left Rome heading for Germany on the twelfth of January. It was unclear how many legions there would remain loyal, if any. Domitian took only the Praetorian Guard; Ulpius Trajanus, himself a future emperor, joined him, bringing the trusted VII Gemina from Spain. Before their arrival, the fighting was over. The Chatti had been unable to cross the ice-bound Rhine, due to an unseasonable thaw. The governor of Lower Germany, an old Vespasian loyalist called Lappius Maximus, had thrown in his hand with Domitian. With his own legions, he had crisply defeated Saturninus and the rebellious troops—the maverick XIV Gemina and uppity XXI Rapax from the double fort at Moguntiacum. Saturninus died in battle.

The aftermath was difficult. Lappius caused controversy by burning Saturninus' correspondence. This may have been to cover

265

his own dubious involvement, or in the light of Domitian's known tendencies, it may have been a wise move to destroy evidence if there really had been a secret conspiracy; violent reprisals against members of the Senate would ultimately have weakened Rome. Merely to have been invited to take part in the treason would have been damning in the eyes of an emperor who was already hostile to the senatorial class.

The rank and file in the legions that had rebelled were treated leniently, though their officers were hunted down, tortured and killed. Their severed heads, along with that of Saturninus, were despatched to the Senate in Rome: a strong visual message. Domitian swiftly introduced measures to prevent future reoccurrence: soldiers could no longer keep more than a thousand sesterces in their legionary savings bank, thus limiting the funds available to any potential usurper. There would never again be two legions concentrated in one fort; the XXI Rapax was transferred immediately to serve in Pannonia.

Three or four months later, with mopping-up operations well in hand, Domitian's personal presence on the Rhine ceased to be essential. He returned his attention to the Danube provinces, this time in beleaguered Pannonia. There was no detour to Rome; he crossed directly overland. Fighting ensued; the Romans suffered a reverse. When the Marcomanni sued for peace, however, Domitian first stalled, and then executed their legation. Having made this declaration of purpose, he finally agreed to make peace with Decebalus and the Dacians.

There was an extremely attractive offer of

Rome paying huge financial subsidies, starting now, then on a regular basis in future years. The terms agreed also provided for Roman engineers and other experts to be sent to help fortify Dacia against threats from other tribes. Dacia would give reciprocal assistance to Rome.

Too wily to expose himself, Decebalus sent his brother Diegis to sign the treaty. Diegis would receive a golden diadem from Domitian's own hands, symbolising that Dacia was now Rome's client kingdom with the Emperor able to validate its rulers. To smooth negotiations, Diegis brought with him and handed over a demoralised bunch of Roman prisoners, men his brother had been holding since the first Battle of Tapae.

*   *   *

For repatriation, they were marched to Carnuntum, in Noricum. In their weakened condition, the effort was exhausting. Only hope stopped it killing them. There, in ancient wine country, the main arm of the Amber Highroad crossed the Danube. There, Vinius and his companions finally crossed back into the Roman Empire.

After four years in another world, they were disorientated to see the familiar lines of a Roman legionary fort, an amphitheatre outside it, nestling in the traditional mess of a small civilian settlement. There was more noise than normal, and many more sentries, because the Emperor was in residence.

Their reception from those at the fort was businesslike, not too much staring. They lined up as smartly as they could, Vinius in the officer's position with a makeshift swagger-stick. A senior clerk collected details: names, previous legions; a short list of those who had died in captivity. Officers began a debrief. The new Praetorian Prefect was notified that a Guard had been recovered; he bustled up to investigate. He found Vinius urgently passing on his suspicion that Decebalus was holding other Romans somewhere. 'I beg you, don't abandon them—'

One of the lads piped up, 'Sir, sir! It was Vinius who got us through—'

Suddenly a new voice exclaimed: *'I know that man!'*

Amid murmurs, the crowd parted. Arms chinked as men sprang to attention. Some tall dignitary, approximately forty, paunchy, familiar turned-up lip, pushed through. A scarlet swirl of overloaded cloak. A moulded gold breastplate showing Minerva. Heavily fringed epaulettes. *Nice sword!*

They all gasped: Domitian. Their commander-in-chief. Their Emperor.

To Vinius he looked gaunt. He learned later just how badly Domitian had been shaken by the revolt of Saturninus, a man he had appointed, a man he trusted. He was hurt to the core that legions had revolted against him, after his care in boosting the pay and status of the army and his sincere attempts to win his soldiers' loyalty. Worse, he had heard the news that back in Rome, his niece Julia, a young woman he undoubtedly loved in his fashion, had died.

Despite his own mental turmoil, it was Domitian who pulled up short. The prisoners had lived day by day with their slow deterioration, not noticing it. They reached Carnuntum underweight and in poor health. Since he remembered the one-eyed Vinius from years before, as fit and muscular, Domitian saw the change. The soldier's grey, dull-eyed appearance shocked him.

The Emperor came right up close. Under the single gimlet eye of their acting centurion, the men strained to attention until their spines cracked. First Domitian clasped Gaius Vinius by the hand. He seemed almost on the verge of embracing him, though that was never his style. Then Domitian passed along the lines; he took his time and shook hands with every man. They all mentioned afterwards how he held on, with a crushing grip. His gaze was compassionate and fatherly. They could see the Emperor was moved by the misery they had endured.

So far, the returned soldiers had stayed in control of their emotions. They were numb and withdrawn, none yet really daring to believe their ordeal was ended. Vinius had warned them they might be received as an embarrassment, or tainted goods, even as deserters.

'Give these men everything they need!'

It was Domitian's genuine kindness that made them finally break down.

PART 4

Rome: AD 89–91

Becoming more cruel

18

Faces. So many faces . . . So much armoured battledress. So many fit men, all reeking of cleansing oils, with wonderful teeth. Such bustle and purpose.

The prisoners shied from their colleagues. Aware of their shabbiness, lost molars, fungal skin and mental rot, the unshaven lank-haired men who had been brought out of Dacia by Diegis shrank into a tight knot, as nervous as colts.

Rehabilitation would be a brisk process. They were given the option of returning to their former units, serving in other legions in quiet provinces with only goldmines to guard, or taking their discharge. Almost all opted to continue in service, some deliberately staying on the frontier in the hope of taking some revenge. They had all sworn to be blood brothers, though undeniably they would lose touch.

Vinius requested discharge. He knew when he had reached his limit.

Domitian generally had two Praetorian Prefects, one military, one with an admin background. Replacing the slain Fuscus, here on the Danube was Casperius Aelianus. He seemed well briefed and perhaps knew of Domitian's previous role as Vinius' sponsor. Whether that, or simply reluctant to lose a man with good years left in him, Casperius Aelianus nagged Vinius to stay on.

'How old are you?'

'Thirty-two.'

'That's nothing. You can't retire; you'll need

employment.'

Capitulating, Vinius demanded the vigiles. Instead, Aelianus offered a headquarters post; he would remain a Guard, with the salary and security. There was an unstated agreement that he could stay in Rome as a non-combatant.

He was to work under the cornicularius, dealing with records; that suited him. A desk job. Some soldiers or paramilitaries, who are prevented by wounds or mental troubles from carrying out the full range of duties, fret against it. Not him. He would suit this posting just as he had enjoyed the vigiles, though without having to put up with a stream of thieves and arsonists.

* * *

Before reassignment, the prisoners rallied slowly. They were all fragile, becoming worse before they improved. Most refused to talk about the past four years. The first time they went to the fort's bath house no one could get them out of there; the bath keeper complained they left him an infestation and stole all the rope-soled footwear. The barracks barber had to work overtime tidying them up. Some rushed to the local good-time girls, though they came back subdued, shocked by their inability to function.

The Emperor gave them what were called generous gifts of money and arms; that meant he confirmed their four years' back pay and rearmed them without the usual deduction from salary. Better, his personal medic attended them. They needed his help. Drink, after four years of abstinence, had disastrous results. Even food caused upsets; they fell on their first Roman meal, only to vomit or to find it dashed straight through them. Vinius fainted; the doctor said it was because he was tall. The imperial quack imposed a strict planned diet to wean them back to proper nourishment. They joked nervously that they hoped he was not the man who had tended Titus in his death throes, which was how they felt. For a time they were all quavering invalids.

Eventually Vinius was despatched to Rome. He wanted to march home, head high, but he was stretched ignominiously in a wagon for most of the trip. It took weeks. From Carnuntum, you had to avoid the Alps. He had a lot of time to think. Mostly he just cleared his mind and waited.

At the Porta Flaminia, he clambered off his transport to stagger into the city on his own feet. As he took the long, straight ceremonial road that ran from the triumphal gate to the Forum, his first reaction was indignant. He had seen Domitian's new buildings going up; yet during his captivity, the Rome in his mind had been the old city, the city he grew up with as a boy, before the fire. This glittering vista horrified him. Rebuilt and improved buildings in the Campus Martius—the Pantheon and Saepta Julia, the Temple of Isis—looked larger, *were* larger, now so fabulously ornate and garish that to him they seemed tasteless. The new Temple of Jupiter, an outsize golden blur atop the distant Capitol, was as unfamiliar as an architectural fantasy on a wall fresco. Instead of feeling he had woken from a nightmare, Gaius was living in one, shaky and disorientated.

He could not imagine the best way to announce to his family that he was home from the dead.

Until now he had done nothing about them. He had enough imagination to become worried what reaction his sudden appearance might cause.

Reluctant to walk in and give his brothers heart attacks, he went for a decent Roman shave and haircut. He sat in the chair with his chin in a warm napkin, as uncertain as a teenage boy on his first visit.

What lotion, soldier? Iris? Cretan lily? I can do you a lovely sandalwood...

Hades. Scrap that muck. Camomile I like. Just camomile.

He decided to go to the Praetorian Camp. This meant he had to cross Rome over the northern heights, a slow, gentle, healing stroll through the Gardens of Sallust; it was a good idea and gave him time to adjust. Then a Guard he knew from the old days took time to visit his family for him, to break the news gently.

Felix rushed to fetch him. Shamefaced, he showed his brother their father's memorial, now with its respectful mention of his own heroic death. 'Shit, Felix—' His brother was in pieces; Gaius also choked. 'Not many people get to inspect their own tombstone. Thanks!'

He ought to be dead. So many colleagues had failed to make it back—why him? Hideous guilt clamped down on him. Although his brother, who had been a soldier, looked as if he sympathised, Vinius was already trapped in bearing all this alone. Seeing the memorial had increased his unspoken shame that he, fortune's random choice, had survived the catastrophe.

That evening screams, tears, embraces, slaps on the back, far too much food and far, far too much

wine were lavished on him. Aunts who had brought
him up—their number now reduced—tottered in to
squeeze him, pinch him, slobber tears into coloured
handkerchieves, grow horribly tipsy on many cups
of sweetened wine. *'Just a finger; you know I never
drink . . .'* His brothers and their wives alternately
sobbed or grinned disbelievingly. The two young
girls, Marcia and Julia, who could barely remember
their uncle, peered around Paulina shyly, then crept
up and put garlands on his neck, while their little
brother hid under a table and peered out, having no
recollection at all of this scary soldier. Even though
they were not his children, Gaius was deeply shaken
by how much the trio had altered in the years he
had been away. The girls were little ladies; the
toddler now a boy.

Nobody mentioned the children's aunt; nor did
Gaius Vinius.

*   *   *

Plum Street next morning looked safely unchanged.

The knife shop was still there. He could have
done with his folding multi-blade in Dacia. The
tassel shop, latterly a sponge emporium, was now
occupied by two beauticians. One young woman
was giving a manicure to someone seated on a stool
on the street; some sixth sense brought the other
dainty practitioner from her customer indoors,
to stare at Vinius. He gave them a nod. Both girls
looked hostile. He needed to work on his act.

They watched him all the way up the stair under
the archway. He had no key. He had to knock.

A cute black slaveboy of about seven answered.
This prettily tunicked novelty was none too keen on

277

today's spare, terse apparition but Vinius forced his way in.

* * *

Peace.

A pleasant central corridor with civilised wall frescos. Wood floors. Household gods in a niche, flowers in a posy-holder. Women's voices, relaxed and conversational.

After the boy scampered anxiously into the workroom, his mistress emerged.

'Don't faint,' said Gaius, as he had been planning to say. 'It's me.'

'*Vinius!*'

She had been tending Aurelia Maestinata who was seventy-three and saw no reason to change her lifelong style. It involved a central parting with three deep formal waves descending to each ear. For denting in the waves, Lucilla used a hot metal rod, which she was holding in her right hand. So, it was her left hand she clapped over her mouth to stop herself shrieking. Gaius immediately noticed her wedding ring.

'Flavia Lucilla.'

He simply spoke her name, in that low, strong voice she had thought she would never forget. The way he said it made Lucilla feel that someone in the world believed her truly excellent.

* * *

Her eyes. Gaius could not believe those great brown, wide-set, exotic eastern eyes that she had inherited from her mother had somehow managed

278

to elude his memory despite all the times he had thought about her. She had beautiful, beautiful eyes.

Lucilla was unable to speak. She was agonised with panic, shock, horror at the changes in him. His stick-thin arms, grey flecks in his hair, intangible hints of suffering. He even smelled different.

I thought you were dead.

No.

I thought you were dead. I thought you were dead.

Well, I'm bloody well not, darling.

*   *   *

'Maybe,' suggested Vinius, very polite, 'once you have finished with your customer we could have a word?' Appalling the slaveboy with his familiarity, he walked uninvited down the hall to the room with the couch—*my room, my couch; get used to it, sonny*—indicating he would wait there.

As he passed Lucilla, unable to prevent himself, he gestured with one forefinger, a vigiles signal: pointing at her gold ring.

'I married.'

'Of course you did.'

Ironically, Vinius had warned the other prisoners, when they were still his men: '*Be prepared. All the luscious girlies who swore they were yours forever will be fat mothers of three and married to tipsy mule-drivers who beat them if their dinner's late. The oldest child may well be your own, but you won't get the bint to admit it, so don't even bother trying . . .*'

How stupid to be caught out himself. How lucky he had realised his error in time. And of course

279

she had never sworn anything; in fact, she ran away from him.

'Yes, I have been married for over a year now. To a teacher of philosophy and literature.' Even Lucilla could hear her voice was flat.

Vinius, still the investigator, hissed: 'So where is he?'

Lucilla faltered. 'In Rome we live with his parents, in the Third Region.'

'With his parents? Trust me, *that's* a mistake!'

As Vinius went into their sitting room his voice and expression did hold a trace of his old good humour with her. After all, what was the point of blaming anyone? She had never been his, so he had never lost her.

He was trying not to let her see how overwhelmed he was by how far the world had moved on in his absence. He really felt like his own ghost. A dead man.

*   *   *

He waited quietly. Half lying on his couch, the one he once constructed from the bag of parts. Gazing into space. Revelling in the luxury of being in his own place, at leisure. Interrupted only by Flavia Lucilla's boy who kept bringing him nick-nack bowls of olives and nuts. His mistress came eventually, carrying two dainty cups.

'I make refreshments for my customers. I've brewed fresh for you.'

'Appreciated.' He gulped. A mulled honeyed wine mixture that must hold a hint of naughtiness for a bunch of women gossiping. 'Bacchus! Your matrons like their tipple strong.'

Lucilla took a throne-shaped chair opposite Vinius with a low table between them, the kind used for serving food at dinner parties: ivory legs, citronwood top, very far from cheap though it must have been her purchase. She stared, finally taking him in properly. Vinius was wearing a tunic Fortunatus had lent him; Fortunatus was a big man and the vast green garment hung in empty swathes on his brother.

She was wearing blue, with deep panels of embroidery at hem and neck. Hair in clouds of curls around her head and down her back. Jewellery; presents from the husband? She had not gained much weight but her body had rearranged itself subtly. Vinius wondered if she had had children; he would never dare to ask whether he himself had left her pregnant.

She was smart, fashionable, fairly composed in the circumstances. He tried to pretend to himself that the way she looked was none of his business, yet he drank her in.

Lucilla felt him assessing her. She knew she must have altered in the past five years, gained aspects of maturity, lost heart in some ways. Her hand shook as she sipped her drink.

'So!—Nice war?' she asked, keeping it wry for safety.

'Every amenity.'

'And what . . .' she finally ventured ' . . . happened?'

'Came home by the long scenic route . . .' Vinius was staring down at the table edge. He sighed, then spoke bitterly. 'No. As you see: a brief idyll in Moesia, then I had four years of ruination—a captive in Dacia.'

'Nobody knew.' Lucilla's voice was low.

'We guessed not. That was the worst dimension.'

'Can you talk about it?'

'No.' He looked up, however. 'Not yet.'

He saw that her gaze was kindly; his in reply held gratitude.

Lucilla burst out suddenly, 'I don't know what to say. It is just so good to see you.' Then, urgently, she had to put things right. Words tumbled out: 'Everything of yours is here. I can give you back your door key. Everything is in your room, except I used the money for the rent—'

'Settle down.'

'No—Your will was read. I was deeply touched. I have to say—I just felt, I was acting as your custodian. I paid for the apartment—'

'So I did the right thing,' interrupted Gaius lightly.

'I kept everything of yours—'

He was startled. 'What—for *me*?'

Lucilla paused. 'No, I won't say, "I knew you would return one day". I never thought that, and I don't hold with mystic nonsense. We believed you were gone.'

'So what would have happened here,' asked Gaius, waving a hand to indicate his side of the apartment, 'if I really had never come back?'

At that, Lucilla dropped her face into her hands, though she soon looked up again, simply at a loss. 'I don't know.'

After a moment, Gaius murmured, 'My turn to feel touched.'

Lucilla was fumbling with her earlobes, tugging off her earrings. 'I must give you these back. Understand, I have been wearing them for you—'

She reached over and placed them on the table beside his empty cup. They were small gold bars, from each of which hung three pendants ending in small pearls. Gaius stared uncomprehendingly.

'I was told they had been your mother's.'

'I can't remember her . . .' He was distressed. 'Please try to calm down. None of this is important. I am finding it—' He faltered. 'Hard. Hard to cope. When people are excited.'

Lucilla fell silent immediately.

*　　　*　　　*

Gaius picked up a snack-bowl, the one with enormous green queen olives. He ate one olive, slowly, then worked his way through the entire bowl. He looked as if he might tear the arm off anyone who tried to remove the food from him. He chewed each olive stone completely clean before replacing it in the ceramic bowl. Once he had devoured every olive, he placed the bowl back on the table, with a small knock that sounded much too loud in the completely still apartment.

Lucilla was grave. 'Shall I fetch you more?'

'No. No, thanks. Back in civilisation now. I must stop gobbling like a prisoner.' He stretched, arms right above his head, gazing at her. 'So. You married. Tell me about the new husband. What's he like, this paragon?'

Lucilla was aware that she flushed slightly. 'As I mentioned, he is a teacher. He taught me to read.'

'You didn't need a teacher!' Gaius felt oddly annoyed. 'You signed your lease. You and your sister were sufficiently competent to forge a "guardian's" signature!'

283

'I meant, Nemurus taught me to read literature.'

'Oh that's lofty!'

Nemurus. She's married an intellectual. Have to give him the once-over. The bastard.

Gaius had noticed that this room contained scrolls. Not in fancy silver boxes, but either in boxwood, or no container at all, just collections tied around with ribbons. Written works as owned by people who either lacked cash or were too miserly to go for expensive containers, but people who read for pleasure.

Out of his league. Out of his sphere of knowledge, anyway. He really had lost her.

'And how are you finding marriage?'

'Oh, we exist in a state of mutual exasperation.' Lucilla's answer was honest, apparently satirical. 'Absolutely normal, I suppose.'

Gaius stood up. Time to be leaving. Lucilla jumped to her feet too, running from the room to fetch his door key as promised.

Out in the corridor he took the key on its old wire ring, which he stuffed in a pouch on his belt. At parting, he offered his hand, feeling her shock at his weak grip. His knuckles looked too large for his fingers. He had lost his rings, stripped off him by his captors in Dacia, she realised.

Gaius then turned Lucilla's hand over, opened her palm and closed her own firm, slim fingers over his mother's earrings. 'I want you to keep these.'

Lucilla said nothing, once more too close to tears.

From the door he turned, asking sadly, 'Are you happy, Lucilla?'

She thought about that. 'As happy as anyone.'

'Oh,' replied Gaius. He sounded depressed. 'Not

284

very, then!'

*   *   *

So that was it. Whatever it was, or might have been.

Gaius had been in love with a memory for four years, but it was all a mistake. Well, it had kept him going.

Lucilla was too polite to say that when she had first walked out into the corridor, she almost failed to recognise him. She was so upset and confused, she never managed to say all she should have said to him.

Once he left the apartment, it was too late.

*   *   *

Gaius Vinius reported for duty with the cornicularius.

Staff officers in the headquarters unit, the Praetorian Prefects' back-up team, were responsible for all it took to quarter, feed, clothe, arm, locate, discipline and, where necessary, bury ten thousand men. He was first allocated the lowest, least-coveted role, looking after the property of the dead. It had been neglected for years. He was put to work on the backlog, which he did not object to, since it involved colleagues who died at Tapae. Identifying bequests and rooting to find legatees, even writing the sad letters to friends and families, was his kind of job.

Gaius buried himself, diligent and methodical, but the task affected him more than he realised. Finally he pulled up short when he came upon the unfinished affairs of his old centurion, Decius

285

Gracilis. He went to his room and wept.

For two whole days he kept to himself, wrecked. Luckily, no one noticed.

Shaking off the misery, he took his unease about the centurion's will to the cornicularius.

'So how much is involved?'

'Savings, plus property in Spain. Some kind of business.'

'Tell you what. We'll split the cash, you sell the land, then we'll go halves on that too.' Though uncertain how to take this, Vinius saw he had been a fool to speak. 'Only joking. Halves won't do. Normally the split is eighty-twenty in my favour. Just check that he never wrote a will.'

Vinius moderated wrath that welled up on behalf of his lost centurion. 'Oh Decius Gracilis was a stickler. There is a will.'

The cornicularius growled. 'Why bother me then? We do not override the testaments of our beloved deceased comrades. Tally up the value, pay the putrid inheritance tax to the putrid Treasury, then hand over the loot to the heirs.'

The officer misunderstood why the new boy felt leery, arriving here and straightway handing a bequest to himself: Gracilis had left everything to him: 'my deserving beneficarius, Gaius Vinius Clodianus'.

For some reason, when he came back from Dacia he started using all his names. At the Camp from now on, he was Clodianus. A weak attempt to distance himself from what had happened to him.

Clodianus pulled himself together.

'Right, sir. The loot goes promptly to the heir. Actually, Cornicularius, my feeling is, our regular split should be sixty-forty.'

'You'll go far!'

'Very good of you to say so, sir.'

I suppose you want my putrid job?

Just looking, sir.

The cornicularius was not all bad. On the verge of retirement, he was a rough gem of limited talent but very long service, who had been posted here when the authorities ran out of other options. Nevertheless, he made few mistakes—that is, few that came into the open; he was liked, as far as anyone liked staff officers.

He knew men too; he was a good superior. He now allocated time for a pep talk with Clodianus, whose vulnerable state he had identified. Even though he must be cursing the powers that had dumped this disturbed soldier upon him, he leaned on his tall desk, acting friendly and fatherly: 'Four years in captivity must have been hard.'

'I'll get over it.'

'Word of advice—that's exactly what you will not do, son. Don't fool yourself; don't keep waiting to recover because, soldier, it is never going to happen. Your experience in Dacia is part of you now, and the only way you are going to cope is if you roll with it.'

His new man, surprisingly, accepted the wisdom. 'I hear what you say, sir.'

'Good. I don't want you cracking up on me. We have quite enough head-cases around here . . . Anything else?'

Vinius spoke meekly: 'Quick technical query, if I may, Cornicularius. I'm trying to grasp the headquarters scene . . . Is "putrid" the new word?'

'It's *my* word, soldier. I don't allow fucking swearing in this office.'

Vinius returned to his work-station. His superior's slightly surreal sense of humour was just like his father's. He still did not want to be his father, but this calmed him, at least temporarily. Now he knew for sure he had come home.

He thought he was fine. But he began visiting too many wine bars.

*　　　*　　　*

The first time Vinius Clodianus was sent to Alba on duty, he tracked down Nemurus. The teacher of philosophy and literature. Staring at Nemurus during a public lecture, he found out that Lucilla's putrid husband wore bifurcated socks.

Clodianus took this morosely. She was a woman of taste, now that she could afford the trappings; she had natural elegance. She would see her mistake one day.

Socks! And I bet he can't screw her properly.
Men like that don't even realise they are useless.
No, but she will. She's had the real thing.

19

Domitian became more cruel. Commentators, writing afterwards, assigned this to the year of the Saturninus Revolt and the Dacian treaty, either a bad reaction to Domitian's betrayal by the German legions and his suspicions of conspiracy, or inability to take criticism heaped on him for buying off the Dacians. Certainly the joy Domitian hoped would greet his return failed to materialise. His brooding presence simply depressed everyone. He knew it.

This idea of his increased cruelty became accepted, a 'truth' that would outlast him by centuries, even though statistically Domitian despatched fewer opponents than emperors before or after him: Claudius, who was seen as bumbling and benign, or Hadrian, so cultured and energetic, both executed their enemies ruthlessly and in far greater numbers.

Even so, with the Emperor in Rome again, nobody felt safe. Anyone of standing who voiced opposition, or was perceived as thinking it, ran the risk of that heavy knock on the door. Sombre men with swords would demand the master of the house, while slaves cowered and women of the family knew not to try to intervene. Execution was a rapid, efficient death. Proud, resigned or terrified, victims accepted their fate. The soldiers were gone almost before neighbours noticed them, the corpse left behind contemptuously for the family to dispose of. There was no public announcement. Other men of standing soon heard about it and were warned.

Cynics said Domitian never became crueller, because he had been a murderous despot all along.

*   *   *

To fuel his persecution complex, in Syria a 'false Nero' popped up, the third since the real Nero died. Pretenders usually appeared in the excitable east where religious cults had an exotic backwoods craziness. Mad emperors gained mad followers. Barmy believers decided that Nero, whose suicide had occurred at a time of political chaos and in a villa outside Rome, never really died at all. People were persuaded that Nero survived in hiding; over-coloured superstitions even claimed he died, yet would be resurrected. A new Nero might arise as a Champion of the East, a heroic conqueror who would overthrow tyranny in the world.

This presupposed there was a tyrant. The sane never dared say so.

All a claimant needed to attract gullible devotees was to resemble Nero and play the harp; if his musicianship was appalling, it was more authentic. The first impostor had appeared shortly after the real Nero died. A decade later, Terrentius Maximus gained a wide following in Syria during the reign of Titus, fleeing with his harp to Rome's old enemies, the Parthians, who only reluctantly handed him over for execution. Now a third 'Nero' threatened Domitian. Obviously a crazyman, yet Domitian himself would never possess such charismatic power; it must be galling for an individual who analysed everything so deeply. He had to send troops to hunt down the new menace, troops who were badly needed elsewhere.

Despite these trials, Domitian made the year one of florid celebration. On his return from the Rhine and Danube, he celebrated a double Triumph; ostensibly it was for defeating the Chatti when they tried to cross the frozen Rhine in cahoots with Saturninus, and also the Dacians. Carpers complained that some Triumphal floats were dressed not with the normal glittering plunder, but furnishings ripped from imperial houses. Other subversives whispered meanly that the Chatti had been thwarted by a thaw, not conquered, while Domitian had not defeated Decebalus, only bribed him.

He renamed his accession date of September 'Germanicus' and his birthday month of October 'Domitianus'. Julius Caesar and Augustus had got away with renaming July and August, and permanently, but they had been very powerful figures. For anyone else, such self-aggrandisement looked foolish.

As the Senate was keen to ingratiate itself after whispers about support for Saturninus, members begged Domitian's permission to dedicate a flattering statue to him in the main Forum. This was good news for the scaffolders' guild: to suit an all-conquering commander and benign bringer of peace, someone had decided the statue had to be eighty feet high. It would tower over other statuary and dominate the public buildings. Domitian was sensitive about honorary sculpture; he had decreed that any images of himself dedicated in temples had to be made of many pounds of gold or silver, which certainly cut out cheapskates.

This was to be an equestrian statue: the Emperor in full uniform with a massive long sword, riding a horse so enormous that the poet Statius felt inspired to create a celebratory poem, bursting with pride at the big beast. He likened it to the Wooden Horse of Troy, burbling that it would last as long as earth and heaven, and as long as Rome saw the light of day. Any gambler who bet on just five years would have made a killing.

Owners of fine horseflesh tripped over themselves offering animals with sufficient stature and character to model. Whoever was chosen would be forced to present their expensive equine as a free gift to the Emperor. He might thank them. The mood he was in these days, he was just as likely

291

to exile them for presumption.

The huge statue would take two years to create. Positioned outside the Basilica Julia, the main law courts, it would face south down the Forum to the Temple of Caesar; an insult to Julius (on his punier horse). The base alone was almost forty feet long. A plinth decorated with processional scenes would support the prick-eared steed's giant legs, its fourth hoof being raised as if it were trotting along in a chippy manner, with delight at bearing its glorious rider. Domitian would occupy the saddle in a relaxed pose, with one arm lifted, palm out, as if blessing his grateful people. The image, which was already being copied by coiners from the Mint, would become an iconic model for future emperors.

Domitian had granted a sitting at the bronze foundry, to enable the sculptor to make a maquette. The Emperor would supply his own sword, cloak and breastplate. He would not have a helmet; that implied military dictatorship. (This detail had been meticulously thought through by a Statue Committee.) He would be bare-headed. For an Emperor 'bare-headed' meant wearing a triumphal wreath, and for Domitian it also meant with hair.

*   *   *

An attractive young matron tripped to the foundry in unsuitable jewelled sandals, carrying a toupee box. Everyone else was shooed out.

Flavia Lucilla introduced herself, while the sculptor peeked in the box. She discussed the hairpiece, perhaps surprising the man with her assurance. 'I have made the curls entirely round and regular. It is not realistic, but everyone knows

292

he wears falsies, so I decided a neat row works better. Even the best wig can never be the same as the real thing, because it just sits, with no movement in the hair.'

'And do I . . .'

'No. You don't have to touch it; someone from the imperial wardrobe department will fix it before they position his wreath. Just look away discreetly while they paint on the glue. I warn you in advance, the wreath they have chosen looks as much like a crown as possible, without actually causing offence.'

'That has been explained,' agreed the sculptor glumly. 'I have to show our Germanicus as regal, but not kingly. He has to be the son of the divine Vespasian, yet seem too modest to be seeking divinity himself.'

Lucilla scoffed. 'I wouldn't want to shock you, but Domitian will put up with it if you treat him like a god.'

'I am not looking forward to this.'

'Just keep saying how honoured you are to have the commission.'

As the crowds had been asked to leave during the handover of the curls, the sculptor gave Lucilla a private view of his workshop. He showed her sketches, plaster busts, wax models, the foundry, and several completed pieces of bronze. The body of the horse was in two hemispherical halves, which would be welded together on site in the Forum. A special crane was being built to lift the pieces.

She was fascinated by the artistry involved, though her general response was satirical. 'Being eighty feet above the pavement is such a good way to hide baldness . . . It's all a farce, isn't it?'

'How true. I told his attendants to give him a

very good pedicure.'

'Rough skin all filed off?'

'Trotters immaculate—though mercifully they will be hidden in fancy boots.'

'So you don't have to model the imperial bunions?'

'Flavia Lucilla, he is hammer-toed. My duty is to hide this aesthetically.'

'Some things must be tricky,' suggested Lucilla. The lack of thrills in her private life seemed to be making her saucy. She could have been twitting the eunuch Earinus again, before Vinius shamed her into respectability. 'Since the public will be gazing upwards in awe, I imagine you must have to be *very* careful in placing the lower tunic folds? We can't have grannies on their way to buy a cabbage craning past his hem braid for a snoop at the imperial tackle.'

'You know no shame, young woman.'

'Do you,' persisted Lucilla gravely, 'have to ask his wardrobe-master which side our Germanicus dresses in the saddle?'

'Now you're being obscene,' grinned the bronze-moulder, as if she had lightened his day.

Flavia Lucilla growled. 'Don't you think the real obscenity is that one man, an ordinary human being with a limited personality, believes he deserves so much reverence?'

'I only make the moulds, dear.' The sculptor sized her up according to the customs of his art. Having invited her to view his maquettes, he ventured into another cliché. 'Could I persuade you to model for me? I'd love to sculpt you as a nude Venus, emerging from her bath . . .'

Lucilla simpered fetchingly. 'I am a married

woman!'

'I can make you famous.'

'No thanks; my husband teaches literature.'

'Fond of the arts? He might be up for this.'

'How can I explain him? . . . he wears socks.'

The sculptor sighed. 'I assume then he must be either a multi-millionaire or *very* good in bed?'

Lucilla was silent, away in a dream. The sculptor kicked himself.

She was not, however, dwelling on that regrettable subject, Nemurus and passion. Her thoughts were of the fabled socks. The foundry's artistic environment had made her realise that the socks signified everything she objected to in Nemurus, because they were a statement. He selected his idiosyncrasies as carefully as the Emperor chose symbolic gear for his public image. What she hated was not Nemurus' footwear as such. As an intimacy of marriage, she now knew he had athlete's foot, though it was unclear whether he wore socks in order to cover the problem or whether in the hot Roman summer the socks caused it.

Lucilla could tolerate Nemurus being eccentric if either he did not realise he was, or he knew it and accepted it honestly. If he felt the cold, or was ashamed of his feet, or sandal straps rubbed his skin, that was acceptable—but she now identified that those socks represented his contempt for people. He was sneering. Nemurus had always despised other people, and now they were married he bullied Lucilla with this eccentricity just as much as the controlling Domitian bullied the Roman people.

In the end, socks were not what caused their marriage crisis. That was precipitated by another man, and not even Gaius Vinius. Nemurus himself was partly responsible.

Lucilla had told him of her work with the Emperor's barber. She had hoped sharing a confidence might help. It did make Nemurus view her as a little more important than a mere women's hairdresser, though he was so snobbish he never really overcame his shame in her work. Nemurus, who was currently in Rome not at Alba, knew Lucilla had an appointment with the sculptor. It had been something to say; conversation between them could be strained. Driven by some tic of distrust, her husband visited too, joining the public who had come to gawp at the half-finished statue. Typically, although Lucilla had given him the idea, when he saw her leave the foundry he made no effort to attract her attention. She dodged through the crowd outside without ever knowing he was there.

Nemurus had come with some of his friends, the evening set who drank and diced with him, men Lucilla rarely met. She still knew the literary circle, though she saw less of them, because Nemurus thought a wife should stay at home in the Greek fashion. Lucilla disagreed, but sometimes establishing her freer rights as a Roman matron was just too wearing.

The men with whom Nemurus shared his private life were coarser, and wealthier, than poets. They had no respect for him, but were denuding him of cash. They did it little by little, never too much so they drove him away, but cynically and systematically. Nemurus was no fool so he probably knew. Gaming for money was illegal in Rome, though it regularly took place; he liked to lurk on the dark side. It was also why he taught philosophy, which emperors regarded with suspicion.

One of Nemurus' unpleasant cronies recognised Flavia Lucilla. He was Orgilius, the businessman who had been Flavia Lachne's lover.

Learning Nemurus was married to Lucilla, this man swiftly engineered an invitation for dinner along with other gambling playmates. Nemurus was shrewd enough to feel uneasy, though he simply told himself the men would be awkward in his parents' company at home. He came from a family of stonecutters. They were good people, who had scraped together funds for his education in the belief he was a genius. Nemurus had never had any contact with his father's employment; his parents were equal strangers to his learning, though they gazed on it with awe.

Lucilla actually liked his parents. They might have been fond of her, had her marriage looked more successful.

When Nemurus brought Orgilius home, she refused to socialise. Her husband raged at her for not entertaining his friends. She gave some reasons. When he belittled her qualms, she even hinted that Orgilius had once seduced her. Nemurus was not a bad man, but whenever Lucilla resisted him, he dug in his heels. Since he refused to listen, she took herself to Plum Street, claiming she was wanted by Flavia Domitilla.

For two days nothing happened. She hoped she had escaped.

No chance of that. Orgilius wheedled the address from her unworldly husband. He turned up there. He bribed her slave to admit him, then kicked the boy out. He was thrilled that Lucilla occupied such a discreet apartment. After a few salacious remarks, he tried to blackmail her by threatening to tell Nemurus she had been his mistress. Then he jumped her.

Unluckily for him, at that moment Gaius Vinius arrived. Vinius had found the little slave weeping outside, clutching a large coin. The Praetorian took the steps two at a time. As he unlocked the door, he heard Lucilla cry out, 'No!'

They were grappling in the corridor, just by the kitchen. The man leapt back, but not before Vinius had glimpsed him, all mouth and teeth, thrusting hands, a hard thigh pushing Lucilla back towards a wall. She, white-faced, was brandishing the multi-tool that Vinius had bought years earlier.

'Everything all right?' Vinius spoke mildly but Lucilla saw his fist clamp on his sword pommel.

'Your lover!' Orgilius was enraged that someone had beaten him to it—while thinking that if Lucilla had *one* lover it would be easier to pressurise her into two . . .

'Landlord!' rapped Lucilla.

'I need a swift word with my tenant—' Vinius shoved the intruder into the couch room and held its doors closed. Though still gaunt, he was stronger than the now elderly Orgilius. 'Quickly—Who is that?'

Lucilla's heart was pounding. 'Orgilius. Lachne's lover. Sadly for me, a friend of my foolish husband.'

'What does he want?'

'The usual.'

Vinius snapped questions like a professional, methodical and neutral. All he needed was a waxed note tablet, and he could be back in the vigiles. 'You object?'

'Don't be ridiculous. I hate him. He forced his way in here. I told him to leave.'

'Why do you hate him?'

'Why do you think?'

'He assaulted you?'

'He will claim I was willing.'

'Were you?' Lucilla made no answer. 'Did he use violence?'

'I was fifteen. My mother had just died. We lived in his apartment. I thought I had no choice. Technically, I did not resist him.'

'Wrong: "technically" he corrupted you.' Vinius was angry, Lucilla thought, surprised by his black tone. 'Once, or was it regular?'

'Once. Once, then I knew it must *never* become regular. At Mother's funeral I found Lara. I escaped to her.'

'Does your husband know?'

'I tried to explain.'

Vinius nodded.

*   *   *

He let the bastard out again, saying to Lucilla loudly, 'I'll have my knife back, please. I've told you before not to borrow my tools . . .' To Orgilius he added, 'You're lucky. The last rapist who tried it, she cut off his prick with my snicketing knife. It took me a week to clean off his blood.'

'I am not a rapist—' Orgilius blustered.

Vinius sniffed. Praetorians had a special sniff,

299

which implied *one*: such hard men could not be bothered with blowing their noses, and *two*: it was a distraction before they disembowelled whoever they were speaking to. 'I heard her saying no.'

'She was leading me on.'

'Not my impression.'

'She was saying no, but she meant yes.'

'Get wise. "No" is simple: you don't touch her.' Vinius still held his sword grip, emphasising that he was a Guard. He was comfortable with his weapon; it was part of him, a natural extension of his arm. His voice was level. 'Not now, nor at any future time. Never. This is an absolute prohibition. If you come within half a mile of this young woman, I will personally rip your heart out. Just in case you think I am joking, you and I are going to take a walk together now . . .'

'What are you going to do to him?' gasped Lucilla.

Vinius gazed at her for a moment. 'I'll think of something.'

20

It was a quiet afternoon on the Via Flaminia. There were no big fires, last night's prisoners had been processed, very little was happening at the vigiles station house. For Scorpus, things perked up when Gaius Vinius arrived. After ten years, he strolled in as if he had never been away. He had even arrested a criminal.

Jupiter, he looked different. Scorpus decided that some of the heavy expression was acting, in order to demoralise the suspect. Not all of it, mind. Talk about gaunt; talk about moody. Once, Vinius took care of himself physically, but now he had lost all his muscle tone.

Heavier these days, Scorpus had less hair but was still clipping it short. He was now chief investigator. The interrogation room had been swapped from the right to the left hand portico at the whim of the tribune, but they had moved the contents exactly: table, writing tools, officer's seat, witness bench, map, nothing else to cloud the issue. Scorpus sat sideways to the door, the way Vinius had done. He, however, leaned back against the wall, with his boots on the table; that way, he could balance a scroll on his knees but whip it out of sight if the tribune strolled in when Scorpus was secretly reading an adventure novel.

Vinius had brought some frowsty businessman of the type Scorpus knew he loathed: pugnacious, oozing with cash that was probably ill-gained, flashing loud hand jewellery. At least seventy, he smelt of myrrh, garlic and unpleasant sexual habits.

Vinius shoved the man onto a stool. With their old teamwork, he and Scorpus settled either side so he could not see both simultaneously.

'How's life in the Praetorians?' Scorpus asked Vinius, ignoring the suspect. Let him sweat.

'I upped to the staff office.'

'Sounds important! Top contacts?' Scorpus, squinting at Orgilius, knew how to wind up pressure. 'Thick with the Emperor?'

'Oh best cronies!'

'So what's this bugger done?'

The ex-investigator clearly remembered how to insult witnesses: 'He is a child-raping, slave-bribing,

301

house-invading, wife-assaulting debauched pig.'

'Nothing too bad then!' Scorpus commented.

His manner bleak, Vinius started to interrogate Orgilius. 'Your name is Orgilius. Ten years ago you were the paying paramour of Flavia Lachne, the mother of a young girl called Flavia Lucilla— Scorpus, you remember her.' Scorpus had no idea what he was talking about. 'Complainant. Poor little scared strip of a thing, all on her own, very immature for her age, which was about fifteen.'

'She was just a slave,' shrugged the suspect.

'Wrong. She was a freedwoman's free daughter. Unmarried—and there is absolutely no doubt that she had kept herself a virgin. Only a pervert would interfere with her.'

Orgilius protested, 'She was over twelve!' Twelve was the legal age of puberty and intercourse for girls.

'Irrelevant,' Vinius snapped. 'Virgins and widows—the crime is *stuprum*. As censor-for-life, his favourite role of course, our beloved Emperor is very hot against stuprum. We cannot, in our civilised society, have respectable women interfered with by filth.'

Scorpus sucked air through his teeth. 'Defilement? That's nasty! Public crime. Comes under the Lex Julia on Adultery.'

'Doesn't every bloody thing?' The Augustan laws on marriage, regenerated by Domitian, were a byword. 'Do we still have the original case records?'

'Unsolved rape of a virgin? Be in the archives,' Scorpus lied. Over Orgilius' head, he shot a look at the Praetorian, trying to rein him in, but Vinius remained unmoved. 'Anyway, Flavia Lucilla can renew her statement—'

302

'Certainly not!' Vinius was terse. 'She won't be put through that ordeal again. I myself will write up the charge for the Praetor, as her guardian.' He added as an explanation, 'I am connected with the family, known them for years.' Both other men immediately assumed he slept with Lucilla. That, they could see, only made him more dangerous.

'Respectable, you say?' asked Scorpus, since the distinction mattered legally.

'Oh give it up!' whined Orgilius. 'She's just a bloody hairdresser.'

Vinius disagreed coldly: 'Flavia Lucilla is a trusted servant of the imperial family. She tends Flavia Domitilla, and our August Empress, and she looked after the late, deified Julia. Any jury will warm to her reputation. She is a hardworking and popular young woman, whose integrity is widely admired.'

'You obviously admire *something*!' The businessman tried turning nasty himself: 'You are not her bloody guardian. She is a married woman.'

'Next charge!' snarled Vinius. 'Not content with ruining her childhood, Scorpus, I came across this piece of dirt attempting to rape her—in her own workplace, her safe haven. He can't deny I witnessed the assault.'

'Oho!' Scorpus took out a notebook, then scribbled rapidly. 'So once the husband hears this, the charge ratchets up to adultery—'

'The husband is soggy seaweed,' Vinius interrupted. 'He won't even use his right to beat the bastard up, or have him buggered by a bunch of slaves. But if he plays soft, we can charge Orgilius anyway then get the *husband* too—'

'—For statutory pimping.' Scorpus finished

303

writing with a scratchy flourish. 'The lovely "brothel-keeper" charge. Encouraging his wife to wander. I always enjoy that; scandal draws such a happy crowd in court! I hope you can afford a decent barrister,' he told Orgilius. 'We want a sensation, not a walkover.'

Vinius viciously grasped Orgilius by his left wrist. 'Married yourself??' He displayed a gold band that vied for attention on the wedding finger among shrieking gemstone signet rings; reluctantly the man assented. 'And you're loaded. Would that be your own money, or are you blessed with a rich wife?'

Scorpus joined in; he plucked at the luxurious nap of the suspect's richly coloured tunic. 'What are you? Seventies? Wrong time of life to give up your comforts, man. Your wife is not going to like this, not at all. If you've kept your habits secret, this will be a ghastly shock; more likely, she already knows, so a public revelation will be just the final straw. A wife can't charge you with adultery, but she can ditch you, telling her reasons to everyone, and you'll have to hand the dowry back, pronto. That's normally the bit that hurts.'

Like all the landlords, thieves and arsonists that Gaius Vinius had reduced to water here in the past, Orgilius saw the game was up. 'How much?' he groaned. 'How much to drop the charges?'

'Not possible,' sighed Scorpus. 'Not for stuprum.'

'I suppose it's a domestic. They *could* settle out of court,' Vinius speculated. The old colleagues were enjoying this. 'Does the First still retain that pimply legal hack who knows the going rates for damages? Virginity must be sky-high.'

'We use an informer,' Scorpus confirmed.

'He knows the value of everything; his livelihood depends on it. I'll have to ask; I've no idea these days. We haven't had a corrupted virgin in this office for absolutely ages.'

Probably never, and you know that, Gaius, my man!

I do; he doesn't.

Vinius leaned down to Orgilius. 'We live in a high moral climate.'

'What?'

'Domitian will jump on this. It's not just informers looking for court pay-outs; Domitian wants the imperial share, to finance his building projects. You're rich—so you're good to prosecute. He's fascinated by trials. I know all about it; the Guards have to escort him. He visits accusers, drops in at their homes the night before a trial, and nitpicks all the evidence with them, to ensure the correct verdict. This is the laudable side of our conduct-obsessed emperor. You are still foul, and Flavia Lucilla still looks like prey to you—but the ever-benevolent Germanicus, censor-for-life, has reasserted ancient rights for victims.'

Nothing was perfect. Without Vinius to defend her, she would have been just one more abused woman who suffered in silence. And Vinius was well aware that he had mixed motives. Even Scorpus suspected it. Orgilius was bloody certain. 'What do I have to do then?'

Vinius helped himself to a note tablet. 'I insist on disincentives. I can't have you walking out of here, thinking you've got away with it.' *And planning to try again.* 'I shall make a witness statement, while you write a full confession. These documents will be locked in a vault—' *What vault might that be?*

wondered Scorpus, as he gave Vinius another look that said he was going over the top—'guarantees of your good behaviour. As I said at the apartment, you are barred for life from ever approaching Flavia Lucilla.'

'I am a friend of her husband—'

'You can bloody well end that.'

'Are you going to tell him?'

'Scared that Nemurus might stab you in the street like Paris?' Vinius finished writing fluently then looked up to find Scorpus with raised eyebrows. 'Yes, it's true. Domitian murdered Paris. I was there. He used my sword.'

'*That* one?' Wide-eyed, Scorpus indicated Vinius' sword, cosily tucked under his right arm.

'Lost mine in Dacia. This is the replacement Domitian personally gave me.'

'You are laying it on thick!' Scorpus reproached him.

'No. I am telling the truth.'

After eyeballing Vinius admiringly, Scorpus shoved writing equipment in front of Orgilius. 'I'll fetch a clerk to help you write your story. He can sign it as a witness.' One more person who would know. 'Adulterers can be held for twenty hours while the wronged husband gathers evidence, so we operate the same time limit. I'll keep you in the cells tonight, for your own safety. That way, Vinius may calm down and not kill you. I'll escort you to your banker tomorrow morning—then what about the cash, Vinius?'

'Bring it to me at the Camp.'

'Oh, so you can pocket it!' Orgilius scoffed.

'Do not judge me by your standards,' Vinius replied. 'Flavia Lucilla will not want to touch

306

money that has come from you but I shall invest it for her.' Scorpus and Vinius went outside to the portico. 'Try to lock him up with a vomiting drunk.'

'Always feasible.' Scorpus had now remembered Lucilla. 'This is the girlie who came calling just before the big fire? Pasty, timid, flat as a board? But you liked her.'

'The one. She's not flat now.'

'You cheeky beggar! You picked her up?'

'She was far too young.'

'You thought she was sweet . . . All this time you've been seeing her?—*Ten years,* Gaius?'

'No. It's not like that.'

'What is it then?'

Vinius sucked in air slowly then expelled a long, enormous sigh. 'What is it?—Scorpus old friend, I don't think I know.'

Scorpus clapped him on the shoulder. 'Apparently, you still like her . . . You look a bit lean. Fancy a Frontinian for old times?'

'I would, though another day, if you can wait. Thanks for your help, but I have to see a man about a dog.'

*   *   *

Lucilla was crouched on the edge of a wicker chair, huddling, her eyes dark with misery, when the Praetorian came in.

'I brought food. Relax now. When I've seen you eat some supper, I'll take you home if you want.'

'Home?' Lucilla felt bemused.

'To your husband?' Vinius suggested pointedly. 'At his parents, in the Third Region?'

'Not tonight . . .' She could not face a quarrel

307

with Nemurus. 'What if Orgilius comes back?'

'He won't.'

'Gaius, I think he will.'

'No. All sorted.'

'How?'

'If that man ever bothers you, go to the vigiles; ask for Scorpus, who will put him on trial. The statements are all there; you won't have to do anything. Orgilius is fixed and he knows it. But we'll take a few precautions.' Vinius, with parcels beneath one elbow, was making his way to the kitchen. 'That slave has to be sold, for starters.'

'He is just a child!' Though full of gratitude for her rescue, Lucilla still hated Vinius being overbearing. 'No second chance?'

Vinius glared. 'You must not have a slave who can be bribed to put you in danger. Promise?' Lucilla resisted mutely. 'Listen to sense. I have to be at the Camp. I can't always stroll in and save you.'

She smiled weakly in consent. Gaius went out to prepare the food; Lucilla jumped up and followed. 'I have not thanked you—'

'Forget it.' Clearing the work space, he came on the multi-blade she had waved at Orgilius. 'I don't recommend facing off intruders with a folding spoon . . . We keep this where?'

'Shelf.' Lucilla indicated. Gaius clipped various parts closed and replaced it. 'Would you care to define your mention of a "snittering" knife, Gaius?'

'Snicketing. Absolutely no idea, darling. Some gadget that men with hobbies use for hours in their den, making awful Saturnalia presents for their rich great-uncles.'

After washing his hands at the tap, Gaius

emptied two kinds of olives into bowls, placed a segmented loaf on a comport, ripped chicory and drizzled it with olive oil from Lucilla's own long jar, pulling down dried herbs from a high hook. Lucilla had never seen him prepare food before, but she knew soldiers could cook. Everything was done fast and extremely neatly. 'Being a man, I always buy too much when I'm shopping. All my wives have commented—'

Lucilla cut across the talk of wives. 'How come the timely arrival today?'

She saw Gaius check. 'Not sleeping. Dacia. Nightmares and flashbacks. It's a known phenomenon. The Camp is noisy, so I thought I might manage better here.' Lucilla started to speak, but he stopped her. 'Don't worry about me! What can we drink?'

'Grape juice.' She reached for cups from the shelf.

Gaius had a fresh mullet to fry; he was kindling the cooking fire, ready to heat oil in his square skillet. He had to use a flint to strike a spark, always a laborious process. Lucilla watched from the doorway; feeling herself sink back into gloom. He noticed she was so downcast: 'Bear up. Could have been a disaster, but wasn't.'

'While you were out, I thought a lot about my life,' Lucilla admitted, hugging a stole closer around her.

Gaius gave her a friendly poke with a spatula. 'I don't want to hear any grim stories.' He filled a beaker, making the juice go further with water, and plonked it in front of her. 'If you're intending to snivel, let me do the talking.'

He poured for himself, with a larger proportion

of juice. Lucilla reached for the flagon and levelled hers. Gaius tutted teasingly. The mood was light, a hint of how things could have been between them.

Lucilla studied him as he continued to work on the fire and the fish, while indeed talking. In profile, with the undamaged side of his face towards her, his original good looks were stunning. He spoke steadily and quietly, as if distracting a badly upset child with a story. He described his new work under the cornicularius. 'It's a big department, many clerks and orderlies. Registrars to maintain documents; copy scribes; accountants and debt collectors. I am curator for the fallen. When Guards have died in service, I secure their property and sort out their wills; sometimes I have to trace their families. I try to see to things properly; do a bit of digging to find out what the man was like. You have to be sensitive.'

'You like it. You are good at it. Was it a promotion?'

Lucilla thought Gaius looked oddly shy. 'Yes. Well, yes, it was.'

'Recognition for Dacia?'

'I'm no hero.'

'You were to me today. And don't forget, I know how brave you are: you left me your golden oakleaves, your civic crown.'

'Oh that old thing. I hope you chucked it out. Come and have your food.'

* * *

They had just finished eating when knocking came at the door. Lucilla froze, flinching with fear again.

'Sit tight.' Gaius went. She heard men's voices,

310

clearly nothing untoward. Goodnights were called.

It was late. The apartment interior had grown dark. Gaius lit oil lamps before coming back. 'Delivery.'

'What?' Lucilla's face clouded with suspicion.

'I thought you could do with a dear little heart-melting puppy. Handily, my brother had one. I bet you never owned a pet?'

'No.'

'Well, I had lots, naturally.' He was talking to calm her again. 'Motherless boy, two big brothers, doting female relatives; naturally I had pups, kittens, doves, goslings, a tame rat—my grandma would watch until I lost interest, then a sad demise would be arranged. Felix gave me a crocodile hatchling once. I didn't take to the snapper at all. One of my aunts helped me carry him to the other side of Rome and we slipped him down a drain. He's probably still somewhere in the sewers, eighty feet long and looking for revenge. I don't hang about in a public latrine even now; just in case he pops up through the seat.'

His portrait of a happy family life that she had never had disturbed Lucilla more than Gaius realised. 'Stop whiffling. You got me a *dog*?'

'His name is Terror.' Gaius acting blasé failed to convince. 'He is a guard dog. His father was a brutally expensive hunting hound from Britain, terrific, beautiful animal, ran like the west wind, breathtaking pedigree—'

'His mother?' Lucilla asked astutely.

'We suspect,' Gaius admitted, 'his father bollocksed an old fur muff. That was the only reason Fortunatus could afford him, because admittedly Terror is a bit of a mixed pickle.

My brother suggests don't make any sudden movements.'

'That scares me.'

'*You* have to feed him. So he will be devoted and will protect you.'

'What does he eat?'

'Raw bloody meat.' Lucilla's face was a picture. Gaius pressed on. 'And really big marrow bones, smelly ones are his favourite. Never, ever try to take one off him, not even if you gave it to him. Ready to meet him?'

'I don't want him.'

'Yes, you do.'

Terror was medium-large, with chunky shoulders, little more than a puppy, still lanky-legged. A wide leather collar hung heavy on his neck, full of metal studs. He had a dribbly snout, long tangled fur, pointed ears and no visible confidence. Fortunatus had washed him, so now he smelled damp. He was sitting up on his own rush mat just inside the front door, looking sorry for himself.

'He has been a night watchdog, guarding tools and materials on a construction site. Fortunatus has to get rid of him. Terror can't bear to be left by himself, so he barks and whines all night and the neighbours complain. He should be fine with you for company.'

'I do not want him.'

'We covered that. He is protection. I paid for him and he's no use to Fortunatus; I can't take him back. You must call him "Terror" out of doors. Let people hear it. Let them feel scared.'

'Does that mean—' Lucilla nervously patted her unwelcome pet, who shrank away from her—'he

312

has some other name?'

Gaius looked coy. 'I believe that in the privacy of a home environment, this dog likes to be called "Baby".'

Baby was sitting on his tail, but managed to wag it when he heard his private name.

*   *   *

The dog lay down and went to sleep. Gaius began to fuss around providing the animal with a bowl of water, then generally clearing up. He said it was late; he told Lucilla she should get some rest too. 'You're safe. I'm here. Leave your door open so you can call if you are worried.' Lucilla was not moving. 'Go to bed, woman.'

'Will you come too?'

'Best not.'

*   *   *

She had made a horrible mistake. Lucilla had acknowledged her desire honestly, but now hot shame rushed over her. Vinius answered at once, as if he had been dreading her request. He was a picture of a man who had taken a decision to distance himself from a woman whose interest in him was becoming tiresome.

He stood well away from her, arms folded defensively. 'Look. I just spent all afternoon pointing out morality laws to your mother's despicable lover. So, beautiful creature, although of course I want to rip your clothes off and throw you over the cooking bench—if I did it, I would be the same as him.'

Lucilla remained still.

'You are very sweet . . .' Gaius at last seemed awkward. 'I am honoured to be asked—and heartbroken that you look so disappointed.'

Gods, I sound pompous.

You must be very proud of that.

Head high but stricken, Lucilla spun off to her room.

She still half supposed he would weaken and come to her. Stoically, he did not do so. She had closed her door. Even so, she remained so alive to his movements she heard him pottering for some time—a long time, in fact—he chinked bowls, washed his face, checked door locks; he blew out lamps; she heard him speak to Terror. She reckoned he left his own bedroom door open, but she also knew he then lay chastely in the darkness alone.

All night neither of them slept much. Stentorian snores filled the apartment, but it was the watchdog.

*   *   *

Dawn came. Creeping out to use the facilities and run herself a cup of water, Lucilla had thought the Praetorian was gone already. But he must have been waiting until she moved about.

He was by the front door. 'I'm off to the Camp.' He paused. 'Friends?'

'Of course.' That was a lie. She had humiliated herself so much she would never be in the same room again if she could help it.

He came up to her. Placed his hands upon her shoulders. Dropped a light farewell kiss onto her

314

forehead, the way people did in families. Fatherly. Brotherly. Unbearably.

From the look in his eye, he then changed his mind and was about to kiss her in a different way. Lucilla was about to let him.

The dog went mad. His bark, as promised, was scarily loud. The moment he saw two people even mildly embracing, he jumped up in frenzied jealousy and put a stop to it.

'Bad boy!' Gaius was appalled, mostly at the dog suggesting he had devious motives. Terror wagged his tail, simply entranced to be spoken to.

'Good doggie,' murmured Lucilla. 'Good Baby!'

Gaius left for the Camp.

*　　　*　　　*

Flavia Lucilla curled up back in her bed and thought about men's fallibility.

She was profoundly aware of the legal position regarding adultery. As a hairdresser for ten years, her clients had often lamented aspects of the legislation which was, to put it mildly, one-sided.

A wife whose husband cheated on her could not prosecute him; she might divorce him and return to her father, but otherwise she had to endure the situation.

Women's adultery was a crime, however. A man whose wife cheated on him not only could take legal action, he had to. There was a special court for sexual offences; it was always busy.

A betrayed husband must immediately divorce his wife. If he tolerated an affair he was guilty of encouragement and, as Scorpus had told Orgilius, he could be accused of pimping. If a husband

315

delayed, after sixty days *anyone* could lay charges against the lover or the adulterous wife, as a public duty.

The law aimed to protect families from illegitimate children; hence the bias against loose women. Penalties were severe. An adulterous wife lost half her dowry and a third of her other property. A convicted woman could not remarry a free citizen. Her lover lost half his property and suffered public infamy, which meant he lost his rights to give evidence in court and to make or inherit from wills. Both the guilty wife and her lover would be exiled—though to separate islands. *Nice touch!* thought Lucilla grimly.

She buried her head under her pillow and thought about the added wrinkle that she knew applied to Vinius. A *soldier* who committed adultery with another man's wife faced dishonourable discharge. All over the Empire soldiers were sleeping around with enthusiasm, but the law was there, if anyone ever made an accusation. A betrayed husband might. So, when Gaius Vinius made love to Lucilla at Alba even though he was married, it was tough on his wife Verania, yet legal. If he slept with Lucilla now *she* was married, it was a crime. Vinius could lose his position, its accrued financial rights, his good name, his legal standing, his ability to receive bequests, his capacity to remarry and, therefore, his right ever to have any legitimate children.

This, Lucilla bitterly decided, accounted for the man's swift rejection of her gauche invitation.

She tried to forget what had happened, yet she went over the incident obsessively.

Vinius had no need of her. For sex he could

316

freely associate with any prostitute, waitress, actress, gladiatrix or slave. If he wanted a regular arrangement, he could remarry.

Neither of them had mentioned Alba. Lucilla never supposed Vinius regretted that. Yet for him, it was a once-only. An opportunity to grasp, but a relationship to shun. He might still speak of Lucilla as attractive and beddable, but men always defined women in those terms. A man with a strong will, who guarded his position and was particularly careful about his money, would not repeat the experience, however powerfully he gave himself up to it at the time.

As he had done. Lucilla knew that. Gaius had been completely overcome, just as she was. If she had stayed in his arms the next morning, she could have asked him for anything.

But Alba would remain just a memory, and not solely because it happened five years ago. He could tick her off. A conquest. Wonderful, but done with. To sleep with Lucilla again was now far too risky.

Only one aspect puzzled her: his loyalty whenever she was in trouble, together with the effort he was prepared to expend on rescuing her. Of course he had saved her from Orgilius. As soon as he unlocked the front door, such a decent man was bound to. Then there was no obligation to involve himself; he could have, *should* have, passed the culprit to her husband for punishment. He need not have made Lucilla dinner; calmed her with his quiet conversation; left his door open because she was terrified; provided a watchdog, at his own cost.

Sometimes he seemed so affectionate. They had an odd friendship, and the only way Lucilla could make sense of it was to think Vinius was drawn to her, but that he did not want to be.

She had to avoid him. She considered giving up their shared apartment, but because of her lease on the ground floor shop, where Glyke and Calliste did so well now, a move would be too complicated; it was not worth doing just to escape her embarrassment.

The awkward incident, combined with unwelcome memories of her early years that Orgilius had brought back, made Lucilla reassess her current life. Men and their deficiencies had put her in a hard mood. She needed none of them. She would be better on her own, which she could tackle now with more confidence than when she was younger.

This, then, was when Flavia Lucilla took her decision to leave her husband.

21

Lucilla went to tell Nemurus face to face.

Various scenarios occupied her head before she tackled him. Mainly she feared an argument, imagining that Nemurus would show how vicious he could be when thwarted. She wondered if he might even hit her.

It was quite unlike that. Nemurus behaved as if expecting her to leave him. Lucilla had forgotten he was a philosopher. Normally she gave it little thought but she knew that every day he practised accepting whatever fate dumped upon him. To endure her departure without anguish was, for him, an exercise in making himself at one with Nature.

For a stoic, a useful test in leading a good life.

'I spoke to your father just now, Nemurus; he is sending someone with a handcart and I shall return all the books you lent me. I do thank you for everything you taught me. I am grateful that you married me. But marriage requires the willingness of both parties to live together; I am afraid I no longer wish to do so.'

'What caused this?' The slight peevishness was regrettable in a stoic.

Lucilla described Orgilius' attack. To explain her escape she said only that 'someone conveniently arrived'. Nemurus looked suspicious, though did not query this. 'I spoke to you of my fears, Nemurus, but you brushed my pleas aside. The most terrible thing was that you actually told that man where to find me.'

Pity the poor woman who had to give a notice of divorce to the man who had taught her literary criticism. He was bound to be thinking about vocabulary, style, tone, imagery, arrangement and presentation of material . . .

But all Nemurus said was, 'Yes. That was unforgivable.'

Then he surprised her, surprised himself perhaps. He spoke with a warmth he had never shown before of his regard for Lucilla; he declared he would miss their companionship.

It was too late. Lucilla knew that if there had been children she would have struggled on with this marriage, but as things were she saw no point. 'Try again,' she urged him. 'Find someone rich, so you have no worries to distract you from your work.'

Finally Nemurus did snap: 'While you pursue your affair with that Praetorian!'

Lucilla flinched. 'I have known Vinius for a long time, but there is no affair.'

'Does he know that, I wonder?' mused Nemurus theatrically.

Lucilla walked out, with no more conversation. She and Nemurus had been together just over two years, though never had a home of their own. The household gods they honoured belonged to his parents. There was neither dowry nor property to redistribute. She had no father to return to, but she had her apartment and furniture; Nemurus never made any claim on those. There she would attend to her customers and live her life quietly.

She told nobody she was divorced. It was no one else's business.

*   *   *

It was a wild time to have upheaval in her life. A menacing atmosphere depressed Rome, with good events only making dark ones more terrible by contrast.

Domitian was pleasing the people. He had given them a *congiarium*, the personal gift from an emperor to his people, traditionally wine or oil in a special vessel, but now more conveniently a cash payment. He held numerous games in addition to other festivals in the traditional calendar, all adding to Rome's carnival atmosphere. He became famous for innovation, allowing foot races for young women and freak events featuring female gladiators and dwarves; he lavished money on spectacles, with regular mock-battles between infantry or cavalry, plus naval fights in flooded arenas. He had added two new chariot teams, the Purple and Gold, in

320

addition to the traditional Red, White, Green and Blue. He created a new Stadium and Odeum in the Campus for athletics and music. People were less than happy when he forced them to remain seated during a sudden violent thunderstorm, allegedly causing some to catch a fatal chill, but they forgave him when he feasted them with an all-night banquet for every Circus spectator, served up to them in their seats.

If the people loved him, the Senate did not. Domitian made no attempt to disguise his antipathy. He strictly controlled admission to the upper and middle ranks. Relegation was the least worry. Banishment and execution were a constant threat. It was said that the Emperor encouraged those who were under a cloud to commit suicide, to spare himself the opprobrium of murdering them; there may even have been some who killed themselves out of misplaced anxiety.

Like many men whose own behaviour is questionable, Domitian regulated everyone else's moral conduct. Vinius had not exaggerated when he warned Orgilius that the Emperor took a direct interest in criminal accusations. Women were charged with adultery while men were just as sternly prosecuted under the law against sodomy with freeborn males. Other crimes were fiercely tackled too. Supposedly one woman was executed merely because she undressed in front of a statue of the Emperor; this caused an extra dimension of fear, because someone in her own home must have informed on her. No one could trust even their most intimate household.

In the privacy of Plum Street Lucilla's clients, a forthright bunch of matrons, preened the

321

immaculate curls their meek husbands were paying for and ridiculed anyone who kept a statue of Domitian in her bedroom. If it really seemed advantageous to own such a statue, the thing could so easily be relegated to a little-used library or the horrible saloon where one's husband greeted his morning clients . . .

Even Domitian's own household became increasingly destabilised. His removal of state servants continued. Finance and correspondence secretaries came and went for no obvious reason, as if merely to keep the others on the hop.

Recent events still weighed heavily on the Emperor. Nobody knew the full tally of reprisals after the German revolt. Severed heads displayed in the Forum had been only one show of punishment. Domitian refused to publish details of those he executed; rumours of 'many' senators being put to death were perhaps false, but the chief officers from the two rebellious legions, who were caught, savagely tortured and killed, were senators' sons. Details of their torture—scorched genitals and hands cut off—were so specific it sounded true.

Some deaths certainly occurred; the governor of Asia, Civica Cerialis, was abruptly executed for unknown reasons, and without trial, possibly because Domitian believed he had encouraged the false Nero. The governor of Britain, too, Sallustius Lucullus, was put to death, ostensibly when he 'invented a new lance and named it after himself'; that seemed absurd but Domitian may have been convinced Lucullus also supported the Saturninus revolt.

In Rome, the vengeful Emperor then played a macabre joke on the upper classes. Members of the

Senate and the equestrian order received personal invitations to dine with him; he was holding a special banquet to honour those who died in Dacia. Everyone was so insecure, the mere offer of dinner with their emperor filled them with anxiety. Unless a man was on his deathbed with physicians' notes to prove it, the invitation could not be refused. All were terrified of Domitian. The more they quaked, the more he enjoyed his power over them.

Flavia Lucilla had joined the background team for this carefully managed occasion. Arrangements were on a theatrical scale. A master of ceremonies had sounded her out on the subject of dyes and skin paints, with which they conducted experiments. She was primed to attend with the necessary equipment, but sworn to secrecy.

One afternoon shortly after her divorce, she was collected in a litter. With her baskets of materials, she was taken down the Vicus Longus, through the new imperial forums, across the ancient Forum of the Romans, and up the steep covered entrance to the top of the Palatine, where she had her first real experience of Domitian's fabulous new palace. Work was still incomplete but already she could see that this was a building of staggering style and innovation. Crowning the Palatine Hill even more majestically than its predecessor, the new palace was designed to give the impression its halls were those of gods.

After the steep climb up from the Forum, the entrance had been positioned close to the ancient Temple of Apollo and House of Augustus. An octagonal vestibule, which had curvilinear anterooms, gave a preliminary hint of magnificence and led to the first inner court. A portico of fluted columns in Numidian yellow marble surrounded a huge pool; it contained a large island over which water continually splashed via complex fountains and channels. Every surface was veneered in expensive marble.

To the left was a staggering audience chamber, roofed with ninety-foot beams of Lebanon cedar; the vast space featured fabulous purple columns and niches which contained massive statues of demigods, hewn from metallic green stone brought from the far Egyptian desert. A monumental outside porch where the heavy columns were grey-green Carystian provided the daily setting for Domitian's formal appearance to be saluted by his people.

To the right of the entrance, Nero's dining hall, once beautiful in itself, had been superseded by a stupendous banqueting suite that would seat thousands at great public feasts. A hundred feet high and lined with three orders of columns, the main hall boasted enormous picture windows which gave views to fountain courts where intricate oval water features stood among yet more multicoloured marble pavements.

Beyond these first formal public rooms lay areas where most people would never penetrate: astonishing second and third courts, exquisite suites, deliberately confusing corridor links, sudden changes of scale or form or level, sunken gardens, bath houses, and a private interior which formed a palace within a palace for the Emperor and his family.

Marble was the principal material—cut, carved, polished, veneered, mosaicked—but Rabirius had been allowed to spend endlessly on gold too. Everywhere glimmered and shone until the interplay of light with the musical counterpoint of water from the fountains dazzled and entranced the senses.

*   *   *

Amidst so much glimmering beauty, Domitian's guests tonight were to have a very different dining experience. None of the glorious banqueting halls for which the palace would become famous were used for the Dacian dinner. A large room had been repainted entirely in darkest black: floor, ceiling, all four walls, plus cornices, architraves, door furniture and dados. On the bare black floor stood bare black couches.

Wives were not invited; each man had to endure the night alone. On arrival, all were separated from their attendants too. No friendly slaves from home would be removing their shoes and handing them napkins tonight. In the hall, they found a formal funeral banquet like those families held for their deceased relations outside necropolis mausoleums. By the dim light of cemetery lamps, each diner found beside his couch a grim black slab that looked like a tombstone. It bore his name.

As guests nervously settled, a stream of beautiful naked boys slipped into the dark room, all painted head-to-toe in black. These creatures performed a ghostly dance, winding around the couches like shadows, ebony against pitch, so only occasional movements and the whites of their eyes showed. The undulating shades finished their performance by stationing themselves one to each diner.

All the solemn sacrifices associated with funerals

325

were made. Black serving dishes were set on low ebony tables. Each spectral pageboy served his diner with strange dark food. Cinnamon and myrrh, the spices thrown on cremation biers, stuffily perfumed the room.

There was no music. No nervous chatter broke the silence. Presiding, more gloomy than Pluto enthroned in his Underworld caverns, only Domitian talked. The sardonic host chose topics all relating to death and slaughter. Throughout the nightmare dinner, his guests expected to have their throats cut.

Finally their ordeal concluded. When they rose to leave, no one could forget that Domitian's family had previously executed opponents when a meal ended. False smiles were a Flavian signature. Tottering back to the great vestibule, the disorientated guests then found that all their personal attendants had vanished. Slaves they had never seen before escorted them home in carriages and litters. At every step of the journey they expected to be dragged out and murdered.

They fell into their houses. As they shuddered in recovery, new terror arrived. Loud banging announced messengers, sent after them from the Emperor. Every tormented man now imagined the worst.

Exactly as Domitian intended . . .

*   *   *

That tense evening had been observed by Vinius Clodianus. Because this dinner was for the fallen in Dacia, as a survivor Vinius had been ordered to be there, to represent the lost army.

326

He was not required to smother himself in black war paint. Thank you, gods! The night was an ordeal for him. It gave him no solace for his dead comrades; it granted no release from his survivor's guilt. He would endure it as a soldier, but his mood was doleful.

He was dressed up in a hybrid parade uniform, with special dispensation for one night only to be armed within the walls of Rome. Over the standard off-white tunic, which soldiers bloused up short 'for ease of movement' (or to show off their legs), he wore a muscled breastplate and military belt, with his most decorative dagger. The belt was composed of metal plates, ornamented with silver and black niello, and heavy with its apron of metal-tanged leather strips. He carried the long oval Praetorian shield, covering his left side from shoulder to knee, exquisitely decorated with a motif of moon and stars behind the Guards' scorpion emblem. He had neatly tied his neckerchief; his cloak hung smartly. Most spectacularly, he had been loaned a gilded cavalry helmet, not crested like the usual parade helmet, but crowned by an eagle's head. Its full-face metal mask, with shadowed eye, nose and mouth holes, looked remote and mysterious, although the only effect for the soldier inside was to make breathing difficult.

'Very pretty!' smirked the cornicularius. He still thought that Vinius Clodianus lusted after his job. He could not decide whether to loathe his cheek or admire his hunger. 'Women who like a man in uniform will be lined up with their legs open.'

'I'm in luck then, Cornicularius sir!' The face-covering helmet muffled how much Vinius disliked the idea.

'Shag one for me, son.'

'Very good, sir.'

'Suit yourself!' the cornicularius grumbled under his breath, as he sensed that this fussy soldier would never take advantage of the hypothetical queues of good-time girls.

The official view of Clodianus was complimentary. From behind the parade helmet, he was conscious of being inspected by Rome's most senior men. He saluted so often, and so smartly, he got pins and needles in his arm. Both Praetorian Prefects approved his turnout as if they had buffed his breastplate and sharpened his sword themselves. The Prefect of Vigiles had a good word for him. The gruff Prefect of the City, most senior of all, was Rutilius Gallicus who had served as Domitian's deputy in Rome when the Emperor left on campaign and opened the city gates to receive him for his double triumph; Rutilius had less to say, though it clearly was not personal. He hardly spoke to anyone. On a night when Domitian was tweaking senators' fears of death, perhaps Rutilius Gallicus was remembering that he inherited his lofty position when his predecessor was executed.

Occasion was taken to award Clodianus promotion: 'liaison officer', a runner for the cornicularius.

'I think I'm going to drown myself?!' groaned that worthy, although Gaius was certain he must have been consulted. His own modest fears about the responsibility were biffed aside. 'Take the money,' ordered his superior. 'For a scroll-worm like you, it will be a piece of piss.'

* * *

328

While the guests choked on their dinner, the Praetorian had to stand sentry outside. He joked with himself grimly that his role was not to prevent unsanctioned intruders but to stop guests making a getaway.

Towards the end, he spotted Flavia Lucilla. She was sitting on the edge of the great courtyard pool. Hugging his knees alongside her was a misshapen figure in red. Vinius saw it was Domitian's dwarf, a man-child with an extremely small head to whom the Emperor often whispered comments on people at the court. Lucilla and the confidant were deep in conversation.

Vinius marched over and put a stop to that.

'Hop it, Diddles.'

The dwarf grumbled but ambled away, while a shocked Lucilla snarled, 'You arrogant bastard, Vinius!'

Vinius Clodianus removed his fabulous helmet. 'How did you know it was me?'

'Footfall. Voice. Bad manners.'

'I've seen you in some company, but that beats all.'

'The lad needs friendly conversation. He listens to terrible things all day: "Do you know why I appointed so-and-so to a praetorship . . . ?" No one will have anything to do with him because he looks so odd and they are petrified he will inform on them to Domitian.'

'You, on the other hand, befriend any freak at court.'

'Yes, I have even been a friend to you in a crisis!'

*   *   *

329

There was a silence, broken only by the soothing splash of waters. Vinius massaged his earlobes where the helmet had rubbed. On another occasion, he might have dropped beside Lucilla, but he would not sit where that dwarf had squatted; anyway, on duty in full uniform, he was obliged to stand smartly. Leaning on his shield, he held the parade helmet in the crook of the other elbow, posing: the noble warrior.

After fiddling with her baskets, readjusting her sandal straps and brushing off water droplets from her hems, Lucilla deigned to take notice.

'Nice rig.' She was really thinking Vinius had a strange hard attitude these days.

'I am glad you've seen me in it.' Vinius then heard himself give her a line even he cringed over: 'Once I'm released from duty, I shall need help taking it all off.'

'You are pathetic.' Lucilla grasped the handles of various baskets and struggled upright. 'Find another handmaid to unarm you!'

*   *   *

She skittered away. Vinius loped after her.

'Is this because I said no the other night?'

'Weak moment.'

'Give me another chance.'

'No. Don't pester me.' Lucilla had not expected to see Vinius, she was tired after painting wriggly pageboys black all afternoon, and the soldier looked so fine tonight that fending him off was killing her. He seemed equally unsettled. Tiptoeing around the matrimonial laws was hard enough,

330

but grappling with their own confused feelings was beyond these two.

'I know you want me.'

'*You* don't want *me*. Too risky. You could be cashiered . . .' Lucilla was testing him, to see if her interpretation of his scruples was right. 'Vinius, you are *so* wise! Think about Plum Street: you could be accused of "making a room available for illicit sexual purposes".'

'*I've* never had any sex there!' grumbled Vinius bitterly.

'Whose fault is that? Pious you, the noblest Roman of them all.'

The dinner was ending. Fraught guests began coming out to the vestibule. Someone whistled to Lucilla and she shot off, as if the summons was expected. She had scampered down a flight of steps. Vinius followed, but slowly; with his one eye, downhill treads always troubled him, and studded military boots could be lethal on marble. By the time he negotiated the obstacle, Lucilla had disappeared.

* * *

The evening was going disastrously wrong. Then Vinius ran into the dwarf again. Jealous of this creature's familiarity with Lucilla, Vinius was filled with loathing and wild fantasies. If the dwarf laid a paw on her, Diddles would find himself hung upside down in the elegant fountain until he suffocated among the sluicing water-sheets and his tiny feet stopped kicking in the spray . . .

'Be careful!' Vinius warned him off. 'You could be had for following a married woman around.'

'Catch up, you prick!' The dwarf spent so much of his time being pleasant to Domitian that when he was released he became filthy-tempered and foul-mouthed. Many men are complete opposites at work and at home. The imperial dwarf was no different.

'What do you mean?'

The dwarf tended to speak too loudly. 'She fucking left him. So get to the back of the queue, soldier!'

*   *   *

Gaius Vinius Clodianus was not a man who queued.

Storming off in the direction he had seen Lucilla vanishing, he followed his instincts and, eventually, much noise. He happened upon her, which was just as well because as he coursed through the spectacular spaces of this palace, he had absolutely no damned intention of asking anyone for directions.

Flavia Lucilla was divorced!

Flavia Lucilla was giving him the run-around.

*   *   *

She had gone to a bath house. It took a while to find her. Then, Vinius stepped into a scene so extraordinary he almost lost his equilibrium.

Every exalted guest at the Black Banquet had had a painted boy attendant; all those boys were now being hastily cleaned up in a vast marble warm-room. The noise was appalling: shouts, squeals and splashes, plus continual clanks of buckets and swooshes of rinsing water.

332

The conceited little midgets would not behave. Swilling the boys down amidst the steam to a tight timetable, slaves and attendants were red-faced and frantic.

Lucilla was near the door, rubbing a sponge over a reluctant child who suddenly made a bolt for it. Vinius blocked him with his shield, then dropped it and grasped the naked escapee. This forced Lucilla to paddle over, through the ankle-high wash of diluted lamp-black, or whatever it was. She was barefoot and wearing just an old sleeveless undertunic, having anticipated this dirty task. Her bare arms and legs disconcerted Vinius briefly.

She resumed sponging the boy so roughly it was easy to see why he fled.

'Explain?' demanded Vinius. '—Ah shit, your little blighter dripped dye on my moon and stars!' As well as the soiling on his shield, he was disgusted to find the hand with which he had grabbed the boy was covered with sticky black goo.

'Next stage of the torture. The diners have been sent home,' Lucilla told him. 'Their last scare will be Domitian sending presents. They will assume it's their personal executioner. But they will get their pageboy, washed and adorned, plus their fake tombstone, which will turn out to be a big slab of silver, and the platters they were served off, also made of costly materials.' Gripping the boy by his hair, she dredged off the last of his paint, sloshing water from a pannikin.

More outrage gripped Vinius. 'You are washing him *all over!*'

'Yes, first I painted his little winkle—what a thrill—and now I have to clean it off . . . One imaginative evening takes hours of unseen work.'

333

Lucilla gritted her teeth as she struggled with the flailing child. 'Don't be pompous. It's only the same as bathing my nephew.'

For Vinius the most hideous aspect was that he had found himself caught in this scene of watery mayhem, while simultaneously trying to start a furious argument with the love of his life. 'It is not respectable!'

'What a prude! You surprise me . . . It's all Domitian's sinister showmanship.' Lucilla released the boy, who ran to be fluffed up and dressed. 'Can you imagine household after household full of elderly maids and set-in-their-ways secretaries, when they wake up tomorrow to find they have to take in a gruesome little stage child with the morals of a rabbit warren. *And* they dare not get rid of him.'

Lucilla reached for Vinius' hand and dabbed at the paint, but his dark mood reached her; she gave up and threw the sponge at him. 'Oh do it yourself.'

As rapidly as the baths must have filled with the blackened boys, they emptied. A parade of imperial gifts, some human, was leaving the Palatine. Relieved officials ticked off addresses on note boards.

'When I said to explain, Lucilla, I did not mean this fiasco.' Thoroughly self-righteous, Vinius sensed he was making no impression. 'You got divorced.'

Lucilla was gathering her equipment, then pushing her way to a changing room. It was almost deserted, since most of the other attendants were still involved in swilling away the grimy water, or just descending into horseplay now their earlier frantic activities had finished.

'Turn your back, Vinius.' Her undertunic was drenched; she intended to remove it before climbing back into her other clothes, which she had retrieved from a manger above the bench. *'Face away!'* Vinius haughtily held up a towel to hide her. She must have forgotten he had once seen her all by starlight.

'You got divorced!'

Lucilla shook down her dry gown and, once decent, began forcing on sandals. As the straps resisted, she snatched the towel to dry her feet roughly. 'So?'

'You bloody well got divorced and never told me.'

Silence.

'Every pervert in this putrid palace knows—but not me. We had a conversation earlier and you never even mentioned it.'

Lucilla bundled her wet tunic into one of her baskets.

'When were you intending to tell me?'

Silence.

'What—*never?'*

'My marriage is private.'

Vinius was livid. 'And this sudden split has no connection with me?'

'Causing a divorce would do you no credit.'

Lucilla was ready to leave. She made her way to the vestibule, gave her name to an orderly, and a litter was called for her. Vinius had tailed her like a hopeful dog. There was no room for him in the conveyance, especially as those who had helped behind the scenes tonight were being sent home with hampers of leftover food and unused amphorae.

Lucilla gave the bearers instructions for Plum Street. A fraught transport queue was building up behind. 'Leave it, Vinius.'

'Am I expected to follow you?'

'Do what you like. Go to the Camp.'

'I thought I meant something to you.'

'For heaven's sake. I only just left one man I regretted—Goodnight, soldier.'

Lucilla was carried away. Vinius was left standing in the vestibule in his gorgeous array, while hard-hearted imperial planners with rotas to organise openly sneered at him.

*   *   *

As the litter bumped her homeward, Flavia Lucilla longed to weep unshed tears on his strong shoulder.

It was the wrong time of the month. For aesthetic reasons, even though her libido was always high, she kept to herself on those days. Had Gaius known her better he might have recognised the signs. She had dark circles under her eyes, she felt uncomfortable in her body, she was prone to making mistakes. Unfortunately, on such days she was incapable of taking precautions against the mistakes . . .

'You never do my hair as well, dear,' her client Aurelia Maestinata had told her frankly. 'Still, once you get to my age you will be blissfully free of all that.' Aurelia also had a view on the male reaction. 'Every month is a surprise. The problem is, dear, *men cannot count!*'

With three wives and many aunts in his history, Gaius had certainly encountered women's sudden flare-ups. He never dreamed Lucilla rebuffed

336

him for that reason. He thought it could only be because she *did not like him* (surely not?) or, more likely, *she was a teasing little bitch*. He called himself an understanding man, yet he loathed women who were unpredictable.

Lucilla knew she had just taken a decision she regretted. In the course of it, she had seen Gaius Vinius in his worst light. Petty, peremptory, authoritarian, unrealistic, self-centred and vain.

Aurelia Maestinata would say, all men are like that, just ignore it. Aurelia's tart good sense being unavailable, when Lucilla got home she drank too much from the amphora they had given her at the palace, and simply added new adjectives for Vinius to her list.

Nemurus would have called it hyperbolic auxesis. Vinius would have called that crap.

Gaius Vinius made one further attempt to court Lucilla: hating himself for giving in first, he called in at Plum Street the next day. Lucilla was not there. (She was curled up among many cushions in the back of the manicure salon downstairs, where Glyke and Calliste had dosed her with hangover and cramp cures; she had done the same for them on many occasions.)

The dog was gnawing his rush mat because he missed Lucilla. He had already torn down the curtain that normally hid the lavatory. He growled at Gaius, having insultingly forgotten who he was. Balanced on a stool to rehang the curtain, Gaius growled back.

He waited around as long as he thought reasonable (not long). Then he reckoned the trollop must be off wasting herself on Domitian's dwarf in some foul palace burrow.

337

Gaius gave up on her.

*   *   *

After that, his life descended into chaos.

He invited his brothers for a men's night out. He still did not want to be his father, but he intended to get drunk out of his skull. Felix and Fortunatus were up for it. Their wives tried to forestall them with requests to put up shelves, which they parried with traditional delaying tactics. Gaius also invited his old mucker Scorpus and even his superior, the cornicularius. Luckily the cornicularius could not make it; he always visited a brothel on Wednesdays where he had been going so long the bawd made him supper and most times he just talked to her.

During many long hours in wine bars, Gaius expressed his current loathing of women so luridly that his brothers thought it was a convoluted hint. They set about what they reckoned they did best on his behalf: fixing up Gaius with a new wife. Soon Felix and Fortunatus were negotiating with a widow who was looking for security; they continued manoeuvres even though their own wives, Paulina and Galatia, cruelly suggested it was a mistake on the widow's part to expect security from fly-by-night Gaius Vinius.

He didn't need Felix and Fortunatus to organise his life, he reckoned. Left on his own in a bar one evening, after those wimps scuttled home, Gaius found his fourth wife for himself. At the time she seemed perfect, being the type of woman who did not mind picking up a new husband in a bar. Just his sort of girl, he thought.

His brothers went ahead eagerly with their own

338

planning. For legal reasons, the widow needed to act fast. Felix and Fortunatus saw no reason why a bridegroom should be conscious at his wedding so they just supported their drunken brother through the event. The priest who took the auguries looked sick, but a cash bonus squared him. The widow's need for immediacy outweighed any wish for a husband who could communicate. So Gaius never told her he had married someone else the night before.

*   *   *

With the lesson of his father before him, Gaius did try to sober himself up. He was helped by the cornicularius. 'This is what I warned about: Dacia's left you a mess, son. Either you start sorting yourself out—today—or you can take your discharge. I don't intend to train you up if you're going on a bender that will see you out, like your old man.'

'You knew my father?'

'This is the army. You don't think I'd have any bugger in this office whose background wasn't known to me?' He always used the term 'this office' as a holy concept.

'What about promotion on merit?'

'Less of the filthy language, soldier!'

A slew of regrettable events threatened to destroy him; Gaius had to overcome his problems. He was supposed to be liaison officer with the military police—a body of investigators, arresting officers, torturers and prison jailers who followed up informers' reports. In his current state, his superior refused to expose him to this shadowy corps, whose methods were notorious and likely to distress a man who had a five-day hangover.

Instead, one day a nervous lictor, a magistrate's escort who attended on Rutilius Gallicus, came to ask for help from the Urbans, whom Rutilius commanded. The three Urban Cohorts were barracked with the Praetorians, though as the City Prefect was always a senator, and so a civilian, he never lived at the Camp. The Praetorian Prefects were quartered there, but a fine tradition of Camp life was that after lunch they were unavailable.

Deputising in his routine relaxed manner was the cornicularius, who found the lictor, wandering lost. Given the Praetorians' traditional rivalry with the Urbans, he decided the Guards must hijack the query. 'I don't think we want some cack-handed Urban twerp making a mess of this . . . Sounds like a situation where we might be helpful, Clodianus?'

'Happy to volunteer, sir.' Even pie-eyed, Gaius knew what to say to an officer.

'Going on what the lictor says, we'll keep this *very* quiet. Use initiative.'

With as much of that commodity as a man with a headache, slurred speech and his feet falling over themselves could muster, Gaius took one Guard to help, choosing a large one. His other equipment included a thin-bladed stylus knife, a large military nail, eyebrow tweezers (one of the centurions had a bisexual servant) and a toothpick (his own). Anyone who had been in the vigiles could open locks, and since discretion was called for, he hoped to avoid having to smash down the door.

Rome had a problem. Rutilius Gallicus, the City Prefect, had locked himself in his office. He was having a nervous breakdown in there.

340

22

Quintus Julius Cordinus Gaius Rutilius Gallicus had locked the office door himself. He was a man on the defensive, which to him seemed the only acceptable condition nowadays. Either the daily dirge of his office or simply the pathos of life in general had become too much for him. He could no longer cope. He found it unaccountably difficult to carry out the most mundane daily tasks; dressing, going to the baths, dining were all beyond him. Without slaves to attend to him physically, he would be curled up in a corner at home, naked and filthy. Everything had to stop. Since he could not do anything, there was no point in people coming in to make demands of him. So he locked the door to keep them out.

Having six names was not a sign of hereditary grandeur. Six names meant you had been adopted by somebody with status, because your original birthline was not flashy. Coming from Augusta Taurinorum was no help either. It was pretty well over the acceptable border and into the Alpine provinces. Senators from outside Italy had a hard grind to find acceptability. Julius Agricola had come from Gaul, and suffered for it. Ulpius Traianus came from Spain and didn't give a damn, but that was the Baeticans all over. A man from a province at least had a province behind him. A man from a north Italian city had to scrabble up every inch of the *cursus honorum*, schmoozing snobbish freedmen, squeezing posts from emperors' pockets, entirely on his own with it. You could get bloody fed up with looking solidly reliable. In Rome you could get sick of having to defend a home city that lay on the rim of the Alps. You could become exhausted by your wife always nagging to go north to see her family.

Rutilius was weary. He could not sleep, yet he was dead tired. He was tired with the heavy weight of the mentally sick, and he knew no way to extricate himself.

He was sixty. Sixty this year. Nobody of sixty thinks they are old; they know they are at the height of their experience, able to show upcoming young idiots a thing or two. Nevertheless, the start of the body's wearing out makes itself known. Hair goes. Heart and kidneys struggle. Energy hiccups. Dexterity falters. Sexual intercourse, if called for, becomes touch and go. At the same time, the demands of high office become greater. There is too much to do; the physical frame struggles to hold up. The mind may be overwhelmed by its burden of responsibility.

Rutilius was a Flavian stalwart. In his early career in the army, he even served under Corbulo, the Empress's father. Luck fell on him, moreover. On Nero's death, he had stepped into Nero's shoes for one useful honour: the prestigious role of priest of the Augustan cult, nurturing emperors who were declared gods. A cynic would say, bloody good training for dealing with Domitian. Later, Vespasian had made him governor of Germany just at the right moment to pop over the Rhine and safely capture Veleda, a German prophetess who hated and tried to destroy Rome. Rutilius never thought enough was made of that exploit. Perhaps by then Veleda's star had faded. When he captured her and brought her to Rome, now in middle age, she seemed neither mad enough herself nor representative of a sufficiently thrilling danger. As a bogeywoman Veleda was a disappointment.

The watchword was conciliation now. A new German prophetess, Ganna, had just visited Domitian along with the king of the Semnones; she was well received and sent back to her forest with gifts. If wild women were merely allies these days, the man who once captured Ganna's predecessor lost cachet.

Domitian did honour him. Rutilius was governor of Asia, a plum post, one of Domitian's first appointees. Then came the City position. Who in his right mind would be grateful for a job where the last incumbent had just been executed on a charge of treason? Arrecinus Clemens, a man known for his gentleness. Too close to Titus though. One of the in-laws who had brought up Julia. Too close to her as well, therefore. Even Julia's influence on Domitian could not save her uncle.

A typical story was told about the end of Arrecinus Clemens: Domitian, who often craftily pretended affection for those he was about to murder, took him for a carriage ride. Passing the sleazeball who was informing on him, as Arrecinus must have been aware, the Emperor murmured, 'Let's not talk to that slave until tomorrow.' It added to the cruelty. Arrecinus was doomed and knew it; he just had to live out an extra day of suspense while Domitian gloated.

City Prefect was a post where you had to work with the Emperor on a daily basis. When he was in Rome the workload was intolerable, the pace pitiless, the stress ghastly. You could not give in to

343

it. Plus there was the tricky stuff: never knowing what Domitian really wanted, never sure he didn't want you dead.

When Domitian was away, the burden for a conscientious man increased. Rutilius was his *de facto* deputy. Who could deputise for the divine?

To be left in charge of the city was immensely important. If anything had happened to Domitian when he went after Saturninus, or afterwards on the Danube, it would have fallen to Rutilius to close Rome's gates and secure the heart of the Empire. He might have been called upon for delicate diplomatic negotiations or, if it all went wrong, he could have died, as Flavius Sabinus died twenty years ago, torn apart on the Capitol by the Vitellian mob. He was unafraid of death, yet the anxiety subtly damaged him.

He worked too hard. He devoted himself to curating Rome, from dawn when good senators arose from their beds to dark hours by lamplight when scrolls became a strain to read.

The Secular Games had been a long trial. Rutilius had to organise them. They were the worst, because they were held only every hundred years, in theory when nobody who had been alive the last time would be still on earth to attend. Domitian altered the prescribed dates; Rutilius had to help fudge that. Then came months of nitpicking detail, dealing with temperamental poets and singers, athletes, equestrians and charioteers, priests, not to mention theatre-sweepers and ticket office staff who by definition chose times like that to threaten to walk out unless they were given a pay increase. There were constantly shifting programme details. New buildings to be finished on time. Then the

344

sheer bloody logistics of bringing everyone into the city and moving them out afterwards through monumental traffic jams, housing and feeding hundreds of thousands, stabling their damned donkeys, finding extra lockups for the influx of festival pickpockets. And, even though it all happened just the same as every other Games, nobody ever remembered just how much extra shit and pee would be washed into the sewers from the public latrines at a time when the public slaves who cleaned those sewers were hoping for six days of public holiday.

That was just one worry.

He was too close to Domitian. He saw the mistakes as they were being made. For a loyal, hard-working state servant it was too depressing to watch a man twenty years his junior wrecking all that Rutilius and his generation had attempted to build and stabilise after the nightmare of Nero. By sixty, you were losing enough friends and colleagues to illness, without watching more sent to their deaths prematurely.

He was going mad. He had stopped functioning altogether. He was sitting now, with unattempted work mounded all around him. Mighty trays of scrolls and tablets. So much work that he placed the surplus in piles on the floor like the short masonry columns that supported the heated floor in a hypocaust. Work arrived every hour of every day; he could not look at it.

He was sitting very still. He had been in a stupor for a long time, days maybe. A dagger was lying close upon his desk, though his lassitude was so severe it prevented him even killing himself. Did he want to commit suicide? He could not even tell. He had no energy. He was lifeless. No one could reach his misery. He himself could no longer analyse what was happening, despite a confused feeling that something must have gone awry. Thought had become jumbled at one point, but now there was no thought.

There was nothing.

*   *   *

He heard the Praetorians arrive. Irregular thumps indicated vague attempts to break down the door, but that was short-lived.

He heard a man say not to damage the décor; stand back and let him fiddle. Rutilius tensed. After some scratching and a muffled curse, the double doors swung gently inwards. A Guard came in, sucking a cut hand. He came in alone. He closed the doors after him quietly then opened just one set of shutters to let in daylight. He came over and sat on the edge of the table, still sucking the blood from his hand where the knife he used on the lock had skidded off and gashed him.

Rutilius did not respond. He made no eye contact.

The Guard had only one eye, in fact. He could have looked terrifying. His matter-of-fact manner belied his scarred appearance.

'Good morning, sir. My name is Vinius Clodianus. I have come along to see if everything is all right?'

The level way the Guard spoke was reassuring. Quintus Julius Cordinus Gaius Rutilius Gallicus managed to speak for the first time in days: 'Something seems a little odd . . .'

346

'Yes.' Clodianus placed a hand—the unwounded one—kindly upon the Prefect's shoulder. Rutilius did not react. The Praetorian lifted his hand immediately, taking the opportunity to pick up the unsheathed dagger from the Prefect's desk. The young man placed the dagger on a side-table and came closer again. 'Yes, I can see things are in a bit of pickle. But you've done a good job, sir, nice holding operation; now you can relax. I am here. Nothing bad is going to happen. My job is to take charge of absolutely everything, so you don't have to worry.'

A group of servants, incapable of following a simple order, pushed into the room, twittering.

'Would you all mind stepping back outside?' The Praetorian spoke politely, though his voice showed annoyance. 'The Prefect and I will ask, if we need anything. A doctor who understands these situations has been summoned. When he arrives, just knock on the door to warn us and let him straight in, please.'

The doors closed. As silence descended, the Prefect of the City found it easier to hold himself together. Nevertheless, he was only just succeeding.

The Praetorian Guard was seated now, long legs outstretched in front of him, ankles crossed. He had positioned his feet very carefully, as if he could only control his legs with great care, as if he needed the top one to hold down the other. It took a trained man to notice that. Despite it, the Guard had never let his single eye stray from watching the Prefect. Meanwhile he was prepared to sit companionably, applying no pressure.

He smiled. It had a wry quality. 'We can talk, if you would like that,' he offered. The Prefect was incapable of talking. He was sunk so deep in depression, he could not even move. 'Or not. Incidentally, I am the Guard who was a prisoner in Dacia. We met at the palace the other evening; you had the goodness to speak to me encouragingly, sir. I have not been myself since I came home and I just don't know how to straighten everything out. To be honest, I would appreciate a few quiet moments myself.' Motionless, Rutilius might not even have heard. 'Thank you, sir,' replied the Guard, as if their two troubled souls had, in fact, communicated.

So, sitting together in that room burdened with documents that should have been dealt with days ago, weeks ago, even in some cases months ago, Vinius Clodianus and Rutilius Gallicus waited for the doctor to arrive. A fly battered itself pointlessly against one leaf of the open window shutter, buzzing at the same spot repeatedly, heedless of the fact that if it just walked around the wooden frame, freedom lay inches away.

23

Ludicrous, thought Gaius. Here is the Prefect, who is in such panic he has mentally shut down. They have sent a man to care for him who is so chronically drunk, he is floating in clouds, hampered by a mile-high headache.

Watching over Rutilius, wafting kindness in that sad man's direction, Gaius considered his own predicament. He was in a foul pit. He had dug it himself.

For three days, he had been a bigamist.

He wanted to ignore the situation, but it could not be avoided and raised a sweat along his hairline. He was so busy nipping from place to place to dodge people, like a servile cook in a comedy, he could neither solve the predicament nor take advantage of the possibility of sleeping with two wives. That was on hold for other reasons too.

Caecilia, to whom his brothers had bound him, was obviously disappointed and intending to endure her new marriage only as long as she had to. For her, Vinius Clodianus was merely a legal instrument. Under the stringent Augustan matrimony laws, as soon as her first husband passed on she had two years to remarry or she would lose a rather pleasant legacy; time was running out. Caecilia was, Gaius supposed, his fifth wife.

Onofria, his fourth, he could hardly bear to think about. Gaius Vinius, who called himself a careful man, a man of sense, had married a stranger he met in a bar. After one terrible, sloppily debauched evening had come a desperate night, now a dreadful dim recollection which rose repeatedly like vomit. At the time, he and Onofria had convinced themselves that their few hours of camaraderie were a sound basis for a lifetime together. In fairness to Onofria, once she sobered up, which took all of four days, she did point out that this was never going to work.

For the last three days, Vinius had also been married to Caecilia, with a wedding ring to prove

349

it, something his fourth wife luckily failed to notice, being most of the time upended with her head in a bucket. With his fifth wife, Vinius was head of household of a neat, small, convenient apartment in Lion Street, and (he was astounded to learn) stepfather to three young children.

Caecilia had actually visited the Camp to find out where her bridegroom was. Onofria could never have made it, since even if she had had such a terrible idea, she was too queasy to go further than the apothecary on the corner of the street for medicines, which she took instead of food. In any case, Onofria would not chase him to his workplace, because she was an easy-going, hard-living, free-thinking, free-spirited woman, who even while recovering from a binge was only interested in wondering where her next night's drinks would come from.

As far as he knew, Caecilia must have been headed off at the Camp (where soldiers were used to getting rid of women who believed themselves married to colleagues), so the cornicularius had not encountered her. Not so far. It was bound to happen. Gaius knew his superior took a dim view of men who bamboozled women into 'marriage' even though it was not allowed. Gaius was heading for more shit than Hercules cleaned from the Augean Stables. He was out of control. It was remarkable he was not having a nervous breakdown of his own.

Perhaps he was.

* * *

Rutilius was deteriorating. Tears began coursing down his cheeks. The doctor still had not arrived.

Pharoun of Naxos: the official choice for this task.

Time for initiative. Gaius gave orders to the Guard who came with him: 'Go to the Ludus Magnus and find Themison of Miletus, who bandages up the gladiators. Mention my name—' He tapped his face. 'Describe this wreckage. Tell him I need help for a friend of mine. Oh—tell him it's a different friend this time; otherwise he'll wet himself. If he agrees, escort him politely. If he quibbles, rope him up and bring him anyway.'

Eager to put one over on Pharoun, Themison came promptly.

Rutilius refused to budge. They had to lift him up from his chair and shift him along physically. Gaius went first, walking backwards, enticing this great Roman figure forwards, beckoning with both hands as if he were catching a particularly neurotic pony. Themison and the Guard shoved the Prefect from behind, using a mix of respectfulness and brute force, as they manoeuvred him to a litter so they could take him to his own house.

'Better come as well,' Themison told Gaius while they got their breath back. 'He seems to have formed a bond with you.'

Gaius had to stay at the Prefect's house for a week before heavy sedation and various kindly treatments worked enough magic for Themison to release him. Before that, if he left the room even for ablutions, Rutilius became agitated.

The cornicularius was to say, 'I told you to use initiative, not get yourself imprinted as a duckling's mother.' Adding, 'At least you came back sober!' Then, snidely, 'Doesn't the Prefect's house have a wine cellar?' And the final put-down: 'Your wife's been here, by the way.'

351

At least the Prefect was recovering. Rewarded with time off for this achievement, Gaius Vinius turned up, not at either of his wives' homes but the Insula of the Muses at Plum Street. Where, so far, neither his fourth nor fifth wife knew he had an apartment.

Terror the dog was tied to a ring outside, so he could watch the world go by. He wagged his tail and let Gaius enter, without savaging his leg, then growled to show he would not let him leave.

Indoors, a couple of customers were having their hair styled by Lucilla and her girls. Gaius walked past this coven and into the kitchen. He made a drink: mulsum. The warm spiced concoction was everyone's panacea, though a man in his disarray might need something stronger. He cooked even a drink in the male style; his method was adventurous and time-consuming, using as many utensils as possible, tasting frequently, admiring his own skill. He was so ambitious, he threw away the first panful as not meeting his high standards.

He carried a jug and two beakers into the workroom, where the clients were now having manicures from Glyke and Calliste. Silence fell. He squeezed through, aware of significant looks that passed between the women; he guessed Lucilla would be on the balcony. He closed the fold-up door for privacy.

         *   *   *

'It's me.'

Lucilla nodded.

'Pax?'

'Pax Romana.'

'I haven't been myself.'

'I bloody well hope not, Vinius! I wouldn't like to think that's what you have become.'

'You were boorish yourself, woman.'

'As you so rightly pointed out, I got divorced—it was a bad moment . . . I'll forgive you if you forgive me.'

In daylight and sunshine, today they were just fellow-tenants. It was probably shaky but neutrality was reinstated between them.

For some time they sat side by side in silence. His mulsum was decent, though not as wonderful as Gaius believed. He gulped. Lucilla sipped hers, looking tired and drowsy.

At one point they both raised their beakers to salute old man Cretticus as he shuffled about down in his garden. They both sat back and put up their feet on the balustrade.

Eventually they heard movement indoors as the customers and girls left; Lucilla went out for polite farewells and, presumably, to take money. When she returned, Terror barged ahead of her; he threw himself on Gaius, putting heavy paws on his shoulders and licking him. Gaius petted the dog, though Lucilla must have seen him wrinkling his nose. Tended by hairdressers, Terror's fur was combed, his skin oiled and ridiculously scented with floral lotions.

With the other women gone, a still afternoon descended. The only sounds now were birdsong and distant street noises. After Terror calmed down and just lolled on him, Gaius continued to rub the dog's great neck for comfort.

'Borrow him if you want. You'd love the Camp, wouldn't you, Baby? . . . What's the matter, Vinius?'

'I'm all right.'

'You look as if you need to talk to someone.'

Dodging the real issues, Gaius described helping Rutilius Gallicus. 'Confidentially.' Rome knew the City Prefect was unwell, though not precisely how he was afflicted.

Succinctly but honestly, Gaius then reported his own troubles.

Assigned a reluctant role as his female friend and confidante, Lucilla listened. Gaius, who would unburden himself to nobody else, never considered how unfair it might be to discuss his personal life so intimately. He had known Lucilla for ten years. He reckoned he had permission to tell her everything. He could not decipher all she was thinking, but her veiled gaze added to the attraction. What man is not thrilled to have the attention of a woman who keeps her mystery?

'What am I going to do?'

Lucilla said briskly, 'You cannot be a bigamist. In Rome, marriage is defined as willing co-habitation by two people. You can only do it once. The second marriage automatically annuls the first.'

Gaius was impressed. 'When did you train as a lawyer?'

'Customer talk. If you don't believe me, take proper legal advice.'

'I can't risk telling anyone. I would be informed on.'

'You just told *me*.'

'I trust you.'

'Thanks!' Lucilla sounded dry.

Gaius rasped a laugh: 'The crazy thing is, anyone

354

who tries to denounce me will come whispering to the very team of inquisitors I now collaborate with.'

He saw Lucilla frown. 'Are you going to enjoy that work?'

'No. But this is the Guards.'

'You will need a clear head then. Stop overdoing the drink. Yes,' Lucilla reproved him. 'Members of your family are very concerned. Paulina had a word. For some reason people think you may listen to me.'

'I do.'

'Then stop being a barfly.'

'I am dealing with it.' Gaius poured them more mulsum; they both smiled.

'All drunks say they are in control, but I agree you are strong-willed.' Lucilla was presumably thinking, *I ought to know*. 'Besides, wine is just your temporary refuge; it's understandable. You never got over Dacia. Are you still sleeping badly?'

'Bad memories.' Gaius scowled. 'I came home, assuming I had left it all behind, yet Dacia won't loosen its grip on me. While I was there, the recurrent memory was something very different.' Time to tell her. Time to open up. 'We have never talked about what happened at Alba.'

Lucilla said nothing.

He stared out over the courtyard. 'That was a special occasion and we both know it. Flavia Lucilla, you could sleep with the man of your heart a thousand times and only achieve such an experience once . . . Mind you,' said Gaius, speaking ruefully for his own reasons, 'you could have nine hundred and ninety-nine other attempts afterwards, with at least some hope . . .' She did not smile. 'I thought about you every day,' he announced baldly.

'I was worth it then?' Lucilla's voice was a whisper.

He turned back. She was sitting on his left, so it meant bringing his head right around to look at her. Graceful in a light flowered gown, with rows of fine neckchains hung from two enamelled shoulder brooches, she made his blowsy wife seem common and his respectable wife seem stiff.

His smile was sad, his voice intense: 'Oh yes, you were worth it!'

Lucilla flushed. He reddened a little. Gaius prompted, 'You could say the same about me? . . .' Lucilla released a scathing puff of laughter, which he hoped meant her appreciation of him as a lover went without saying. 'Still, not anymore,' he confessed hoarsely, bursting out with it. 'Dacia seems to have done for me.'

*   *   *

While Lucilla slowly grasped what he meant, Gaius writhed unhappily. He was innocently unaware that she was thinking he had two wives, a sympathetic commanding officer and a large family; it was unfair to burden her. Still he insisted: according to his fourth wife, when he came round after that first night in her squalid lair, he had significantly failed to function. 'Apparently, I just cannot do it.'

Lucilla exhibited very little shock. Gaius would have been amazed how often impotence was a subject of conversation with hairdressers. 'That must be enormously distressing for you.'

Gaius swallowed, unable to say more. Broken by the relief of sharing his trouble, he dropped his face into his hands, elbows on his knees, welling up in shame and misery.

He heard Lucilla's chair scrape as she rose and came to him. Leaning down, she put her arms around him. He smelled her own perfume, plus echoes of other lotions she had been using in her work. As if held by his mother, he was enveloped in warmth and sympathy. Clearly there was no sensual element to this close embrace; even though Lucilla stroked his hair, her touch was professional. 'This grey over your ears . . . I could darken it for you; still, it looks distinguished . . . You are a man who has lived. Gaius, living means suffering.'

When crouching became awkward, she loosed him and resumed her seat. Gaius had recovered his composure. 'Time, Gaius. You will have to heal. Have you talked to a doctor?'

He flared up. 'There is nothing wrong with me!'

Lucilla forbore comment on the contradiction. 'Were you wounded?'

Gaius was still tetchy. 'Why is that the first question women must ask?' Onofria had done so. 'No. Not in the groin. I was hit on the head.'

'But might a head wound affect you?'

He exploded again: 'I don't use my brain—'

Lucilla toughened up with him. 'When fit, you used everything, including the wits you have thrown away today. Experience, observation, curiosity, ideas, responses . . .' *Alba again.*

'Hands, lips, breath, muscles, heart—but mostly the all-important dingle-dangle,' groaned Gaius bitterly.

There was silence.

*   *   *

357

Lucilla braced up to the easier question. 'Well you have to decide which you want. You can't have two wives, one of them must go.'

'Both.'

'The loud Onofria *and* the quiet Caecilia?'

'Both. Absolutely; both.'

'Well Gaius, make this the last time you let your brothers boss you. Stop them pushing you around. Grow up. Take responsibility for your own life.'

Now it was the turn of Gaius Vinius to make a massive, unthinking mistake.

'I know what I want—who I want. Get free of both these bloody nightmares and make a vacancy.' He meant so well—for both of them. He said it so wrongly.

Lucilla was hearing unpleasant contempt in the way he spoke of Onofria and Caecilia, even though he just told her he had voluntarily made drunken promises to one and exchanged formal vows with the other. He sounded hard, coarse, a little crazy. For herself, she would never fear any harm from Vinius, yet she was glimpsing a changed man here; she understood it might be temporary but he was a man out of control, a man she did not like.

At Lucilla's silence, he made matters even worse: 'All right, I know I'm a mess. But you can excuse the battle flashbacks, the drunken nights, the dried-up sap . . . Here I am, darling. Battered, but now all yours.'

*   *   *

Oh no. Calling her 'darling' was terrible. She had always hated the mocking insincerity of the

358

way he used that word. But that was just the tip of her wrath, and Gaius could see how his lack of refinement was destroying their relationship.

Flavia Lucilla jumped to her feet. Deep in her eyes burned a fierce message that a man with five wives recognised: a diatribe was about to fell him like a tree struck by lightning. 'How convenient—I can be sixth in the parade?'

The dog slid down off his lap and quailed against his chair. 'That came out wrong,' Gaius admitted hurriedly.

'Really? You forget—I have seen how you treat wives. Who wants to be pushed out of the way while you grease your way off to some new refuge, your next secret "investment", to confide in some new safe co-tenant, who may let you seduce her when she's desperate but who will have no claim on you?'

'I have had my faults—'

'Yes.'

'But you would be different.'

'The promise you made to all those neglected wives!'

'No!'

'Two believe they still own you, even while you are pouring your heart out to me.'

'*Because* you are different—'

'Because you take me for an idiot. You imagine I am just waiting to be a substitute, the next chained captive in your pathetic triumph.' Lucilla shuddered. 'This is my home. Don't come to my home and behave like a dumb soldier. I have been a wife—to a good man, who for all his faults offered affection and respect.' She knew how to make Vinius jealous.

'I respect you.'

'Don't insult me. You are a disgrace, Vinius.'

'So my wives tell me.'

She stormed off. The dog, who knew how to make choices, slunk after her. Vinius sat on the balcony with the wreckage of his hopes, until there was no point sitting alone any longer. He left the apartment without speaking again to Lucilla.

That was that then.

He had ruined it.

Everything was over.

*   *   *

The Praetorian knew it would be self-destructive to spurn Lucilla's good advice. She would have been surprised how much of it he followed. Step by step he reclaimed his life.

He said goodbye to Onofria. He took her a generous amount of money and was surprised when she good-heartedly waved him and his cash away. He left the pay-off even so.

He agreed with Caecilia that although he was retreating to the Camp, she could consider herself married to him until she received her legacy. He could be civilised about it. There was no rush; he would not be marrying anybody else. Being honest, it was a fair certainty he would never be married again. He wanted no more second best. There were financial and career penalties for unmarried men, worse for those who refused to be fathers; he would live with that.

He consulted Themison of Miletus about his dysfunction. Themison paid great attention to the wound on his head, noting with interest how irascible interest in the skull depression made

360

Gaius, who still considered it irrelevant. Then the doctor told him this happened even to gladiators, happened to those sex gods regularly. Give it six months. Be abstemious with drink. Then stick with his best girl, relax and keep in practice. Gaius amused himself wondering what his best girl would say, if asked to make herself available for therapeutic purposes.

He returned to the Camp. He smartened up for the cornicularius. He approached his work in a mature and conscientious manner, as he always used to do. He was now assigned to investigating the public. He stuck with the task without self-loathing, though it made him twisted and cynical. That worked well as a state of mind for a Praetorian.

He drank no wine for a month. He resumed only at his old measured pace, apart from occasional evenings with Scorpus, though they tended to be more interested in the aniseed and savoury delights of Chicken Frontinian, or for Scorpus, sausage in a ring, with double fish pickle. Once a month Gaius submitted to a night in a bar with the cornicularius, which they called 'catching up on the paperwork'. Those rather stiff occasions cemented what became a gruff friendship. Now that Gaius had to deal with Domitian's informers, with their sour reports of adultery, sedition and treason, he needed somebody who understood his work. His duties were grisly, verging on the unacceptable.

*   *   *

He imposed new rules on Felix and Fortunatus.

He took them to a bar, set up the most expensive

flagon to show there were no hard feelings, then announced: 'Every time I look up from picking the fluff out of my bellybutton, you two have married me off again. Some woman I never met before, who wants intimacy five times a night and thinks I'm made of money.'

'You know we always look after you,' said Felix, moved by this appreciation.

'You are our little brother,' Fortunatus added fondly.

'I don't want to appear ungrateful, but there are limits.'

'What brought this on?' marvelled Fortunatus.

Gaius refused to answer.

'Give him another drink,' urged Felix.

Gaius insisted: 'It has to stop.'

Felix paused to effect his famous fart, then commented portentously: 'Titan's turds! Baby Brother must have found love.'

'Shit! Is it because Caecilia is a widow?' Fortunatus wheedled. 'Are someone else's nippers too much to take on?'

'Now you've done it!' muttered Felix.

Gaius stood up. His brothers assumed he was going off to order a new round of drinks, but he was leaving.

'No,' he announced. 'It is because I am thirty-three years old, and I don't need nursemaids. Next time I get shackled to some horrible mistake, I want to pick my own.' Then he added, in a steady voice, considering: 'But it won't happen. Marriage is for procreating children and I cannot do it, lads. I've got Sailor's Wilt, Soldier Boy's Droop, Ex-Prisoner's Prick. You just tell your next lovely widow that it wouldn't be fair.'

For once both his brothers were reduced to silence. After Gaius had marched from the tavern, the horror-struck Fortunatus did fart again, but it was involuntary, caused by shock, and far from his usual heroic standard.

After a time Felix found his voice. 'Be fair to the boy. It must have taken guts to tell us that.'

They continued to drink, without speaking, for a long time.

*   *   *

Gaius Vinius Clodianus lived at the Camp and got on with being what Flavia Lucilla had called him: a dumb soldier.

PART 5

Rome: AD 91–93

Our Master and God

24

The quarrel between Gaius Vinius and Flavia Lucilla was hard and upsetting. It involved pointed, bitter silences aimed, from behind closed doors, across the corridor at Plum Street. They easily sustained the feud for a year.

Both became adept at avoiding each other. Sharing the same apartment could have been impossible, especially as Gaius now made a point of being there to irritate Lucilla with his ownership. They mastered a fine art of leaving a dish carefully positioned, to mark kitchen territory; Gaius would elaborate this by rewashing a supposedly cleaned saucepan of Lucilla's to show how scouring was done by experts. Doors would open silently but click closed again, avoiding a face-to-face meeting. The watchdog became a constant battleground over petting rights, though Terror was in heaven, rightly thinking he now had two doting owners. Gaius brought him horrendous marrow bones, deliberately leaving them in the corridor, so as soon as the dog lost interest Lucilla would kick them out of doors furiously, with their comet-trail of flies. Gaius returned them. 'Here, Terror—nice boney!'

Once, once only, Gaius came upon and ate two cold artichoke bottoms that were not his.

This was a dangerous moment. Lucilla spent a wrathful night, mentally planning vile torrents of recrimination, but she overslept and he hastily bought a whole netful next morning before he had to face her. She would have to prepare and marinade the new chokes, which caused plenty of bile, but Gaius kept out of her way for a month.

Once she did weaken. Coming home between visiting clients, she heard a troubled shout. From the open doorway of the sitting room, she saw Gaius had dozed off on the couch. He was frowning, his jaw clenched, one hand forming a fist. As dreams distressed him, he let out fitful gasps. Aware of his deep need for sleep, Lucilla slipped among the furniture, to close the heavy wooden shutters, muffling light and noise. After she finished lunch, she looked in again. Now Gaius slept peacefully. The watchdog had shoved in beside him. Although Baby was not allowed up on cushions, he had mastered sneaking up onto the four-foot-wide couch one paw at a time; Gaius must have woken enough to allow it and massage the loose skin under the dog's collar, where his hand remained. She left them together.

*   *   *

In between were long periods when she and Gaius were in different places and so never had to meet. Lucilla was able to focus her antipathy on the distasteful work in which he was now involved, the results of which were well known at court and throughout society.

Rome had never been a liberal environment, but its atmosphere had decidedly altered. One man could not single-handedly wreak this change. Domitian relied on people's indifference, their compliance, their complaisance. He also needed his soldiers, his undercover inquisitors, his brutal enforcers. He needed the Guards.

The Praetorians' remit had always been

368

threefold: imperial protection, suppression of public disturbances and discouraging plots. An emperor's measures against plots could be as innocuous as Vespasian's edict ordering food shops to sell only lentil and barley dishes, so boring that nobody would hang around talking politics. Or they could extend fear and betrayal like sinister tentacles into all areas of home and business life. That was Domitian's way. Vinius Clodianus now had to work spreading the fear.

Strictly speaking, the wider supervision of law and order, including intelligence collection, came under the Urban Cohorts, governed by their Prefect, Rutilius Gallicus. He had a reputation for restraint and fairness, although trying to reconcile such an attitude to Domitian's punishing regime could well have helped his mental health deteriorate. The Urbans supervised the triumvirs, a board of three who organised the ceremonious burning of seditious books—or books that Domitian called seditious—a bonfire in the Forum that was now lit with depressing regularity. They ran the political espionage team who investigated treason and social crimes. They carried out interrogations, often using torture, even though that was recognised as unreliable because some suspects were too tough to give in, while others collapsed at the first hint of menace and would say anything they thought the arresting officer wanted to hear.

As censor, chief magistrate and as Pontifex Maximus or chief priest, the Emperor himself judged many criminal proceedings. If Rome was a collective household, Domitian was its head. He presided over serious trials. Theoretically, he

369

would never initiate charges himself, but when names were handed in by informers, the facts (or fantasies) had to be checked to gauge the likelihood of securing a conviction; where Domitian was the judge, his Praetorians liaised closely with the Urban Cohorts. Vinius Clodianus helped the Urbans evaluate cases and gave them ideas for following up evidence.

He was startled by what he saw. As censor, Domitian's actions were meticulously correct, yet some seemed crazy and unjust; he ordered that when a juryman was convicted of taking bribes, all his colleagues on that jury should be punished too. He expelled someone from the Senate because he had acted in pantomimes. An ex-centurion was proved to be a slave after many years living as a free citizen; he was returned to slavery with his original master. Charges that the Emperor hounded married women for adultery were coloured with tales that he had often seduced the women himself first—though at Plum Street Clodianus once overheard one of Lucilla's clients maintaining that if true, the women would not submit quietly but would come out and accuse him openly. What was there to lose? And why should Domitian get away with it? (Lucilla realised Vinius was in the apartment and shut the woman up fast.)

Sometimes accusations revived old injuries: Vespasian had once decided not to prosecute an opponent called Mettius Pompusianus, declaring that leniency would force him to be grateful and therefore loyal. Domitian first exiled Pompusianus to Corsica, then put him to death for having a map of the world painted on his bedroom walls, indicating supposed political ambitions. The man had also taken an interest in historical royalty. Studying bad rulers from the past was always seen as suspicious by bad rulers of the present; a philosopher died after an unwise speech criticised tyrants.

Domitian had no compunction about making an attack personal. Aelius Lamia perished; his only crime was to have been Domitia Longina's first husband. Although at one point Domitian had made him consul, Lamia was never reconciled; he took his loss hard and made no secret of it. Someone complimented him on his voice; he joked that he had given up sex and gone into training (as vocalists did). Then when Titus once urged him to remarry, Lamia scoffed, 'Why—are you looking for a wife yourself?' In the end, he was prosecuted on a trumped-up charge. He was supposed to have composed libellous verse.

The written word was always dangerous. Suspicion was so invasive that on two occasions issues of intellectual freedom drove Gaius and Lucilla further apart. What Lucilla had heard about Vinius at work, in gossip from his family, convinced her that he had become an accomplice to Domitian's repression.

The first time they clashed was at the home of Felix and Paulina when Lucilla was invited for Marcia's birthday. Vinius did not attend the meal, but turned up with a present for the young girl afterwards. It was raining; he was wearing his hooded military cloak and although he unfastened the front toggles, he kept it on so was clearly not staying. To avoid him, Lucilla stepped out on a sun terrace 'for air', but he followed her.

It was ages since he had spoken to her directly.

He came out munching cake in a casual way, but the confrontation was preplanned because he quickly broached the unusual subject of a poem by her friend Statius, about Rutilius Gallicus. This happened after the City Prefect regained his health and resumed his duties. How Vinius knew about the poem was never clear, for Statius had not yet published his collection; an informer must have gone to one of the poet's popular readings, heard him recite a draft addressed to Rutilius, and made an insinuating report.

'The piece began, "Rutilius has recovered, thank you, gods; you do exist!" Makes you vomit,' declared Vinius, a frank critic.

'Papinius Statius writes in what is called the mannerist style,' Lucilla replied in a haughty tone, staring out at the rain which had come on suddenly earlier and still drenched the empty streets. A damp breeze chilled her arms; she huddled in her stole. 'Much as I like him, I agree the heavy classical allusion can seem overdone.'

'He must be taking the piss.'

'He writes occasional poems to mark public events, or poems of friendship. Celebrating a marriage, bon voyage, a new bath house—'

'Lament for a dead parrot!' snorted Vinius. Lucilla was already dismayed, then he went into startling detail: 'Listen: in this Rutilius effort, according to your crazy poet friend, the god Apollo and his medico son Aesculapius personally flew here and saved the Prefect with a mystical infusion of some herb called dittany from Crete. What rubbish. It's an insult to the excellent Themison of Miletus, who I know used a very successful healing regime based on sympathy and rest. One passage

372

described Rutilius sprawled and inert—it mentions overwork, lack of sleep, how he was frozen in inactivity—'

Alarmed, Lucilla interrupted, 'Is this an official visit?'

Vinius stared at the depressing weather.

'Gaius Vinius, are you *interrogating* me?'

'If it was official I would have the militia outside.' *Inside in fact, with you tied to a chair . . .* 'One question: I see nothing to be ashamed of in the man's collapse. Rutilius seems open about it. Everyone knew he was unwell. But to avoid a crisis of confidence, it was officially decided not to give out exact details.'

Lucilla finally understood. 'You think *I* told Statius what happened?'

'I am trying not to believe that.'

'You're scared you'll get into trouble for having said too much to me!'

Vinius glowered. 'Think that if you must. So, Flavia Lucilla, did you pass on what I told you?'

'No.'

'Thank you.'

Although bitterly resentful, Lucilla tried to diffuse trouble: 'Rutilius writes; he attends the literary circle. During his recovery he talked freely about his symptoms. He told Statius himself.'

'Fine.'

'Is that it? You are not much of an interrogator; what if I am lying?'

'Are you?'

'No.'

'Case closed then.' Vinius shrugged. Refastening his cloak toggles, he appeared to be leaving. 'Sorry. Mistrust festers, until even the innocent are seen as guilty. The worst is, it takes almost nothing to make you *feel* guilty.'

'It must be hard to do your job,' sneered Lucilla.

'Better I do it, than somebody less scrupulous,' said Gaius briefly, as he left her alone on the wet terrace.

Perhaps he really believed that.

* * *

She called after him from the doorway. 'I thought you might mention artichokes!'

All the family indoors were listening. Gaius gave her a pleading look that had been known to win over the sternest of aunts. 'An accident. I just couldn't resist. I had hoped my replacement met your schedule of reparations.'

'Nobody buys me!' Lucilla hooted.

* * *

Pretty well everyone else in Rome was being bought. Vinius Clodianus was fielding accusations more often than he liked his friends and family to know. Having to keep secrets from your own circle was part of the insidious process. He tried only to take action when he thought action was justified, but sometimes he was given orders from above against his inclinations. If people were guilty, he supported arrests. But sometimes it went too far, he had to admit.

Informing ran through society from highest to lowest level. At the top, where Clodianus was little involved, were members of Domitian's own council, senators who had been informers under Nero or advisers to Vespasian; some now claimed to have given up, yet remained as shadowy presences behind the scenes. Domitian encouraged senators to accuse one another; he liked the divisiveness. A stigma attached to great men who indulged in prosecutions against their equals. If encouraged by the Emperor, that stigma disappeared, so a star orator might put himself at Domitian's service almost on a salaried basis. To challenge such activities would question the legitimacy of Domitian's regime. Few attempted it. Lower down society snuck weasels who would independently lay an information in the hope of being allowed to prosecute for profit, or who even sometimes named names anonymously. These professionals came from all levels, including very baseborn profiteers. Clodianus saw their work all too often.

Sometimes an informer's involvement was casual. Every evening the actor Latinus would drop by the imperial quarters while Domitian was relaxing, and amuse him with the day's gossip. Names to investigate then came into the Praetorian office the next morning on chits from Domitian's palace freedmen.

At the lowest end of society were slaves who betrayed their masters and mistresses. Strictly speaking, it was illegal for slaves to act as witnesses against their owners, but a device had always existed to get around that; they were first bought by the state, using compulsory purchase orders. Although penalties for disloyal slaves were severe, in practice they stood to gain large financial rewards, plus their freedom. One harsh word at home could make them eager for that.

Domitian used defecting slaves as a constant

resource nowadays. No one was safe from hostile eyes in the dining room, hostile ears in the bedroom. Clodianus was not obliged to involve himself in domestic enquiries, the Urban Cohorts did that; but as ex-vigiles his expertise had been recognised. He could give the Urbans a steer about which doors to knock on, when the door should be kicked down instead, whether interviewing slaves in a discreet bar might work, or when the slaves should just be picked up and tortured without ceremony.

Although the moral conduct laws offered the most notorious possibilities, many other charges were made. It was not all bad news. Abuse of office had once been rife—either overseas governors who acted like bandits in their provinces or officials in Rome who took bribes. Proving bribery could be difficult because the donor had also committed an offence and if they achieved what they wanted, they kept quiet afterwards. In fact, Domitian's reign showed a marked decline in abuses of office, due to his obsessive control over appointments.

Otherwise, the crimes Clodianus regularly looked into were usury (which was illegal but of course happened everywhere), inheritance fraud (often keeping quiet about a will in order to avoid paying tax), and religious deception; that mainly involved Jews who, for financial reasons, pretended not to be Jewish. A tax of two denarii per head was imposed on Jewish men, women, children and the elderly, and also converts; it was used to build and maintain the Capitoline Temple of Jupiter, a deliberate humiliation as it replaced a tithe previously paid by Jewish males to maintain their Temple in Jerusalem, which Titus had destroyed.

Many tried to escape this tax. If there was no other solution, men's tunics were lifted to see if they were circumcised.

There were fictitious adoptions or supposititious births (frauds for inheritance reasons, occasionally to conceal adultery, but sometimes just because a couple were childless). Absenting oneself from the Games or public feasts drew attention; maybe someone just had a reclusive nature or was easily bored, but it was viewed as a protest against the government. For a man to abstain from public office when he was qualified to stand looked similarly dubious, a subversive refusal to support Domitian—which he took personally. Publishing, or just privately writing, seditious or libellous material was inevitably fatal. Using magic (anything from witchcraft to mathematics), or possessing somebody else's horoscope, especially that of the Emperor, was illegal and carried a scandalous frisson that enlivened a trial and generally guaranteed a conviction.

Many thought such cases involved unpalatable intrusion into domestic life. Once an informer had handed in a name to the authorities, even on a spurious excuse, investigation inevitably followed, often carried out with physical violence. Clodianus did not beat people up. He just sometimes gave the orders and occasionally had to watch.

There were risks. To make an accusation that could not be substantiated ultimately ran up big financial penalties, plus lasting disrepute. In order to be seen cleaning up the courts, Domitian made a point of being harsh with informers who laid false claims. To expose rotten prosecutors suited his austere image of himself, however guilty he was of the same evil. Danger from Domitian's judicial rigour threatened even the highest; a potentially illustrious career could be ruined by one misjudged court case.

On the other hand, lucrative careers were made out of prosecuting malicious informers . . .

*   *   *

Vinius Clodianus thought himself dispassionate. He genuinely fought the temptation to slip over the boundary from fairness into something much blacker. It would have been easy for him to become corrupt. That threatened to happen over Flavia Lucilla's ex-husband, the second time she and Clodianus clashed about his work. With so many victims being denounced, endless people feared they might come under suspicion after some slip-up. One, it transpired, being Nemurus.

Domitian's annual games at Alba in honour of his patron goddess Minerva were close to his heart. That March, Statius had submitted a poem called *de Bello Germanico,* 'On the German War', a honeyed paean to the new conqueror of the Chatti and Dacians. Its author was thrilled when he won the poetry prize and received a scintillating gold wreath from Domitian's own hand.

The Capitoline Games in Rome in October were a much grander occasion. These were a revival of ancient festivities, the famous Naples Games which had ceased to be held after the eruption of Vesuvius. Modelled by Domitian on the Greek Olympics, they were held every four years in Rome and lasted sixteen days. Competitors came from all over the Empire. Statius absolutely

378

expected to repeat his success in the Latin poetry section, hoping to beat off scores of rivals and win international acclaim. He thought Domitian was his patron, not seeing that Domitian's sponsorship could be capricious. For one thing, the Emperor loathed any suspicion that his actions could be predicted. Once it was assumed he favoured any individual, that person was finished.

Statius was stunned when this time he failed to win. He was so devastated, it would drive him home to Naples, abandoning the stress of competition. That caused family problems, because his wife Claudia was reluctant to leave Rome; her daughter was sixteen, a talented musician making a career, entirely the wrong age to be left alone. But once Statius felt he had lost Domitian's patronage, retirement seemed the safe option. At least Domitian never turned on him. Statius would now quietly teach, write his intended masterpiece about Achilles, and publish poems he had previously only circulated informally.

From the moment Statius lost the prize, his friends were unsettled. Lucilla learned that some were questioning their safety. Even Nemurus thought he was vulnerable, despite the fact teachers were generally respected. Domitian, who remained childless with Domitia, had recently named two young sons of his cousin Flavia Domitilla as his heirs and made much of appointing the grammarian Quintilian to be their tutor at court. Quintilian was an advocate and rhetorician, the first to be awarded a state salary, under Vespasian. After teaching for twenty years, in a school that had brought him unusual wealth, he retired to write a groundbreaking treatise on rhetoric; it

379

defied contemporary taste by favouring content over style, it was a treasure trove of sane rules for composition, humane advice to teachers and good sense.

When Quintilian was made imperial tutor, Nemurus was vain enough to be jealous. Lucilla had heard about it from friends, laughing because anyone could see Nemurus was not in the same league. Lucilla ran into him at the Capitoline Games, when the old literary group clustered to commiserate with Statius after his loss. Milling among them was her ex-husband.

Nemurus approached Lucilla with a manner so friendly she was suspicious at once. He had even brought her a present: Ovid's love poems. The gift itself was unexpected, and it seemed an odd choice.

'I should never have insisted you return all the books I had lent you, dear. I am proud to have fostered your love for reading. This is a peace offering.' Lucilla had worked at the court long enough; she recognised a bribe. 'Please, I need to talk to you . . . In private.'

Curiosity made her agree. As it seemed so urgent, they left the others temporarily and walked off together outside the theatre in the centre of Rome where the poetry contest had been held. Though October, the night was mild and the atmosphere civilised. They found a bench.

'This is a delicate . . .' Sighing, Lucilla waited for details. 'They are rounding up philosophers and exiling them.'

It was not new. Even in Vespasian's time it had happened. New expulsions were imposed by Domitian last year, with the philosopher Epictetus among his victims. More seemed unavoidable.

380

One reason was that a hardened group of Flavian opponents, connected with the stoics, routinely insulted whoever was emperor. They had tackled Vespasian then Titus; Domitian must be due his turn—and like his predecessors, sooner or later he would be driven to react.

Nemurus, a stoic himself, was highly agitated. 'I need a favour. Spies are everywhere. If anybody questions you about me, will you say that I only teach literature? That I never touch philosophy?'

'Come clean: what have you done, Nemurus?'

'After our divorce, perhaps unwisely I decided to devote myself to philosophy—which is of course merely the pursuit of a virtuous life.'

'Who could argue with that?' Lucilla knew the authorities did.

Shyly, Nemurus owned up: 'For a time, I let my hair grow. I had a beard and wore the philosopher's robe. I even refused to eat meat, and only took what nature gives us without the need to kill fellow creatures.'

Lucilla tried not to laugh. People had told her Nemurus was despondent after she left him, yet becoming a vegetarian and wearing a long beard seemed an extreme reaction to divorce. 'How Greek! But, sadly for my profession, there is no law against terrible hair.'

'Please do not joke. My beard may have been noticed by the wrong people.'

'Well, dear, I can truthfully say I knew nothing about it.' Lucilla wondered what Nemurus looked like with a beard—and winced. 'But why would anybody ask me?'

She saw Nemurus' face cloud. 'Your Praetorian Guard might take a vindictive interest.'

'No! He has no reason to pick on you.'

'He was staring at us earlier outside the theatre,' Nemurus insisted. Lucilla thought he must have imagined this. 'It is not the first time he imposed his baleful presence!'

'What do you mean?'

'Once he marched into a lecture I was giving.'

'Vinius?'

'Had to be him. One-eyed man, scowling like thunder. Came and sat at the back.'

'So what was your lecture?' demanded Lucilla, in amazement.

'On metre. "Dactylic Hexameters or Hendecasyllabic Iambs? Epic glide or elective limp—the poet's dilemma".'

When talking informally, Lucilla knew, Nemurus had insightful views on how poets chose their metre and line length. Given wine, he could even be amusing on scansion. Set on a public platform, however, he was a nervy speaker, who muttered down at his notes even though he was trying to show off. She commented with a smile, 'That must have been uncomfortable—for both of you.'

'He did not linger!' Nemurus admitted.

They had been married, successfully at one time. Now anybody watching would have seen them burst into shared laughter, ruefully and with their heads together, like children giggling at a rude word.

'Well,' Lucilla assured him kindly, 'I shall protect you. But Vinius and I are not as close as you think. We never even speak these days.'

'I find that odd.' Nemurus sounded sarcastic, as he rose to depart. 'Especially as the man is standing in the shadows over there, observing us right now.'

Lucilla refused to look that way, but she made

a point of jumping up and kissing Nemurus on the cheek before he left her. Startled, he made a clumsy half-response, but she dodged that and sat down again.

*   *   *

She remained waiting on the bench, pulling her light stole up over her hair and rearranging the bangles on her arm.

As she expected, Vinius came into the open and marched over.

'Cosy scene. Does he want you back? He bears gifts, I see!'

'Rather out of character. There must have been a remainder sale.' This was disloyal to Nemurus but Lucilla hoped to distract Vinius. 'Ovid. *The Art of Love* contains advice for women on how to look attractive—"a round-faced girl should pile her hair in a topknot"—hardly news to a trained hairdresser.' At the end of the poem, Lucilla happened to know, were extremely frank lists of positions for lovemaking. Some she would never have thought of. Most seemed feasible. She wondered: had Nemurus been using this book as pornography? 'This will interest you, Vinius— Ovid was exiled, for mysterious reasons, which may involve promiscuous relations with the Emperor Augustus' raunchy daughter. They stuck him in Tomis which is, I believe, at the far edge of Dacia.'

'Poor bloody bugger!' exclaimed Vinius forcefully.

Lucilla tightened her grip on the scroll and rattled her bangles again. 'Why are you spying on my ex-husband?'

'The man does not concern me.'

'So I told him. But you once went into a lecture he gave?'

'Just curious. When you were married, did you have to knit his socks?'

Lucilla tried not to react. 'His mother makes them. Vinius, don't menace him; leave him alone, will you?'

'Oh, have I got him worried?' demanded Gaius cheerfully.

'Don't abuse your office. I rely on you to be fair.'

'Fair?' *Rely?*

'Your decency was the first thing that struck me when you worked with the vigiles. Vinius, I want to believe in you. There have to be good men, when everyone swims in a sewer of treachery.'

Gaius listened, looking unemotional.

'I wish you were back there,' Lucilla told him in a morose voice. 'You made your own choices. You were aware of human failings, yet you stood for enlightenment. You were honest. You were even kindly.'

'Within reason.'

'I would take your reason over Domitian's fake benevolence any day. Don't lose your humanity.'

'You think I changed?'

'Dacia changed you.'

'*You* changed me.'

'Do not blame me. Working for the Emperor is your own choice.'

Gaius thought Lucilla's assessment was right. Society had tipped up and gone topsy-turvy. While Domitian pretended to nurture correct behaviour, he undermined it. Everyone now behaved like shits. As the despot supposedly reinforced Rome's moral system, he was destroying it. He, Vinius Clodianus, was helping. He was an instrument of the police state. He had taken the oath. He accepted the not inconsiderable money. He followed orders.

In doing so, had he lost his own values and his independence?

Lucilla stood and began to walk away. She did not give Vinius the farewell kiss she had given Nemurus; Vinius noted that bitterly. As she marched off to find her friends again, he called out one last appeal.

'Flavia Lucilla! I don't suppose you have ever considered that somewhere in all the years we have known one another, I might have fallen in love with you?'

Lucilla stopped and looked back. Since people had told her he was still married to Caecilia, this soul-baring did not endear him. 'Never!'

'You might give it thought.'

*　　　*　　　*

The last thing Gaius wanted as he strode away in the opposite direction was for a wraith to manifest itself among the monumental architecture, then to be confronted by her bloody husband.

'Clodianus!' cried the ghastly Nemurus, as he popped up like a ghost in a bad Saturnalia story. 'I take it amiss that you destroyed my marriage, stole away my wife—yet you have not had the decency to make her happy.'

The man was ludicrous. When seen close up he was also much younger than the fusty, self-neglecting academic that Vinius wanted to envisage. Nemurus must be similar in age to

385

Lucilla. He looked as if he might even throw a ball around at the gym, though probably one stuffed with feathers. He bit his fingernails, perhaps absent-mindedly while reading.

'Not my fault!' retorted Vinius. 'I would have taken her on—the poor girl deserves some excitement—but she loathes what I stand for.'

'I heard that,' Nemurus exulted. Vinius cursed. It was doubly annoying for a spying Guard to discover he had been spied on. 'You need public speaking lessons. Decorum, man! Telling a woman you love her ought to be an act of worship—not hurled at her as a punishment.'

This was where Vinius became tempted to abuse his power. He was too frustrated to hold back. He lowered his voice and threatened Nemurus: *'I have seen your name on a list.'*

Nemurus, no actor, was visibly perturbed.

'Luckily for you, it is not my list.'

Nemurus could not know whether to believe this: if any list really existed; if so, what list it was, or whose; or what Vinius proposed to do about it. That was how fear worked these days.

Whether or not Nemurus had been denounced, his panic told Vinius that he must be guilty of something, even if it was unprovable chicken-stealing. Nemurus had just given himself away before he was even under suspicion.

'I do not descend to the personal,' claimed Vinius piously. 'If I am ordered to exterminate you, you're done for. But I don't lean on people without evidence. What is your secret, by the way?—I bet I know. I bet you are an undercover republican. Or are you a conspiratorial philosopher? What's your fancy? Cynic? Sophist? Stoic?'

386

'I am slightly unnerved to think of the Guards studying ethics.'

'You would be surprised!' Vinius boasted with relish. 'Know yourself, the old sphinx said—and I say, know your enemy. I produced a memo only the other day to warn my troops that not all philosophers wear convenient beards, so watch out for a devious mentality too. For example, we know the stoic creed is avoidance of anger, envy and jealousy . . . Would that apply to you?'

He had guessed right—not difficult, because most educated Romans with a liberal outlook were apt to call themselves stoics.

'How can I look at you and set aside those regrettable emotions?' Nemurus fought back.

'Believe me, I see *you* and feel anger in enthusiastic quantities—though I am not troubled by envy and jealousy,' returned Vinius as spitefully as possible. 'Sadly, Flavia Lucilla has enough reasons to despise me. Perhaps I shall not add another by arresting you.'

Perhaps . . .

Nemurus tried to engage him: 'Flavia Lucilla assures me you are not malicious.'

This was what nobody could know about anyone any more. Who would act ethically? Who would destroy others before others could destroy them? Who would do it for a vengeful reason? For amusement? For the Emperor's favour? For money? Or to save their own neck? Who for no reason at all?

Vinius laughed bitterly. 'Oh she thinks me a dumb soldier.'

Nemurus looked him up and down. He raised one eyebrow; he did it far too archly, being awkward socially.

'*Does* she?'

He taught oratory. As a young man, he himself had taken lessons at the fine Quintilian school. He knew how to pose a rhetorical question to be subtly destructive, causing doubt to linger with his hearer for a long time afterwards.

25

It was the Cornelia case that finished the cornicularius. Until then, he had been refusing to give up. He had served his time, his sixteen years as a Guard. He just could not bear to leave the military life. With this trial, the unpleasant aspects proved too much for him. He did not care that the evidence was minimal, but hated a crisis involving a woman, especially the Chief Vestal Virgin. The cornicularius was not alone in loathing what happened, which would become notorious. Once proceedings against Cornelia began, he got out fast, leaving Vinius Clodianus as the proverbial safe pair of hands.

Clodianus had been waiting, with surprising impatience, for his superior to go; he found he fancied the job. Also, his own position had become awkward. His association with the Urban Cohorts had gained their admiration. They wanted him on full secondment and Rutilius Gallicus officially applied for him to be transferred. Naturally, that made the Praetorian command more determined to hold onto him. A tussle ensued. Rutilius was of senatorial rank, the Praetorian Prefects only equestrians—although there were two of them. Even when Rutilius emphasised his personal gratitude to Clodianus, the transfer request failed. As the Praetorian Prefects recognised: Domitian invariably dug in his heels over anything somebody else wanted.

Then Gallicus died, apparently of natural causes, nothing to do with his mental problems. Clodianus waited cynically for some mannerist poet to write an elegy sobbing, 'Gallicus is dead! Curse you, gods; you cannot exist after all!' With his maverick streak, he even told the seditious materials team to watch for such dangerous verse. This team was composed of soldiers who claimed to be poetry-lovers and playgoers, though Clodianus suspected they all knew exactly what they were doing when they volunteered for the undercover censorship job; it would get them off fatigues. On receipt of his order, they devoted much time to listening for atheism at public readings. Disappointingly, the god-cursing lament failed to materialise. Rutilius was old news.

'Wise Minerva!' cried Clodianus in a mock strop. 'What is wrong with authors today? If someone doesn't get a move on, I may have to write the putrid ode myself.'

He was cheerful for a reason. For him, the death of Rutilius Gallicus removed the Urbans' hope of poaching him. Their new Prefect was bound to reverse all requests made by his predecessor. Anyway, the cornicularius had at last asked to retire, and it was confirmed that Clodianus would replace him. The cornicularius must have put a word in. Like Decius Gracilis, here was yet another patron who had known his father. Gaius went along with it. He was older now. He wanted the job and he submitted to the system.

He was briefly an optio, a man chosen for promotion. That supplied a clarity he liked, for he hated hints and supposition. It also meant that at their monthly nights out in the Scorpion, it became 'Gaius' and 'Septimus'. Well, sometimes it was still 'Gaius' and 'Sir', but it was good to show respect, especially when a senior soldier was right: you really were after his job.

'*Septimus*' was after something else, and with an adroit manoeuvre obtained it. When, just before the Cornelia trial, the cornicularius applied for his discharge, he set himself up with a complete retirement package. He would receive the bronze leaving diploma, signed by Domitian himself as a sign of the Emperor's personal relationship with members of his Guard. He would have the notably attractive financial grant. And, since senior officers in the Roman army were the world's greatest schmoozers, he organised an extra little treat for himself.

The fifth wife of his much-married optio had called at the Camp one day (because the optio never called on her) to confirm that she had finally obtained her longed-for legacy. Since Clodianus had hidden in the clerks' room until he was sure of what his wife wanted, the cornicularius dealt with her. The nervous optio emerged to hear 'Septimus' uttering the ghastly chat-up line, 'Caecilia—*that's* a pretty name!' To this he coupled a technical explanation that although the authorities turned a blind eye, no serving soldier could legitimately be married (thus putting her legacy in jeopardy), whereas a soldier taking his discharge would be given that privilege legally (thereby, if she wanted, rescuing her money for her).

So, despite his hackneyed wooing technique, Septimus acquired the widow. Caecilia was youngish, prettyish, and genuinely relieved that a strong man had offered to shelter her. She brought Septimus the very nice apartment in Lion Street, which he could sublet profitably; he already had a bigger home of his own which needed, he cooed romantically, only a woman's touch. He became head of a ready-made family, the stepchildren whose adoption would give him the instant rights of a father of three. He might yet have children of his own too, for although Caecilia had not slept with Gaius, she had looked at him very hopefully. Expeditionary moves by Septimus had ascertained that she approached marriage as a dutiful woman, in other words was deliciously eager for any new husband to fulfil her needs. He got the legacy too. Moreover, in filching Caecilia of the lovely name and assets, Septimus had won the gratitude of his optio.

Gaius lost no time in letting his family know these new arrangements, so the news would reach Flavia Lucilla. His only regret was a suspicion that the gossip would be: 'Poor Gaius has had his wife *stolen* by his senior officer!' Or worse, a suggestion that Caecilia was a necessary bribe to buy his promotion, making Lucilla think he gave up his wife reluctantly.

Money had changed hands for the job, of course. Sweeteners were the unwritten axle-grease of Roman army postings. It was done in a routine fashion, and selling your wife would not normally form part of the process, not least because a soldier was not supposed to be married. Selling your sister, daughter, grandmother or Mauritanian concubine might be different, Gaius supposed gaily, but as Septimus had Caecilia for extras while the Prefects were satisfied with their usual exorbitant scale of charges, this never came up. Gaius would have been prepared to throw in a couple of his aunts, just to hear those stroppy women's squawks.

Yes, he was so happy with his promotion, it put him in a silly mood.

*   *   *

Another change was cheering him. Whether the end of his final marriage helped, or whether Lucilla and he had both simply reached exhaustion, their long feud began to thaw.

It first showed when Gaius found renewed interest in music. After Dacia, at first he could not tolerate any kind of melody, but now his old love returned, seeming to mark new inner peace. He had wanted to go to a recital by a celebrity harpist called Glaphyrus. Somehow, he lost the ticket. They were like gold-dust; as he desperately hunted, he sent his servant from the Camp to see if he had dropped the precious seat token at Plum Street.

Lucilla had to let in the servant, so she helped search the apartment, though with no luck. What happened next was instinctive. Working at the court, she was able to call in a favour and good-naturedly sent Gaius a new ticket.

Fresh from the recital, Gaius spent all the next afternoon at a bookshop, deciding on a suitable thank-you present. With the aid of a fascinated shopkeeper, he came up with the odes of Horace. He placed his offering on the table in the sitting room at Plum Street, tossing aside the Ovid that he knew Nemurus gave her. Lucilla had left her bookmark at a poem about a girlfriend with beautiful natural hair, which had all dropped out when she used too much lightener, while attempting to go blonde.

Gaius wrote no message, but on subsequent visits he could tell that his own gift was being read instead of the sock-wearer's. Lucilla liked Horace for his decency and punchy good humour. And what hairdresser enjoys reading about a bleach disaster?

Gaius found marinaded artichokes left under a cloth in his favourite bowl.

At Saturnalia, Gaius paid a painter to make a family portrait of Felix, Paulina and their children, which was to be his gift to them. The artist, no fool, also sketched the two young girls, Marcia and Julia, informally. Gaius bought this charming little picture, telling the girls to give it to their Aunt Lucilla, since she was very fond of them.

'Is it a present from you, Uncle Gaius?'

'You can say it is from you.'

She will guess you paid for it.

I hope so!

*   *   *

Meanwhile the season's big event threatened to make Lucilla less well disposed. At work, the new cornicularius inherited the Cornelia kerfuffle. Domitian had decided to try the Chief Vestal Virgin for having lovers. It was the second time she stood accused. Guilty or innocent, she was unlikely to get off.

Women throughout Rome were riveted and horrified. Apart from the imperial ladies, who kept their lips sealed, every client of Lucilla's raised the subject during her coiffure. Most women of any standing knew Cornelia socially.

There were six Vestal Virgins, who were selected by lot between six and ten years old. Taken from their parents, they spent ten years learning their duties, ten years conducting the rituals and ten more teaching new girls. Instantly recognisable with their hair braided with white fillets, and with Hercules Knots on their girdles to symbolise chastity, every day the Vestals walked to a sacred spring and fetched water for the ritual cleansing of their beautiful round temple. Every day they were responsible for keeping alive the flame of Vesta, goddess of the hearth, which must never go out (though it did sometimes) because it had been brought from Troy by Aeneas who founded Rome (in one version). Upon the eternal flame depended Rome's survival.

As part of their initiation, Vestals took a vow of chastity. In return they received exceptional privileges. A lictor attended each of them everywhere as a sign of their power. They could make their own wills, were not obliged to have guardians, took special seats at festivals and rode in carriages. This perhaps provided a freedom of movement that was useful for the few who erred. Not only did they attend the Games, they visited respectable homes, where it was considered a privilege to have them to dinner. As guests, they came to know not only the matrons of Rome, but over their oysters, rich meats and fine wines these revered women had a chance, if they were so inclined, to flirt with men.

Given that early in Domitian's reign three of the four adult Vestals had been exiled for taking lovers, it was clear that their inexperience was theoretical; flighty ones could flirt most efficiently. Varronilla and the Oculata sisters had been found guilty. Domitian exercised leniency, so instead of exacting the traditional brutal punishments, he only banished their lovers and let the three guilty Virgins choose their own deaths. Cornelia had been tried too, but acquitted on that occasion. This time, it was clear she would not escape so lightly.

Interfering with a virgin was normally challenged in the courts as stuprum, the same crime that Vinius had held over Orgilius. Because of the Vestals' special symbolic role, their purity was a religious commodity. As it ensured the continuing safety of Rome, its loss was a national calamity. Yet upon their appointment Vestals were taken from their relatives and the whole of Rome became their family, which meant anyone who slept with a Vestal was committing incest. That was the charge against Cornelia and her lovers now. Punishments had been devised in the remote past. Guilty lovers were hung from a cross in the Forum and thrashed to death with rods. A convicted Virgin must be buried alive. It had happened, although not for a very long time.

Lucilla's customers divided: some were appalled at the obsolete penalty being meted out in a now-civilised society; others were disgusted that a woman who had enjoyed enormous privileges could not manage to keep her vows and keep her legs together. All were fiercely indignant that Domitian tried Cornelia in her absence. It had always been traditional that, with their unique legal position, unlike other women Vestals were allowed to attend a trial and to represent themselves. Charges would be heard by the college of priests, in the Regia, the pontifical offices. There, a Vestal would be like a disgraced daughter facing a family council, which in Rome carried the force of law yet was dignified and private.

This trial took place at the Emperor's Alban villa. It was not held in secret; other emperors had been severely criticised for political hearings held behind closed doors. Domitian summoned all the priests to him there and, as Pontifex Maximus, he presided as if in open court. Cornelia remained in Rome, in the House of the Vestals—which had been newly enlarged and restored by Domitian as part of his civic building programme, though not really with the intention of providing a more luxurious place for wicked women to endure house arrest.

Ironically, there was a special sanctuary of Vesta at Alba Longa, associated with the sacred flame, which Aeneas' son Ascanius was supposed to have first deposited there after arriving from Troy. Cornelia could have been moved to Alba and permitted to attend her trial. Domitian, who had tunnel vision when it suited him, overlooked this.

Mettius Carus prosecuted. He was an informer setting out on a career of supporting Domitian, whose examination of witnesses would become famous for its cruelty. One senator, allegedly, was so stressed by Carus' harshness, he collapsed and died in the Curia.

Despite rigorous questioning, the case proved extremely difficult. It began to look as if the

Chief Vestal would be acquitted again, leaving Domitian shamefaced. He wanted to be seen as an unflinching keeper of religious observance. To charge a guilty Vestal would be painful, but he would endure it for the welfare of Rome. However, to charge an innocent Vestal would be criminal and an offence to the gods. If she was exonerated, he would come out of this looking far worse than when he began.

Cornelia's supposed lovers ranged from an equestrian called Celer to the highest, Valerius Licinianus, a senatorial ex-praetor, just one rank down from consul. No one of that status could be tortured, nor even have arresting hands laid on him. The lovers all had legal training; Licinianus was considered one of the best advocates in Rome. As praetor, he had been the city's senior magistrate, presiding over the legal code. The prosecutor, Carus, carried much less weight and for a long time could make no progress in trying to extract confessions. The only evidence against Licinianus appeared to be that he had given refuge to one of Cornelia's freedwomen, though that did argue for friendship between him and the Virgin beforehand.

Seeing the case slip away without witnesses, Domitian began to ferment with anxiety. Then, at the last gasp, friends of Licinianus persuaded him he was doomed either way. Domitian was intent on pushing through the charges. To escape dying under the rods, Licinianus needed to admit guilt and beg the Emperor for mercy. He suddenly confessed—or, as Herrenius Senecio described it dryly, speaking for him in court: Valerius Licinianus 'withdrew his defence'.

Ecstatic and relieved, Domitian bounded

through the villa at Alba, crowing that Licinianus had exonerated the prosecution. The ex-praetor's life was spared. He was exiled, but first allowed to take as many of his possessions as he could carry away before they were officially confiscated. Licinianus was never asked to give details of his admitted affair, even though in the absence of formal evidence the question of Cornelia's guilt or innocence would remain permanently clouded.

The other purported lovers continued to deny the charges. They were condemned by association and beaten to death as tradition demanded. Celer, for one, died under the rods still protesting his innocence.

The Chief Vestal herself was condemned to the old punishment of interment underground, an example of Domitian's rigid adherence to the law. The punishment would be supervised by the college of pontiffs, fifteen fusty priests of the state religion; if he decided to join in, Domitian would be there as Pontifex Maximus. However much Domitian longed to enhance his reputation, the whole affair was extremely unpopular. There were, therefore, concerns about law and order on the day. The college of pontiffs would take responsibility for the woman's burial. Otherwise, oversight of security on this unpleasant state occasion was assigned to the Guards: an ideal test for their new chief-of-staff, Clodianus. He found himself lumbered with ensuring there were no disturbances.

Vinius Clodianus happened to be good at logistics and in his odd way even enjoyed practical arrangements. The more unusual, the more he rose to the challenge. That was why he had this job. He had been sidekick to not just one but two of the army's best scamming, bluffing, fiddle-fixing senior officers: Decius Gracilis and the previous cornicularius, a pair of tough old soldiers who had consistently escaped from hairy moments as if going for a stroll on a beach. He had learned much from them. He knew he must prepare in meticulous detail, on the basis that if the worst could happen, it would. He was unfazed. He could plan the unplannable—as this was, given that no one could remember the last Vestal Virgin interment. There was no entry in the manual for ensuring a live burial went off quietly.

He conducted research. He pored over historical records. He familiarised himself with the traditional order of events. Much was shrouded in secrecy but he made an intelligent guess at the protocol.

He organised a runner to liaise with the college of pontiffs, so even though the snooty priests were ritually intent on not telling him anything, with luck he would at least know when the party was about to start. The Praetorians would arrive on time. If Domitian suddenly sailed down from Alba to watch, Clodianus would make sure the tribune of the day supplied an appropriate honour guard. Once the target had been dropped tidily inside her tomb, the only requirement was for a very discreet detail to conduct observation at the site. A small daily presence. With perhaps tighter precautions nightly. Just in case any subversive idiots—stoics, Christians, sons of senators out on a drunken spree, do-gooding women who should be at home weaving—scuttled up under cover of darkness to start removing earth.

A couple of rotas would do it. That, and maniacal supervision, which he would undertake himself. Clodianus would take no chances. He would be on duty throughout.

It was sorted. He ought to be confident. However, it was his first major exercise, when he had yet to get his feet comfortably under his new desk. It would be fair to say the new cornicularius had a few collywobbles.

What a boy needed for that, his old aunties would tell him, was a nice big cake oozing with a lot of honey.

So, with the Vestal's descent programmed for evening like any traditional funeral, earlier that afternoon Vinius made his way down from the Camp towards the Forum, where the procession would start. He had had a haircut and shave. He wore the most formal degree of Praetorian city dress: hobnails, the red tunic that distinguished an officer of his standing, with his sword concealed by a toga. No helmet. A notebook with his many comforting lists was tucked in his military belt.

He had an hour or two in hand. On the way, he was sufficiently early to call at the bakery on Ten Taverns Street, where he obtained two of their largest and gooiest confections, one for himself and one for Cretticus, his amicable landlord at the Insula of the Muses. He would have bought three, had he realised that when he walked into the peaceful courtyard garden he would find Flavia Lucilla gossiping with the old man. Undeterred, Gaius tore his own cake in two and handed her half before she could start simpering and pretending not to be hungry.

This had the advantage of forcing her to stay there while she ate it.

To daintily manage a thick, layered pastry, oozing with honey and dropping chopped pistachios, which had been crudely dismantled by a man with strong hands, who was now watching her, took all her concentration. Lucilla had a good excuse to stay quiet.

It was a sunny day in early spring, warm enough to let a nonagenarian lie out on a daybed in a colonnade, with a rug over his scrawny legs and torso, while his two younger friends sat on fold-up stools.

'Delightful young lady!' the old man confided to Vinius, after he had wolfed down his cake. 'I can never understand why you are not screwing her.'

Horrified silence struck both his companions. Lucilla quickly licked her fingers clean, preparing to flee. Gaius already knew Cretticus was a crude old bugger, though it looked as though Lucilla had previously thought him harmless. Cretticus might always have been uninhibited, or perhaps extreme age had removed his social graces.

It was not over. The lewd old boy went on, 'I don't suppose you can offer any kind of an explanation, soldier?'

'I can, in fact.'

Both Cretticus and Lucilla sat up sharply.

Gaius spoke conversationally, as he sucked the last smears of honey off his lips. 'It is because I am an idiot.'

'Well then!' cried Cretticus.

'Exactly!' said Gaius, aiming this at Lucilla.

He looked at her. She looked at him.

'Why don't you take her upstairs now?'

demanded the impertinent old fellow.

Lucilla jumped up, about to sweep off like an affronted goddess, vanishing in a rainbow trail.

Gaius swung himself upright too. 'A grand idea,' he told Cretticus as levelly as possible. He had risen too fast and was in danger of cake repeating on him. Lucilla waited to hear how he got out of this. 'But she's looking a bit inscrutable. Besides—' he indicated his formal dress—'sad as it is, my duty calls.'

Then he reported directly to Lucilla in a low voice, 'I have a bad task. Assisting the college of pontiffs.'

*   *   *

The old man saw they were conversing without help from him, so closed his eyes and seditiously let them get on with it.

'Cornelia?' Lucilla had always been quick. 'You have to . . .'

Chewing a fingernail, Gaius shook his head. He thought about what it would have meant, if he and his comrades had been ordered by Domitian to conduct the cold-blooded execution with weapons of a middle-aged woman whose position in Rome they had all been brought up to revere.

'No, no.' He was as reassuring as he could be. 'But some of us have to attend at the scene.'

'Which entails?'

'To stand on guard today, then afterwards, to ensure nobody interferes with the vault.'

'Trying to release her?' Lucilla knew him well enough to believe he was not looking forward to any of it. 'You were at the trial?' she demanded.

Gaius nodded. 'Did she do it?'

'Probably.'

'Or possibly not?'

Gaius assented again, ruefully. 'Either Licinianus really was guilty and turned state's evidence to save his arse, or he was innocent, but so shit-scared he lied to the court. The end result is, he has saved his skin and also saved a lot of his property—which you could call being paid for his evidence. We don't approve of that, do we? Without any doubt, he grassed up the other lovers, and of course he condemned Cornelia. No one has heard her story. This is about as unedifying as it gets.'

Lucilla was pleased at the way he put the story; she thought he had told it the way he really saw it, not aiming to impress. 'It's a terrifying death. One would hope some sympathetic friend will find a way to slip the poor woman a vial of poison . . . Gaius, please don't search her.'

'Not if I can help it.'

'Will you have a choice?'

'Ritually, I believe it is forbidden. Nobody will touch her.'

'Are you in charge?'

'The priests are in charge.'

Like him, Lucilla hated everything about this trial and punishment. Gaius only hoped she was satisfied that as the Chief Vestal went to her grim fate, he at least would feel compassion. 'So you must see the tomb sealed and guard it. Then what?'

'I suppose we'll receive orders.'

Again, Lucilla was appalled on his behalf. 'You mean—*you* may have to open up the chamber, to see if she is dead?'

'I couldn't find out from the old records whether

403

anybody checks. I hope a priest will simply declare formally that it must be over. After, let us say, enough time passes . . . It will take—' Gaius paused fastidiously '—some days.'

Lucilla's voice was low and intense. 'Then will you come home?'

'I will,' promised Gaius, looking into her eyes like a man who could hardly bear to leave.

'Good luck' seemed inappropriate so Lucilla murmured, 'You will be in my thoughts, soldier.'

Vinius Clodianus snapped to attention, kicking up dust with an expert heel-grind, as he gave her a full Praetorian salute.

*   *   *

Lucilla's departure across the garden and through the exit gateway to the street allowed him a pleasant survey of her elegant rear view. Gaius rather thought old man Cretticus, who had opened his eyes again, was enjoying the same vision salaciously.

He stayed a few moments longer in the peristyle, as good manners.

'When you do manage to bed her, leave the window open so I can hear.' Cretticus was shameless. 'Go on,' he wheedled. 'I'm ninety-one. I don't get many thrills these days.'

26

The House of the Vestals lay towards the southern end of the Forum. Its enclosed precinct contained a large quiet garden among colonnades, with accommodation for the six Virgins, who lived there throughout their thirty years of service, only leaving if they were taken so ill they must be nursed by a respectable matron in her home. Some stayed even after they retired. No men were allowed in the Vestals' house; the precinct was locked up at night as a precaution.

The small round Temple of Vesta stood just outside in its own enclosure. Across the Sacred Way, the odd-shaped triangular college of pontiffs completed the religious sanctum, buildings whose origins, perhaps as a palace in the days of the old Roman kings, were long lost. A delicate contrast to that jumbled group, the beautiful white marble temple had no cult statue. It did contain the sacred fire and the palladium, a venerated object of uncertain form which had supposedly come from Troy and which, like the flame, symbolised the health and survival of Rome. It was secret; nobody ever saw it. Clodianus thought that, given what the Greeks did to Troy after they got in with the Wooden Horse, the palladium's efficiency as a form of protection might be questioned. He did not voice this outrage. Standing among a subdued crowd at the end of the Forum, his role was to prevent trouble, not cause a revolution.

This was a very ancient area. Rituals carried out by pontiffs and Vestals were the oldest, and occasionally the oddest, the Roman people still followed. The daily procedures of the Vestals went back deeply into history and myth: carrying water, tending fire, cleansing, and making ritual salt cakes. Today's archaic punishment belonged with that tradition, a tradition rooted in darkness and retribution just as much as the Vestals' life was central to survival and hope.

The Forum had long been the starting point of funerals for aristocrats. Here many a noble family would still bring a bier with the dead body of their loved one lying on a costly mattress among precious spices—a consul or general, or even a great lady who had married famously and endowed provincial temples. They would assemble their procession of mourners, with musicians, masks of their ancestors, irreverent clowns mocking the life and characteristics of the dead. Here they would hear a public eulogy, before wending their way by torchlight and amidst the sound of flutes to their chosen great necropolis on one of the major arteries out of Rome; there the corpse would be cremated and its ashes collected in a costly urn of porphyry or alabaster, to be kept forever in the family mausoleum and, at least in theory, regularly visited.

Today there was no corpse. Instead of an open bier, a tall closed litter was carried from the House of the Vestals. It arrived without the normal ceremonies and a leaden silence greeted its appearance. Everyone knew that Cornelia was there inside, though the interior was hidden by heavy coverings and the coverings had been tightly fastened down with cords. People made way. As a procession formed, those who were most curious followed in gloomy silence. If Cornelia's birth family were present, the observing Praetorian could not identify them. The other five Vestals stayed in their house. Her lovers, if such they had been, would definitely not be paying respects.

Activity in the Forum ceased. Idlers playing board-games on basilica steps, entrepreneurs fleecing contacts in the shade under ancient arches, patrons and their struggling clients who had met beside water bowls or the Golden Milestone, all stopped gossip and negotiation. Workers high up on the scaffold that housed the nearly completed statue of Domitian on horseback gazed down with curiosity. The courts were closed. Trade ended. Even bankers took a pause. If prostitutes continued their crude business at the back of temples, they did so furtively. Despondency fell upon everyone, like a cold shadow when the sun passed behind a cypress tree.

The sombre procession set off. After crossing the Forum, participants travelled on foot to the far edge of the city; homes and businesses were shuttered all along the journey and people stood, mute and unhappy, while the severe cortège slowly passed. Its destination was beyond the Praetorian Camp, where the ancient embankment called the Servian Walls was broken at the Colline Gate, as the Via Nomentana emerged from Rome. Outside the walls was the Praetorian Campus, the Guards' massive parade ground, empty today. Inside the walls was an area of unused, scrubby ground called the Campus Sceleratus, which meant profaned, criminal, accursed, polluted. In this bleak haunt, guilty Vestals were entombed.

Vinius Clodianus was glad to see the public

slaves had done their job; the vagrants and stray dogs had been moved on, the clutter and windblown detritus that gathers at such isolated places had been collected and cleared. There were no dumps of broken amphorae, burned-out carts, halves of dead sheep or abandoned shoes. A couple of extremely old whores who liked to sit around a bonfire offering migrant workers either a bunk-up or mild fortune-telling were keeping away today. He had personally suggested that the aediles responsible for street affairs should sign a petty cash voucher for the women's all-day bar bill.

Into the earth bank, a small chamber had already been dug. Temporary steps led down inside. At the bottom were a covered couch, a lighted lamp, and very small quantities of bread, water, milk and oil. This symbolic sustenance exonerated everyone from causing a Vestal Virgin's death. They would not last her long. At some point, presumably, fresh air would run out. The lamp would falter. Perhaps before that, panic would set in. Possibly madness. For anyone who thought about it too much, this inescapable entombment in darkness and silence was horrific, the most terrifying human fear.

*   *   *

A second covered litter had turned up from out of town. It halted, as if the occupant was watching, though the dark curtains never seemed to move. Gaius guessed who was lurking. He gave the Guards a discreet nod.

Upon the Vestal's arrival, the cords on her litter were released by the chief priest of the old religion, the Flamen Dialis. He and his fourteen colleagues had assembled in their traditional hairy woollen cloaks and leather skullcaps, each with a tuft of wool and pointed prong of olive wood, items of long-forgotten significance. They were the archaic face of Roman religion, as the Vestals were themselves.

The convicted woman emerged stiffly, while priests enacted mysterious ritual gestures and prayers; Gaius reckoned those were really intended to stiffen the priests' own resolve. She was not bound or chained. For one thing, that would cut across the complicated rules imposed on the Flamen Dialis, who was never allowed to see anyone in chains; by tradition, he could not even wear a finger ring.

Heavily veiled, Cornelia advanced to the steps, where unfortunately her gown caught on a splinter. An attendant moved to help unfasten it but, professional to the end, the Virgin beat him off with a shudder of disgust, unwilling to be defiled by a man's touch.

The Guards stood together in a small group, as respectful as a prisoner escort can be under the discipline of an execution. They were iron-jawed and so rigid they seemed corseted, all masters of making their very impassivity reveal distaste. Less clear was whether their distaste was for what Cornelia had done, or simply for today's events.

Cornelia behaved with nobility, at least in the subsequent judgement of male intellectuals. Pliny, a prig devoid of emotional imagination (who had not been present), later reported this occasion to add a sensational touch to his published letters, yet with no real sense of its sordid tragedy. It was a miserable twilight scene. Every participant who walked away afterwards would be permanently soiled.

She did not go quietly. She had been refused the right to defend herself in court, but nobody would physically gag a Vestal, so she had her moment. After calling for assistance from Vesta and all the other gods, Cornelia shouted to the assembled men (they were all men): 'How can the Emperor imagine I would have broken my vows, when it was I who performed the sacred rites that brought him his victories?'

This subtle undermining of Domitian's cherished role as conqueror convinced many people that Cornelia was innocent. Had she been unchaste, surely the gods would not have responded to her ritual prayers and sacrifices when she begged for military success? The Chatti, Marcomanni and Dacians would never have succumbed. Her purity could be presumed, therefore, and it made a bitter contrast to the hypocritical licence of the Emperor, who many believed had seduced his own niece, perhaps causing Julia's death with an enforced abortion.

Cornelia had the last word. Perhaps she guessed that her cry would resonate from the verge of the tomb, one bitter sliver of self-defence that Domitian could never silence.

She took her time. Well, why not?

The watching cornicularius felt most nervous at this moment: what if this robust Chief Vestal refused to descend underground? If she would not cooperate, he foresaw that the situation might deteriorate. Getting her down the ghastly hole was up to the priests, whom he sized up with a sinking heart. They were inbred patricians, men who were

410

neither young nor in any way handy. Slaves did everything for them. Most could barely lift a finger to scratch their own dandruff.

Indeed, wondered Gaius glumly, who in his senses, priest or otherwise, would try to manhandle a furious mature woman, who had spent nearly thirty years having her own way? He would certainly not order any of his men to corner her, grab her, strike her, push her or otherwise force her onto those insecure wooden steps. This was one situation where he himself would not volunteer either.

Fortunately, Cornelia was conditioned to comply with rituals. She protested her innocence loudly enough, but made no attempt to dig in her heels or thrash about.

The priests averted their gaze. The Vestal, who could never have been on a ladder before, climbed down; she tumbled the final distance, but managed to control her garments to preserve her dignity. Those who did look (Clodianus and anonymous public slaves who had to do the manual work today) glimpsed not so much as an ankle. The steps were pulled up quickly. Heavy loads of earth were piled over the entrance. The soil was beaten flat, levelled with the remainder of the embankment, so in years to come once the ground-cover grew back, the location of the chamber would be permanently lost.

Lost? Oh, be reasonable! thought Gaius tetchily. He had noticed the city surveyor had sent a representative; in that practical department they would need a discreet mark on their charts, for whenever the old embankment had to be maintained. Even the priests would want to avoid the bad omen of turning up a skeleton, supposing

411

they ever had to bury another culprit.

The black-covered litter with the anonymous occupant had already gone, heading out of Rome. The priests removed themselves from the scene promptly. Off for a stiff drink in one of those putrid pontiffs' fancy dining rooms, no doubt. The chief of them, the Flamen Dialis, was bound by a ridiculous system of prohibitive rules for his daily life, but presumably nothing barred him from a very strong restorative after he had buried a woman alive. His wife, the Chief Priestess, would have known Cornelia well, so he might be going home to a very frosty atmosphere.

The Praetorians remained discreetly at the lonely scene. They would deter any rescue; none was attempted. They would observe whether the goddess Vesta resurrected the virgin who had been consecrated to her for so many years, as a sign that Cornelia was innocent. As Gaius expected, all the gods chose to abandon her.

A small detachment guarded the Campus Sceleratus for days. Since normal funeral ceremonies were forbidden, anyone who attempted to lay flowers or tributes was prevented; not many tried. Vestals might be honoured women, but they were haughty and self-important, therefore more revered than loved. Veiled elderly women of all ranks appeared occasionally and were persuaded to go home. A few passers-by came up to make enquiries, though nobody wanted to gossip with Praetorians. No one wanted to attract their attention. People were afraid it might get them arrested.

The Guards' task was grim but at least when the watch changed, the Camp was nearby. Details marched to and fro quietly, and since their own parade ground was immediately the other side of the Colline Gate, they were virtually at home and often their abnormal duties went unnoticed by the public.

Vinius Clodianus attended the scene as much as possible. When he was desperate for rest, he slept at the Camp. He ate and bathed there. He visited his office daily to check correspondence. He made no move to go into the city, even when by any standards he had the right to be off duty.

It was a draining vigil. The soldiers were well able to imagine what was happening underground.

Eventually there could no longer be any hope of life. Without being required to check the tomb, the guard was quietly stood down. Clodianus returned to his office where he wrote a short, clear report, should anybody want it, to state that the dismal episode had passed off without incident.

He took himself to the Praetorian baths, where he scraped himself over and over again with a strigil as if it was he who had been defiled. He sat in the steam in the hot room trying to cleanse his spirit. Inertia claimed him for a while, but eventually he pulled himself out of that.

Then will you be coming home?
I will.

*   *   *

When Gaius walked into the apartment, Lucilla took in quickly that he had bathed and changed. He was in a white tunic that looked old and comfortable, with a civilian belt, and apparently unarmed. The back of his head was wet, since

413

tough men rarely towel-dry their hair. They claim you cannot catch a cold that way, and are always surprised when they do.

'Is it finished?'

He merely grunted.

'Do you want anything?'

A shake of the head, only just short of annoyance. He went into his room, closing the doors. Their rules forbade her to follow.

Lucilla addressed the dog clearly, so Gaius had to hear: 'Bad grumpy Master! Anyone would think I had married him!'

No sound came from inside the room, but perhaps he was grinning.

Despite his refusal, she prepared him food: a segment of loaf, filled with sliced cooked meat and gherkins; half a cup of wine; a full beaker of water; figs in a saucer. With this snack on a small tray, she knocked firmly and, without waiting for permission, entered his sanctum.

Gaius was sitting on the edge of his bed, elbows on his knees, head down, completely slumped. Lucilla walked around him and placed the tray on a small table he had recently bought, marble, one leg shaped like a dolphin. The dog, who recognised a food tray, came in eagerly, claws scratching the wooden floorboards.

'No, leave Master. Let him settle. Come on out; you are going to see Glyke.'

Before she left, she brushed one hand briefly over Gaius' clean, springy hair. 'Ignore me then! I could dance off in a huff. But I'm just going to the baths, Gaius.'

He had not moved. He was taut, morose, a man who had come in from his work, still worked

414

up over a project he had hated. But that was temporary. Gaius would soon be himself again. Lucilla was tolerating this mood because she understood him; equally, he was allowing her to manage him because she had that understanding. They knew each other inside out, like people who already lived together.

When the front door had closed behind her, Gaius raised his head, letting the silence of the apartment seep into him. His movements were slow, yet relaxed. He ate the bread and meat, though left the wine, also the figs, but gradually drained the whole beaker of water. Then he lay on his bed resting, while he waited for Lucilla to come home to him.

*   *   *

There were two tacticians in their relationship. Now Lucilla not only left the watchdog with Glyke and Calliste in the shop, but made arrangements for the girls to forestall her clients tomorrow morning. They exchanged looks; she ignored that.

She went through the baths hurriedly: warm room, hot steam, cold plunge. She strigilled the oil off for herself, talked to no one and refused the masseuse.

Back at the apartment, all was quiet. No sound came from Gaius, though he had evidently been about. It was late enough to need light in the corridor so he had placed a pottery oil lamp on the shelf in front of the Lares. Lucilla lit another lamp, which she took to her room. She left the door open. Other than that she made no overtures to Gaius. The next move was up to him.

When he appeared in the doorway, it was the first time, to Lucilla's knowledge, he had ever seen her bedroom. Gaius smiled slightly, entering her private place. She watched him look around, inspecting everything. In his room, the bed was close against the wall, but Lucilla had hers positioned centrally, with purple and black striped rugs either side. There were rather good cupboards, with panelled doors, curved legs and pointed pedestals. A folding stool, composed of slats, sat in front of a side-table where she kept her personal cosmetics, pins, perfumes, combs and ornaments. The window shutters were half open. For his own reasons, Gaius went and closed them.

She had not tidied specially. Things were neat but casual. Her clothes from today were piled on a chest, except a light undertunic she was still modestly wearing. She was lying on her bed, barefoot, ankles crossed, hands folded at her waist, as if she had just spent a long time thinking. She was lying on her hair too, its vibrant chestnut length well combed, but simply tied on the nape of her neck with a snaggle of blue ribbon. It was the first time for many years Gaius had seen her as she was, with neither face paints nor jewellery, and her hair only one tug away from flowing out freely.

He too was now clad only in an unbleached undertunic, and shoeless. Seeing his bare feet for the first time, Lucilla rather liked them: the well-kept feet of a soldier who regularly practice-marched twenty miles and could not afford to get blisters. The tension had drained out of him,

416

though he still looked weary. He tipped his head on one side and gave her a soft look while he said, 'I would really like your company.'

Lucilla nodded.

Gaius came to the free side of her bed. He lay down alongside her, mimicking her pose with hands demurely folded. Neither was quite sure of the other, yet nothing seemed to need explaining.

Lucilla's bed possessed only one pillow. She had most of it. Masterful, Gaius pulled more to his side. Lucilla hoiked it back. Gaius reprised his tug. Lucilla gave in and angled her head towards him, so they were sharing.

'Come here,' said Gaius. 'Come properly.'

'Properly' meant tucked up against his side with his arm around her and her head on his shoulder, nuzzling his neck, absorbing his warmth and his familiar scent. He had put back the weight and muscle he had lost as a prisoner. His ribs, hip and thigh were solid to lie against; the clasp of his arm, though casual, was strong.

'I'm sorry,' he whispered.

'You were upset.'

'No, I mean sorry about everything.'

Lucilla hugged him closer. Then she stretched up, turned his face towards her with one palm, and kissed him quietly. Gaius was welcoming, though seemed restrained.

Had he never recovered? Was he incapable? She feared the worst. He read her thoughts: 'I don't know. I never tried. I only wanted you.'

Despite years of hairdressing gossip, Lucilla realised she had no idea how to deal with this. One false move could be fatal, she guessed. She let him lead.

'Too tired.' Gaius shelved the issue. 'Here is my plan: we will lie here like this, cosy and comforting. In due course we'll sleep. When we wake, we'll do it.'

Lucilla teased him: 'Does everything in your life have to have an agenda?'

'Nothing beats it,' Gaius assured her gravely. He ticked off items: 'Opening remarks. Snuggle. Sleep. Love you. Any other business . . .'

Lucilla accepted it, settling against him as if this had been her place for years. His hand struggled under the neck of her tunic, not exploring, not sensual, simply seeking her shoulder's bare skin. She curled her own hand lightly around his wrist. It was the touch of ownership, on both sides. They lay together, relieved, relaxed, contented, resting.

Time passed. They did not sleep. Neither could bear to lose the intensity of this companionship.

*   *   *

Gaius moved. It seemed more than a readjustment for comfort, and at Lucilla's small murmur, he gathered her so they could kiss again. His lips tasting hers were positive; some decision had been reached. Her heartbeats speeded. Still mouth to mouth, Gaius rolled them, so Lucilla was in the position that would always be her favourite, feeling his weight on her. He was tender, appreciative, leisurely but purposeful. She had no doubt where he was taking them.

As a master logistician, Gaius removed his clothes and hers, somehow without spoiling the moment. Taking his time, he positioned Lucilla and himself as he wanted them to be. 'Never fear. The omens are promising.'

'Omens?' She kept it light. 'You went to a *priest,* Gaius?'

She felt him shudder; he had had enough priests at the Campus Sceleratus to last him a lifetime. 'You sent me to a doctor.'

'*Sent* you?'

'I'm obedient. Take the auguries yourself.' He moved Lucilla's hand down so she could see there was no problem now. She heard him gasp and felt him tense as she touched him. Neither could bear to wait.

'Ready?'

'Ready.'

They gasped slightly, as they always would, at the moment they joined together. An exquisite welcome, which they would never take for granted.

On that first return to each other, they made love as their ancestors the old Romans must have done, when the man came in weary from ploughing and the woman who tended his hearth welcomed him in their rustic bed before they slept. Nothing fancy, nothing too drawn out. The straightforward unashamed pleasure of two people who would share life as long as they were allowed to do so.

There would be other times to be adventurous, for more extended passion, for raucousness and ribaldry. This was the uncomplicated, intimate communion of a couple who liked to end their day by expressing their love.

27

Light altered subtly throughout the apartment, although it was still dark. Outside, a bird began to trill a piercing and joyous soaraway song that suited Lucilla's waking mood. The last few delivery carts trundled away into the distance, trying to beat the daylight curfew when wheeled vehicles had to leave the streets. The earliest workers were out in Plum Street, visiting the food shop on their way to menial jobs. Their voices came loud, seeming thoughtless, as if *they* had to be up and about, so why not others?

Inside, everywhere lay still.

Gaius, beside her, had curled on his side, facing away in such deep slumber that at one point Lucilla had wrapped herself around him, pressing against his back to listen to his lungs as if she needed to check he was still alive. She knew without asking, he had not slept so well for years; some long-held grief had slid away last night, to give place to healing.

He sensed she had woken. Dragging himself from unconsciousness just enough, he struggled over towards her, flung arms around her, hauled her into his embrace, then sank back into further sleep. His warm palm was spread against her head, his fingers had run into her hair.

Lucilla held him, shaking and overwhelmed with gratitude for what she now had. Gaius roused enough to make a small protest at her emotion, his fingertips stroking her temple until she too was soothed and began to sleep again.

He came awake soon afterwards. He lay on watch, as the morning sun grew in strength to flood

420

through gaps in the shutters, while street-sweepers came and went in Plum Street, then shoppers and people on business occupied the neighbourhood. For half an hour schoolchildren clamoured uninhibitedly on their way to lessons. Then the voices were less shrill. After a while, Gaius drowsed gently, waiting until Lucilla awoke so they could spend their day together.

He was a happy man. It went beyond the morning bonhomie of any fellow who had screwed a girl he liked. He knew their lives had altered fundamentally. Still, he would have to exert himself to hang on to this—fight off all the other bastards, keep her permanently sweet—he was looking forward to the process. When she stirred, he greeted her with kisses, unable to stop smiling.

At first they lay in silence, foreheads together, blissfully lost in their reconciliation. As they gazed like soulful doves, Lucilla realised she rarely thought of Gaius as one-eyed. She knew him so well she would read his expression, tell his thoughts, just as if he had two eyes to communicate like anybody else. Whether he was handsome or hideous did not matter either. All she loved came from his character.

'What are you thinking?'

'Your action list got abandoned!'

'Perfectly decent action list,' declared Gaius. 'I shall complete it.' Lucilla smiled and Gaius enjoyed her benevolence like a dog lapping gravy. 'Any agenda of mine,' he offered, at his most cheerful, 'always receives systematic treatment, item by item, as steered by a man who knows the lazy, incompetent bastards he is forced to deal with . . . Listen, sweetie, this is important stuff; stop tickling my balls for a moment—'

'Can you not be fondled and talk nonsense at the same time?'

'Can't concentrate. I am not a demigod ... So: in my office there is an agreed programme, but other activity may be authorised, if I decide it necessary. Loving you last night was a special exercise. The agenda remains active. I *will* work through the damned thing. Clear?'

'Perfectly. When does it start?'

'About two heartbeats from now.'

Then Gaius fulfilled his agenda in an orderly manner—with passion, inventiveness and the energy of a man who had had a thoroughly good night's sleep.

*   *   *

Later, they let half a morning go by, talking and teasing and languidly exploiting their first real chance to spend time together, with no pressure to do anything.

While they were still in bed, Lucilla could not resist asking, 'You said something outside the theatre that time, but you were angry—Was it true?'

'This is what a grammarian would call "a question expecting the answer yes". Let's not play games. You know I love you.'

Thinking of his dogged pursuit, how could Lucilla doubt it? She lay gazing up at the old wooden ceiling. 'And are you going to ask me?'

Gaius folded her hand into his, linking fingers. 'You will tell me when you want to.'

'That sounds as if you think you already know.'

422

'So am I very conceited?'

'Not really. Just a trained observer.'

Gaius had found the end of the blue ribbon; remarkably, its knot was still intact. Inevitably, he pulled it. He spread Lucilla's shining hair, loosening it around her head, tenderly laying strands upon her shoulders.

'Ironic,' she concluded ruefully. 'I devote my life to doing women's hair, to make them attractive to their men—and all the time, what men really like best is hair worn long and loose, without adornment—'

'On a pillow!' exclaimed Gaius enthusiastically.

*   *   *

'So what happens now?'

'Breakfast.' Gaius pulled himself upright and sat on the edge of the bed, stretching what he must know was an impressive torso. 'I have to get up. Traditionally, the boy in a family goes out for breakfast rolls.'

Are we a family? 'I meant—'

'I know.' Gaius stopped her. 'I am not letting you get away this time.' He rolled back and hung over her. He knew how uncertain Lucilla's life had been, and how determined he himself was to avoid any more stupid mistakes. 'Let's get it over with. You need to know I am a permanent fixture; I need to know that if I nip off for a pee, you won't disappear on me.'

'Tell me what you want, Gaius.'

'What do you think, love? I've been mooning after you so long, it's all pretty obvious to me.'

'No guesswork. Too many of my clients have

come to grief through relying on presumption.'

'You want a written agreement?' Lucilla was amused to hear he sounded as if, had he had a waxed tablet here in the bed, he would have jotted contract notes. 'Whatever you will agree to,' Gaius said. 'Whatever you choose to call it. I won't push my luck; you made it clear, you think I'm a bad bet for marriage and I don't blame you . . . Just be my girl, Lucilla. Be kind, and let me be loving to you. When work permits, we shall be together. One bed, one hearth, one table—one bloody dog, who already thinks he owns us both. One life, one set of dreams.'

Lucilla caressed his ruined cheek with her knuckle. 'I notice you put the bed first.'

Gaius nibbled her finger affectionately. 'No, the dreams come first. I am just frightened to admit that, in case you think I'm soft.'

'So what are your dreams, Gaius?'

'Who knows?' He was completely honest. 'Maybe I have to come to you to learn them . . . Give me a chance, girl. You know you want to.'

Lucilla smiled so sweetly her happiness was translucent. She shimmied to her knees and held him close, before despatching him to fetch their breakfast.

'Shall I bring the dog up?' They could hear Baby howling piteously in the salon downstairs. He knew he was missing something.

'May as well. He has to get used to it.'

'He either accepts it—or he goes!'

'Gaius, as a pet-owner, you are ruthless . . . Do I have to do what you say, too?'

Gaius scoffed. 'Oh no. I know my limits.'

The bakeries would be nearly sold out. He

424

washed, pulled on his old tunic, and went out to find bread rolls. Lucilla heard him all the way down Plum Street, as he filled his lungs and, just like the blackbird earlier, sang his heart out.

Heads turned. Gaius Vinius knew it, and he did not care.

28

They would have five years as lovers in Plum Street. More than most lovers could hope for. In their city's political history those were dreadful times, but people could, if they were careful, find normal human happiness. The apartment Lucilla and Gaius shared had always seemed isolated from the world's troubles. Even though Lucilla worked there, once customers left it was domestic and private; for Gaius it had long been his secret refuge.

They saw each other regularly now. When they did, everything seemed quite natural. As other people noticed them as a couple, Lucilla was surprised how little they commented.

'They all think we've been sleeping and living together for years,' explained Gaius.

Lucilla was indignant. 'Who says so? Who thinks that?'

'Anyone who has ever seen us in the same room together, precious.'

The first time he came back after spending time at the Camp, Lucilla heard him fuss the dog and ask, 'Where is she then?' in a familiar way that brought a lump to her throat. He only kissed her quickly on the forehead, taking himself off to dump a parcel of shellfish then wash his hands before

425

he really gave attention to her. When he did, his affection was unforced.

Despite all he promised, she had been torn between belief in his return and doubt. 'Hey! I'm a soldier—don't cry on me; you'll break my heart . . . You knew I would come back.'

'Yes.'

'Better like it then, because I can't keep away from you.'

She would not cry next time.

This was good. Gaius was a householder coming home with their supper, which he had chosen and which, she guessed, he would insist on cooking, since frying up a batch of prawns with garlic had to be man's work. Lucilla would edge around him in the tiny kitchen, preparing other things for the meal, sharing the tasks without needing to consult. Now they were lovers they could squeeze in together, the more intimate the better. They touched all the time. It was more than reassurance; they liked to be in continual contact.

This was how life would be. Lucilla realised with a thump in the chest that overnight they had become one unit. They were friends, lovers, partners, co-conspirators against everyone else. They would eat together this evening, drink a little wine, talk, complain about others, enjoy the evening twilight, then tidy the house, walk the dog, chat to neighbours, return home, conduct ablutions, go to bed cheerfully, and turn to one another between the sheets with wonderful excitement.

Lucilla had decided to avoid having children. They discussed it once, when she knew Gaius had seen what she was doing. She did believe he would look after her, and love any child they conceived

426

together, yet there were uncertainties in his own profession and she still remembered his warning after Lara died about how children would affect her work. Besides, who wanted to bring a baby into Domitian's Rome? It was no place for innocents.

Gaius seemed to accept her decision. At least he said so. Men could be sentimentalists. Men wanted heirs to continue their line. But he applied no pressure. The other thing about men was that, if they were honest about it which none of them were, they wanted their women to themselves. Lucilla had learned that wisdom from her customers.

Crucially, they both now discussed everything together. A definition of Roman marriage said a wife was the one person with whom a man shared his most intimate thoughts, thoughts he would not divulge even to his close male advisers, his amici. In Gaius' case, his amici were his two brothers, his old vigiles comrade Scorpus, and his predecessor Septimus; he was restrained with fellow-officers because in any organisation a good chief-of-staff trusts nobody. Gaius admitted, at least to himself, he had never shared much with his wives. By agreement he and Lucilla would not call themselves married. But he confided totally in her now, and she did the same with him. They discussed work, politics, society, their neighbourhood, family matters, friends, music and literature, absolutely everything. Many a conversation was held on their balcony, in the room with their reading couch, while out walking, in bed. Neither had been known for talking, but when they were together they talked to each other constantly.

Perhaps they talked too much. Where so much was said, if ever some topic was to be kept unmentioned the silence would be telling.

They laughed a great deal. Sometimes an outsider would be hard pushed to know why. Their amusement was based on a shared opinion that most of the world was ridiculous, but it also derived from the complex weave of their past conversations. Sometimes they just looked at each other and laughed, without needing to speak.

Lucilla never went to the Camp. She knew what it was like: about two-thirds the size of a legionary fort, said Gaius (that meant little to her), with room for ten to twelve thousand men if needs be: a small army. Accommodation was packed in, with unique two-storeyed barracks and even extra buildings crammed against the inside walls in a way that would be unsafe in a campaign fort, where a clear berm was always left to catch enemy missiles and allow emergency manoeuvring. Lucilla knew the exterior, a mighty square beyond the north-eastern city gate, with red-brick-faced walls about ten feet high; these walls were not entirely daunting, yet their extreme solidity seemed forbidding, beside a city that was mainly unfortified. The Camp's sheer size, with its massive parade ground outside, helped it dominate that area.

Gaius worked at the centre, on the main interior crossroads where all military forts had impressive command posts. His office adjoined the suite used by the Praetorian Prefects. Gaius saw that as only a mild disadvantage; if one of them dropped in for a moan about a colleague, he generally managed to stop picking his teeth before they noticed. If not, stuff them; it was his office. He had his own secretary, a couple of clerks and a runabout, whom Lucilla knew because that cross-eyed lad would sometimes be sent to let her know when Gaius intended to come to Plum Street. In his personal quarters, which had almost the space and amenities a cohort tribune would expect, a body servant looked after him, his uniform and his equipment.

Lucilla liked to think that since he left the liaison post, his work had changed. The Guards' involvement in rooting out crimes continued, but she let herself believe Gaius spent more time on personnel issues, supervision of clerks, monitoring the savings bank and checking granary records. He was content to give the impression that his life was a long round of ordering new note tablets. He never wanted to worry her.

*　　　*　　　*

Their first year together passed quietly. Domitian's huge equestrian statue was unveiled, so there was Praetorian interest in the formalities, but that was a passing excitement. They were not yet in what would be known as the Reign of Terror, but had certainly reached constant anxiety.

The Emperor liked inventive punishments. A senator and informer called Acilius Glabrio was summonsed to Alba and ordered to fight a huge arena lion single-handed in the small amphitheatre. Glabrio unexpectedly got the better of the lion. Domitian then exiled him. He had allegedly been stirring up revolution.

'True?' Lucilla asked Gaius.

'Probably said the wrong thing a few times. Which of us hasn't? It's the lion I feel sorry for. He can't have expected to lose.'

'You don't mean that.'

With her, Gaius allowed his conscience to show. 'No. Good on Glabrio, for not consenting to get mauled—though much good it did the poor sod.'

Glabrio had been called back from exile and executed for 'atheism'.

*   *   *

The following year a new war erupted on the Danube. Sarmatian tribesmen, the Iazyges from the great plains, joined with the Suebi and attacked Pannonia, wiping out the XXI Rapax legion. Once again, the Emperor put on uniform and went to war.

Domitian was away for a good eight months. This time, Gaius was not required to go. That meant eight months of comparative peace, although he did act as the absent Praetorians' focal point for their communications with Rome. It was extra work, but work he relished. He dealt with correspondence swiftly and was able to spend more time than usual with Lucilla. They both enjoyed that, though they accepted this would be a limited treat.

Perhaps it made both of them consider having a full life together. A life where they lived in one home, as one domestic unit, all the time.

While Gaius was kicking his heels at the Camp, he sometimes mused over investment calculations. This, he knew, is traditional in bureaucracy where, when you are not scooping your ear wax, or reading love letters under the desk, naturally you work out financial projections for your retirement on the back of an old report. He began to correspond more closely about the import-export business in Hispania Tarraconensis that he had inherited

430

from his old centurion, Decius Gracilis. He had never sold that; maybe an inspection trip over to Spain would be something to do if he ever retired. He certainly thought it a good idea to frighten the freedman he had inherited with that possibility. After he wrote to the manager, income picked up. Impressed, he even looked up Colonia Caesaraugusta on a map. Just in case.

He had served with the Praetorians now for almost thirteen years. If he wanted, he could leave after another three. He was thirty-six. In his prime, he reckoned, with years to come; even though many men never made it to his current age, he was still fit and full of energy.

He had been earning a high salary for a long time and had barely touched the money. It struck him that he and Lucilla could have a very pleasant life ahead of them. He told her. Seeing him as a dedicated career soldier, she did not take this too seriously, though she noted how Gaius was thinking.

*　　　*　　　*

Gaius had been involved in the flurry of intense commissariat activity that preceded the Emperor leaving on campaign; there were similar japes on Domitian's return. The Emperor had been successful in quieting the Suebi and Sarmatians, although from intelligence coming back from the frontier, this was viewed as only a temporary respite. Military action along the Danube might continue for years. Indeed it did, though what Domitian had achieved would serve as a sound basis for future campaigns, one day to be immortalised on Trajan's

Column.

A Triumph was suggested for the January of Domitian's return to Rome. But this time, even he took a muted view of his achievements; he only accepted the minor celebration called an Ovation. It involved some pageantry, in which Gaius was tangentially involved, and culminated in the Emperor dedicating a laurel wreath to Jupiter on the Capitol. It lacked the elaborate street procession of a full Triumph but, for the third time, Domitian handed out a congiarium of three hundred sesterces apiece, so as they clutched their big gold pieces the public were happy.

That year there was a serious grain shortage, with a long period of famine. Even the Praetorian cornicularius had to attend extra victualling meetings with a slightly furrowed brow; he had ten thousand men to feed daily, plus supplying horse fodder for fifteen hundred cavalry. If the military granary ran low, it would be grim. When Rome was short of food, supplying the Guards took some precedence, but that had to be handled carefully to avoid unrest. Good public relations in a time of distraught bread queues were essential. A cornicularius who had family in Rome could grasp the sensitivities.

For Gaius the grain shortage was an interesting aspect of his job. A political solution was not his remit, thankfully, but he was called to occasional tactics meetings. A Prefect of Supply had oversight of grain acquisition, markets and distribution, so at such mainly civic gatherings Gaius was an unimportant contributor, with his report scheduled last on the agenda, so it would be summed up in a minutes appendix if discussion overran. Nobody reads appendices.

'Another action meeting,' he would groan to Lucilla. 'Memo: an "action meeting" is one where an "action list" will be produced, probably the same as last time—and resulting in no action.' Like all the best administrators, his outlook was pessimistic. Like the very best, his office usually out-performed his cautious forecasts.

He learned more than he expected about the great provincial grain baskets that supplied Rome's hungry mouths: the endless golden wheatfields of North Africa, which produced nearly two-thirds of the city's requirements, and Egypt which sent a large contribution, with additions also from Spain, Sicily and Sardinia. He cared more than he had expected, too.

It made him think about the enormous trade in commodities around the Empire. Both necessities and luxuries were shipped and carted in all directions. Most Romans enjoyed the benefits automatically, especially since trade was barred to the senatorial class, so they loftily sneered at it. Clearly there was a packet to be made. A constant theme at the provisioning meetings was how to avoid speculation. How to encourage the provinces to grow and send what the great greedy city of Rome constantly needed. How to keep the negotiators and shippers sweet, especially since so many of those slippery buggers were foreign.

Vinius Clodianus was no snob and at heart he would always be a logistics man. He had learned that from his father, who as a vigiles tribune had kept order across two districts of Rome, balancing the needs of disparate communities and the differing demands of law and firefighting, balancing the books, keeping his superiors at a safe distance, keeping one jump in front of the criminal and corrupt, keeping his head. Glimpses of the business world brought Gaius back to his own small involvement in trade, with his inherited Spanish wine enterprise. He knew he could be an entrepreneur. He filed that thought away, though an intrigued Lucilla was watching him.

Eventually Domitian passed an edict that in order to encourage cereal production, no new vines could be planted in Italy, while in the provinces at least half of the existing acreage was to be torn up. On this almost unique occasion when Domitian ventured into legislating for the Empire as a whole, the plan failed to work. After petitions from the eastern provinces, the Emperor rescinded his edict.

Next, he tried a clear pavement law for Rome: the city was like a vast emporium, its highways clogged with barbers' stools, vegetable stalls, money-changers' tables, pots and baskets for sale. Goods hung off every pillar and awning. Most clutter was tawdry. Some was dangerous. Domitian passed a law that all this encroaching paraphernalia must be kept back behind the frontage line. That failed to bring him popularity, too.

Some people rejoiced that Rome had been restored to them; most bewailed the inconvenience and loss of character. In Plum Street, the previously spreading tables outside the Scallopshell were folded away, though Cretticus allowed the bar to use part of his garden instead. Even Lucilla's assistants, Glyke and Calliste, had to stop carrying out manicures outside their salon and make everyone move indoors. It was a nightmare for gossipmongers. Closeted in the narrow shops or workshops that lined the streets, they missed half of what was going on.

While people grumbled, worse happened. This was the year when, for those in public life, real fear began.

*   *   *

Domitian said an emperor who had to execute only a few opponents was just lucky. Compared with past and future emperors, he was in fact restrained, though there was a keen sense that he hated the Senate, and many who escaped with their lives were exiled instead. Trajan was to say pithily that Domitian was the worst emperor but had the best amici (Trajan himself being one). Trajan was safe; he earned Domitian's trust during the Saturninus Revolt and now he was serving as governor of Pannonia, one of the Empire's danger zones.

Crucially aware of his own competence, during the Reign of Terror, Trajan was on the up. Still, he would have seen other governors of provinces executed without trial when Domitian doubted their loyalty. He would also have seen what happened to Agricola—a man whose unusually long posting of seven years had added most of Britain to Roman control, despite climate, terrain and implacable natives. But to Agricola's disgust, when Domitian then needed troops on the Danube, the vital British legions were reduced and the army ordered to retreat from its hard-won territory in Caledonia. On Agricola's return to Rome, he received triumphal honours, though it must have seemed grudging since he was then denied the plum posting to Africa or Asia that should have been his right. His son-in-law Tacitus would even claim that Domitian tried to poison off the slighted general.

Ingratitude was there, certainly. It rankled more when Agricola died that year. Those loyal to him felt Agricola had been finished off prematurely by the Emperor's poor treatment. Gaius Vinius, for one, thought so; he had served in Britain under Julius Agricola and soldiers are traditionally nostalgic about the commanders of their youth. Every time Domitian's antipathy to the senatorial classes led to some spiteful act against an individual, such ripples spread. He could kill a man who offended him, yet he left everyone who had ever been impressed by that man feeling angry. He had enough acumen to feel the growing backlash, though that only increased his isolation and mistrust.

Domitian's friends had lost any management of him. Julia's softening influence was gone, and Domitia seemed powerless. Perhaps, in what had become an empty marriage, she lost interest in trying. With the gradual deterioration of the Emperor's mind came crueller and more abrupt actions. A man was overheard saying that a Thracian gladiator might beat his Gallic opponent but was no match for the patron of the Games— Domitian; the speaker was dragged from his seat and immediately thrown into the arena to be torn apart by dogs.

Such was the Emperor's reputation that people actually shook with terror in his presence. As despots do, he noticed with grim amusement. Everything was summed up in his known wish to be addressed as *dominus et deus*, Master and God. 'Master' was commonplace; it would ruffle no plumage, because it was a normal mark of respect used by everyone from soldiers to schoolchildren. But to call any living person a god aroused revulsion. Even deified Roman emperors were a recent phenomenon; they had to be awarded transubstantiation by their successor or the Senate, and they definitely had to die first. Domitian's own father had made a joke about that, as Vespasian realised he had a fatal illness.

Domitian publicly denied any formal claim to Master and God, yet he accepted the title, seemed to want it—and openly used it in his own correspondence. Sycophants took the hint.

As in all courts full of terror, shameless fawning occurred. In the glistening halls on the Palatine and the remote citadel of Alba, Domitian basked in flattery. People bowed; visitors flung themselves into inappropriate acts of obeisance; there was vile foot-kissing. The careful myth promulgated by the Emperor Augustus, that Rome's leader should be a normal man living modestly, merely the 'first among equals', had always been a sham; it was now completely cast away.

*   *   *

There would never be an organised intellectual opposition. Nonetheless, even though life under a despot grew nerve-racking some still dared to react against it.

First, the Younger Pliny and Herrenius Senecio, himself a Spaniard, joined forces to prosecute Baebius Massa, the governor of Hispania Baetica, for maladministration. It was all the braver because Baebius was a friend of Domitian's. They won

437

their case. Baebius had to surrender his property to pay off the provincials he had swindled, but with Domitian behind him he survived politically. He retaliated and prosecuted Senecio for treason. The charge failed, but then Mettius Carus, the man who had prosecuted the Vestal Cornelia, took it up in his usual abrasive style.

This was the final stage of a long confrontation with a group of entrenched republicans with stoic beliefs that went right back to the reign of Nero. It led to deaths, and to suspicion of philosophers. It even led to the unlikely spectacle of Nemurus, the closet practitioner of stoic values, visiting his ex-wife to beg for information, hoping she could squeeze her tame Praetorian.

The bony academic managed to turn up at Plum Street not only when Lucilla was out, attending to a customer at the woman's home, but Vinius was in. For Nemurus this was the worst possible scenario. It forced the two men into an awkward tryst, seated on the balcony in the late afternoon with a bowl of fried stuffed dates and cups of watered wine, while they awaited Lucilla's return. Nemurus writhed. Vinius (handing snacks po-faced) thought it was very funny.

'I hope you like these. I made them myself.' He guessed Nemurus was helpless in a kitchen. The man looked horrified. 'I don't expect Lucilla to do everything at home. She works so hard on her own account. She deserves spoiling.'

After a frozen silence, Nemurus caught on. 'Are you two . . .'

'Oh! Sorry. Yes, we are.'

Nemurus became desperate to leave but was too gauche to extract himself.

438

Flavia Lucilla arrived shortly. Vinius left the balcony, deliberately pulling a door closed. Nemurus heard him greet Lucilla in a low voice, 'Your ex is here.' A silence followed. Nemurus imagined them canoodling. A petrifying dog then pushed open the folding door and growled at him.

Vinius came back, bringing a third chair which he placed close to his own. 'Put him down, Terror! . . . She's coming.'

Nemurus was now trapped on this small balcony, in the kind of evening the couple must enjoy regularly, either alone or with friends or family. Muted sunshine. Wine and titbits. Pleasant conversation. Laughter. Things that made him nervous.

The awful dog clambered on top of the Praetorian when he resumed his seat. He played with the beast, airily showing off how easy and commanding he was with it.

Lucilla appeared. At once she dived into the stuffed dates, eating with one hand while with the other she removed her sandals and rubbed her feet. Always a wearer of silly shoes, the straps had dug into her, not badly but enough. With her mouth full, she said nothing to Nemurus, just raised an eyebrow questioning his visit. The dog left the Praetorian and lay down by her chair. Using the creature as a footstool, Lucilla buried her bare feet in its horrid fur, wriggling her toes. There could be no doubt, this dreadful pet was beloved of both of them.

'Oh—would you two like to be left alone?' Vinius asked suddenly, as if he had only just thought of it. Polite. Considerate. Sickening.

Of course he made it impossible. Nemurus had

to say no, no; nothing he wanted to discuss was confidential . . . This cut across the first principle of the great stoic philosopher Epictetus, who said that people should not lie.

'So what *do* you want to talk about?' demanded Lucilla bluntly.

Nemurus had to come clean. He harboured a suspicion Lucilla and Vinius were laughing at him. He felt constantly uncomfortable.

One of the charges against Domitian was that in the aftermath of the Saturninus Revolt he had forced confessions by ordering men's genitals to be set on fire. Vinius Clodianus had reduced Nemurus to a wreck by simply handing round canapés. Lucilla was still enjoying the sweetmeats, unaware that her ex-husband was imagining her lover ramming snacks down a suspect's throat . . .

Nemurus said he wanted to ask about the implications of recent opposition trials. Lucilla professed she was confused. Nemurus carefully offered to explain. (The Praetorian, he noticed, said nothing; presumably he kept details of previously condemned subversives all on file.)

'It began about thirty years ago with a senator called Thrasea Paetus, who stood up to Nero. For example, he walked out of the Senate without voting when asked to approve the letter Nero sent to justify murdering his own mother, Agrippina.'

'A terrible woman?'

'Agreed, but it *was* matricide. Paetus offended Nero, then retired to private life. But his role model was the upright Cato, who had drawn attention to the ambitions of Julius Caesar; Paetus wrote Cato's panegyric. The simple style of living that Paetus adopted seemed an affront to Nero's crazy court.

He was charged before the Senate, who caved in and convicted him, it is said, due to the presence of large numbers of intimidating troops.'

'Hmm,' commented Vinius: some uninterpretable professional remark.

Nemurus swallowed. 'Paetus went home and opened his veins. His daughter Fannia, who was charged in this latest trial, was married to Helvidius Priscus, another ardent stoic. He survived from Nero to Vespasian, though he was banished by Nero at one point for demonstrating approval of Caesar's murderers.'

'That is illegal?' Lucilla asked Vinius.

'No wise man displays busts of Brutus and Cassius, nor celebrates their birthdays.' His tone was neutral, suspiciously so, Nemurus thought. Vinius now joined the discussion: 'Wouldn't you say Helvidius Priscus embodies how these stoics deliberately confront emperors?'

'You mean his quarrels with Vespasian?'

'Yes; he was lucky that Vespasian was a tolerant old fellow, who let him continue his abominable behaviour for so long. Helvidius refused to acknowledge Vespasian as emperor in his judicial edicts as praetor. That was bloody rude. He resolutely called Vespasian by his private name, instead of his title. For the Emperor it must have been galling.'

Nemurus explained, 'Helvidius was disgusted that Vespasian wanted to found a hereditary dynasty. He always refused to compromise, until Vespasian felt obliged to execute him. Vespasian is said to have tried to rescind the order.'

'An old trick, but looks good!' answered Vinius, smiling.

Nemurus was a little shocked. It had never struck him that Vespasian could have been devious about it.

'Now,' said Vinius, 'Senecio's treason must have been deliberate: he wrote a sympathetic biography of Helvidius Priscus.'

'But it was a funeral eulogy . . . Have you read it?' A teacher's question. Nemurus noticed that Vinius avoided answering. He found it extremely hard to gauge this one-eyed man's expression. Presumably if a Praetorian Guard did read republican literature, it was for obnoxious state reasons.

'Gaius went to the trial.' Lucilla leaned forwards and spoke earnestly across her lover's lap, 'You do realise the position Gaius Vinius holds now? He is the cornicularius—the Guards' chief-of-staff.'

'Just a bean-counter,' Vinius put in, this time definitely smiling.

'Congratulations,' said Nemurus in a hollow voice.

Vinius stood up. 'I'll fetch more bites.'

*   *   *

An interlude followed, during which both Vinius and Lucilla came and went, bringing items for an informal supper. They clearly assumed that Nemurus would stay. New wine appeared. Perhaps by an oversight, Vinius only poured it for Lucilla and himself, but Lucilla seamlessly reached over and filled Nemurus' beaker. It was a very palatable red from Spain. Clearly, they lived well.

'Tell him about the trial, Gaius.'

'Seems a shame to spoil a pleasant evening.'

'Well he already knows it stank.'

'These are good; where did you get them?' Vinius was asking about seafood rissoles. It was not a distraction; intrigued, Nemurus watched their relaxed interplay between political and domestic subjects. Lucilla answered, then Vinius smoothly summarised the controversial treason trial as if the interruption never happened.

The seven accused included Arria, the fanatical widow of Thrasea Paetus and Fannia, his equally determined daughter, widow of Helvidius Priscus. Arulenus Rusticus, a friend of Thrasea, was convicted for writing a panegyric on him, a work which Domitian had had burned. Rusticus' brother and sister-in-law were also on trial.

Senecio's oration for Helvidius Priscus had been written at Fannia's request and in court Mettius Carus forced her, using brutal interrogation, to admit she lent Senecio her husband's notebooks. Senecio had further damned himself by refusing to stand for public office.

Helvidius Priscus junior, the late stoic's son, was on a different charge: he had written a play. Based on the story of the Trojan prince Paris abandoning his first wife Oenone for Helen of Troy, it looked like a jibe at Domitian for divorcing Domitia over the actor, also aptly named Paris, supposedly to enable his passion for Julia.

'Domitian made both Rusticus and Helvidius junior consuls last year,' Vinius pointed out. 'Diffusing the opposition through friendly overtures.'

'Buying them off,' scoffed Lucilla. 'It never works!'

Three male defendants were now to be executed;

Domitian had banished the other four, three of them women, to remote islands. The whole affair had become another cause célèbre. This show trial would always be cited as proof that Domitian was a despot.

*　　*　　*

'If you are worried about your own position, Nemurus,' said Vinius, 'forget it. Domitian has no quarrel with stoics as such. The condemned committed very public sins: parading their republicanism, a long family history of enmity with the Flavians, withholding themselves from public duties—plus writings that made saints of previous martyrs.'

'Don't write any eulogies,' instructed Lucilla crisply.

'So much for my proposed Life and Times of the Late Herrenius Senecio . . .' Even Nemurus could make jokes. 'I teach, dear; I don't write. Just tell me,' he pleaded with Vinius. 'Are there to be banishments of philosophers?'

'Sorry. Privileged information.'

'I think it will happen, Vinius.'

'I think you are right.'

'You said it was privileged.'

'The information is. I gave you my opinion.'

'Subtle! Luckily you have freedom of speech.'

'True,' said Vinius. 'What a glorious regime we live in, under our Master and God.'

Lucilla put a hand on his arm. 'Gaius, stop teasing. What should he do?'

'Does he need to do anything?' Vinius shrugged. 'I don't want to insult the man, but he is well below

444

the sightlines. Why would anyone bother to attack you, Nemurus?'

'We live in dark times—but not for most people.' Lucilla reinforced Vinius' comment.

'Be realistic.' Vinius was blunt. 'You are not worth it. The old prosecutors of Thrasea Paetus gained five million sesterces from it. The latest lot will make their pile, plus Domitian's gratitude. If you are anxious however, get out of Rome, man. Go now. Go of your own accord, so you can choose your destination and find a quiet life.'

'He cannot afford it,' protested Lucilla.

'*Exactly!* A poor teacher is not worth prosecuting.'

Nemurus remained silent and despondent.

'So what's perturbing you?' insisted Vinius.

'What happened to Juvenal. He was in the circle I move in.'

Lucilla growled. 'The idiot cannot expect to get away forever with saying Julia died after popping out a series of aborted foetuses, "each the image of Uncle".'

Vinius winced, then nodded. 'Nor his descriptions of Domitian's council in that turbot-cooking satire. He was brutal—about important men, many of whom are professional informers: very shortsighted.'

'You know the work of Juvenal?' Nemurus was amazed. The Satires had not yet been formally published, though drafts had been read at private parties; presumably, Vinius had been informed by spies.

'So what has happened to this bloody daft author, Nemurus?' The Praetorian pretended not to know.

445

'Apparently there were whispers of "a promotion"; Juvenal is an equestrian. He thought he was to have an honourable military posting; instead he was packed off to an oasis miles from civilisation, stuck in a quarry in the Egyptian desert.'

'Classic Domitian!' Vinius guffawed unkindly. 'I have a thought,' he then offered. 'If you do consider moving, Nemurus, I know someone with a working farm on the Bay of Naples. It's towards Surrentum and escaped the volcano. She might welcome a respectable tenant living there as a rent-free caretaker.'

'Who is this?' asked Lucilla a little too quickly.

'Caecilia.' Vinius twinkled. 'It's her famous legacy. Decent size, room for you to take your parents, if that's a worry, Nemurus; great views; the best weather in the world. Domitian's villa is safely on the opposite side of the Bay. The area is being revived after the eruption and there is plenty of culture for a man like yourself.'

'Have you been there?' Lucilla demanded.

'No. Septimus took a look.'

'He would!' They had dinner with Septimus and Caecilia occasionally now; Lucilla felt ambivalent about the friendship.

'Who are these people?' Nemurus sensed undercurrents.

'My ex-wife and her husband. Nice couple. Obviously,' said Gaius, teasing Lucilla, 'Septimus owes me a favour for freeing up Caecilia and her fabulous farm for him.'

'Bastard.' Lucilla showed him no real malice.

Gaius then reached across the arm of her chair and clasped her hand, looking at her tenderly.

446

Public displays of affection between men and women were traditionally un-Roman, but even with Nemurus awkwardly watching, the couple continued to hold hands. Nemurus could tell they did it frequently, whether anyone was there or not.

*   *   *

The meal ended. The wine flagon was not refilled. Nemurus decided to mention that he must be going.

Lucilla merely waved him off, staying where she was. It was Vinius who saw him out. The Praetorian actually came onto the landing, holding the door closed behind him. 'I meant what I said about Naples. If it seems good, let me know.'

'That is unexpectedly kind of you.'

'I want something,' Vinius admitted. His tone was unexceptional, but his stare was harder. 'Don't look so worried. My affection for Lucilla has always shielded you. Sincerely, I do not expect anyone else to betray you either. Our Master and God permits honest philosophy; what you believe, even what you teach, is your own affair. But I want to protect Lucilla.'

'What do you mean?'

'Don't contact her again. This is not personal, though I suppose you are entitled to think so. If ever any informer should look at you too closely, I do not want them to pick up a silver snailtrail leading to her.'

The teacher chewed his lip.

'She is defiant in her choice of friends,' said the Praetorian softly. 'She will not drop you; so *you* have to do it. "*The point is, not how long you live, but how nobly.*" Seneca,' Vinius spelt out. 'You know:

447

wise, compassionate, amiable—one of those worthy men of literature who got himself killed by a mad emperor.'

29

One day, in his thirty-seventh year, when he ought to have known better, the Praetorian cornicularius Clodianus was called in to the Prefects' office and invited to join a small committee of like-minded men. He could see no way to wriggle out. It was proposed to him, as such nightmares always are, as an honour.

Privately, he thought the term 'like-minded men' carried the same whiff as 'concerned citizens'; it meant madmen with unpleasant designs on society. He had served in the vigiles. He had kept the surveillance lists of mathematicians, Christians and astrologers. He knew what like-minded men who gathered in furtive groups were generally aiming for and as a soldier he disliked it.

'There has been bit of toing and froing on this,' the Prefect admitted. It was Casperius Aelianus, the man Gaius first met after Dacia. 'Usual nonsense. Changes of mind. Waiting for a decision. Still, we seem to be clear now, and you'll be glad to know it has been agreed you are absolutely the right man for the job.'

No one else will touch it, thought Gaius. Luckily, keeping his private thoughts hidden was one of his talents. It was essential to his job. Being one-eyed with a wrecked face gave him every advantage in appearing inscrutable. With the Prefect, he played on it shamelessly. 'Thank you, sir.'

His tone was so benign the Prefect shifted on his seat, caught by a riffle of uncertainty. He suspected that under the grave veneer, this Clodianus could be a subversive bugger.

The new committee was official, yet it was secret. Clodianus was given to understand that the Emperor was aware of its existence. That implied Domitian approved. Perhaps he had even suggested it—always a worrying aspect.

'May I ask who chose me, sir?'

'Abascantus. Know him?'

'Vaguely. I know who he is, obviously—chief correspondence secretary. I have dealings with his people.'

There were hundreds of palace clerks, specialising in either Greek or Latin paperwork; Abascantus sat at the top, supervising both. The cornicularius received documents from various officials who had worked out that he was a safe person to push queries out to (where 'safe' meant, if the item looked harmless, he would not bother to relay tricky questions back but would diligently lose the original). He had even seen bumf with Abascantus' signature on it, especially while the Emperor had been away in Pannonia, taking his chief officials with him. A lot of dross had floated back to the Camp then. Gaius had pigeonholed it with good-nature, though he could always be relied upon to find it again if unexpectedly requested.

Indeed, should that happen, he would even add a note or two, prettying up the document so it looked as if trouble had been taken to deal with the matter. Usually that sufficed to get the bumf lobbed back to him harmlessly for filing. He would

449

put it away in the cache he had labelled very neatly with a Greek word for round objects. His symbol of two circles, he would explain sombrely to new clerks on their first day, meant the documents filed there had already been on two full circuits for comment, or as the cornicularius called it 'chugging to Pannonia and back'. If the new clerk had not twigged the code by the end of the week, he would be transferred to granary records.

Perhaps Abascantus, who came from a family of imperial scribes, had noticed the devotion with which Clodianus tended the altar of bureaucracy.

'An old-style freedman,' said Casperius Aelianus. 'Younger than you might expect, horrible hairstyle, you must know him by sight . . . I have him down as one of Domitian's personal choices, not inherited from Titus.'

'He involves himself in postings?'

'Don't they all?' The Prefect looked demure. 'I think he prepares most of the Emperor's personnel suitability briefings.' That was a new definition, which the cornicularius noted approvingly. He collected jargon.

'Right,' said Clodianus. 'Well, better than having a ballet-dancer in charge of promotions, as that dodgy poet once claimed.'

'Oh quite!'

'I once rashly asked my predecessor what happened to promotion on merit.'

'Oh merit works,' the Prefect told him, in an offhand tone. 'So long as you back it up with a large enough thank-you package for the freedman who gives out posts.'

'So what exactly is my remit, sir?'

He thought the Prefect looked slightly

embarrassed.

Aelianus explained that the superstitious Domitian regularly had the hour and manner of his death foretold by astrologers. Such prophecies went back so long that even his late father had chivvied him about it on an occasion when Domitian was handed mushrooms—the famous medium used for poisoning the Emperor Claudius. As his leery son refused the dish, Vespasian had joshed, 'You'd do better to worry about swords!' But Domitian was becoming increasingly afraid of assassination, and in the near future.

'So when's this scenario due to occur, sir?'

'Don't ask me. Highly confidential.'

'Right,' murmured Clodianus, feeling depressed. 'A few details would have helped with planning. Date and time would have been perfect.'

'Of course. But possessing the Emperor's horoscope, that would be treason.'

'Understood! If anybody told us, we would all have to be executed.'

'Bloody ridiculous,' agreed the Prefect.

He had been in post a good nine years. He thought he knew everything. He and Clodianus had worked together for long enough to develop an easygoing relationship. Although Aelianus saw his chief-of-staff as slightly maverick, he also thought he saw a steel backbone there.

According to the rule of thumb Clodianus used, after nine years, the Prefect was well past his best. In the Clodianus system, you spent the first year fumbling through everything, the second getting most things right, and the third absolutely tiptop efficient. From then on, you—and even perhaps your superiors—believed you were perfect, but you stopped trying. He himself was at that point. A sad moment to be noticed by some loopy freedman . . .

The caustic Clodianus had remembered Abascantus now. Way back, when he used to be on imperial escort duty, before he went to Dacia, he had been present one day when Domitian announced that freedman's promotion to chief secretary. Abascantus had a pushy wife, Priscilla. She had thrown herself to the marble mosaic in front of Domitian, exuding gratitude for their princely master's honour to her husband.

Sickening, Clodianus thought. Then he corrected himself. Flattery was only one way to proceed: you lied. You lied and praised him until your teeth hurt, in case Domitian's mood changed abruptly.

'We want trusted men to work on this.'

'Absolutely, sir!'

'Abascantus is setting up the committee to put the Emperor's mind at rest. Domitian should now feel reassured, because you are out there, looking for the people who intend to fulfil that wicked prophecy. He has convinced himself there are enemies who hate him; he suspects a conspiracy.'

'The idea is, I will infiltrate any desperados and observe . . .'

The Prefect looked embarrassed again. 'Assuming they exist.'

Which we are assuming they do not, sir? This is all a fantasy.

Too right. Just keep the stylus-pushers happy. 'So— are you up for it?'

'I suppose so, sir. Let me go along and give the wise ones my investigative expertise.'

'Good man! That's all anyone is asking.'

No formal minutes were taken for the Prefect—

452

or not that Clodianus could see—but he felt convinced that whatever he had replied would go on his record. He was doomed if he did this and doomed if he turned it down. A wrong answer might look positively black. He was a Praetorian, whose job was protecting the Emperor. Any hint that he was lukewarm in respect of this committee would be the end of him.

He felt secret meetings were a stupid way to go about it. Still, he felt that about most things.

He had accepted a place on a body that he guessed would mutter away for years, calling for ineffectual papers, reviewing false evidence and vacuous submissions, making lists of action-points that no one subsequently reckoned were their responsibility, generally losing sight of its original mandate. Its mandate was in its title: the Committee to Preserve the Emperor.

'Sheer bloody madness!' complained the Prefect. 'Chasing bloody shadows.'

Encouraged, Gaius suggested, 'If there's no real evidence, I could hire a few dodgy characters to look like activists, get them to behave suspiciously; then we could watch them at it and report back.' Enjoying himself, he grew more inventive. 'Dress them up in hooded cloaks, buy them all drinks in a seedy bar on the waterside . . .'

'You are being frivolous!' grinned the Prefect, glad of any light-heartedness to ease his constant burden of facing up to his emperor's resolute anxiety. He knew the cornicularius was whimsical only to stay sane in Rome's deadly drowning-pool where they all desperately dog-paddled. He would do the job. 'I hardly need remind you how important this is, Clodianus. It is the highest grade of top secret.'

'Yes, sir.'

'Don't mention this to anybody—not even your wife.'

'No need to worry, sir. I am a soldier,' Clodianus assured him gravely. 'I cannot have a wife.'

He went straight home and told Lucilla all about it. Lucilla said, 'Look on the bright side, love. If *you* cannot be told the hour when the old horoscope says our Master and God is doomed to die—then no plotters will know when to arrive with daggers either.'

'What a woman!' exclaimed Gaius. 'What a mind! Jupiter, I love you, girl. Let's go to bed.'

*　　　*　　　*

Gaius was perfectly right. There was no conspiracy to investigate.

Well, not then.

PART 6
Rome: AD 94–96

Few tyrants die in their beds

30

Abascantus, freedman of the Augustus, *ab epistolis*—receiver of correspondence—chirruped from the top of the tree.

Titus Flavius Abascantus—important to distinguish, because there were many Abascanti and they worked for more than one emperor. Imperial freedmen, dedicated members of the palace *familia*, kept their old slave name. They unabashedly used it as their third, personal name while their first two signified the Emperor who had liberated them. So, in the great tribe of imperial servants, *Tiberius Claudius* Abascantus had once flourished under the Julio-Claudians, as secretary of finance. He was still alive and would survive to ninety-seven. That put him well above the worn-out slaves who worked on country estates in toiling battalions, let alone the grey-faced workers who were sent to die of hard labour and metal poisoning in Rome's great silver and gold mines.

Being the emperor's slave was no penalty. Living the good life, moving in high circles, gaining influence and property. The long-surviving Tiberius Claudius Abascantus had had a son with the same name who held the same important position under Nero, but predeceased his father. Yet even that son lasted longer than most grocers before earning an expensive terracotta memorial, with two fine winged gryphons to guard his tomb eternally:

Tiberius Claudius Abascantus,
freedman of Augustus, finance secretary,
lived forty-five years,
Claudia Epicharis, his wife, to her
well-deserving husband.

Wasn't there some trouble with Epicharis?
She killed herself.
The Piso affair?
Don't ask.

Titus Flavius Abascantus, today's man, had different parentage. It was unlikely his slave name was a gesture to either past finance secretary, and once scandal attached to them, as it had done, he shunned any connection. He worked in a separ??ate branch of bureaucracy, correspondence. He liked to suggest he honoured a different code of loyalty. Perhaps that was true.

He had gained his high position at a very early age. He was called 'this young man' approvingly by the poet Statius. Abascantus was claimed as a friend by Statius, yet Flavia Lucilla, who knew the poet, his wife and also the chief secretary's wife, reckoned any 'friendship' with Abascantus was one-way. Poets fluttered around the most senior freedmen, desperate to have their work noticed. Even Martial, whose writing Domitian apparently enjoyed, had pleaded with a chamberlain to slip his book onto the Emperor's bedroom couch at some well-chosen moment.

Parthenius, another chamberlain, handled such requests now. He organised the Emperor's personal existence; he lived in Domitian's company

458

and controlled access to him. Poets believed the Emperor was most likely to browse epigrams when he was secreted in his private quarters. This could have been lucrative for Parthenius, except that poets notoriously had no cash. *They* needed to extract money from the Emperor, which was why poems were so glutinous with flattery, flattery he believed: he was the new Jupiter, Jupiter on earth. He knew everything, saw everything, could cure sickness; his gaze struck terror like thunderbolts, he could kill with a thought . . .

Parthenius had told Abascantus that nowadays Domitian never read poems. They joked that Jupiter was not renowned for having his nose in a scroll. Heavenly Jove was too busy fornicating. People said Domitian did the same (presumably not manifesting himself in a shower of gold or disguised as a swan, else the rumour mill would have gone wild). Parthenius, a highly discreet state servant, neither confirmed nor denied any of it.

Parthenius was another *Tiberius Claudius*: the older generation. Even so, he and Abascantus thought the same way. One thing they knew was that the imperial administration would always outlive the current office holder. Emperors might come and go; their grand secretariats would roll on unflaggingly. It could be argued—and was certainly believed by some bureaucrats—that the secretariats, with their archives and forward planning and well-established means of conducting official business, were more important than the Caesar Augustus on the throne. That especially applied during the reign of a bad emperor. To a true bureaucrat, such periods were when the administration really came into its own. A weak emperor would be steered by his freedmen, as Claudius was by the magisterial Narcissus. A doomed despot might even be helped to remove himself, as Nero was by Phaon and Epaphroditus.

*   *   *

Titus Flavius Abascantus, the youthful high-flyer, was a person of such style he verged on the vain. He had hair he was proud of; he wore it thick and long, so he had that affected way of tossing back his luxuriant locks that always annoys everyone else. He was blond. In a man it never helps. Touch of the playboy.

Unquestionably one of the Empire's finest minds, Domitian's Abascantus had all the traditional talents: an all-round, incisive intelligence, elegant drafting skills, a clubbable personality, astute judgement of when and how to approach a difficult master. It went without saying, he had been educated to high standards at the palace; both his Latin and his Greek were perfect; he could dip into his treasure chest of literary allusions and produce an apt quotation like a jeweller plucking an expensive gem for a rich client. Better still, Domitian liked him.

Redraft that: Domitian *seemed* to like him. Domitian never relished having to be grateful to anybody else.

Abascantus became wealthy. He accumulated money and property. On duty, which was most of the time, he wore the white livery with gold trimmings that was standard at the palace—though he clad himself in a particularly lavish version, multi-thread cloth with heavy gilt embroidery. Plus

460

bracelets and fistfuls of finger rings. Even earrings. And he walked in a miasma of extraordinary oriental perfume.

Some people disliked him. Inevitably there was jealousy of his talent, even after Abascantus ceased to push himself, merely enjoying his reputation and his position at the top. Minions ran around and did the work; one of his skills was knowing how to choose his juniors, then where and when to delegate, or on other occasions, when to step up before his Master and be seen to give personal attention to some delicate and demanding matter.

All of Domitian's slaves and freedmen were celebrated for their calmness and for showing respect to visitors. So, Abascantus had been slickly groomed. He was never obsequious, yet always polite. Nobody had ever seen him lose his temper. He would listen, as if whatever was being said to him was genuinely interesting. He made even idiots feel they had a place. Up to a point it encouraged them to raise the standard of their contributions to papers and meetings.

Unfortunately, with the truly inept, that could only ever be up to a point. In contrast to Abascantus' own glittering mind, idiots would always stand out as what they were.

*   *   *

Abascantus gave the impression the safety committee had been all his own idea. Perhaps it was; perhaps not. He was the kind of administrator who would steal other people's cherished initiatives without even realising he had done it. (He would also distance himself smartly, once an initiative went wrong.)

He kept things informal, which meant there were comfortable seats, with cushions everywhere. Attendants greeted committee members by name, as if each was regarded as a special expert. To show how far he was different from normal hidebound bureaucrats, Abascantus served almond tuiles and peppermint tea. That is, he had them served, in silverware, by very polite young slaves.

'May as well be civilised.'

Fuck me! My snooty Auntie Viniana would feel at home in this place.

'This place' was Nero's Golden House, across the Forum from the Palatine: secure, luxurious, well staffed with clerks and messengers if needed, yet now slightly apart from the main centre of court business. Once past the Colossus which stood in the vestibule, awed visitors entered famous rooms, such as the octagonal dining room with a revolving ceiling from which perfumes had once rained down on Nero's guests; there were intricate marble fountains; there were tall corridors painted with exquisite designs that would influence European art for many centuries. As soon as Domitian's new Palatine palace was finished, all these grand rooms had been abandoned as regular office space. The Golden House was then ideal for an official committee whose subject was top secret.

Apparently serious, the Praetorian cornicularius, the chief secretary's most recently co-opted member, asked where the freedman acquired his almond fancies. For once, the urbane Abascantus was thrown. He had no idea. A man of his status had probably never bought anything from a street stall or shop; it was doubtful if he even carried cash

462

on him. He managed to mutter something about the work of palace pastry chefs. Still, Clodianus had wrong-footed him; the Guard had slyly established his own credentials as a true citizen of Rome. Abascantus lived remotely; the cornicularius was a regular in the Street of Patisserie Makers. Wherever that was.

The chief secretary had perhaps presupposed that a Praetorian would wolf food down with disgraceful manners, but Clodianus held a pastry daintily between one finger and thumb, while he talked good sense about anonymous letters: 'Composed with the left hand to disguise the writing. I used to wonder why these people don't just dictate their secret note to a slave—but of course if they do, then a slave knows.'

'Do we take them seriously?'

'We do. Such letters must always be scanned very carefully. I read this horrible batch you circulated, and while I am open to other opinions—' The Guard made a graceful gesture with his tea bowl (though he did not pause to let other committee members interrupt) 'to me these are all low grade. A mix of genuine mental illness and crackpot idealism: nothing that I anticipate will end in a serious attempt. Solo efforts, scribbled by loners in garrets, people who will never in reality emerge from their hidey-holes.'

'You cannot detect organisation?' asked Abascantus, to demonstrate his grasp of the issue.

'No, although you clearly understand that is what we have to fear. But nothing suggests a plot. If we trace these senders, they can be dealt with in the usual way.' Nobody wanted to ask what that was.

Someone did risk enquiring what would happen

463

in practice if a deranged loner turned up with a weapon outside Domitian's audience room.

Clodianus replied patiently. 'As I'm sure you know, Vespasian made a public point of ending the tradition that visitors were checked for swords.' The others all tried to look well informed. 'Well, don't believe everything you read in the *Daily Gazette*. The new ruling was meant to end senators having to endure the indignity of a search. Old Vespasian had had it done to him and he loathed the experience. But believe me, the Guards frisk everybody else. *We* carry swords, but otherwise, not so much as a pocket fruit-knife passes in. Even attendants are forbidden arms.'

'Have I not seen Parthenius with a weapon?' sniped Abascantus.

'The bedchamber man?' Clodianus smiled. 'Yes, Domitian gave him a special dispensation. It makes the favoured Parthenius feel like a big meatball, I'm sure. Last time I looked, he had a bit of a toy in that fancy scabbard. I assume we discount Parthenius as an assassin?' he threw back.

Abascantus assented primly. 'Parthenius is one of the Emperor's most trusted servants.' The Guard had a shadow of a grin, as if he was thinking, *Top of my suspects list, then!*

Clodianus continued his assessment of the most recent death threats, down-to-earth yet never disrespectful. Eventually Abascantus spotted what he had been up to. By a sleight of hand while he was talking, the hungry cornicularius had whisked all the nibbles his way and cleared the platter.

*   *   *

464

Even though they constantly lost out to him on refreshments, other members soon came to regard this Clodianus as their rock. He brought commonsense and clarity to what could all have been rather hysterical. Abascantus preened himself on his sound choice. (He overlooked the fact that his co-optee had been put forward in the first place by the Prefect, Casperius Aelianus.)

Once during a discussion, Abascantus caught a fly, crushing it between two fingers in mid air. It was a sign, should one be needed, of how sharp the chief secretary was. Nothing wrong with his reactions. Nothing squeamish there. As the freedman wiped his fingers clean on a napkin, he noticed the Praetorian shot him a fast gleam of admiration, the way someone would indicate '*Good catch!*' on the move, while flinging beanbags at the gym. Even so, Abascantus always had a feeling that Vinius Clodianus viewed these proceedings with some sly undercurrent of satire.

For a long time that fly being caught was the most exciting thing that happened at their meetings.

31

It was comparatively quiet, the year many would call the Reign of Terror. Maybe that very quietness increased the fear. Nobody knew what was happening.

What's he up to?

Who knows?

Rumours were everywhere.

Nonetheless, for domestic slaves buying leeks at a stall, for market-gardeners, for young men wrestling in a gymnasium, for toothless old folk dreaming in the sun, for small children trying to keep awake on uncomfortable outdoor benches while primary school teachers drearily intoned alphabets—and for their bored teachers—or for matrons having their hair dressed, most of the time nothing special happened. People who kept diaries would have found them dull reading afterwards.

No one with any sense did write a diary, in case it was ever held against them.

You never knew. That was the problem: doubt that festered and smelt like unnoticed spilt milk, all of the time. Everyone was clenching their buttocks in a permanent state of anxiety and the only people who did well out of *that* were apothecaries who sold greasy haemorrhoid ointments from discreet little booths down suburban side streets. For body-slaves who had to apply these suppositories to the inflamed rear ends of groaning masters, it was not such good news.

A good masseur could make a pile from fees and tips. Uncertain times caused psychosomatic bad backs. Hylus, the top masseur at the public baths that Vinius Clodianus liked, declared that an impacted disc was the signature symptom of political gloom.

Vinius had no problems with his spine; Hylus put this down to regular sex. Vinius smiled mysteriously so Hylus took that as affirmative. He knew when a client was much happier these days.

Booksellers were having a hard time. Statius had published his *Thebeid* two years earlier and it sank like a stone. (Not even the frankest critics told him that was because even as epics go, it was awful.) The first three books of his *Silvae* were now on sale,

466

his occasional poetry. That little scroll struggled too, but then most of his friends and many members of the public had already heard him read the pieces. 'The New Bath House of Claudius Etruscus' held little interest for anyone except Claudius Etruscus, especially since the show-off freedman was not inviting the sweaty Roman public to enjoy his marble plunge pool and silver pipes, only his elite friends—the ones who had already sat through the poem at far too many dinner parties. Otherwise, Rutilius Gallicus was now not even old news but a forgotten man, and what was the point in praising his recovery from the nervous breakdown when he had since died of something else? An epitaph for an arena lion was limp; sceptics said the poem was so short, and weak, because Statius had shied away from saying this was the enormous lion killed by the unfortunate Glabrio when Domitian tried to polish him off. Statius chickened out. Still, he would not waste a poem he had started, so here were thirty rather soppy lines to the late Leo . . .

His friends expected free scrolls with florid inscriptions. Lucilla did buy one; she was thoughtful and supportive. Even she decided Statius was unworldly. When Gaius found the scroll hidden under a cushion, Lucilla was prepared to admit that, on being shown stylised verses entitled *Forest Leaves,* most readers would exit quickly from the bookshop and splurge their cash on street food.

'Bright idea. While you work up an appetite reading how our Master and God graciously invited wonderful Statius to a Saturnalia party—free cheese puffs and belly dancers with big breasts; *ooh how exciting!*—I'll nip out and fetch us a chicken supper.'

'He does *not* specify the flirty-girls' bustband size.'

'Too rude. Make him too popular. This silly bugger describes your Earinus—'

'Not mine.'

'Having his eunuch operation, without even saying "testicles". The bum has no idea how to write a bestseller. He dreams of being read by an adoring minority in two thousand years' time, when he should be putting loaves on the table now . . . Do you want a delicious Frontinian?'

'Yes, please, dear heart.'

'Any sides?'

'Just a green salad and a kiss from you.'

'Good news!' chortled Gaius. 'Kisses are this week's special offer. Ask for one, get a hundred free.'

That was, thought Lucilla, slightly derivative of the poet Catullus although it must be accidental. Gaius would maintain no putrid poet suggested his lines, and Lucilla accepted that they came from his own heart.

*   *   *

Domitian was suffering a bad period, that much was known. His paranoia had flared up like a boil; the fear was that it would escalate with no remission. Full details of his illness were carefully concealed, because the illnesses of the great are privileged information for supposed national interest reasons.

'I would have thought,' groaned Gaius, 'it was in the national interest to know if we are being governed by a maniac.'

He was having his own flare-up—of gloomy

468

cynicism. Many of the Guards were in low spirits. They preferred to be protecting a ruler who set an example of splendid control, not a head-case. Some of the old hands were spending time in drinking dens remembering how much they had liked Titus.

Despite precautions, hints leaked out. People at court had overheard tantrums and slammed doors. They noticed how the palace slaves slunk along corridors keeping close to the wall, heads down and unwilling to be spoken to. Imperial freedmen were jumpy. The Empress never gave anything away, yet even she seemed even more hard-faced than usual.

In the rest of the Empire things seemed quiet. The bad result was that Domitian stayed in Italy therefore, either in Rome itself or at Alba or Naples or some other place too close for comfort. Some resort where the inhabitants thought he was marvellous (because the lower class never saw much of him) while the uppercrust (who did see him close up) were beginning to get itchy about hosting him on their patch.

There were occasional upsets. A tribe in Africa, the Nasamones, rebelled against brutal Roman tax gatherers. There were savage reprisals, but they fought back and invaded the Roman commander's camp. Then, drunk on wine they had looted, the rebel tribe were wiped out. When details were reported, Domitian proudly announced, 'I have forbidden the Nasamones to exist.' Uncompromising words. Liberal minds were shocked.

Eventually new war loomed on the Danube. He enjoyed war, and it kept him occupied. Taking his time, absorbed in every detail, he was at his best. For once, his introverted character made him

469

ideal. It combined his strange personal mixture of brooding with his talent for strong, obsessive planning. He was as good at second-guessing foreign tribes as at scrutinising perceived rivals in Rome; they were all his enemies. But nobody else could decide whether to be reassured or nervous. Which did make them nervous.

All his advisory council were agitated. 'Nothing new,' said Gaius. 'But perhaps some of them may one day break out in spots and tackle him.'

'Is that a hope, love?'

'I'm a Guard. I would have to give naughty boys a reprimand.'

'Since it would mean burning off their goolies and putting their heads on spikes in the Forum, they may hold back.'

'I fear so,' replied Gaius. 'He's got them all so hypnotised with dread, we must be stuck with him.'

Domitian either became more solitary or in public revelled in bad-mannered behaviour. He would finish an evening at court forcing the bullied diners to endure not just wrestlers, tumblers and jugglers but troupes of seedy entertainers from the east, or horrible fortune-tellers. Given the legal attitude to magic in general, and anything that touched on the Emperor's personal fate in particular, this was doubly cruel. Reluctant participants were coerced into applauding these acts, although at any moment their host could contradict himself and turn on them for taking part in forbidden activities.

Even at dinner, he would scarcely eat but would prowl and watch others, while belching or throwing food at his guests. It might seem uncouth but harmless, yet when people were too scared even to

470

be seen wiping off the gravy with a napkin, it was an ugly abuse of power.

'Anyone brought up by a batch of aunts knows that good rulers have good manners,' Gaius grumbled. 'Every time he burps in a senator's face or flips a meatball, I hear my old granny mutter darkly from the grave, "courtesy costs nothing". Of course you would never *choose* an emperor for his table habits, but it's not unknown to be rid of one for crass behaviour—when a Praetorian Prefect finally snapped and murdered the Emperor Gaius, aka Caligula, the reason was that Caligula had given the Prefect, who was sensitive, an obscene watchword to pass on once too often.'

'Who was that?'

'His name was Cassius Chaerea. Domitian should worry, because first the Guards ambushed the mad tyrant themselves, and then that was the time *they* created the next emperor: they found old Claudius hiding behind a curtain and proclaimed him on the spot.'

'For a joke.' Lucilla knew that story. 'Is Casperius Aelianus sensitive?'

'Not sensitive enough. A wood-block traditionalist. All "my Emperor, right or wrong"— so hard luck, Rome.'

*   *   *

Domitian was determined to validate his own divinity, using that of his forebears. He inaugurated the splendid Temple of the Flavians, which he built on the site of his uncle's house in Pomegranate Street. Domitian had been born in that house during the period when his father lacked funds,

471

then he had spent a lot of time there later, with his uncle Flavius Sabinus, while Vespasian was away abroad.

The new temple was spectacular. It dominated an area outside the traditional sites of public monuments, on the Quirinal Hill. Set in a large square porticus and magnificently elevated on a podium, it was striking even by the high standards of Domitian's building programme. Marble and gold decorated the huge domed mausoleum; there were many very fine reliefs showing celebratory scenes that involved Vespasian and Titus, scenes which associated them with the mythical founders and heroes of Rome, such as Romulus, who was himself turned into a god, according to legend. Domitian brought the ashes of his father and brother, with those of Julia and other relatives, and installed them together here. For generations to come, this great temple would signify the permanence of Rome.

Lucilla visited the Temple of the Gens Flavia along with other old family servants; it was a duty of Flavian freedmen and freedwomen to show formal respect. She had known Flavius Sabinus' house from her earliest years and was saddened to see that comfortable private home turned first into a demolition site and then a strange new monument. Contrary to Domitian's intentions, she felt that the family she had served with her mother and sister were now lost, rather than reaffirmed. Her patron Flavia Domitilla was married to Sabinus' younger son, Clemens, who could, in theory, have felt he owned the original house even though Domitian had taken it over.

Insofar as Domitilla spoke of her reaction, she

472

seemed to share Lucilla's saddened feelings. It was the first real sign of unease between the Clemens family and their cousin the Emperor, though more was to come.

Turning the house into a temple had not rendered Clemens and Domitilla homeless. As the Emperor's only surviving relatives and as parents of his designated heirs, they lived at the palace. Their two eldest sons had been renamed by their imperial uncle as Vespasian and Domitian. The young boys had been subtly separated from their parents; they had a good tutor in Quintilian, though he was getting on in years. Domitian himself gave them little attention. Lucilla knew their mother worried about their isolation.

Nobody yet took them seriously. A lot could happen in Domitian's mind before those boys inherited so much as an old cloak.

The fact that he had identified two young brothers to succeed him had precedents. A spare was prudent. On the other hand, it could be divisive and among the conspiratorial Julio-Claudians it had never worked. Augustus' heirs Gaius and Lucius both passed away from natural causes too soon but when Tiberius inherited with Gemellus, Gemellus quickly suffered fatal effects from a suspicious cough linctus, and when Nero inherited with his stepbrother Britannicus, almost his first brazen act was to have Britannicus handed a goblet of poisoned wine at a public banquet. If Domitian had been right when he claimed that Vespasian intended that Titus and he should rule jointly, and that Titus forged their father's will to avoid this, then duality did not work among the Flavians either.

It was now clear that Domitian's mind churned with greater suspicion than ever just when, if the establishment of the great family shrine meant anything, he should have been most secure. Not only had he alienated himself from the Senate, but he harboured increasing doubts about the trustworthiness of his own servants. Imperial freedmen could no longer rely on the safety of their positions.

As always, and as Themison had once suggested to Vinius and Gracilis, there could be a grain of reality in his decisions. An example was his dismissal of an elderly freedman called Epaphroditus. In his heyday, Epaphroditus had been Nero's petitions secretary. He had served Nero faithfully, especially when a senator named Calpurnius Piso plotted with others to organise a coup; loyalists revealed details to Epaphroditus, who immediately reported everything and the conspirators were arrested. To mark him saving his Emperor's life, Epaphroditus was awarded military honours; he also became very wealthy. He remained close to Nero to the last. After Nero was declared a public enemy, Epaphroditus helped him flee and, when requested to do so, he assisted his quailing master to kill himself.

Subsequently he continued in service. To be a remnant from a previous reign was never a good idea, nor did Epaphroditus endear himself by owning as a slave the leading stoic philosopher, Epictetus. Suddenly, Domitian banished the old scribe because of this connection to the opposition.

Sometimes, it worked the other way. Early in his reign Domitian had dismissed a secretary of finance called Tiberius Julius, whom he recalled now, ten years later, allowing the elderly man to die in Rome at the grand age of ninety. Statius wrote a consolation to his son, another senior freedman called Claudius Etruscus.

'He would!' commented Gaius.

'A nice gesture,' reproved Lucilla.

'Crass. Claudius Etruscus really does not want to be reminded that his papa was banished under a cloud. Not least, my darling, because it might make Etruscus scared that with Domitian in his current spiteful mood, the same thing can happen to him.'

*   *   *

Once Gaius took against someone, he was merciless. 'Look, he wrote a verse to celebrate the anniversary of the poet Lucan's birth—'

'You snaffled my scroll!'

'I was tidying the couch like a good boy. It tumbled on the floor from under the headrest. I assumed it must be saucy so I sneaked a look. Listen, your foolish friend says, when he and the widow, Pollia Argentaria, were discussing the birthday commission, "that rarest of wives wanted it written and *billed to her account*"—surely the most revealing words he ever wrote? He has done it for the money! Well done, honest poet!'

'I like his Lucan poem.'

Gaius lowered his voice abruptly. 'Well don't say so publicly.'

'What's wrong?'

'Don't you know that Lucan and his Uncle Seneca were executed for involvement in that big conspiracy against Nero? The very plot that our recently exiled Epaphroditus once exposed? Piso was the ringleader and would-be replacement emperor, but a wide range of other people died for supporting him. Seriously, I am astonished that your poet friend associates himself with Lucan publicly. This is the equivalent of celebrating Brutus and Cassius. It is all too, too reminiscent of the kind of plot with daggers that Our Master and God thinks is aiming against *him*.'

'Maybe Statius is a brave man.'

'No, he was lured by the money, and just slipped up. He'll be writhing with fright once he thinks about it properly.'

Gaius was obsessed with plots, plots and the history of imperial plotting. Although Lucilla knew he had an airy enjoyment of his work on the secret committee, she was in two minds about how it affected him. The only thing that saved him from complete commitment was his double-edged verdict on the mandarin Abascantus. Gaius judged him extremely clever, but found him subtly unreliable. Such mistrust was endemic in Domitian's Rome.

Lucilla had owned up to something: 'Gaius, you do realise I know Abascantus' wife? Priscilla? She is a friend of Statius' wife Claudia and has been a client of mine for years.'

'So what's the gen? Do you like her?'

'She is not my favourite. Being in the height of fashion with the same hairstyle as the imperial ladies is all part of her plan to push Abascantus. She wants to look the part. He married up, quite a long way up—'

'The freedman's ideal.'

'Yes, I'm waiting to catch some consul's eye myself, Gaius darling . . . Priscilla seems to have decided to make Abascantus her life's great project.

His service to Domitian is a holy calling—I do so loathe that! Still, she has money and she tips well . . .'

'He's her second husband?'

'Yes and she is significantly older. They seem a little odd together; I can never imagine them in bed. Theirs is one of those marriages where the couple work for the sole purpose of furthering the husband's career.'

'Vomit-making. When Domitian promoted Abascantus, Priscilla flung herself down like a human carpet and practically licked the floor at the Emperor's feet, thanking him. I do wish people would stop doing that. It encourages his delusions.'

Lucilla smiled serenely. 'Would you like me to kiss our Master's tunic hem for you, darling?'

'No! You know I try *never* to be noticed by the great.'

'You have not done too badly then, Gaius.'

'Yes, my father would be ecstatic.'

'I think I'll have a cameo carved to celebrate your glorious career. You will ride in a chariot with gambolling cupids, wearing your oakleaf wreath and looking shy of the attention. It will be titled, The Triumph of Diffidence.'

'Have you kept my golden oakleaves?'

'They are a swine to dust. But maybe one day the name Clodianus will be famous.'

'If I thought that,' said Gaius, with feeling, 'it would really worry me!'

*   *   *

Lucilla was one of the first people who knew the wife of chief secretary Abascantus was ill.

477

Hairdressers notice the health of their clients. Hair becomes lacklustre or even falls out, sometimes before any other symptoms of disease present themselves. Clients share bad news with their hairdressers too. Their special intimate relationship encourages people who would not normally open up to trust their stylist. It is understood that nothing said while the comb is plied will be passed on.

Priscilla needed a confidante. She shared her fears with Lucilla early on, yet she was concerned to keep the information from her husband for as long as possible. This was how they lived; his work for the Emperor was too important to be disrupted by anxiety for her. Domitian, of course, took Abascantus' devotion for granted.

Priscilla was *very* ill. That quickly became obvious. Abascantus had to be informed. Although Priscilla had not previously been a favourite customer, Lucilla was upset by the situation. She tended Priscilla gently on her sickbed, making her more comfortable and tidying her when her ravaged appearance embarrassed her. Doctors came and went, but despite the very best attention it was clear there was no hope. Soon, Priscilla no longer wanted the fuss of being touched, though Lucilla continued to visit her.

When Priscilla died, Abascantus was with her. Lucilla witnessed the human side of what was supposed to be faceless bureaucracy. The man was devastated. He had lost the driving force of his life. Theirs had been a partnership where the husband was the public face, yet the powerful woman made decisions, kept him to the mark, gave him his energy and his will to prosper. While he worked late by lamplight, instead of sending slaves, Priscilla

478

herself tiptoed in with refreshments—frugal snacks of course, because that was what Our Master and God himself liked.

Losing her, Abascantus was crushed.

A year later Statius wrote a poem of consolation, where he claimed the chief secretary had been so bereft he raved, threw himself upon his wife's body, threatened suicide. Certainly when Gaius took Lucilla to the funeral they were both shocked by the extravagance of the cortege and the opulence of the tomb Abascantus provided, even though by that time the freedman was conducting himself with dignity.

Lucilla herself had been shaken by Priscilla's death. It was by no means the first time she lost a customer but she was caught off guard. Gaius had accompanied her to the funeral to support her; he had some obligation to Abascantus as a member of his committee, but he would probably not have attended otherwise.

After seeing the flamboyant parade the freedman gave his wife, Lucilla muttered grimly, 'I give it a year. You see; he will soon remarry.'

'Men are all bastards, you think?'

'No; he just won't be able to bear being on his own.'

Lucilla and Gaius were at home by then. Struck by melancholy, she asked him, 'What would you do, if you lost me? Would your grief be so outlandish?'

'I would not show my heart to the world.'

'No; you are very different.'

Lucilla knew Gaius would not stagily finger a sword blade, nor would he run to a high crag and threaten to jump off, as Abascantus was supposed to have done. Gaius did not issue 'cries for help' like *Daily Gazette* advertisements. He was sentimental but he either endured his feelings in private or got on logically and dealt with the problem. This was in part because he was a soldier, but it also derived from his character and heritage. Although Lucilla had never met his father, from what she had heard, Gaius was still influenced by that strong-willed tribune.

Nevertheless, Gaius showed unexpected sympathy for Abascantus. 'I can see why he splashed out on myrrh and balsam, why all those expensive statues in the tomb and the elaborate funeral banquets. He must be thinking, what is the point of the money now she is gone? What was it striven for, if not to give them a good life together? . . . If I lost you, I would feel the same. I would send you off in style, my love, if it seemed the appropriate gesture—I know there are plenty of people who would want to mourn, and I would let them. But privately, I would never, ever be consoled.'

'Would you take up with someone else?'

'No.'

Lucilla doubted men's claims; that was why she distrusted Abascantus' exaggerated display. But she believed Gaius.

After Dacia, neither needed to ask the other question: how Lucilla would feel if she lost him. But she had been younger then, and not bound to him. When she curled up against him now and cried, it was more than her grief for Priscilla. It gave belated relief for the pain she still remembered. Gaius held her, comforting her, and as she clutched his hand against her cheek, he was again moved by her deep feelings.

For Abascantus, difficulties continued. It was reported that Priscilla's last words had been to encourage his devoted service to Domitian. That must continue at all costs. The ethos of public service was to bury yourself in your work, solace in itself.

Once the freedman was able to return to his duties, Gaius expected to be called to a new meeting of the safety committee. When it failed to happen, he risked wary enquiries. To his surprise, he learned Abascantus was no longer in Rome. Domitian's distrust of his freedmen had claimed another victim. The Emperor continued to work his way across the secretariats, replacing imperial servants with men of equestrian rank he had chosen himself. Now he had dismissed Abascantus.

The circumstances of any freedman's banishment were by convention murky. There was only one reason a senior official was removed: embezzlement. Fraud need not have taken place. Even if the real reason was that his imperial master could not stand the sight of him, mishandling funds was a useful public excuse. It would be ungrateful to dismiss a freedman otherwise, someone born and bred to palace service, someone completely devoted to the Emperor. (Any emperor he was stuck with.) There had to be rules, all the more so in times of upset.

Otherwise, unless imperial bureaucrats became completely decrepit, they never expected to leave; their duty to the emperor was for life. That sometimes meant their life ended prematurely.

Nero famously disposed of his predecessor's chief minister, the legendary manipulator and plutocrat Narcissus, by making him go into exile 'for his health'. Understood by everyone as an order to commit suicide, Narcissus swiftly took the hint.

So, Abascantus had unexpectedly retired. What, Gaius wondered, would happen to the committee now?

He went next door, intending to ask Casperius Aelianus. He had another surprise. The Prefect's office was empty, his clerical staff moping in corridors, frightened and miserable about their futures. In the latest cull of officials, Domitian had also decided to terminate the ten-year unblemished career of his Praetorian Prefect. 'My Emperor, right or wrong' had failed to shield the commander from suspicion: he, too, had been dropped.

Casperius Aelianus went quietly. Keeping his dignity, he made no complaint. Prefects had been replaced before; he knew there was no stain on his record. Even so, he had been popular. Men were loyal to him. Around the Praetorian Camp the musty whiff of imperial ingratitude now hummed, as if there was a problem with the drains.

Gaius had known the man since his own release from Dacian captivity. He owed Casperius Aelianus his move to the headquarters staff. He found such a change without warning hurt like a kick in the guts. He was as loyal to the Emperor as the next Guard, but he reeled for a moment, uncertain where this left him.

32

The following year Domitian awarded himself his seventeenth consulship. Statius wrote a poem.

Oh go on, surprise me!

I knew you would mock.

Grovelling bastard.

There were always two consuls. This was a Roman measure to avoid abuse of power, though it was incapable of curbing a deluded emperor. Once an annual appointment, there was a faster turnover nowadays to give promotion to more; one year, clearing a backlog, Domitian had appointed a bumper series of eleven. Hardly time to read the files before moving on.

Alongside him now in the position of honour, Domitian appointed his cousin Flavius Clemens, husband of Flavia Domitilla. Domitian's own consulship was notional, a few days only, but Clemens was listed to serve until April. If Statius ever contemplated a poem to celebrate this public appointment, he thought better of it. For Clemens and Domitilla, it was the beginning of the end.

*   *   *

Lucilla became concerned. Whenever she visited, she could see Flavia Domitilla feared the consulship. She lost weight and became abstracted. From the moment the couple had been informed, when the list of consuls was published the previous autumn, Domitilla had believed they were fated. There was nothing they could do. Clemens could not refuse. No Roman turned down a consulship unless he was gravely ill, let alone when he was to hold the role at the same time as the Emperor. It was announced. It was inescapable. And it boded ill.

When Domitian became emperor fifteen years before, his first partner as consul had been Clemens' elder brother, Flavius Sabinus. Keeping it in the family. That was the Flavian system, the way Vespasian and his own elder brother operated. Maybe Sabinus upset Domitian by his presumption he was the imperial heir. Perhaps he flaunted his hopes. He was the senior family member and events had not yet shown how dangerous Domitian could be. But Domitian executed Sabinus without offering a reason, immediately he gave up his post.

Later, Domitian repeated the pattern: Arrecinus Clemens, in-law of Titus and close to Julia: consul, then killed. Then Glabrio, allegedly impious and plotting revolution: first the honour, then lion-fighting, exile and death. Next, the stoics, Rusticus and the younger Helvidius: both consuls, both tried for treason and killed. Aelius Lamia, Domitia's first husband: the same grim sequence.

Who would seek this supreme Roman honour now? Especially if Domitian could convince himself in his dark private ramblings that a consul had an eye on his throne?

Flavius Clemens would never put himself out to usurp. Unqualified for anything, he was despicably lazy. He had held no military or civic posts, content to enjoy his position as a fortunate member of the ruling family. He accepted the benefits without the responsibilities. It was a far cry from the Flavians' origins, dedicating themselves to acquiring not just position and money, but honour. Vespasian and his brother Sabinus both seized every rank, packed with political energy and driven by a genuine belief that lifetime service to Rome was the highest goal.

Clemens accepted the status they won as his birthright. Vespasian and his brother would have been scathing. They would have shaken him up, too, in the way Domitian had been compelled to live with his father, in order to control inappropriate behaviour and to be trained in statecraft. Instead, as long as Lachne and Lara had served the family, as long as Lucilla herself had been associated with them, Clemens and his wife Domitilla had led an existence on the fringe of the imperial family that had little meaning or worth. They were only ever respected for who they were, never for anything Clemens achieved, for he achieved nothing.

Conversely, they did no harm. Flavia Domitilla, the daughter of Domitian's long-dead sister, was pleasant and loved by those who knew her.

Lucilla had groomed this woman's hair for over fifteen years now, weaving her coronets of curls since helping Lachne. Rank distanced them, yet tending Flavia Domitilla was a routine of her own existence. They exchanged little gifts at Saturnalia and on birthdays. They spoke frankly of ailments, Lucilla grumbling about the pains in her neck and shoulders that were a consequence of her profession with its frequent standing and working with raised arms. Saying she served the Emperor's niece had undoubtedly helped Lucilla build her wider clientele.

Domitilla was now almost the only person Lucilla dealt with who had known Lachne and Lara. She would occasionally reminisce about them, a kindness which showed she understood their significance to Lucilla.

Lucilla knew the Flavians generally treated their women well. Vespasian's mother and grandmother had brought status and money to the comparatively undistinguished provincial men they married. Both women had been astute and forthright. Vespasian had been partly brought up by his grandmother on her estate at Cosa on the north-west coast of Italy; everyone knew he had liked to return there. His mother was another strong character; she was said to have bullied him into public life when he showed reluctance. So, although their women seemed to stay in the background publicly, that was from choice. They were traditional. That had never meant subservient.

Domitilla was an only child. She had lost her mother when she was very young and whoever her father was, he faded from the scene or died too. Like her Uncle Domitian and Cousin Julia, she was brought up by others in the family. She saw no reason to treat her uncle deferentially, but sniffed at his grandiose ideas and deplored his conceit with eye-rolling glances.

It was inevitable Domitilla would be married early, and to another cousin, Clemens. Despite what people said about the repeated intermarriage of such close relations, she became the mother of seven children, for which in Roman society a woman was greatly honoured. After producing her third, the Augustan laws gave her the right to run her own affairs without a guardian although, as far as Lucilla could see, this made little difference in practice. She was never aware of Flavia Domitilla possessing estates of her own; if she did, her husband probably assumed nominal control but left everything to managers. Clothes and jewels were suitably abundant for a niece of the reigning emperor who appeared with him at court and in the imperial box at festivals. Her hair, of course, was immaculate. Lucilla's bills for this were slow to be honoured, though she was eventually paid.

Even when the couple lived at the palace in association with Domitian, Flavia Domitilla had her own household. Her staff were loyal—as Lucilla herself was loyal—though sometimes snobbish. Tatia Baucylla, the hard-working nurse of the seven children, was prone to describing her charges as 'the great-grandchildren of the Divine Vespasian', adding much less proudly that Clemens was their father, and immediately reminding people that their mother was the Divine Vespasian's granddaughter. Stephanus, the steward, called himself 'freedman of Domitilla'. Lachne always did the same, Lucilla remembered. She was herself Domitilla's freedwoman, come to that.

So, Flavia Domitilla was now in her mid-forties, discreetly menopausal, facing serious fears as Domitian turned his neurotic attention on her husband. She had never particularly enjoyed court life, preferring the country existence when the Flavians returned to their Sabine homes in the Apennines. True, they owned grand country villas set in well-run estates, but there they lived out Italian summers with long wooden tables set in the open air for relaxed family parties, while quarrel-free children scampered about under pine trees: rustic breads, earthy wines, simple cheeses, bountiful vegetables and fruits, wild honey. They enjoyed harvests and visits to local markets; hunting in the woods, truffle-seeking, river fishing; entertainment by travelling musicians and traditional dancers. Long sunny days followed by a good night's sleep.

Lucilla had been on these vacations in her time, and much enjoyed them, although since she became lovers with Gaius, she tended to decline invitations so she could spend time with him.

Her closeness to Gaius had slightly distanced her from Flavia Domitilla, who accepted the change with knowing smiles, pleased for this lively young woman she had known from childhood, who was part of her own domestic history.

*   *   *

Gaius began that year with insecurities. Having two new Prefects rocketed into post like unpredictable comets caused tension; it was the first time he had gone through this since becoming cornicularius.

The newcomers had to settle down. They came up with ridiculous ideas for restructuring— not feasible in a legionary organisation, as their cornicularius had to point out gently. There was the usual talk of budget cuts, although any commissariat man could kill that dead using adroit threats to his superiors' perks. Then they scrutinised the complement. All the senior officers became jumpy, in case they were to be weeded out. It came to nothing in most cases. The irritating bastards everyone else had hoped to lose clung on in their posts as irritating bastards always do.

One Prefect, Norbanus, was a dedicated Domitian supporter; he arrived here via the army route, after making his name during the Saturninus

Revolt. He had taken troops from Raetia to aid Lappius Maximus in defeating Saturninus, earning himself Domitian's gratitude and the reward of this prefecture. The other new man, Petronius Secundus, had risen through civil positions, including the prestigious post of Prefect of Egypt. It was unclear how well, if at all, the two men had known each other previously; there were signs they did not gel. That was the point of having two. While they jostled for supremacy, they were unlikely to acquire too much power at the expense of the Emperor. Nobody had ever forgotten how the brutal Sejanus tried to grab the throne from Tiberius.

Domitian must remember this: his favourite reading, perhaps his only reading nowadays, was Tiberius' Memoirs, a book most people would place on the highest shelf of their library to gather dust. Gaius had a copy in his office; one of the scrolls had just the right flexibility to whack flies.

Petronius Secundus kept his head down at first. He let Norbanus lead. Gaius felt irritated, though not entirely surprised, when Norbanus had his personal secretary (a creepy hack who had come with him from Raetia) send a stiff little note in spidery writing to say it would be of value if the chief-of-staff dropped by for a review of his duties. For that, in the ludicrous way of public service, Gaius prepared career notes on himself.

He took his draft to Lucilla before he submitted it. She made him beef up the parts where he had shown bravery in the field.

He highlighted the Abascantus safety committee, because he knew that among his handover notes from Casperius Aelianus, Norbanus possessed a secret file on Preserving the Emperor. Gaius, who had drafted most of the file, had much entertainment outlining his own role, in the third-person narrative he conventionally used when briefing seniors: whether it would be cost-effective to remove Clodianus from his important work on granary records to be co-opted onto the safety committee, the verdict of the suitability assessment, plus exactly what security checks on Clodianus had revealed. He gave Clodianus the all-clear for loyalty.

When Gaius sauntered along, the Prefect was wearing his full uniform. He always did. Praetorian commanders were military and Norbanus enjoyed that. Guards judged a Prefect by whether, in the privacy of his quarters, he felt it necessary to retain formal marks of status or threw off his huge cloak with a groan of relief as anyone sensible did.

Norbanus had little to say about the cornicularius duties. He wanted to thrill himself sick with top secret subjects. 'I noticed you mentioned Abascantus and his special group.'

'Yes, sir. I hope it did not come across as flippant.'

Norbanus thought for a nerve-racking period. 'No.' He considered some more. He was a slow thinker. Gaius had learned to pace him. 'No, I like your attitude.'

Gaius said nothing.

Norbanus suddenly produced a beaming smile that his officer distrusted. 'So, Clodianus—this is a tricky one!'

Hades!

'"Preserving the Emperor"—that's what we're all here for . . . What's the mood at barracks level,

490

tell me? Talking to cohort commanders, do I sense a dangerous yearning for change? Are any Guards wondering, at what point do we have to start making awkward decisions? What do you think? Have you noticed whispers?'

Shit! What change? What decisions? Surely the man was not making dangerous suggestions of a new regime?

The Prefect was staring directly at him, twitching up one hairy eyebrow in enquiry.

'We take the Oath, sir.'

'And the rest!' Norbanus spoke low. 'Our Master handed out a whacking bonus to secure the Praetorians, back when he became Emperor. Your curriculum shows you on the complement then, so you were one of the lucky ones.'

'Yes, sir.'

'That was fourteen years ago. If the term in service for a Guard is sixteen years—well, you see my thinking. The number who received the bonus must be dwindling fast. Do new boys feel the same obligation, in your opinion?'

'They are proud to serve, sir.' Gaius sounded like his father. They had got him at last.

Norbanus whistled. 'Gods, you're a cool one! I can see why they appointed you, Clodianus.'

Longing for this to be over, Gaius applied a cool man's close expression. As a soldier he was good at it.

'Well, I want you to keep attending this committee. Watch what they are up to and report back to me personally.'

'Yes, sir.'

'I don't entirely trust these freedmen—load of funny buggers wearing fancy necklaces. I weep no tears for the loss of Abascantus.'

'No, sir. By the way, sir; with Abascantus packed off, I have been wondering who I should liaise with instead?'

'Parthenius!' Norbanus announced. 'Don't ask me how they fixed it up between them, but Parthenius is your man now.'

Gaius went so far as to raise his eyebrows. 'The *chamberlain*? Doesn't he spend his life counting pillowcases?' He could not envisage it working, but until he had the measure of this change, he decided not to protest. The chamberlain shadowed the Emperor and controlled his visitors, so it could be appropriate.

'Well, the same aim applies. The Emperor's safety is paramount. That will always have my personal attention. Now Clodianus, this briefing is absolutely confidential—just between ourselves.' Norbanus addressed him in the manner of a slightly sinister uncle. 'I don't need to tell you that if anything goes off, it is absolutely essential the Guards nip trouble in the bud. Vigilance! We need absolute vigilance.'

'Absolutely!' Gaius knew how to pick up jargon. 'Just one query, Prefect. On the safety issue, do you know the position of Petronius Secundus?'

Norbanus looked guarded. 'He has his own ideas. I am sure we can count on him.' So he viewed Secundus as treacherous. 'I don't want you to feel inhibited. Any problems, come to me.'

'Jolly good, sir!'

'My door is always open.'

It was closed at the moment so nobody could overhear Norbanus insinuating disloyalty in his fellow Prefect.

Once Norbanus had meddled enough to establish himself, Secundus started his own exercise. Gaius monitored the interplay between them as a kind of scientific experiment for an encyclopaedia, a section with insects.

Secundus decided to emerge from his chrysalis and interview all his cohort tribunes about their careers: he called this 'the personal touch'. To anyone who had been in the army twenty years the phenomenon was well known. The cornicularius patiently took charge of the diary to book in the ten tribunes for their little chats, then he produced helpful briefing notes on each man's history. Straightforward stuff. It was no different from when, in the vigiles, he had sent a criminal to the City Prefect, appearing to ask for advice on the case but giving a strong steer on what the culprit had done and how to punish him. He gained a few drinks out of this exercise, as the more astute tribunes tried to influence what he said about them.

He could have landed one or two of them in it, had he been that type. Which they must hope he wasn't.

Of course not.

He watched them return from their interviews, seeing who looked deflated and who swaggered. One or two would receive their discharge diploma quicker than they had expected; Gaius, who gave instructions to the calligrapher who incised the tablets, had already set this in motion. The Prefect's exercise was excellent man-management, although like most such party games it severely unsettled the men who were being managed, even those who survived the process. Although there was never any suggestion Domitian know about it, this was just the kind of mental cruelty the Emperor himself enjoyed.

Gaius had to submit to the 'personal touch' himself. Secundus set him at his ease—always embarrassing for both parties. The Prefect plodded through various aspects of his work as cornicularius. Ever thoughtful, Gaius had prepared a list for him, to smooth this process.

The truth was, little needed attention or alteration. The office was well run. There were few complaints; most of those could be discounted. A decent commissariat made for a smooth-running corps. Secundus knew he had a good chief-of-staff, who was abreast of everything. The Guards were fine. Of course Gaius had already established this with Norbanus.

'Excellent!'

'Thank you, Prefect!'

They had reached the moment that always happened in interviews, when the discreet Clodianus had to decide exactly when to pick up his note tablets and slide out of the office. Sometimes—and his antennae prickled that this was one of those occasions—he had to stay for a stiff period of informality. The tone would lighten up. A Prefect would discuss the Games, the weather, or even mild anxieties about his children; a particularly jolly incumbent would have a laugh about any sex scandals which involved children of absent colleagues (though most thought it bad form to openly libel their equals in rank). According to tradition, there was a possibility Secundus would

494

produce his set of wine glasses, while a previously unseen slave would pop out with wine to put in them.

Last Saturnalia, with Casperius Aelianus, there had even been a bowl of olives. Since Gaius had to stock the Prefects' refreshments cupboard, he had made sure they were Colymbadian, and whenever he was at a meeting where tuck came out, he took home the leftovers. Such are the quiet rewards of honest public servants.

Today neither the glasses nor the slavey turned up. They had hit the friendly part, but had not finished business.

Gaius had thought this time he was getting away without mentioning the safety committee. Secundus left his big throne-like chair and flopped in a more comfortable seat. As he placed his boots on a low table to indicate they could relax, he brought up the subject after all. Gaius picked at a thumbnail despondently.

Secundus suddenly remembered the etiquette. 'Time for a noggin, yes?' He plonked his boots back on the floor, jumped up, went to a cupboard and now did produce glasses. They were enormous greenish tumblers, with cheery skeletons advising, *'Drink, for tomorrow we die'*. He burrowed in the wine stash without involving a slave.

He came back, arranged stuff on the low table between them, poured. They raised glasses. It was excellent wine. Prefects always brought their own in because they wanted a decent vintage; with the best will in the world a military negotiator could not afford quality, else Treasury Audit dug in their heels. Gaius had had to explain this tactfully when the two new Prefects were appointed. It was about the third point down in some Guidance Notes for Induction of New Commanders that he had inherited from predecessors. Where the first point was telling the incumbents why their offices were not big enough and the second was pointing out which latrine was specially reserved for their use. For them—and for Gaius, when he knew they were out of camp.

Petronius Secundus regarded him with a wry expression. 'Well! . . . Delicate, is it not?' He did not mean his wine.

'Yes, sir.'

'I don't have to remind you, anything said in this office stays here.' Gaius gave a twist of his head, the universal sign; Secundus could feel happy that in no circumstances would his colleague Norbanus hear what they had said. 'You worked with Abascantus, so you understand what he was trying to do.'

Gaius sipped like a girl. Wine on an empty stomach, together with a feeling that the discussion was escaping him, made him moderate his input.

'I assume you approve, Clodianus?'

'Yes, sir.'

'Well, let's be open about all this. The Abascantus initiative continues and I believe our involvement needs to continue with it. Either the Guards can limit their service to a simple role as bodyguards, or we aim for the survival of Rome. Are you with me?' he checked again.

'I think so, sir.' Gaius was always amazed how much a chief-of-staff was taken into his superiors' confidence.

'The days of an armed insurrection are past.'

Luckily Gaius had just swallowed, so he did not splutter his wine. Now he knew that the so-called career discussions Secundus had been holding had a specific purpose: to sound out his officers' opinions, in preparation for a coup.

When Secundus was frank, he pushed the boat out: 'It may have worked for Caligula, but trapping Our Master and God in a tunnel with a bloody stabbing organised by us is just not on.'

'Really, sir?'

'The field army love him far too much. He has endeared himself to the troops by his personal presence on the Rhine and Danube. An uprising back home would be very unpopular. The legions would never wear it.' Gaius had to remind himself this man came up by the civil route; his colleague Norbanus would not have spoken so regretfully about the army. And 'an uprising at home' must mean, by the Praetorians. 'There would be civil war throughout the Empire all over again; we had enough of that in the Year of the Four Emperors. What is necessary now is a smooth transfer of power. As I see it—' Secundus paused.

'Hypothetically?' Gaius prompted. He was always considerate.

'Oh good man! All of this is *sub rosa*. You know the risks. Anybody asks us, we both deny everything . . . Clearly, any move would necessitate the Senate, the Guards and the imperial staff all working together. In this scenario, you realise, the Guards' role would be background support.'

'We won't *do* anything, but if somebody else tries it we refrain from intervention?' Gaius felt he had abruptly ended up with his toes on the edge of a very deep trench; he was struggling to hold his balance, about to topple forwards and fall in.

'A bugger, isn't it?' Secundus asked confidingly.

497

He drained his glass in one relieved gulp. 'Well, I'm glad we had this little chat. Just wanted you to know, any problems, anything at all, my door is always open.'

Gaius could now extract himself. He stood up to leave. 'We all know we can rely on you,' smiled the Prefect. 'Your watching brief is vital. You won't let us down, I know.'

Gaius reached the door. He turned back. 'Just one query, sir, if you don't mind. How do you see the position of your colleague Norbanus?'

'Good question! Could be tricky. Don't worry; no hiccup. If and when things ever kick off, you can leave Norbanus to me.'

'Good to know that, sir.'

Jupiter Optimus bloody Maximus!

*　　　*　　　*

Gaius walked next door to his own office. A couple of clerks looked up, but read his expression and decided not to engage with him.

There was one rather unpleasant possibility, as Gaius was fully aware: his conversations with Norbanus and Secundus could be a cheat. Perhaps one, or both, was attempting to draw out their chief-of-staff's opinions in order to report him for treason.

That was how people thought in Rome. Domitian had had that dire effect.

*　　　*　　　*

He went into his private area, where he sat sweating for some time. *You worked with Abascantus, so you*

498

understand what he was trying to do . . .

He had been a fool. He had entirely missed the point.

Even while Petronius Secundus hedged and hinted about a transfer of power, the cornicularius had quaked at the implications. There *was* a plot. Officials were themselves running it. Everyone who mattered was supposed to know all about it already. Even people like Norbanus, who was unsympathetic and had not been invited, suspected what was going on. Of course it was not signalled. Nobody was going to have a big sign up on his door saying 'Conspirators, Enquire Within', were they?

Now as Gaius pondered in amazement, he saw that the Abascantus 'initiative' was extremely clever—no less devious than he would expect. No one became a disgraced civil servant without expertise in double-dealing. It was simple. All the safety committee members, other than him, were insiders. They were hidden from notice by meeting in plain sight. The people being canvassed for support were a much wider group than had turned up at meetings to munch almond biscuits. *The Senate, the Guards and the staff* . . . Most of Rome, apparently.

As for him, Abascantus had requested someone from the Guards, and Casperius Aelianus, a loyalist and a man who had missed the point, just sent along someone who enjoyed bureaucracy. Now Norbanus assumed Gaius was spying; Secundus assumed Gaius was plotting. Jupiter, what was he supposed to do?

Abascantus made him nervous: there could be a reason why Abascantus was so suddenly dismissed. Some whisper had reached the Emperor. That was seriously bad news for everyone involved. Even poor idiots like Gaius who had had no idea of anything.

Still, he knew now. Now he would have to make choices. Either he went along with this, or he must do what he had thought he was there for in the first place: observe the conspirators—the *real* ones—and eventually report on them. At least he had two different superiors assuring him he was their man. That ought to guarantee protection!

Once again in his life Vinius Clodianus felt that other people were pushing him into something. He had acquired a dangerous level of involvement without even understanding that.

He knew how things worked; if people were exposed for plotting, he would probably go down with them.

When he talked it all through with Lucilla at home, he managed to convince himself that until an assassination attempt was imminent, which might be never, this could not be problematical. But he felt dispirited. Nothing was clear-cut, and to Gaius that meant there was a very high chance all this would go wrong.

*   *   *

If he needed reassurance, it came in the absence of action from Parthenius. If the banished Abascantus really had passed a torch to the chamberlain, Parthenius must have immediately doused it. Nothing happened. There were no further meetings.

Domitian meanwhile grew more unpredictable. Nobody knew the rules. People were lazy and wanted no trouble. They would knuckle under to any system, even bad ones, provided they could understand what was expected of them. With a ruler who was mentally disturbed, quiet periods lulled them into hoping everything had settled down, but then he offended them with some new outrage. They could not even rely on previous behaviour as an index. He would go back on himself, reviewing past incidents and reaching newly disturbing conclusions. It left everyone hysterical.

A case in point was Epaphroditus. Epaphroditus had not only survived being close to Nero, Domitian too had accepted him as a secretary for years. When he suddenly banished the man, that was perturbing. Now he brooded again and suddenly recalled Epaphroditus from exile. As the freedman hobbled back to Rome, it was nearly three decades since his first master Nero committed suicide. Everyone knew that Epaphroditus helping him had been at the cowardly Nero's own request. A loyal act, simple compassion.

That did not stop Domitian deciding he would now make an example of his elderly secretary. He wanted others to see that causing the death of an emperor, even if he asked you, was a crime.

Epaphroditus was executed.

*   *   *

Worse followed. Domitian suddenly turned on Flavius Clemens. Even before his cousin's consulship ended in April, there was a mysterious charge of 'atheism'. Clemens and Domitilla were said to have engaged in 'Jewish practices'. What these practices were remained obscure. When

Vespasian and Titus returned from their conquest of Judaea they had brought many Jewish prisoners, so some of the war booty slaves may have ended up in the Clemens household; if so, none were specifically accused of converting their master. Christians, too, would subsequently claim the couple as saints, yet there was no evidence there either.

The nebulous charge seemed to derive from Domitian's own twisted imagination. Families tend to speak their minds. Perhaps at some private family occasion his cousins had scoffed at Domitian's interpretation of himself as a god on earth. To them he was just a very tedious relative. Whatever Flavius Clemens did, or whether his mere existence as a potential rival coloured Domitian's fears, the usual men with swords arrived one day, and that was the end of him.

As soon as Lucilla heard, she rushed to Flavia Domitilla. Although the poor woman had been living in dread for months, Lucilla found her in a complete daze. The couple had been married over thirty years. There was no trial; there had been no time to get used to the possibility of losing her husband. This was hideous, far worse than illness or a fatal accident.

There would be no public funeral. Certainly no interment in the great new Flavian mausoleum that had once been Clemens' family home. Arrangements had to be scrimped and secretly conducted; Domitilla's steward, Stephanus, arranged it.

Domitilla had nobody to turn to. A woman who lost her husband ought to rely on family support, but Domitian was now her only adult male relative;

he was also her terrifying enemy.

Domitilla's household staff were appalled. They clustered around her, most in tears. She was not condemned to death, but the Emperor had ordered that she should be taken from Rome to exile on the Island of Pandateria. Anyone who thought about it realised he could still change his mind and give worse orders. Even if not, Pandateria had a terrible reputation.

While hasty preparations for this unsought journey were made by distraught slaves, Domitilla gave tremulous instructions for the welfare of her children, whom she had to leave. She was given no time even to explain the situation to them. No one could guess what fate lay ahead for the two sons Domitian had previously named as his heirs, though it seemed unlikely he would continue to view them in any friendly light. They and the five other distressed children were orphans in a harsh world. No one who feared Domitian would dare to show them kindness.

Coming from outside, Flavia Lucilla had a clearer head than many. She discovered that although her heart was racing, she could stay calm in an emergency. She buckled to, helping Stephanus make rushed arrangements. An escort of soldiers arrived, while Lucilla was comforting her patroness; they were from the Urban Cohorts, none of them men she recognised. They were fairly polite, all awkward at having to give orders to an imperial lady, but there was underlying menace.

A small group could travel with Domitilla to the coast. Stephanus insisted on going. A couple of hastily selected maids were taken. When the party set off, Domitilla seemed to welcome Lucilla's presence, so she volunteered to go too. She had not thought about this in advance. She had no time to notify Gaius properly, though she sent him a message, keeping it vague so as not to implicate him in Domitilla's disgrace.

The journey to the coast took a couple of days, although the troops hurried them. Pandateria was a tiny volcanic island thirty miles off the fashionable Bay of Naples resorts of Baiae and Cumae. This remote dot in the Tyrrhenian Sea had long been a favourite location for imprisoning disgraced imperial women. The island hosted several of the Julio-Claudian family, some of whom had died there of deliberate starvation; others had been sent surprise executioners. Hardly any survived to leave. Few ships called there. The inhabitants must be accustomed to seeing themselves as jailers, jailers from whom cruelty would be welcomed by the authorities. Flavia Domitilla could only view her lonely incarceration with horror.

She was to be transferred to the inhospitable caldera by a navy ship from the fleet at Puteoli; its oars were already manned in readiness. Stephanus was forbidden to accompany her. The loyal freedman tried to insist but was dragged back. As distraught farewells were said on the quayside, Lucilla was horrified that only pallid little slaves were to be companions for their mistress. She herself abruptly offered to continue to the island. She meant it; nevertheless she was relieved when Domitilla turned her down, telling her to enjoy her life instead. So they parted.

Flavia Domitilla looked suddenly older. Despite her pampered prior existence, during the journey to Puteoli her face had acquired the lines of an elderly woman; even her hair, simply wound by Lucilla in an old-fashioned style today, seemed to have greyed, thinned and faded. Though widowed and torn from her children, she was still the granddaughter of the Divine Vespasian; she walked unaided up a narrow gangplank to be received by a naval captain who looked shamefaced. She spoke to him graciously. She never looked back.

Lucilla waited with Stephanus on the quay until the ship had sailed out to sea so far they could no longer see it. Even when travellers are expected to return, the slow dwindling of a vessel into the far distance is a mournful sight. Lucilla knew she would never see Flavia Domitilla again.

*   *   *

On their journey together back to Rome she and Stephanus spoke little. They were both raging at the injustice, but under Domitian no one openly showed such feelings if they wanted to survive. By the time they reached Rome, nonetheless, they had a shared understanding.

Hurrying to Plum Street, even though it was late, Lucilla could tell Gaius was at home. They normally slept in her bed, but she found him in his old room, with the dog on his feet, forcing him to curl up. She crept into bed behind him. Gaius greeted her only with a bad-tempered grunt and did not turn around.

Pressing her face between his shoulder-blades, Lucilla murmured pleas against his unresponsive back. 'I am sorry. Please don't be angry. I was her freedwoman. I discovered that it meant something.'

Gaius, a free citizen from birth, had spent the best part of a week depressed. He knew freed slaves had an obligation, but until now its importance to Lucilla had escaped him. He was jealous, he knew it. Lucilla heard his misery: 'I thought you had left me.'

'Don't; please don't upset yourself. I am here. I would have gone as her companion,' Lucilla admitted. 'But she knew you had a claim on me. I am so glad she said no. I wanted to come home to you.'

Gaius pushed the dog off the bed with the flats of his feet so he could stretch out and turn round. He hauled Lucilla into his embrace. 'Oh gods, am I glad to have you back . . . !' He was warm-bodied and warm-hearted; despite the scare she had given him, he remained deeply affectionate.

'It's over. She is gone, Gaius. I know she will die there. She will never be allowed home. He means her to die. They will neglect her, and probably starve her, and because she has no hope she will surrender to her fate. That is how he wants it. So he does not have to see what happens, and can shed all responsibility.'

Gaius wrapped himself around her until she felt like a kernel, safe in its nut. 'There; let it out. You need to cry.'

Lucilla took his comfort but she said, 'I have not shed one tear since I watched her sail away. I am too angry.'

Gaius was silent. He recognised that she had changed. He saw that he could indeed lose her—though of all the wild doubts he had ever harboured, losing Lucilla would not be in any way he had dreamed. No other man would lure her, nor would she tire of him. Even her long exposure to poets, teachers and philosophers had not achieved this. Flavia Lucilla had joined the opposition to Domitian.

'It has to end.' Lucilla's voice was quiet, her tone stripped, her mood fatalistic. 'People must do something. Whatever it takes, he will have to be stopped.'

33

Over a year passed, after Flavius Clemens died and his widow was banished. Nothing significant happened. It could be argued that this was because the conspirators took their time and planned things properly. Excuses, said Lucilla.

Organisation did occur, however. A slow current of hatred had begun its drag. In the Senate, men confined themselves to muttering complaints, while Domitian knew they did so, and loathed them more as a result. At the Praetorian Camp, officers and soldiers took another New Year Oath, pledging loyalty to their emperor with set faces. Their Prefects waited, each with his motives. The army loved Domitian; legionary commanders and their provincial governors, with power in their hands, were his loyal appointees. He chose them personally, and they had seen what happened to anyone who challenged him. The public neither loved nor hated, grateful for gifts and favours, yet finding him a cold, distant ruler. The benefit of efficient government with many costly state occasions was that there were no riots—nor would there be, if their ruler was to fall to a well-constructed palace revolution, with the promise that life for the public would continue undisturbed. Juvenal's famous slur was right; given bread and circuses, people would tolerate anything.

A group of dedicated people worked secretly to identify who was sympathetic, indifferent, suspect or hostile. They rarely met formally. When they did, they chose the summer, so absences looked like normal holidays. Some of these people were senior officials, who were used to running the Empire. They knew how to hobnob. Because they were careful, their meetings often took place far from both Rome and Domitian's fortress at Alba. So, in the middle of summer, Gaius Vinius and Flavia Lucilla travelled together down the Via Valeria, setting off like cheerful holidaymakers with light luggage, an obvious picnic basket, and their dog.

*   *   *

There was a villa in the hills which by reputation was the farm given from his rich supporter Maecenas to the poet Horace. A will produced in a hurry when the poet died in delirium had bequeathed his entire estate to the Emperor Augustus. Horace had enjoyed imperial patronage and he was a childless bachelor, so no suggestion of sharp practice should be inferred.

The poet's beloved Sabine farm was swallowed up into the gigantic imperial portfolio, from which imperial freedmen were sometimes rewarded with spectacular presents. Some of the best properties in Italy passed from an emperor to a servant who worked hard, or who knew where the bodies were buried. When the state budget was tight, those who had made a packet from bribes could buy auctioned property at wincingly favourable rates, though sometimes there was a quid pro quo.

Nearly a hundred years after Horace died, the small farm at the head of the wooded valley was in new ownership. Approached by its own informal road, it was encircled by low, scrubby hills with a crown of trees. The dark soil was thin, but supported modest agriculture; Horace had had his own flocks and was able to seal demijohns of his own wine. A small spring provided fresh water. A brook chattered.

The living quarters remained modest, at least by contrast with the gross spreads flaunted by tycoons along the Bay of Naples. Even so, a luxurious redesign and make-over in the reign of Vespasian had improved both facilities and décor, with plenty of white and grey marble, all worked to a high standard. The most important rooms on the ground floor had impressive geometric mosaic floors in black and white, announcing that this was a high-status home. Pleasant suites occupied two storeys; some rooms opened onto internal courtyard gardens. The master dining room had a splendid view across a peristyle down the main axis towards a particularly striking hill in the distance. A short flight of steps led to a gently sloping garden, surrounded by shady colonnades, that included the usual topiary and urns, a large pool and scallop shell grotto. Natural woodland complemented the formal plantings.

Only a staggeringly outsized bath house showed that although this delightful and very secluded house was in single private ownership, it was occasionally used by travelling rulers and their large, demanding retinues. Freedmen lived here.

An emperor could enjoy the attractive dining and sleeping rooms, in the suave company of a host he knew and trusted, while his swarming backup team was foisted onto local villages or bivouacked in the grounds. This rural villa made an ideal stopping point on the way to Nero's spectacular country palace in the hills at Sublacium, too far from Rome to be reached in one day, which had continued in use by the Flavians. Alternatively, with only a slight detour, this could serve as a way-station en route to Vespasian's birthplace at Reate and other Flavian family compounds. Though close to the Via Valeria, the house lay down a minor road which lent privacy and made it very secure.

A daytrip from Rome, Horace's Villa had seemed in the past a superb place to plot. An equally long way from Alba, it still was.

*   *   *

The current owner was Domitian's great chamberlain, Parthenius. He took on the villa after other wealthy and influential freedmen and women, as he explained on the first evening while his group of visitors relaxed with nightcaps after their hot and bumping journey from Rome.

'I find it entertaining—' Perhaps because he had worked for so long for an emperor with a macabre sense of humour, Parthenius was amused by situations that made other people feel faint—'that one of my predecessors was Claudia Epicharis. In view of our purpose, this seems a peculiar irony.'

For those of his guests who either never knew or had forgotten, the genial host elucidated: Claudia Epicharis had been an influential freedwoman involved in the famous Pisonian plot against Nero. Epicharis tried on her own initiative to suborn the commander of the Misenum fleet, Volusius Proculus. She made a mistake there. He betrayed the plot to Nero's chief secretary, Epaphroditus, the freedman Domitian had just eradicated.

Epicharis was arrested and tortured, yet never identified her fellow-conspirators. After being broken on the rack, she was being carried for a new day's questioning in a chair, since the injuries already inflicted on her meant she could no longer stand. Though in hideous pain, she managed to remove a bustband she was wearing; she fixed it to the chair and by straining on the material somehow throttled herself.

'The courageous Epicharis owned this villa. I like to think the Pisonian conspirators may have met and discussed their intentions here,' Parthenius ended. 'Where they failed, we must prosper.'

*   *   *

A short time afterwards, the urbane freedman bade everyone goodnight; he sauntered out into the garden. There he noticed the tall figure of the one-eyed cornicularius, Clodianus. Arms folded, the disfigured Praetorian stood lost in thought. The impression he gave was gloomy.

'Are you enjoying the balmy evening—or reviewing your options?' asked Parthenius, coming up to him. 'Not reconsidering, I hope?' Clodianus acknowledged his presence, though did not respond to the question. Around them moths and insects darted, while the fountains on a great square water feature still tinkled, lit with dim lights. 'Oh, I am so sorry—did my story of Epicharis and her suicide upset Flavia Lucilla?'

'It upset me.'

'You are naturally anxious about Lucilla's safety.'

'She is her own woman. I can only urge caution.'

'I am sure she values what you say.' Parthenius could be bland. She was not his girl.

They were all putting themselves in great danger by this conspiracy and Gaius was suffering as he imagined the disaster of exposure, with Lucilla being tortured or suffering a hideous death. Alone of those here, he had in the course of his duties witnessed torture. Not often, but enough.

Parthenius was married. His wife had been sufficiently visible for politeness, though it had been clear she would stay safely out of discussions tomorrow. There were children. Gaius had glimpsed a boy, Burrus, about twelve or thirteen; he was loafing about like any adolescent, staring at the new arrivals yet unwilling to communicate with his father's visitors.

'The Piso affair,' Gaius challenged bluntly. 'Total cock-up, I recall. Debauched candidate. Huge group of conspirators—over forty people, no?—all with conflicting motives. Action delayed until it all unravelled hopelessly; slaves snitching on masters; promises of immunity that were filthily broken; suicides; betrayals; amoral prosecutors, out to make a mint. None showed a jot of the morality of Epicharis.'

'No, indeed. Faenius Rufius, the Praetorian Prefect, was originally right in it,' added Parthenius, who must have been an official at the time. 'Became one of the most vicious accusers, covering himself. He died anyway.' Mentioning this reprehensible

Prefect was a mean sideswipe. 'Lessons must be learned, Clodianus. We rely on you to keep *our* Prefects in order!' Gaius sniffed at that. He would need to be ambidextrous. Parthenius lowered his voice, though it was hardly necessary on his own property and so far from Rome: 'I am entertaining your esteemed Petronius Secundus later this week.'

'After the rest of us leave?'

'He will feel happier. A happy Prefect is a friendly one, I hope . . . Well, to your bed, man,' Parthenius urged. 'Our delectable Lucilla will be wondering what kept you. I hope your room is satisfactory.'

'We have simple tastes,' Gaius assured him.

A chamberlain was bound to fuss about domestic matters. 'I want everyone to be comfortable.'

'Appreciated.'

Gaius would not be packed to bed like a teenager. He stood his ground until Parthenius wandered off on whatever household rounds were necessary in such a remote location, then he deliberately stayed longer in the garden. Above, the open sky had faded to a magical violet hue. A few faint stars became visible.

Once alone, Gaius mused despondently on the likelihood that a half-baked, behind-the-scenes bunch of fancy factotums might actually one day (the day in question being one of tomorrow's agenda items) manage to dispose of Domitian.

Kill him.

Kill the Emperor. Words a good Praetorian Guard was conditioned to find outrageous. Any Praetorian. Including Gaius Vinius Clodianus.

*   *   *

513

Blundering noises from the nearby woods announced arrivals; nothing sinister, just Lucilla, holding a leash, and Terror, dragging her excitedly. Previously a complete town dog, Terror had been here less than an hour when he disgraced himself by assuming the horticultural plant pots buried in the garden had been put there with hidden bones for him. He had worked his way down half a row, destroying the elegant specimens they contained, before he was stopped. Gaius and Lucilla had underestimated the hard work involved in bringing a spoiled pet from Rome to the wilds of the country.

'Done his business?'

'Eventually. You take him next time!' Lucilla grumbled. 'It's so dark! I was petrified—you know Horace once saw a wolf here when he was strolling about singing. It ran away from him, luckily.'

'Any wolf that turns tail from a poet is a crap wolf.'

'And a tree fell on Horace once and nearly brained him.'

Gaius, now softened by the quiet country night, enveloped her and kissed her. 'You might be brained by a windowbox in a city street just as easily ... I could live in a place like this.'

'On a *farm*?'

'I own a farm,' Gaius reminded her. He made it sound significant. 'In Spain.'

The dog had covered his snout and legs with leaf litter and had rolled in a pungent substance that had been deposited by a wild animal with a foul diet. They had to take him to the baths to be washed before he could go back in the house. There was no one about, but the single slave on duty

514

volunteered to clean up Baby, keeping him well outside the pristine suite of hot rooms. Gaius and Lucilla had arrived too soon before dinner for more than basic ablutions, so as there was still hot water they went in and enjoyed the rare thrill of bathing together.

Gaius thwacked into the plunge pool, emerging to find Lucilla laughing as she watched him. After shaking off showers of water drops, he floated on his back naked and cheerful—the Gaius that Lucilla loved to see.

'Oh I could get used to this! In Tarraconensis, I am told, my old centurion's estate includes a farmhouse, like the simple place Horace had here originally. My manager says it's become a hovel, so I could transfer money out there and rebuild. Mosaics and my own bath house to chase you round—there's a thought.'

'*That* much money? And *Tarraconensis*?' repeated Lucilla in pretend tones of horror.

Parthenius' slaves had kindly left snacks and wine in their bedroom. The bed was soft with feather mattresses and pillows, in the lush, almost effeminate taste most wealthy palace freedmen had. Giggling, they made the most of it. At least they tried to, until Baby began howling.

Later, when they were back in Rome, Lucilla realised that must have been the night she became pregnant.

*   *   *

In fairness, Gaius did like the Parthenius plotting agenda:

Why?
Where, when, how, who?
What unlucky bugger do we choose to go next?

For obvious reasons this was never written down.

Gaius approved of the fact that *Why* was never taken for granted, but was formally considered. 'Our once caring and conscientious ruler has become a cruel tyrant. There is no chance he might leave voluntarily. We must remove him.'

Agreed.

Where: they decided it must be done in Rome. Alba was remote but Domitian was equally protected there. In view of the rumours that started when Nero died outside the city, even only four miles away, Rome would make the event appear more open.

Those gathered at Horace's villa never introduced themselves, though some were recognisable, including Entellus, the petitions secretary, another bureaucratic mogul. He sought advice from the cornicularius. Lucilla was surprised Gaius cooperated, though she then realised his contribution was so factual anyone could safely say such things openly: they should avoid the horror of a death in public. So not at the Games. The palace offered a secure, containable location, 'where any balls-ups can remain hidden.' His soldierly belief that hitches were inevitable made the others look nervous.

A long argument ensued, with people faffing about whether to tackle their victim at dinner or the baths. At dinner, it was thought he might be relaxed and off-guard—although Domitian's main meal was generally lunch. In the baths, anyone

516

was vulnerable. Clodianus pointed out dryly that an armed, clothed assassin would stand out among the oiled nudes, plus there was a risk the would-be killer would slip on a wet floor and go arse-over-tip. He spoke gravely, yet appeared insidiously satirical.

Too difficult: the dinner or baths debate was dropped. Parthenius ordered up a buffet lunch. They ate in the garden, to the sounds of cicadas and tumbling water. Baby was having the time of his life in the elegant pool; the young boy Burrus was boisterously playing with him.

When depended on Domitian being in the capital. Parthenius would keep a close watch on his diary for a suitable moment; first he wanted to wait until there was a favourable consul, to keep a grip on senators. Then the Senate could be summoned quickly, too, and the next emperor proclaimed fast. *Whoever that was.* They discussed other important people in Rome. With the Praetorian Prefects sympathetic (or Secundus sympathetic and Norbanus somehow dealt with), the Prefects of the City and Vigiles would probably acquiesce, locking down Rome until everything had settled. If Rome stayed calm, there would be more chance of avoiding mutiny abroad.

They had to consider Domitia Longina. While afternoon refreshments were brought—for this was a very comfortable kind of conspiracy—Parthenius asked if Lucilla could transfer her services to the Empress, now Domitilla was gone.

'To observe?' asked Gaius, with a narrow look. 'Working for the plot?'

'An idealist would say, she is working for Rome,' corrected Parthenius.

Lucilla smiled. Gaius did not buy that crap.

Neither did she. 'Is Domitia Longina aware of us? If not, is she to be told?'

'What would you advise, Lucilla?'

'Say nothing. Never force her to choose sides.'

'My feeling is,' Parthenius said, 'she is now trapped with him, in fear for her life.'

'Don't underestimate her loyalty,' Lucilla warned. 'She married him for love, and in their way it has been a successful partnership. Despite his mad behaviour, she has shown she means to stick it out.'

'But she must feel certain he no longer loves her.'

'So? I don't suppose she still loves him. How could she? Women stay married for plenty of reasons. She has always been conscious of her position as Corbulo's daughter; she is equally proud to be the Augusta, with her crowns and carriages. Those two still have the habits of enduring one another that come from any lengthy marriage. So, for safety, keep her out of it.'

How? Poison was problematical, and a woman's method. Nero's attempts to murder his mother had shown that trick beds, drowning accidents or the like were foolish and dented public confidence. Strangling was a punishment for criminals; in Rome, it was important to respect rank. This was an emperor; they were terminating his career for decent reasons. Ever since Julius Caesar, despots had been killed with blades. That was the mark of noble killers, killers with consciences.

Who became a poser. People tried to pressurise Clodianus, the only soldier present; he refused the honour, citing what his Prefect Secundus had said: that the Guards should only refrain from intervention. Parthenius said he had some ideas, but deferred a decision.

What unlucky bugger do we choose next? Everyone pitched in to discuss a replacement emperor.

Entellus, the petitions secretary, went through a list, apparently without notes. Emperor was hardly a job anyone could apply for, in the way of requesting a sideways move to Supplies or an upgrade to Transportation. On the other hand, if the position ceased to be hereditary, this was no different from putting together any promotion board.

'Ought we to consider the two Flavian boys?'

'No!'

'No boy emperors.'

'No relations of Domitian either.'

Their team had to headhunt a man of standing and calibre, but critically, someone who would agree to do it. Based on Entellus' suggestions, names of men to approach were shared out among people who knew them. Previous attempts to interest a candidate had miserably come to nothing. Those asked had changed their minds, were waiting for their wives' reactions, had already been told to say no by the wife, were too cautious, or ill, or had an ill grandfather they were suddenly very fond of, or were aware of the situation and thought these were novel proposals but unfortunately could not make full disclosure of their intentions at this stage . . .

Some front-runners were abroad, acting as governors of provinces or generals. Others were too old. A few with the right level of experience had foreign origins and there had never been a foreign emperor; Trajan, who certainly believed himself up to the job, was Spanish.

'Unfortunate!'

'His bad luck . . . What about that fellow who did all those years in Britain and whopped the natives? Agricola? We should not dismiss him simply because he had the bad luck to draw a ghastly province and got stuck there. Mind you, isn't he from Gaul?'

Entellus was discreetly consulting scrolls. He whispered to Parthenius, who informed the gathering that they were spared having to consider the ex-governor of Britain, since he had died. Nobody had wanted to denigrate a province simply for being obscenely remote, or a candidate for having had to serve there. Nobody wanted a Gaul. Gaius, who cynically watched this performance, noticed veiled relief all round.

Another ex-governor of Britain, Julius Frontinus, was on their list; he had governed Asia too, which was more reassuring. Frontinus was born in Italy, so he must be sound.

There were other difficulties. Half the possible candidates had a close allegiance to Domitian—or might do; it was not always easy to tell how they would jump. He chose good men; good men had ethics; but ethical men might think it their duty to oppose a despot . . .

Everyone was drained by the intense discussion. Lucilla nudged Gaius to signal that one man had gone to sleep. Another kept getting up and going out; either he was whispering information to a hidden accomplice or he had a weak bladder.

The agenda was abandoned and they adjourned for dinner.

Towards the end of a fine meal, accompanied

by flutes and decent conversation that deliberately ignored the conspiracy, Parthenius approached Lucilla. 'Tell me about the cornicularius.' Parthenius suspected Clodianus had only attended the meeting to keep an eye on his girl, now she had become so passionate about Domitian's removal. If Clodianus became too anxious about her, he might be a risk. What were his own loyalties? Did Clodianus even know?

'He has one Prefect sending him to spy, and one who wants to help us. Opposite orders . . . Don't push him,' Lucilla urged. 'He hates it.'

'Can we rely on him?'

'I do,' stated Lucilla unquestioningly. 'He cares. You can trust him.'

'With that wrecked face, I find it hard to decipher him. But you manage?'

'I have known him a long time.'

'How long?'

'Over fifteen years.'

'I never realised. You have both been extremely discreet.'

'Long story!' chuckled Lucilla. 'In my view, Vinius Clodianus is completely decent. When things matter, he never hesitates.'

They watched Gaius. He knew they were observing him, and he knew why.

He had cornered Parthenius' freedman Maximus to enthuse about his favourite scoff: 'Your portions must be well roasted in olive oil. They need to be glossy and golden. Then the gravy is the real point. Chicken Frontinian is not for mimsy eaters who only pick at finger food. Serve the chicken in a decent bowl of sauce, either to mop up with a lot of old bread, or, well, you can just pick up your bowl

521

and glug it down at the end.'

'Gaius, you are a barbarian!' Lucilla called.

He shrugged off the tease. 'And pepper is essential. A good sprinkle all over, before serving.'

'Not a dish for the poor then?' joked Maximus.

'No. I take my own peppercorns if I'm eating out, in case the waiter is mean.'

'He really does,' confirmed Lucilla, as she made her way over to Gaius. 'He makes them bring a mortar to the table. You have to find it endearing—or you would cringe.'

Reclining alongside Gaius, Lucilla unexpectedly made a declaration to the company at large. For Gaius and her, this was a rare public appearance as a couple. She surprised herself with the confidence that gave her: 'I know we agreed to have no business talk at table, but this is what we want. Don't we need to recover a world where you can dine at ease, at home or in public, enjoying the fabulous ingredients our Empire makes available? Enjoying skilled cookery and service? Most of all, enjoying such good company as we have here tonight—without getting heartburn because you are racked with tension, and without constantly looking over your shoulder in case an informer reports unguarded words to a cruel tyrant?'

'Being able to trust dinner companions, hired waiters and the little slave who helps remove your shoes,' Parthenius agreed.

Even Gaius took a hand, smiling: 'A world where Parthenius can safely bring his boy to listen in on the grown-ups.' The sleepy-eyed young Burrus woke up and blushed. Gaius went on seriously, 'Where you never have to look sideways at your wife nor keep your opinions hidden from

522

your girlfriend—assuming you can get one as fine as I fortunately have to share my couch this evening!'

Lucilla smiled at his compliment. She could see that Parthenius was still wondering if this was a clever ploy from Gaius or if he had genuinely opened up. Was it the wine talking? Gaius had been quaffing in Praetorian style. He was mellow though not drunk, she thought, even though he turned and smiled back at her with giddying sweetness.

*   *   *

They returned to Rome the next day. Many decisions had failed to materialise, yet the project had moved on. People took away tasks—even though Gaius claimed knowledgeably that at the next meeting there would be complaints of inaction, caused by plotters being too terrified to approach anyone.

Lucilla was buoyant. Gaius, too, felt a hardening of purpose, which became all the more fixed after a couple of months when, simultaneously, they realised that Lucilla was to have a child.

A pang of uncertainty passed between them, before it was obvious they both welcomed this. Although pregnancy was unpredictable and birth a threat to both mother and baby, they were both happy that they were now to become a family. Ironically, they also treated their news like diagnosis of an incurable disease: during the next months, both began putting their affairs in order.

Gaius had decided to leave the Praetorians

as soon as he had served his sixteen years. He informed both Prefects that his girlfriend was carrying, so he wanted to legitimise their relationship, and he started training an optio. The conservative Norbanus was particularly solicitous; it was a good Roman tradition to father a family and he assumed Gaius intended to produce a row of soldiers.

Strictly speaking, a retired Praetorian would be in the reserves for two years. 'That assumes they can find me!' muttered Gaius.

Lucilla meanwhile had learned about the compensation money Gaius squeezed from Lachne's lover, Orgilius. She split it between the two slavegirls she worked with, giving them their freedom too. Calliste wanted to get married; Glyke in all probability never would, but Lucilla saw no reason for her to lose out. She treated them equally, letting them know that if ever she and Gaius decided to move away from Rome, she would leave them her business.

The couple vaguely prepared people for the idea that they might relocate one day, if they were not too disorganised to manage it. There was mention of Campania, where unclaimed land whose owners died in the Vesuvian eruption was being made available. Gaius cracked jokes about returning to Dacia as one of the Roman experts sent to support King Decebalus under Domitian's unpopular treaty. Lucilla dropped other hints: that the prospect of a baby had given her the freedwoman's dream to see the eastern homeland from whence her mother was originally taken . . .

'Rome is a glorious city,' claimed Gaius, 'but not the only city in the world.'

'Oh you do like a laugh!' Felix and Fortunatus chortled.

*   *   *

Gaius wrote a new will.

'Everything will come to you, Lucilla. Listen; you won't like this, but to make it easy legally, I named you my wife.'

'Then we are heading for divorce.'

He gazed at her, with that wry tightening of muscle at one end of his mouth that Lucilla knew so well. 'Just go along with this, precious.' He produced a gold ring. A woman's wedding ring. 'Wear this to look good.'

He saw Lucilla's expression. 'How many of your wives—?'

'Be easy. The last person who wore that ring was my mother, Clodia.'

Lucilla knew how he thought of his mother. She did try it on. 'I am supposed to accept this for the child?'

'Let our child be born a citizen! If anything should happen to me, I want to think you are both provided for—otherwise the state will deny your rights and snaffle everything.'

'Nothing is going to happen to you.'

'Not if I can help it . . . I found this, when I was burrowing.' Gaius produced an elderly tablet, the wood stained and the wax hard. It was from his time in the vigiles, and on it in his handwriting was her name. '*Flavia Lucilla*; some girlie who made an impression on me in the vigiles. Look, I never smoothed it over in nearly twenty years.'

'Oh Gaius, why?'

'I didn't know.' He grinned at her. 'But I know now.'

He still had a handsome profile, and Lucilla still thought he was too aware of it.

34

On the first of September new consuls were sworn in.

The conspiracy revived. They had considered the mid-year consuls unsympathetic to their aims: one with a military background had worked with Domitian closely in Pannonia, and another came from Reate, Vespasian's birthplace, the Flavian heartland whose politicians were intensely cliquey. Both men looked dangerous to the plotters. With two powerful consuls against them, they felt stymied.

Those consuls were replaced for the last four months of the year by Calpurnius, whom nobody knew much about although they knew nothing against him, and a much healthier prospect: Caesius Fronto. He was the son or adopted son of the famous lawyer and senator, Silius Italicus, who was now swelling the ranks of retired poets in Campania; Italicus was writing an epic about the Carthaginian war, a work which was bound to involve reminiscing about the good old days when politicians had sanity and integrity. He came from Patavium, birthplace of the martyred philosopher Thrasea Paetus; this town had produced many members of the stoic opposition, men who tended to meet and collaborate when they went to Rome.

The son, Fronto, mingled with those men, held the same views and was, like others before him, awarded a consulship by Domitian to mitigate his hostility. Parthenius believed in Fronto as his ideal controller of the Senate if the plot went ahead.

That finally seemed likely. Flavia Domitilla's steward Stephanus suddenly learned he was accused of theft. Everyone knew what that meant. He was next up for banishment, if not execution. He approached Parthenius and offered to carry out Domitian's murder.

*   *   *

Stephanus looked suitable. So far, he still worked at the palace, so he could get close to the Emperor. Stephanus was angry enough and strong enough. He still raged at the injustice to his mistress and her family; he loathed Domitian. With both career and life under threat, Stephanus had nothing to lose. They would have to act fast though, because of the theft accusations. Delay only increased the chance of discovery.

Domitian was in Rome. That was what they wanted. He was officiating at the Roman Games which, ironically, began on the fourth of September, an extra day that had been added in honour of the murdered Julius Caesar. The Roman Games ran for over two weeks, until the nineteenth; on the thirteenth, the September Ides, fell the important anniversary of the founding of the Temple of Capitoline Jupiter, which Domitian would obviously want to honour. By coincidence, Titus had died on the Ides of September, so the fourteenth, which by another grim coincidence was traditionally a black day in the calendar, had become Domitian's own anniversary as Emperor. So he had a lot to celebrate—while others were also thinking about his anniversary and evaluating his reign bleakly.

The period of the Roman Games would be their last chance. Insiders knew that as soon as these Games ended, he would slip away. An enormous expeditionary force of five legions plus auxiliaries had been assembled for the next war on the Danube. Domitian had been closely involved in planning and he intended to go. Militarily, time was tight. Even if he dashed off straight after the Games ended, he could not arrive in Pannonia until the start of October; that allowed a maximum of six weeks before winter set in and campaigning had to end. An initial excursion across the Danube had in fact already started, under an experienced commander called Pompeius Longinus, who had years of frontier service.

That could be helpful. Once Longinus committed troops, he was unlikely to pull them back even if he heard that the Emperor had died. The Danube army was the dangerous one for the plotters, so it was good to have it tied up in an active campaign. The legions in Britain and the east were tricky, but hopefully too far away to cause trouble.

*   *   *

They still had no candidate to replace Domitian. Their objective of a smooth transfer of power depended on producing someone who would be willing and acceptable. Frantic manoeuvring began.

The Games, with their bustle and socialising,

provided good cover. They were triumphal, beginning with a parade, then dancing, boxing, athletics and drama; the finale was four days of chariot races in the Circus Maximus, which the Emperor was currently repairing after fire damage. Domitian would watch from his splendid new viewing gallery on the Palatine, which dominated the great southern bulwark side of the imperial palace, right above the Circus. As fire-walkers and rope-dancers entertained vast crowds, amidst the constant scent of flowers, smoke, donkey shit and street food, everyone important was conveniently in Rome. Associates could meet and mutter, without causing suspicion. Canvassing went ahead apace.

One after another, the most prominent men said no. Intriguingly, none reported the plot to Domitian.

*   *   *

No one, said Domitian, ever believed in plots until the victim was dead. He believed. He was all too superstitious. He felt convinced people were out to get him—a reasonable fear since it was true.

To the agonised Emperor, Rome became full of portents. He had dedicated the new year to the care of the Goddess of Fortune but the omens were dreadful. That summer, lightning struck several monuments, among them the Temple of the Flavians, the Temple of Jupiter and the new palace; a flash damaged Domitian's bedroom, which he took as particularly significant. Had the Emperor not been so insanely superstitious, no one would have thought anything of all this. It was approaching the autumnal equinox. The

Mediterranean often had thunderous storms. Flurries of severe weather came up suddenly, passed quickly, left the air fresher.

Astrologers prophesied when the Emperor would die; they knew his fixation. He had such black thoughts, they could safely make such forecasts, even though producing imperial horoscopes was illegal. If nothing happened on the day they named, their predictions would be quickly forgotten, especially by Domitian. Anyway, he believed that if he knew in advance what was planned for him, as a clever schemer he could outwit the fates. To prove it, he challenged one prognosticator to foretell his own death; on hearing it would be soon, and that the man expected to be torn apart by dogs, Domitian crisply had him killed and arranged for his funeral to be conducted very carefully.

A storm blew up and scattered the pyre; dogs did descend on the half-burned corpse, and Domitian's informer, the actor Latinus, unhelpfully told him.

*　　　*　　　*

During this crazy period, Gaius found himself summoned to attend at the palace with Norbanus, the more loyal Praetorian Prefect. From what he heard and saw, he became horrified that the plot was on the verge of being exposed.

Domitian would still go for walks, brooding bleakly on the danger he was in. His latest extravagance was to have huge plaques of moonstone set up, polished mirror-bright, so he could see if anyone crept up behind. Gaius reflected tetchily that there was a beautiful,

530

completely private garden where the Emperor could have walked instead in perfect safety.

Domitian was defying danger. If the danger was real, this was bloody stupid.

Norbanus and Clodianus accompanied the Emperor as ordered. It was a fitful stroll. Domitian paced in short, agitated spurts, gaining no benefit from the exercise. He never relaxed; he was tight with anxiety.

The fragments of conversation Gaius managed to overhear as the Emperor and the Prefect marched up and down ahead of him confirmed everything that was said about Domitian: he was secretive and treacherous, he was crafty and vindictive. He must have got wind of something. He was excitedly giving the Prefect orders about senators. Gaius recognised several; these men were on the plotters' list to canvass as replacement emperors. They had said no. Despite that, Norbanus was being told to eliminate them.

'Clodianus!'

The Prefect gesticulated for his officer to approach. It was the first time for years he had been up so close to his master. They were two feet apart: Domitian with his glorious purple robe stretched taut over the chunky Flavian paunch, Clodianus tall and strong in his red tunic, expression clear despite his nerves. Perhaps he imagined it, but that oddly curved lip of Domitian's seemed more pronounced, the backward tilt of the head ever more peculiar.

For the soldier, there now began the most difficult conversation of his life. Domitian demanded a report on the secret committee. He wanted details. Who attended? How had they contributed? Which seemed untrustworthy?

531

What signs had been observed that they aimed at his destruction? Names were put directly to the cornicularius. Domitian fired them off: names Clodianus knew, names he knew for certain were innocent, even names he had never heard of. The catalogue astonished him. Half the Senate and large numbers of imperial freedmen seemed to be under suspicion. Domitian had picked these out for himself as people who were against him, faces he was about to have arrested.

The cornicularius assumed a boot-faced, solid attitude, still trying to reconcile his duty with his inclinations. He was giving nothing important away, yet his act must be unconvincing. Norbanus shot him filthy looks and although Domitian apparently took it all in without resistance, Gaius felt queasy.

Quite suddenly, his interrogation ended.

The Emperor gave him a long, hostile, knowing stare. Domitian did not say this time, *I know that man!* Nor did Vinius Clodianus mention their past encounters. The cornicularius had failed his test.

There was no recognition that this was the soldier who had saved the priest and sympathised with Domitian on the Capitol all those years before, a Praetorian Guard with long years of steady service, the prisoner whose suffering in Dacia had so shocked his master. Anyone else built up trust through shared experience; for the Emperor, the past was irrelevant. With his flawed temperament, Domitian only lived for the suspicions of the moment.

Domitian was convinced the Guard had betrayed him. But Clodianus had been true so far. Once the Emperor discounted his whole career of loyal service, everything changed. He swore the oath and took the money. But he had remained his own man. Themison had diagnosed it: *to be constantly under suspicion while innocent may exasperate his associates until they do turn against him. Those who love him will feel rejected . . .*

He understood that look in Domitian's eyes. He knew what all those men must have gone through, those the Emperor invited into cosy confabulations at the same time as turning against them. Now he stood in danger himself. A cornicularius, with access to the entire Praetorian budget, could easily be accused of mishandling funds, for example. He, Vinius Clodianus, was in line for some harsh accusation of misdemeanour; for disgrace, exile, even death. Untrue; unjust. But impossible to refute, even if opportunity was given—which would not happen.

'I want a list.'

'Of course.' A commissariat man knew always to agree; in his own time he could ignore instructions. *'Domine.'* He meekly said 'Master'—but he would not call Domitian 'God'.

What kind of list? This was the nub of the problem. Brooding intently, Domitian would not specify. He thought anyone loyal ought to know what was needed; to force their response was a good trial of their honesty. He did not care what they told him; he made up his own mind anyway. Any list would do. Any names would answer. The list need not be complete, it need not be relevant or truthful, it just had to provide him with his next victims. Confirm his suspicions. Validate his fear.

After a curt dismissal, the unhappy cornicularius marched off. He felt the Emperor follow him with another baleful stare. Norbanus remained behind, probably so Domitian could order him to discipline and destroy Clodianus. One of the slaves who assembled within call slipped past. Domitian had asked for a note tablet. He would make his own list.

That stare said Vinius Clodianus would be on it.

*　　　*　　　*

Domitian believed that he would die on September the eighteenth, at the fifth hour.

The previous day, someone gave him a gift of apples; he ordered them to be served tomorrow, saying darkly, 'If I am spared!'

'He is like some miserable uncle that nobody wants to sit beside at Saturnalia!' Lucilla complained to Gaius. As Gaius remarked, at least it gave the conspirators a diary date.

'The last day to choose is when he expects it,' Lucilla demurred. Gaius smiled quietly. He was abstracted, still burdened by that meeting with Domitian, anxious for himself, more anxious for Lucilla. 'Oh Gaius, surely we must hope to catch him by surprise!'

'If he anticipates an attack, he may accept it. *"This is the prophecy, your time has come, give up now."* Then killing him becomes much easier.'

Gaius thought the inexperienced Stephanus would falter. Stephanus might look strong, but a palace freedman had no martial training. They had brought in a gladiator to instruct him in basic attack moves. Parthenius produced one of Domitian's own professionals, who helped them in return for the promise of freedom and presumably a large cash payment. Gaius never knew the fighter's name. He had no great faith in what the gladiator could achieve with Stephanus in just a few days of secret working out.

Stephanus had bandaged his forearm as if he had some injury. He wore an obvious sling, like a hypochondriac, walking about the palace that way until everyone had seen him. By the end of a week, the Guards grew bored with searching him for concealed weapons. That was when Stephanus hid a dagger under the bandages.

*   *   *

When Gaius confessed his fears that Domitian was composing written details of the plot, Lucilla decided to do something; she pretended she had to see the Empress.

Domitia Longina rarely asked for her these days, not since Flavia Domitilla was exiled; the Empress was probably afraid Lucilla would want her to beg Domitian to let his niece return. Lucilla would not waste her breath. As far as she knew, Domitia had never once tried to influence a political decision.

Lucilla guessed where Domitian would be keeping his notes. Like innocent children, emperors tucked secret things under the pillows in their bedrooms. At the palace, she used her skills. She made friends with one of the naked boys who flitted about the court, generally up to mischief. She sent him in to look. Rather than be spotted lurking suspiciously, she told the lad she would come back for anything he found, after she had paid her respects to their imperial mistress.

When she entered the room, everyone was discussing Domitian's fears for tomorrow. Apparently, he kept exclaiming dramatically,

'There will be blood on the moon in Aquarius!' Domitia retorted, in that case she would make sure she was away seeing friends.

The Empress allowed Lucilla to kiss the rouged regal cheek, then Lucilla began inspecting what Domitia's maids had done to her hair, tweaking her coronet fussily.

'You look pregnant! Do you know whose it is?'

'Yes, Madam. He will be a good father.'

'Well, that's lucky.'

The inevitable happened. The boy had found Domitian's note tablet. He brought it to Lucilla. Domitia spotted him. She demanded the tablet. She read it.

Holding up a mirror behind the Empress's head, Lucilla craned to look over her shoulder. There, in Domitian's fervent handwriting were packed columns of names, some of them accurate.

Domitia was silent for a long moment. Expensive jewels rose and fell with her strained breathing. She slammed shut the double-sided note tablet, almost crushing her own fingers with their burden of heavy antique rings.

'The appalling little thief has no idea what this contains. Luckily I was shown it.' She grasped the tablet firmly. Standing beside her chair, Lucilla stayed motionless, expecting the worst.

The Empress turned her head and looked straight at her. Domitia Longina of the compressed lips and uncompromising attitude murmured scornfully, 'He will not be deterred by losing a few notes!' Then, as if to herself: 'These people need to hurry up, if they really mean business.' Suddenly she passed the note tablet across. 'Flavia Lucilla! Your man is a Praetorian?' She seemed bored now.

'Show this to him, will you? I presume he will know what to do about it.'

Astonished, Lucilla nodded faintly. Domitia turned immediately to someone else, closing her association with the tablet.

The Empress must be not unaware of the plot, not unaware that the names she had read were significant. She knew the implications if she told the plotters how close they were to detection.

Of course there were dangers to Domitia herself in an assassination. When Caligula was killed by his Guards, his wife Caesonia was also brutally murdered, and the brains of their infant child dashed out. Domitia had no reason to think the new conspirators intended to deploy only minimum violence. Domitia had watched her husband's deterioration at close quarters. Had she decided there was no hope of recovery and his exit was inevitable? Cynically, if she survived her husband, that would be her release from misery too. People thought she was terrified he intended harm to her.

Or maybe Corbulo's daughter chose to act in the national interest: that noblest of motives for any Roman, man or woman.

Lucilla lost no time in informing her colleagues they must act immediately.

*   *   *

The hunt for the next emperor assumed desperate urgency.

The last man they approached was Cocceius Nerva. He might be sympathetic because he had had a nephew, Salvius Cocceianus, who had also been related to the Emperor Otho, a rival to the

537

Flavians back in the Year of the Four Emperors. Domitian had executed Salvius for honouring his Uncle Otho's birthday.

Nerva was a long-term politician, now in his sixties, looking frail and some thought faintly sinister. Childless, and not particularly liked, he had little experience of provincial government or the army. He was a stalwart Flavian, but conversely this might help smooth over any backlash because he would be acceptable to Flavian supporters. In the course of a chequered history, he had helped Nero put down the Piso conspiracy with much harshness; it was said he also heavy-handedly helped Domitian's retribution process after the Saturninus Revolt. At least, said Gaius dryly, it meant Nerva knew how plots worked.

Everyone, including Nerva himself, acknowledged that because of his age he was a stop-gap. This would allow a second look at the succession, time to interest a worthy successor. For Nerva, his life was drawing to a close, so why not take a risk?

He was in Domitian's advisory council, the amici, one of Caesar's friends. Not that that stopped him. Nerva agreed to do it.

*   *   *

The eighteenth of September came. Domitian spent the morning in court, giving cases his usual pedantic attention.

At noon he adjourned. He was intending to take a bathe and his usual siesta. He demanded to know the time. Attendants assured him it was already the sixth hour, knowing his dread of the

538

fifth. Parthenius then mentioned discreetly that a man had something significant to show him, in his private suite. Obsessed with threats, the Emperor was all too keen to hear what this person had to say. Parthenius controlled access to the Emperor. He trusted Parthenius to vet admissions.

Domitian fearlessly set off alone. A perfectionist, he always wanted to be in sole control of anything vital.

In his bedroom, he found Stephanus, still with his arm bandaged. He handed Domitian a document. As Domitian intently perused this, Stephanus produced the concealed dagger.

* * *

At Plum Street, Gaius and Lucilla had spent the hours after breakfast together in their apartment. Their mood was quiet, sober though resigned. They took a special pleasure in the routines of this morning, as if it might be their last time together.

'This was our home.'

'Wherever we both are, that's home.'

Gaius gave Lucilla his discharge diploma. Ordinarily the tablets were signed by Domitian; using his authority as cornicularius, Gaius had had these completed and Lucilla did not ask him if the signature was forged.

'Released from my oath.' She understood.

They clasped hands. Each thanked the other for the life they had had together. Neither wept, though both were close to tears.

Gaius was going to the palace to see what had transpired; he had a plan for them to vanish safely afterwards. If anything happened to him, Lucilla would have to manage on her own. There was money. They had plenty, much already sent on ahead.

'I am coming with you.'

'No. Stay here.'

'You never give me orders!' One hand on her stomach, Lucilla allowed him a let-out. 'You fear for the child.'

'For the child, yes—but above all, I am afraid for you, Lucilla. Wait for me here until an hour before the vehicle prohibition lifts. If I have not returned, you must leave at once without me. Think of the baby, think of me and how I love you. Then go and be safe.'

Lucilla gave her promise. Gaius kissed her, came back and kissed her one more time, and left. He was dressed as a Praetorian, in a red tunic, soldier's boots and military belt, and wearing his sword.

*   *   *

As he walked down the Vicus Longus, he was struck by the normality of Rome. Nor was there anything extraordinary about his own behaviour: a tall man with long legs, walking with a slow tread to his workplace. Though approaching forty, he had kept up the twenty-mile training marches; he was strong and solid. Not yet forty: still plenty of time yet to cause havoc.

It was towards the end of summer, but days were long and the sky cloudless. In September, the sunny side of Roman streets was still uncomfortably hot, though the shade felt clammy. Lines of washing and bedcovers flung over balcony rails to air hung motionless. When, heavy with his mission, the

540

cornicularius sucked in a deep sigh, the air was warm in his lungs.

The fifth hour was when most shops drew across their shutters. People were at lunch; the sixth hour would be their rest period. Few people were about. In this traditionally quiet time, Rome basked. Shabby dogs curled against house walls, asleep. From behind upper floor window shutters came the sound of an unhappy baby mithering. Further along, Clodianus smelt fried food and heard the routine knock of cutlery on pottery.

He turned left, to reach the Forum at the western end, marching faster as he passed the Arch of Titus; he was still relaxed but purposeful. With the House of the Vestals on his right, he crossed the uneven ancient slabs of the Sacred Way then climbed up the steep approach to the Palatine. All the Guards on duty knew him. They nodded in their cornicularius without question.

Inside the palace, there was no Praetorian presence. Secundus must have given the right orders.

*   *   *

Everything in the public areas seemed otherwise normal. Visitors, in Rome for the Games, milled around in the massive state rooms immediately beyond the grand entrance. The cornicularius pushed through the crowds and kept going.

The architect had designed this complex to astonish, delight and confuse people. Knowing it would be his last ever visit, Clodianus took more notice than usual but he did not slow down, apart from when he took care on a flight of steps.

Knowing his way around, as all Guards did, he entered the imperial family's private quarters, exquisite suites nesting deep within the more public areas. He saw no servants in the corridors.

He went quickly to the agreed rendezvous. Parthenius was there, among a small group of others. With them was Nerva, a good-looking elderly senator, who had crinkled hair above a triangular face and a gentle manner. No spare flesh on him. He looked as if he was wetting himself with terror. Clodianus recognised another man as the consul, Caesius Fronto. Fronto looked calm, though keyed-up.

Parthenius gave him a breathless update. Domitian and Stephanus were locked in; Parthenius had arranged locked doors to keep out attendants. The combatants had been closeted for a long time, too long. Noises suggested that they were still fighting, with Domitian very much alive.

Clodianus cursed. He was not surprised by what he heard. Without hesitation, he took over.

He left Parthenius fanning Nerva, who had almost collapsed with terror. They had always had a secondary plan in case Stephanus failed. Clodianus took Entellus, the secretary of petitions, with Sigerius, a junior chamberlain. Parthenius sent one of his freedmen, Maximus. The gladiator who had tried to train Stephanus tagged along.

All the doors to the private suite were still locked. Screaming was audible inside. Two voices.

Clodianus could have crashed in, using a shoulder, but he chose the quiet method. He had taken a key from Parthenius. That way, once they reached the bedroom, his arrival went almost unnoticed during the crucial first moment.

He assessed the scene: a mess. A total bloody mess. But retrievable.

Domitian and Stephanus were grappling on the bedroom floor. Both looked exhausted. Stephanus had stabbed Domitian in the groin. There was blood, blood everywhere. The Emperor had grabbed the dagger with his hands; his fingers were lacerated. The dagger was lying a long way from where they were now.

Stephanus had facial wounds. Domitian had tried to gouge out his eyes. Stephanus must have been stabbed too at some point; his condition looked critical.

Someone else was there, someone who should not have been. Crouching petrified was the long-haired boy who tended Domitian's personal gods in a bedroom shrine. Palpitating with terror, the Lares boy had frozen beside the massive bed. The Emperor must have screamed for him to bring the knife he kept under its scented, silken pillows. A scabbard had skittered across the marble. All the boy was holding was a pommel with its blade removed: again, Parthenius' work.

Attendants loyal to Domitian were battering at other doors. Time had run out.

Armed with daggers by Parthenius, the men who came in with Clodianus moved in and tackled Domitian. Entellus, Sigerius, Maximus stabbed him, one after another, a further seven times. Still, he refused to die.

The squad stood back, shaking their heads at Domitian's resilience. The freedmen were cool enough; they did well. Only the gladiator had no heart for it. Elsewhere in the imperial suite, doors abruptly crashed inwards. There were shouts;

people approaching. Clodianus signalled the others to make themselves scarce. They disappeared, leaving a swathe of bloody footprints. Stephanus stayed, too badly hurt to escape yet struggling again to come at Domitian.

Attendants burst in. Making a concerted effort, they pulled Stephanus away from Domitian and killed the steward. Fair enough. It was always convenient if a murderer was finished off at the scene. No messy trial, one neat culprit to be blamed. You could almost wonder cynically if Parthenius had planned that.

Parthenius came into the room.

Domitian was gasping grotesquely, and still snaking sluggishly around the floor. Seeing a Praetorian, Clodianus, his protégé, he desperately tried to speak. Clodianus gestured to the others to stay back. He heard Parthenius give calm orders to the servants. That still left the problem.

What was your thinking when you involved yourself?

He was going to die anyway . . .

Clodianus trod carefully across the floor. Astonishing how far one small drop of blood could spread, as it flattened on the marble in a fine spray. Astonishing how much other gore from the two combatants had spurted, pooled and jellied. Above one glistening, bloodstained area flies already circled with morbid fascination.

Domitian was now nearly gone. His eyelids drooped, probably no longer seeing anything. Impossible to say whether he knew this man standing above him, or realised what his final assailant was about to do.

Without a word, Clodianus drew his sword. He

544

knelt beside the Emperor and thrust it in hard. The flesh closed and gripped his blade, but he twisted it out with the savage pull that legionaries used when despatching an enemy: a second wrench that made the original blow certain.

He did not need to look. Domitian was now dead.

*   *   *

Clodianus pulled off his red tunic, hauling it past his belt and sword scabbard. He wiped the blood from his sword, cleaning it thoroughly, sheathed it and tossed the wet garment away. Underneath he wore another tunic, like a civilian. As he walked past Parthenius, he met the chamberlain's eyes and nodded. Mutual respect passed between them. They would not meet again.

In the enormous public spaces, no one seemed aware anything had happened. He walked, with his hand casually on his sword pommel, back through the palace, past the oblivious Guards on duty, out into the shock of brilliant September sunshine.

With a steady pace, Gaius Vinius—never again to be Clodianus—retraced his route down from the Palatine, back across the Forum and along the Vicus Longus. The same dogs were asleep in almost unchanged positions and the same baby was fretfully crying. This time he had the sun behind him. He could feel it, warm and cheering on his back, as he returned to the Sixth Region where for years he and the woman of his heart had rented an apartment, the apartment they were now leaving.

He reached Plum Street, found his waiting girl, picked up her hand luggage, shouldered his own, whistled the dog, and walked them briskly to the station house of the First Cohort of vigiles. Scorpus had kept the cart safe for him: a builder's cart bought from his brother and already laden, an unassuming dray with a comfortable ox, nothing to make anyone look twice. Builders' carts had a special licence to be on the streets during the normal ban on wheeled vehicles. Leaving now, they would avoid the incoming surge of evening traffic.

'Ready?'

'Ready.'

Gaius was withdrawn now, in shock. Lucilla accepted his silence. He would talk in due course; he would tell her everything. She draped a cloak around him, taking the reins herself. She pointed out how this was hardly an unusual sight on the Empire's roads—a lazy scoundrel husband simply staring at the scenery, while his poor pregnant wife did all the hard work . . . Somewhere deep, a response glimmered; Gaius dropped one hand onto her lap. *Just drive, darling.*

They would turn out onto the high road, close to the Saepta Julia, as if they were heading past the Horologium and Mausoleum of Augustus, en route for northern Italy. Instead, they would turn off left, drive across the Field of Mars and reach the Tiber. Crossing Nero's Bridge, they would change direction one more time, to follow the river down to the coast at Ostia, where their ship was waiting.

Behind them in countless local neighbourhoods, citizens were still enjoying lunch and their rest period, unmoved by events on the Palatine. There at the heart of the city, important men had frantic work to do, but nothing of this would become public until tomorrow. Today, Rome, the eternal, the Golden City, lay bathed in sunlight peacefully. There were no alarms. It was a quiet afternoon on the Via Flaminia.

Author's Note

Writing about this period is tricky since, apart from a few fixed events, it is notoriously difficult to plot dates with certainty; I made the best sense of it I could. Novelists have to choose. When in doubt about what happened, whether something happened, why, or when, I have generally taken my lead from the magisterial Professor Brian W. Jones.

Domitian's assassination passed off quietly. His body was consigned to a public undertaker, but famously retrieved by his childhood nurse, Phyllis, a freedwoman of the Flavians. She had him cremated at her villa outside Rome, then took the ashes to the Temple of the Flavian Gens and mingled them secretly with those of Julia.

Next morning the Senate convened and proclaimed Nerva, ushering in the Era of the Five Good Emperors. Domitian was *damnatio memoriae*: obliterated from history. Senators rushed out into the Forum to oversee removal of his images, including the enormous equestrian statue. Roman historians and many who followed them would denounce Domitian and belittle his achievements, although these are being reassessed, particularly his work on the Roman frontiers in Europe and aspects of his building programme in Rome, projects like Trajan's Markets, which we now think Domitian began.

Nerva's reign was short. Its most dramatic event involved the Praetorian Guards: under their new Prefect, the reappointed Casperius Aelianus, they furiously demanded that Domitian's killers be punished. The Guards actually took Nerva prisoner in the palace, holding him hostage until he was forced to capitulate and produce two of the leading conspirators. Stephanus had been killed at the scene. The ex-Praetorian Prefect Petronius Secundus was executed. As a freedman who had betrayed his master, Parthenius was killed in an excruciating fashion; his testicles were cut off and stuffed in his mouth, then he was strangled, very slowly. We do not know the fates of Entellus, Sigerius, Maximus or the anonymous gladiator, but since nothing is mentioned, perhaps they survived.

In the two historical accounts of the murder (by Suetonius and Dio Cassio), only Suetonius names the cornicularius Clodianus. What happened to him is not disclosed. I have given him names and a history. I have also assumed that a Praetorian chief-of-staff would have had the opportunity and skills to disappear. So Clodianus, if he really existed, took all that was his, including his family if he had one, and slipped safely away. His bravery is without question.

Of the imperial women, Domitia Longina's supposed involvement in, or awareness of, the plot is ambiguous, though in later life she continued to call herself 'wife of Domitian'. No one knows if Flavia Domitilla ever returned from Pandateria or if she died there; no one knows the fates of her children. Flavians are afterwards absent from recorded public life.

Despite what happened to Parthenius, his son Tiberius Claudius Burrus became owner of the lovely villa that some of us like to think had once belonged to Horace, and to the courageous Claudia Epicharis. I owe great thanks to Professors Bernard

Frischer and Jane Crawford, for alerting me to this and for the great treat of our day at Alba and Licenza.

Finally, let me just say that anyone looking at the hairstyles worn by ladies of the Flavian court, or at Domitian's surviving statues, will see that they had at least one extremely inventive (and quite possibly satirical) hairdresser. I have given her names and a history too.

Lindsey Davis
London, June 2011

Acknowledgements

'The Girl I Kissed at Clusium'
The legionary song in *The Eagle of the Ninth* by
Rosemary Sutcliff

'The Boy I Kissed at Colonia Agrippinensis'
Invented by Gaius Vinius